MW01169117

THE HITMAN'S GUIDE TO MAKING FRIENDS AND FINDING LOVE

SPECIAL EDITION

ALICE WINTERS

NOTE FROM ALICE

Thank you so much for checking out the special edition! When I wrote Leland and Jackson's story, I had absolutely no idea how much love these characters would get (especially Leland). Leland is such a special character who can say everything you wish you could say (and some things you'd never want to). Since I'm an introvert, it's fun seeing Leland run out there, forcing people to be his friend, never fretting or worrying about what others think, and just being all around chaotic. He's not afraid to tell it like it is, and he can make friends with *anyone* no matter how reluctant they are. I know I'll never write another character as wonderfully unique as him, and that's okay. I could never replace that fence-loving man. Speaking of The Fence (can't forget the capitals), I never knew that The Fence would become such an important thing. I never planned for Leland to bring that chunk of wood home to terrorize Jackson with for years. I actually started Leland's story around seven years or so before I published the one you see here. The character wasn't named Leland and really didn't have a whole lot in common with him (beyond being a hitman who was trying to woo a PI), but he was the reason Leland came to be. And the character who became Jackson was able to scale that fence with ease (so let's all agree that this version is much superior). Once I started publishing, I stumbled across that story that was really only around 15k words (completely unfinished), but the idea stuck with me, so I decided to try my hand at it again and write something fun about a hitman and a PI. This time, Jackson didn't make it over that fence and Leland fell in love at first sight. When Leland hit the scene, I had absolutely no idea about the love he'd gain. I remember the first conference I went to, I was absolutely blown away that people KNEW about him... and they wanted more of him. Well, I hope you continue to enjoy the chaos that is Leland, as well as Jackson, who really does his best to keep an eye on the man of his dreams. And I hope you enjoy the special edition where Leland and Jackson sit down and look back on how they met. I hope you continue to join Leland and Jackson on their journey. They have many more stories to tell and more people to drag (some kicking and screaming) into their found family. Thank you so much for taking a chance on this book and showing me how much one chaotic hitman can do.

WANT TO ENJOY THE NEW SNIPPETS ON AUDIO?

Flip to the back for the book for a link to access the audio version of the snippets. In order to access the file, you MUST be a newsletter subscriber. If you are not, you can become one by going to my website and joining the newsletter at the bottom.

www.alicewintersauthor.com

Leland: Jackson, my love. My sweets. Come, come.

Jackson: This is horribly suspicious.

Leland: You're... you're suspicious because I'm lovingly telling you to trot your tush on over and enjoy the most beautiful story ever told?

Jackson: You're literally just wanting to relive how we met, aren't you? As if I wasn't there with you.

Leland: Who the hell else is going to sit here and listen for *hours*? I mean... if they knew what a fine man you are and what a fine fence that is, they'd be *enraptured*, but alas... you're my only vic... uh... not victim... no, no... um... *clears throat while thinking hard*

Jackson: Just go with victim. Willing victim.

Leland: Perfect! Now let us begin with the night we met. The night your tush changed my life *forever*.

Jackson: Could we skip that part? Maybe just jump over it to something *better*?

Leland: I'm going to jump over it like you jumped over The Fence... not at all.

Jackson: *mumbles* I'm not so sure about that.

Leland: And so our tale of two unlikely but beautifully destined for each other men begins with that fateful night... and a fateful fence.

Jackson: *sighs*

ONE

LELAND

I wonder when stakeouts became boring. In movies or crime novels it always sounds fun. Let's go stake out the supervillain like a badass! What they *don't* show are the five consecutive days of staking out whatever it is.

It's clear that I'm bored when I'm not using my binoculars to watch the house I'm supposed to be watching but am, instead, staring at the neighbor's TV. What's worse is that *The Bachelor* is on. Since I can't hear them, I like to pretend I know what they're saying.

Big tits: Want to see my dildo collection?

Tiny dick: So *that's* what a dick is supposed to look like.

I've never handled idle work very well. My mind wanders far too much, and then I'm not paying attention to what I'm supposed to be paying attention to.

Like the guy climbing over the fence to get into the house I'm supposed to be staring at. He even managed to walk over to the tall wooden fence without me even noticing, so who knows what else I've been missing.

There was probably an orgy I missed out on watching as well.

From my spot on the roof of a nearby video store, I stare at the man clad in black as he grabs onto the fence. Clearly, he knows he's not supposed to be there with the way he's decked out like a teenage goth.

He leaps up to grab the top of the tall fence and hoists himself up. Just as he's starting to lift his foot, he teeters and does a face dive off the other side. The issue is when his pants catch on the top of the fence as he falls over it.

With my binoculars, I'm given a *very* nice view of his bare ass as he hangs on the fence, feet kicking. Thankfully, there's enough light from the streetlamps that I get to zoom in right on it.

This is *so* much better than *The Bachelor*.

I'm honestly disappointed when he hoists himself back up, frees his pants, and continues his fall.

He's up in an instant and moves toward the house like he's not even embarrassed. If that happened to me, I think I would just give up and get a job at a grocery store or something that doesn't require stealth.

As he walks up to the house, he turns enough that, even with the black hat hiding his hair, I get a decent look at his face and realize that I wouldn't mind another look at his ass. Maybe a little closer, if he didn't care.

"And what are you up to, handsome?" I mumble.

While his fence-vaulting skills need some work and were leading me to believe he didn't know what he was doing, his quick entrance into the house makes me change my mind, but it's clear he's not supposed to be there, what with the fence scaling and all. When he passes through the door, I lose sight of him, so I can't tell what he's up to.

For a moment, I wait on the roof and watch the house, but I'm not getting anything from this distance. I toss my binoculars into the backpack that's waiting next to the spot I'd climbed up. I zip it closed and swing it over my back. Then I grab the case holding my gun before looking down at the dumpster I'd used to help climb onto the roof. I jump down, trying to stay as close to the edge as I can since the lid isn't guaranteed to hold my weight. Not that I'm overly heavy, since I'm pretty average in height and weight, but because I broke the lid when I climbed on it yesterday and ruined my brand-new stalking shoes.

Once in the alleyway, I take the sidewalk toward the house. That's when I notice a car that hadn't been there when I'd come in. While it could be a nearby resident's, it hasn't been there any of the other nights I've frequented this place. I pull off my glove and set my hand on the hood where I find it warm to the touch.

I bet it's his car. With my gloves back on, I try the door, but of course it's locked. Doesn't mean I *can't* get into it, but I feel like my time might be better spent seeing what he's doing inside the house. I open my backpack and pull out a notepad where I jot down his license plate number. It's a clean notebook, and I haven't handled it without my gloves, so I write a little something down, tear the paper out, and tuck it under the windshield wiper.

Now, off to see what Bare-ass is up to.

JACKSON

The house has clearly been evacuated in a hurry, which could be a good thing. They might have made mistakes in their rush and left something behind, but is there anything I can use? There's a possibility that they'll send a cleaner in to strip the place, so it'd probably be a good idea to watch it for a few days and see if anyone comes back for anything they might have missed.

Currently, the house is trashed. I don't want to shine too much light, so I have a tiny penlight to help guide my path. Beer bottles and takeout boxes are scattered everywhere. I find the living room where a stained couch sits, cigarette holes burned into the armrest. The DNA that's surely scattered throughout the place won't help; the people that were here are petty thieves and drug dealers. I doubt any of them are the man I'm looking for, *but* they've associated with him and might have information on where they've taken the girls to.

I walk into the adjoining room, which is the kitchen. It smells like rotting food, and I can hear the buzzing of flies. Who knows what else is crawling around in here? That's when I see a door sitting ajar. As I walk toward it, my foot kicks a padlock that'd been lying on the floor.

It slides across the stained linoleum and strikes the wall. I pull a plastic baggie out of my pocket and pick the padlock up, zipping it in tight, before tucking it into my jacket.

The open door leads to a staircase which I head down. It's clearly where they were keeping the girls, if the pile of blankets in the corner and the five-gallon bucket are anything to go by. Since there aren't any windows in the room, I turn a brighter flashlight on and pull out my phone. I take pictures of the room before carefully going through it, but I don't want to tamper with it too much. Anything I *do* tamper with, the court might not be able to use when the police invade the place.

I spend another half hour poking through the place before stepping out of the house. This time, when I need to leap the fence, I make sure that I don't tear my pants off in the process. When I make it back to my car, I unlock the door and get inside. That's when I see a paper tucked under the windshield wiper. Thinking it's a flyer, I get back out of my car and grab it.

I like your ass.
-the Sandman ♥

At first, I'm mortified about someone seeing my failed attempt at leaping the fence, then I'm confused about *who* saw my failed attempt. The writing is sloppy and almost hard to read—and is that a *heart* next to the name?—but it's clear that they were watching me. They even knew that this car belonged to me.

That's not good.

Leland: Ahhhhhhh, the most beautiful memory. Something that will last me a lifetime. I wish I could frame it.

Jackson: Can we hurry to the next part?

Leland: I actually think we should start over from the beginning.

Jackson: And they lived happily ever after, the end.

Leland: What the hell, Jackson? You can't just skip to the end! Who does that? You're like one of those people who ruins the movie before others get to see it just so you can get your kicks out of the misery of others. Here, I can do a summary of it for those who are struggling to follow along. "It was the dead of night when the beautiful man trotted onto the scene! With a battle cry and a flick of his luscious mane, the PI turned to his nemesis—the fence —and declared 'I will mount you!' and mount that fence he did! He clambered and clawed, but the fence was an enemy unlike one he'd ever seen before! For you see, The Fence required a toll to pay, and that toll was the mighty man's majestic moon!

Jackson: I'm calling it. Please, let's just get to chapter two. Better yet, let's stop reminiscing here.

Leland: Never!

TWO

JACKSON

Instead of going to the private investigation office I work at, I head to the police station. Once inside, I greet the secretary and go to the back where the chief of police's office is. I knock on the door before pushing it open.

"Hey, Jackson," Henry says.

"Hey, I have something for you from the Hardek trafficking case," I say.

While I don't work for the police, Henry occasionally consults with me and I with him. I'd been hired by the parents of one of the two missing girls to help find her. She and a teenage friend went missing from a college party five days ago and haven't been seen since. There is talk that she's a victim of human trafficking, and the parents are prepared to do anything to bring her back. While the police have been stuck on leads, I've been tracking down information about the young man the girls had been hanging around with from place to place until I found the house.

Through all of that, I began to speculate that they were involved in a crime syndicate led by a shadow of a man who we think is called Hardek.

"I found the house they were being held in," I announce.

Henry's eyes shoot up. He's a man I've known for a few years now, ever since I got out of the military and decided that I couldn't sit behind a desk again. He's older than my thirty-nine years at around fifty. His tightly curled black hair is starting to gray.

He's waving his hands in a manner that tells me he's not too pleased about the information I just gave him. "And you didn't call it in? What the hell are you waiting for?"

"I want to stake out the place for a couple days and see if anyone goes back to it. If I let you guys at it, you'll scare them away."

"Or we could go in and find something in there worth following."

"You already ran a ton of fingerprints from the last drug house you raided and got nothing. Even the men you arrested, you couldn't hold them for *anything*. And *none* of them spoke a single word about Hardek. Let me watch it. Two days, tops. But I did get you this to see if the fingerprints matched the last house," I say as I drop the lock on his desk.

He picks the bag up and scrutinizes the lock. "This was on a door?"

"It was on the floor, but it was clearly used to lock up the basement. One other thing…" I pull out the note. "Is this anything?"

Henry reaches out and grabs the note. The look on his face tells me there's definitely something about it that I didn't get when I first saw it. Clearly, my instinct to bring it in was right.

His dark eyes grab onto mine and I realize that there's something more there than I thought. "This was in the house?" he asks.

"No, on my car."

His brown eyes widen. "On your car?"

"You know who wrote it?"

"Eh…" He shrugs. "We believe he's a hitman, if we had to guess. No one's ever seen him, but he likes to toy with his victims. He leaves them little notes, and always leaves a note for us on their bodies. You remember Vince Hart?"

I think about it for a moment. "Wasn't he that guy convicted of raping those women, but got away with it because they couldn't prove it was him?"

"Very same guy. Ended up dead days later. Shot through the head."

"Yeah, I remember hearing about that. You're saying this guy did it?" I ask as I motion at the note.

Henry does something on his computer before turning it toward me. On the screen is a picture of a note much like this one, lying on the chest of the man we'd been talking about.

I took care of this one for you.
-the Sandman

"This isn't good. Don't touch the note again," he says. "I'll have someone run it for prints for you. You need to be careful."

"You think someone put a mark on my head?" I ask. "What else do you have on this guy?"

"Jackson… I hunted that man for years. He killed my partner almost ten years ago."

"What?" I ask in shock. "Are you sure?"

"He left a note. I'm positive. What I'm saying is, you'd be best to keep your nose out of his business. Stay away. If he wanted you dead, you'd be dead. So back away before he can do something else to you."

I want to ask more about his partner, but he doesn't seem to want to talk about it. "Can I at least have some information on him so I know what I'm up against if he comes after me?"

Henry sighs. "I can send you everything we have. If you could bring him in, you'd be one lucky man. Let me get some stuff gathered and email it to you. Thanks for the tip, and you'd better have that address in my hands come Monday morning. Don't make me regret this."

"I won't."

"Find us something."

"I'll try."

I head out of the police station and over to my car. The office I set up with a buddy from the military is only about five minutes away. It's above an old bookstore that has been owned for years by an elderly woman named Rose. She's in her seventies now and generally gets so caught up in what she's doing, she forgets to flip the closed sign to open. To get upstairs, we have to go through the bookstore, so I unlock the door and find Rose hurrying around.

"Did you want the closed sign still up?" I ask.

She looks over at me and sighs. "I left it up? I was *wondering* why no one was showing up!"

I don't have the heart to tell her that the sign isn't the issue but the fact that her newest book was written in the nineties is. "That's alright," I say before switching it for her.

"Thank you, dear. You're such a sweetheart."

I try not to snort. It's not too often I'm called a sweetheart. "You're welcome." I walk past rows of books to the stairs that line the back wall and head up the stairs to my office.

When I open the door, I find that Mason is already at his desk, dutifully playing solitaire. He looks up and smiles at me. "'Bout time you decide to stroll in here."

When we opened the place together, I had high hopes that Mason would actually help me with the cases. What Mason does is play on his computer while I take care of the cases. He's much more like a secretary, but he does help pay the rent and expenses, so I let him play secretary all he wants. During slow spells, I'm not sure if I could have held this place together without his donation to the monthly bills.

"Oh, ha ha," I say sarcastically.

"Got a cheating case for you that a woman is wanting looked into. Interested?"

"I'm kind of busy at the moment. That'd be a good one for you."

He sighs but nods. "Fine, fine. I'll do it, this once. Just for you."

"Just for me."

He grins at me. "That, and she's *hot*." He's a little older than me, in his early forties, with blond hair and a beard that's started to get out of control. I met him in the army, where he'd spent a good five more years than I had before being discharged because of an accident while in the field. While overseas, he took a bullet to the arm, which left him with mobility issues. At least, that's what he tells me. It seems to work just fine when he's playing solitaire.

Our tiny office is so small it's almost suffocating, but my desk is close to the window, so that's one good thing. I head over to it and turn my computer on. I don't plan on spending much time here, since I want to get some sleep before tonight so I don't doze off while watching the house. But before that, I need to get a few things done. The first thing I notice as I slide into my chair is the email from Henry titled "Sandman."

> To: Jackson
> From: Henry Johnson
> Here's what I can give you. The Sandman, as he calls himself, has been the focus on a couple of investigations, but he's a shadow. No one's gotten close to figuring anything out about him. He's wanted for at least four known cases of murder. When he sets his eyes on a target, he doesn't stop until they're dead. Be careful and don't fuck with this guy. I don't want to be pulling a note out of your pocket.

I open the pictures first and look at the different notes the Sandman has left on the bodies of his victims. I want to know more, but Henry doesn't give me any names or anything else. From what he does give me, it doesn't sound like any of the Sandman's victims were innocent, but that doesn't mean this man can go around killing anyone he likes.

LELAND

They're watching *The Bachelor* again. Did they record it? Someone actually wanted to watch it so much they *recorded* it?

Blonde bitch: Look at my tits. They're so perky.
Tiny Tits: Oh—

. . .

Hold up.

I swing my binoculars to the right as I notice something moving in the darkness of the night.

Well fuck me sideways. Assman is back. I zoom in and watch as he walks down the sidewalk on the far side of the street. After last night, I'd looked up the man's license plate to see if he knew anything I needed to know.

Name: Jackson Stein

Age: Thirty-nine

Light brown hair and hazel eyes. Served in the military until the age of thirty-four. That's when he opened his own detective agency. I got bored at that point. He clearly isn't involved but is investigating the case for some reason. Probably one of the parents reached out to him to find their missing daughter.

I watch as he slips into the dark, and I lose him for a moment. Where the hell did he go?

I debate climbing down to get closer to him, but that's when I see movement on the balcony of an abandoned house. He must have climbed up the side since he wasn't gone long enough to break into the house. The house had been my second choice, but from there, I couldn't clearly see the back door.

Hmm… I really would enjoy seeing his ass again. Especially hanging over the fence so I could have a good laugh.

It's too dark to get a good look at him, but I see that he has something shiny sitting on the railing of the porch.

I know I need to stay focused; he's of no concern to me. What I need to do is turn my attention back to the house or even *The Bachelor*.

Oh… but that ass. It was love at first sight.

I grin.

I gotta fuck with him.

Before the part of my brain that holds any intelligence can wake up, I unlock my weapons case. When I flip it open, I beam at my sniper rifle sitting in its cushioning.

JACKSON

The house is quiet. They might not return, but I'm going to be here and ready for them if they do. I reach out and grab my Pepsi before popping the top. I *have* to find something by Monday. I know that once the house goes to the police, there won't be anyone revisiting it.

I set my pop back on the railing.

This might be my only chance.

And that's when my pop can explodes.

It hits the wall, Pepsi spraying me as I drop to the ground. My military training tells me that when shots are fired, I have to find some cover. On the small balcony, I have nowhere to go but over the side, where I'd crawled up earlier. I pull my gun out as I lie in the pooling pop and wait for another shot.

Do they think they hit me?

But fuck, I didn't even hear a gun go off. Where the hell did the shot come from? Maybe it *wasn't* a shot at all. Maybe the can exploded… for some reason.

I scoot back to the wall where the pop canhad slammed into it. From the direction the can flew in, it tells me the shot came from directly in front of me. Is there someone in the house? I reach up to the wall and run my hand along it until I feel a bullet hole buried deep. Definitely a gunshot. The hole isn't at an angle, so the shot almost had to have been straight. The railing also would have stopped anything low.

For a few minutes, I remain on the ground before reaching into my bag and grabbing my thermal binoculars. I aim them toward the house, but they're not picking up on anything. What they *are* picking up on is someone walking toward my car.

What the fuck?

Quickly, I pull out my camera and zoom in. There's a figure walking over to my car wearing a dark hoodie. They have a backpack slung over their back and a case in their hands.

Is it that man from yesterday? The Sandman?

He tried shooting me. Does he think he got me?

I watch him, but he doesn't try getting into my car; instead, he turns around, *waves* at me and walks away. He knew I was watching him. Cocky asshole.

I wait until he's far out of sight before dropping off the balcony. Slowly, I move back toward my car which I'd parked in a different location than last night. When I get near it, I see the note sticking out from under my windshield wiper. I don't want to get shot through the back, so I'm careful as I move toward the car and grab it.

> *Sugar plum,*
> *You shouldn't drink pop. It's bad for your teeth.*
> *-Love, the Sandman* ♥

What the fuck? And that's definitely a heart drawn next to his name.

Clearly, I'm being messed with.

But why?

Leland: Do you ever get jealous over how phenomenal my flirting skills are?

Jackson: You… think some part of that was flirting? Shooting at me? Destroying my drink? Toying with me?

Leland: *quiet for a moment* You… didn't… think that was flirting? Jackson… Jackson, have I been flirting with you all wrong? No… don't do this to me. Don't tell me that I'm not as suave as I thought I was.

Jackson: Why yes, babe. I was overcome with how phenomenal you were at flirting! Like… my heart skipped a beat, not because I thought someone was going to shoot me, but because I felt myself get hit with Cupid's arrow!

Leland: The amount of sass and sarcasm in your voice right now is *criminal*.

Jackson: Not as criminal as the idea that shooting equals flirting.

Leland: Well, I got the man, didn't I? Now tell me this, if my flirting was bad, would you be here with me right now?

Jackson: If your aim was bad, I sure wouldn't be.

Leland: I would *never* put your life in danger. Well, mostly never. I mean… the only time I ever did was when I met your mom. Really, your life is in danger every time she walks into view… how *much* do you like her?

Jackson: You can't replace my mother.

Leland: What if… I found a woman who looked *just* like her?

Jackson: Let's get back to the story. We're going to be here all night if you keep distracting me.

THREE

LELAND

I climb the stairs to the third floor of the apartment I've called home for three years. It's a shithole, but it's much easier to hide in a shithole than a mansion. It's not like I *need* a bigger house, although a home theater would be nice.

As I shut the door behind me, I contemplate my actions. No one should stick a person who has trouble paying attention on a stakeout and expect them to do a good job. And then on top of that, give them a mouse to play with.

Oh, but the way he jumped brought far too much delight to my evening.

So much better than *The Bachelor*.

It's already seven in the morning. After giving Assman his letter, I moved to a different location to finish out my night before heading home. The apartment is an open, one-bedroom space, mostly bare but for a couch, TV, and a fridge. I didn't plan on staying here very long, so I didn't think I needed much. I was going to do a couple of jobs and move on.

Three years later, here I am, taking any job that brings me in a few bucks and gives me an adrenaline high. It's like I'm always looking for something different or something better and never finding it.

I was hired by a man who asked me to kill Hardek, the person involved in the trafficking. The man who hired me never told me his name or why he wanted Hardek dead, but the sum he offered me made it worthwhile.

The issue is finding Hardek.

I open the fridge and stare into the empty void. While I have cheese singles, I don't have bread. But I *do* have crackers. So I open up the cheese, fold it between two crackers, and feast on my meal.

I'm going to starve to death out of pure laziness.

Sounds about right.

The room is hot as I make my way over to the couch and grab my laptop off it. I flip it open and continue my search on Jackson Stein. When I stumble across a picture of him in his army uniform, my interest is piqued. I've always loved a man in uniform.

I hope he's back to play tomorrow.

JACKSON

I have Henry on the phone with me as I drive to the abandoned house. "He shot at me."

"Well, if he wanted to kill you, you'd be dead. With every victim of his, there's never a fight or a stray bullet. He shoots once and his victim ends up dead. One shot," Henry says. "Why don't you pull back, let us deal with it. I don't like you around the man. He did some… horrible things and I think you'd be safest staying out of it."

This is my last night staking out the house before I give the location and everything I have to the police. This time, I park the car as far from the house as I'm willing to walk.

"I don't like the odds, Henry."

"If you told us your location, I could have a team there in fifteen minutes ready to take this guy down. If he was there the past two nights, he's probably there again."

"Just one more night. Then you can do what you want after that."

As I turn the car off, I look around the grocery store parking lot.

The main reason I picked this place to put my car is because it's open twenty-four hours a day; the second reason is that I know this place has a security camera out front. If he's smart, he'll figure that out, but if he's not, I might get a better look at his face.

"I'll give you the address at seven," I assure Henry.

"I'll be ready."

After ending my call with Henry, I gather my stuff, make sure my gun is loaded, and head toward the abandoned house. As I walk, I keep an eye out for where that man might have shot at me from. I also need a new location to scout from.

When I see a video rental store with its lights off, I head over to it. Around back is a dumpster that gives me enough height that when I climb onto it, I can grab the edge of the roof and pull myself up. The lid of the dumpster is cracked, making me wonder if he cracked it climbing on it.

When I pull myself up, I look around in case he's hiding somewhere, but the flat roof has little to offer. But it does have a good view of the house, so I stay crouched as I move to a good spot and lie down in hopes of not giving anything away.

For hours I wait, attention snapping from spot to spot at each noise or movement. I feel like I'm waiting for the Sandman to jump out of nowhere and shoot me again, but either he can't find me or he isn't here to harass me.

When six comes around, I know it's a lost cause. Who knows how long the house has sat vacant. With all of this, I could be losing the lead the police could have had. It's still dark as I walk back to my car, but it would be strange for them to show up at the crack of dawn instead of during the night.

When I reach my car, the first thing I look for is a note, but there's nothing on the windshield. Did he not show up? Or could he not find my car?

I pull the car door open and slip inside before buckling my seat belt. I'm sure Henry is chomping at the bit, ready to send his team flying in, but there's something disappointing about not having any leads *again*.

Maybe I'll take one more drive around the block, just in case I missed something, then I'll call it in. I start the car and pull out of the parking lot before driving toward the house. That's when I feel something on my shoulder and look down as a hand slides around my neck.

"Hi, Jackson," he says in my ear from the back seat.

"Fuck!" I cry out as I jerk the steering wheel. Thankfully, I wasn't going fast, but it does nothing to stop me from slamming into the mailbox of the abandoned house. The decapitated mailbox crashes into the windshield as I hit the brakes.

LELAND

"What the fuck?" I cry out as I look at the man like he's nuts. "That was a bit dramatic, was it not?"

He tries turning around in his seat to face me, but I grab his hair and yank his head back so he can't. Why's his hair ridiculously silky? And he smells good, almost woodsy.

I take a deep breath while trying to imagine he smells this good because he knew I'd be here waiting for him. Well, maybe not *here* since he seems to be surprised about me being in the car.

"What the fuck?" he yells like he's irritated.

It's not *my* fault he didn't notice me sitting in the back seat of his car. All he had to do was look. "I wasn't even hiding," I say as I stick my finger in his ear. I'm thoroughly satisfied when he jerks away. "Everyone knows to *always* look in the back seat before you get into a car."

"Get out of my car," he growls as I lean forward and smile at him. Even though he's looking at me in his rearview mirror, he can't get a good visual on me when I'm donning this sexy ski mask that really makes my blue eyes pop since he literally can't see anything else other than my mouth.

"Why?" I whine. "I have a tip for you. Oh, not *that* kind of tip, you dirty boy. Unless you want that kind of tip. Although, if I'm being honest, I like the tip more than giving the tip, if you get me?"

He grimaces, and I can't imagine why. My only conclusion is that he doesn't like my mask. Or maybe hostage situations don't really turn him on. Or maybe he didn't get my joke.

"Did you not get it? Penis. Tip of your penis." I try to reach for it in case he needs further explanation, but he smacks my hand away.

"I got it."

"Are you offering?" I ask eagerly.

"No?"

Ooh. "Why did that sound like a question?" Now he's got me all excited.

"What? That was *not* a question! It was my confused brain trying to make sense of your ludicrous… statement."

"That makes sense. This is generally not how I try to get laid either, but hard times call for desperate measures. Get it? Hard times?"

He doesn't get it. "Who the hell are you, and why are you in my car? Are you going to kill me?"

"What? Why would I kill you?" I ask in surprise.

"You *shot* at me."

Oh. *That.* "Well, that was just like flirting. Like how a boy pushes a girl he likes."

He looks at me in the mirror like I'm crazy. "You *shot* at me."

"That's my version of pushing. You were like three houses away, how else was I supposed to get your attention?"

"You *shot* at me."

Clearly, that's the only thing he knows how to say.

"You know what, you're getting less attractive by the moment. So, I have a tip for you. I found out that a man who goes by the nickname of Buster is who tipped Hardek about the interest in the house. He might know where the girls are at."

"Why should I trust you?"

This man is obstinate. I was expecting him to pop a boner at my investigative work or, at the very least, give me a thank you. "Because I've seen your butthole and that pretty much makes us BFFs."

His face turns grave. "That's… no."

"What do you mean? I looked it right in the eye."

He cringes. "That's… no… just… no."

"I think it even winked at me."

"Oh my god. Get out of my car."

I start laughing. "So? BFFs?"

"No!"

"Fine, but the spot is open."

"I can't imagine why."

"What's that mean?"

"You shoot at people, break into their car, talk about their… their *ass* and then claim to be…"

"BFFs," I supply.

He sighs. "Yeah… that, but the first thing to being BFFs is telling me your name."

"I'll whisper it to you." I lean forward so my mouth is next to his ear. "They call me… Massive Dong."

Then I lick his ear before pushing the door open and slipping out. "Oh, I left my sex playlist in your CD player."

And then I drop to my knees and start crawling away because it's not easy to just "disappear" like they do in the movies.

JACKSON

I grab for my gun, ready to apprehend the clearly fucked-up man, but by the time I turn to look, he's gone. I twist in my seat but I'm completely alone. How did he get away so quickly?

And what the absolute hell was that? The man is clearly insane. I just lived through an encounter with a deranged man.

I quickly back up the car, planning on pretending like I had nothing to do with the smashed mailbox. Then I reach for my phone, but before that, I turn the radio on and click to the CD so I can hear this "sex playlist" he left behind.

"I'll Make a Man Out of You" from *Mulan* begins playing.

I sigh and dial Henry's number. As it rings, I think about the Sandman's tip. Not the penis tip, but the actual tip. Buster? What am I looking for, a dog?

At least it's something to go by, as long as it's not useless information. But if it isn't, why give it to me? What did I do to deserve it? And why is he targeting me?

Henry answers with, "Found nothing?"

"Well… I have something, but you're not going to like how I got it."

. . .

Jackson: You know what I learned from that encounter?

Leland: That we were always meant to be BFFs?

Jackson: To always look in the back seat before I get into a vehicle.

Leland: Good! You should have already known that. You never know who might be lying in wait for you, and while your bestest love will keep you safe, I still want you on your toes. I wasn't even *hiding,* and you just waltzed right in… or were you hoping I was waiting inside, you sly, sly man?

Jackson: That was the last thing I was expecting *or* hoping for.

Leland: The real question is whether you kept my sex playlist.

Jackson: It was… oddly good. Definitely would never have sex to *any* of those songs. *None* of them were sexy.

Leland: That's a defeatist attitude, Jackson. Honestly, I'm just loving all of these wonderful things you told Henry when talking about me. It's like a teenager running home to tell Poppop about his crush.

Jackson: We have wildly different ideas about what a crush means.

Leland: I have two types of crushes. 1) Watch me crush this motherfucker like the badass motherfucker I am. And 2) Dat Jackson is *Fiiiine* with a capital F for Dat Fine Fucker Could Fuck Me.

Jackson: I'm glad you never got those two mixed up.

Leland: Right? Like I don't wanna crush the motherfucker and then realize I wanted to fuck him!

FOUR

JACKSON

When I walk into the office, Mason smiles at me. "You have a new client."

"Why didn't you take them?" I ask a bit sourly. I've spent the past four hours searching for anything that could lead me to a "Buster" and have nothing to show for it.

Mason waves to the woman sitting in front of him like she's a good excuse for why he didn't take the new client. While I did see her when I came in, I didn't feel like acknowledging her since I'm positive Mason's wasting far too much time talking to her.

"Where's the person at?" I ask, since it's clear they're not in the little office.

"He got tired of waiting for you and went down to look at books," Mason says. "I told him to keep an eye out for a guy with a 'no fucks given' attitude and a permanent scowl on his face."

I scowl at him because I don't have time for this. "What's his name?"

"Oh… I think Donny. Something about a cheating fiancée."

I sigh and set my bag on my desk before heading through the door, and I nearly run into the person I was sent looking for. "Donny?" I ask.

His blue eyes go wide as he stares at me from where he stands on the steps. "I'm really sorry for not watching where I was going. And no, I'm not Donny. Do you need a Donny? I didn't see anyone else down there."

He looks behind himself as he nervously runs his fingers through his dark brown hair. His hair is longer on top and shorter on the sides, but it's currently sticking straight up, telling me he's been repeatedly running his fingers through it.

"What's your name?" I ask.

His eyes snap up to mine. "Tommy... oh... were you looking for me?"

"Yes, I apologize. Come along."

He smiles at me and I realize that when he's actually looking at me, he's quite attractive.

"It's okay. I get called other names a lot, and I should have realized."

I do *not* have time to deal with this guy. My dick tries to tell me that he's attractive and that I haven't gotten laid in months, but my mind is fixated on this Buster guy. And the guy in my car.

Mostly the guy in my car.

What a cocky asshole.

I wave at the plastic chair in front of my desk. "Have a seat."

He sits and nervously picks at his dark blue shirt while looking around with equally blue eyes. I wonder if they're contacts to be that blue.

"So, Tommy, what can I do for you?"

He turns his attention back to me and gives me a sad smile. "Well... my friend said that you could help me with my fiancée. I think she's cheating on me, but maybe she's not... This is stupid. I'm sorry. I'm probably wasting your time."

My phone dings, and I look over at the text that just came in.

Henry: I might know who Buster is.

"I apologize, give me one second," I tell Tommy. He seems to sink in his chair, and I realize that I'm being really rude.

"You seem kind of preoccupied... do you want me to make an appointment? I can come back later."

I shake my head. "No, I apologize." I fall into this issue where I get caught up in the exciting cases and don't want anything to do with the cheating or suspected cheating. The issue is that the stressed spouses pay the bills. This other stuff rarely happens. "Just one second, and I'll be all ears."

He smiles and the expression brightens up his entire face. Suddenly, I find myself smiling in response. "Okay. Thank you," he says.

Whoever his fiancée is would be stupid to cheat on him. Although, he's more adorable than sexy, what with the way he's timid about everything. I suppose that might not be much of a win for a woman looking for a manly man, and instead, they get a timid kitten.

I grab my phone so I can text Henry back.

> Me: Give me everything you've got.

I turn back to the man. "Alright, so tell me about your fiancée."

As he talks, I write down everything I can while occasionally glancing down at my phone.

> Henry: Some of the guys think they've heard the bartender over at Stone's Pub being called Buster.

I listen to everything the kid is saying, but to me, it sounds like he's insecure and looking for something to pin on his fiancée. Or maybe some type of reassurance.

> Henry: I'm going to send someone over to the pub and see if he's working.

"Is there anything else you need?" Tommy asks.

"Just your phone number."

He fills it in on the paper I give him then smiles at me as he stands. "Thank you so much for your time."

"You're welcome."

Henry may already be on top of it, but he can't do anything without proof about Buster, unlike me. As soon as the young man is gone, I grab my bag. Mason is still talking to the woman even though I'm positive he doesn't need to talk to her for this long. Why's she giggling so much? What could *possibly* be worth giggling about to this extent? It's a good thing Mason helps pay for this place.

"I'm headed out," I say.

Mason nods at me, barely looking away from the woman long enough to acknowledge me. "Got it. Be safe."

"Thanks," I say as I head down the stairs. Just as I'm passing through the bookstore, Rose waves me down.

"Jackson, hold up!" Rose calls.

No one is going to let me rush anywhere, are they?

I see her looking around for a moment before grabbing whatever she'd been looking for. She holds up a thin book that looks like a graphic novel. "This is from the sweetest young man that was just in here."

"Yeah? That's good."

I need to go and not be distracted by the sexy young man. Oh, with that timid nature, I bet he'd be fun to show a thing or two.

"He said he bought this book for you and asked if I'd give it to you. Not sure why he didn't want to give it to you himself, but who am I to judge what kids are doing these days?"

Interest now piqued, I walk over to her. I'm pretty sure kids these days aren't going around buying private investigators books. Although, maybe it was as a thanks and he was too embarrassed to give it to me.

"Thanks," I say as I take it from her.

I flip it over and see that it's a Neil Gaiman book. While I haven't read any of his books, I've heard of him, but none of that matters when I see the title.

Sandman.

Holy shit.

"Rose!" I yell, making her jump and grab her heart. "What did he say when he gave this to you? Exact words."

She raises an eyebrow. "Boy, I don't even remember what you said to me a minute ago. He just asked me to give it to you."

"And this was that young man? Mid-twenties? Dark brown hair, about five inches shorter than me. Thin?"

She nods. "Yeah. He went upstairs after talking to me. A client, I assume?"

I just sat in my office chair while the fucking *Sandman* pretended to be a client. And I was too busy *thinking* about the Sandman from my car to pay attention to the Sandman sitting in front of me.

Fuck.

I tuck the book under my arm and race out the door, but I know he won't be anywhere within sight. I have to be the worst PI ever.

Hold on... he gave me his information, address, phone number. Could any of it be real? Did he use my pen or his? Do I have his fingerprints?

I rush back in and up the stairs. The pen he'd used is gone, but the paper with his information isn't.

LELAND

He's adorable.

That's all I can decide. He was like a man in love. Mind preoccupied, surely by me. While I *know* it was risky showing my face, I *needed* his attention. The look on his face when that old lady gave him the book was priceless.

From my spot by the science fiction bookshelf, I watch him zoom out the door, clearly looking for me. What's he going to do when he finds me?

Hopefully, award me for my cleverness by showing me a good time.

In retrospect, it probably wasn't intelligent showing him my face. Of course I checked to make sure he had no security cameras up before I walked in, and I didn't give him any information he could do anything with.

Well, besides the phone number.

And what's he going to do with my face? Even if he remembers everything about it, he's not going to be able to track me down. I'm like a ghost. A nobody. Even if he had my name and dragged me right into the police station, they wouldn't be able to pin anything on me. I'm careful... most of the time.

It was still really stupid, especially when I'm *always* so careful. I would never make a mistake like this, so why'd I willingly do it? I think I've lost my mind. Am I love blind? Lust blind?

I'm bored. That's what it is. Definitely *all* it is.

The bell on the door sounds as he comes rushing back in. Then I watch him race up the stairs before taking my leave. No one notices as I step out onto the street.

As if on cue, my burner phone starts ringing. I pull it out of my pocket and accept the call.

"Hey, sexy," I say, all thoughts of how stupid this is rushing right out the window with my eagerness to talk to him.

"Who is this?" he asks.

I chuckle as I walk down the sidewalk to my car. "I-It's T-Tommy. Did you need more about my unfaithful fiancée?" I ask as I use the timid and low voice I'd used with him earlier.

"Why are you targeting me?" he asks.

"Targeting? You're not my target. Unless you're talking about your penis. That's my target."

For some reason, he doesn't seem amused *or* turned on. "Why don't you come back here so we can talk?"

"Honestly, I would, but my feelings are hurt. I was spilling my soul to you, but it was like going on a date where your date just stared at their phone the entire time. It really made me feel sad."

"What's your interest in me? Does someone want me dead?" he asks.

"I hope not. I already explained it to you, but clearly, you're quite dense. That's okay, you're really cute and that makes up for it."

"You're a wanted murderer, this is not... you should just turn yourself in."

"A murderer, huh?" I think about it for a moment. "I suppose I have killed people. What about you? Have you ever killed anyone, Mr. Stein?"

"It's different. I'm doing my job. I'm legally doing what has to be done."

I reach my car and unlock the door. "Fine, I'll leave you alone if that's what you want."

"No, I told you I'd meet you."

"And let me guess, the guys with the shiny lights will be waiting with you?"

"They won't have their lights on."

"Hm… I've never been arrested before; it might be fun. Would you handcuff me and show me a good time first? Pat me down? Do an *all* over exam on me?"

"If that's what you want," he says.

"You're such a liar. Why are you cute even when you lie? I'll see ya around, hot stuff," I say before hanging up.

Why the hell am I being so reckless? Just because of a nice-looking man?

A part of me doesn't care what happens to me. This is the most alive I've felt in a long time. Sometimes it gets tiring hiding who I am and only getting close to people I'm going to kill.

I push reckless thoughts away and switch them to Hardek and Buster. Whoever the person texting Jackson was, they said that Buster worked at Stone's Pub. I guess I'm going to be making a pit stop to see what Buster is up to.

Jackson: Why *did* you risk so much for me, Leland? I mean… showing your face when I knew who you were could have ended very badly for you.

Leland: Hmm… honestly? I think I was a bit… I don't even know if I want to say bored. I was… careless because I was tired… you know? Something I didn't know growing up, and that took me a long time to realize, even after I met you, was how much people need others. I'd gotten to the point where I just... didn't care anymore. And then suddenly you were there, and you were something *fun*. It'd been so long since something piqued my interest like that. And then I became far too intrigued by the idea of this PI that I could pester.

Jackson: I'm sorry that life turned out that way for you.

Leland: Okay... nope. This is getting to be too much. Feels icky and gross; let's go back to reliving the first chapter. "Sexy man! Towering fence—"

Jackson: You know with me, you don't have to run from your feelings.

Leland: Oh, Jackson. I'm not running from them. I'm fleeing like the motherfucking wind!

Jackson: How is that any better?

Leland: I'm a whisper in the night. Fuck those feelings!

Jackson: Don't fuck the feelings.

Leland: Fuck 'em. Fuck 'em, Jackson!

Jackson: Baby steps. Someday... you will walk right up to me and go "Jackson, let me tell you all about how I'm feeling."

Leland: And that is the day you will know that I have been cloned. You will then spend days and weeks searching for the real me... and when you find me... you'll have to face the hardest decision of your life. Would you choose to have sex with both clone me *and* real me at the same time?

Jackson: I'm not engaging in this conversation.

Leland: It's not cheating. I will permit it. Clone me and real me could climb on top of you like a mighty naked Jenga tower.

Jackson: And with that image in our minds, we're on to the next part of the story.

Leland: You're welcome.

FIVE

LELAND

Over the past day, I've figured out that employees of Stone's Pub come in through the alleyway door. They park out back and walk down the alley, since there's not enough parking out front for them and patrons. I sit in my car and watch the parking lot for the man called Buster to show. After perusing the Stone's Pub Facebook page, I found some pictures of him and have a good idea of what he looks like. There were a couple of photographs where he was in the background, serving drinks to customers when the shot was taken, and someone tagged him in it.

He's a beefy man that wears shirts he clearly paints on every morning. When he parks his car, it's not until I see the man up close and personal that I realize the pictures did *not* do the big man justice. When he gets out of his car, the suspension seems to spring back to life. Buster looks like he should be the bouncer instead of a bartender from the way his muscles make him look like he could pop my head off with a pinch of his fingers.

I slip out of my car just as he walks toward the alleyway. No… "walks" isn't what he does. Maybe struts works better, but in a way that he swings his rock-hard arms back and forth with each step he takes. Then I realize that during my assessment, I forgot my keys, so I quickly open the car door back up. I snatch them off the seat and hurry toward the alleyway. My luck, he'll have already gone inside.

Oh, but I should have known that recently, I've had the best of luck because when I peek into the alleyway, Buster hasn't gone inside, Buster is confronting Jackson.

Whatever Jackson said to him before I showed up must have been pretty bad because Buster is towering over him, the back of his neck red out of anger. He's also wearing this unique expression like he wouldn't mind punching Jackson's face in.

"Hey, Jackson!" I yell.

Startled, Jackson looks over at me, and that's the moment Buster decides to punch the man of my dreams in the face. Because Jackson was too busy scowling at me, he never saw it coming. The punch is hard, and Jackson drops like a deadweight.

For some reason, I kind of feel like that *might* have been my fault.

Like… a teeny tiny bit might have been my fault.

So teeny.

But this will be the perfect opportunity to show that I'm a perfect mate. I shall do a mating dance for my unconscious mate-to-be. "Hey, asshole. I like his pretty face," I growl as I strut up to the man like I'm something to be feared.

The man turns to me, towering over my five-foot-eleven frame with his six-foot-seven body. "What the fuck do *you* want?"

"Tell me where Hardek is," I say in my best "bad guy" voice. I kind of sound like a smoker, but cigarettes kill, so it might work.

He laughs as he moves toward me, like he's going to scare me off. Since I can't rightfully shoot him in the alleyway during broad daylight, I decide a taser will have to do. The poor man almost walks right into it. He drops nearly as fast as Jackson did, and I realize that I might have a manic grin on my face. Wiping it off and getting my bad boy expression back on, I leer over him.

After he's done flopping around like a fish, I squat down on his chest as he tries to figure out if life has ended for him. Once I'm strad-dling him with my legs spread as wide as they can go to accommodate his size, I begin to question if I should have just squatted next to him. Should I sit on him? Would that be weird? Would that be more menacing? I'm spending far too much time thinking about this. "Hey, buddy, you tell me where Hardek is or I'll…" I look around and notice a thin rock which I snatch up.

He's watching me with wide eyes as I press the rock to the right of his eye.

"Or I'll dig your eye out with this rock."

I press a little harder to show that I'm "serious" and the thin rock snaps in half. Little rock pieces fall into his eye and he howls as he flips onto his side. The force of it sends me falling off him as he rubs vigorously at his face.

"I told you," I say as if I planned that. "I'll put rock dirt in your other eye if you don't cough some shit up. Now, where's Hardek? I ain't asking again, *motherfucka*." I stand up so I have the higher ground.

Not for long because he gets to his feet and turns to me, ready to murder me. I decide that my specialty clearly isn't my threats or my rock dirt attack, but guns. So I pull my silenced gun out and aim at him.

"I'm done playing games. Answer the fucking question."

He starts laughing like he has the upper hand even though there are tears running from the one eye. He can't even fully open it and his hand is clearly itching to rub it. "Do you even know how to use that, kid?"

I shoot him right in the foot, and you'd have thought his balls never dropped by the noise he makes. "Where's Hardek?"

He falls against the wall. "Fuck! Fucking! My foot! What the fuck is wrong with you?"

"Answer the question. Where's Hardek?"

He seems to be interested in taking me a little more seriously this time for some reason. "L-Last I heard, he was hiding out with Caleb Garvin. He's protecting him."

"Thanks, bud. And let me just say that if you're wrong, I'm going to come back and sprinkle rock dust into your eyes again."

He flips me off.

"Now you patiently wait there while I head off with my friend," I say as I look down at Jackson who has to just be napping at this point. The man didn't hit him *that* hard.

I tuck my gun away, lean down and grab Jackson around the midsection. The issue is that he's a good four inches taller than me and outweighs me. But I am nothing if not an overachiever.

I grab onto him and carry him a few feet before realizing that he's heavy as fuck, and I *really* don't want to pull a muscle. I guess I could leave him here. I mean... he's just so *heavy*. Yeah, he has a very nice face, but his personality is mediocre at best.

Fine. I'll do my good deed for the year.

I dutifully drag him the rest of the way out of the alleyway. He'll probably have a little road rash on him when he wakes up, but it's honestly the saintly thing of me to do to help him out.

I find his car and decide that I'll drive *to* him, so I drop him on the ground. Maybe a bit too hard because I think I hear his head smash into the pavement.

"Please don't remember that," I whisper as I pat him over for his keys.

Once I find them, I drive his car up to him before dragging him into the passenger seat. Then off we go on an adventure together to a nearby shop that I'm *positive* he'll love. It'll be such a delight for him when he wakes up.

He's still not awake when I arrive, so I check to make sure that he *is* alive. That'd be a real downer if I strained myself by carrying him around and he dies three minutes later. But he's breathing just fine. I scavenge his car over until I find something to write him a note with so he's not confused when he wakes up.

JACKSON

I groan as I come to. There's an insistent knocking that I fight to ignore, but the pounding in my head drives me awake. I open my eyes and look out at the man peering through the window.

"Dude, you alright?" he yells through the car window.

I have no idea who it is, but I nod and try to wave him off.

"Looks like you might have partied a bit too hard. Maybe you should call someone to pick you up."

"I'm fine, thank you."

The man nods and heads away.

As I sit up, something rolls off my lap. I reach down to the floor and pick it up only to find that it's a twelve-inch massive dildo.

Where the fuck did this come from?

That's when I notice something making a strange noise. At first, I think it's my phone vibrating, but when I look down, I realize that it's a vibrator buzzing away. My lap is littered with… stuff. There's a ball gag, a fluffy handcuff that is attached to my right wrist, and I have some kind of lacy underwear wrapped around my neck that I pull off.

For a moment I can't remember what happened. I have no idea where this stuff came from or why I'm wearing it like a sex fiend. Then I remember that I was talking to dickhead Buster when that *man* came waltzing onto the scene. He distracted me and I was punched in the face.

My head is fucking pounding and it makes me want to strangle that guy even more than I wanted to before. Figuring out his identity is driving me insane. I *have* to find out who this asshole is.

I yank everything off me, tossing it all onto the ground before getting out of the passenger seat to get into the driver's seat. That's when I realize where he got all the stuff he dumped on me.

At the Swings and Things Adult Store.

Of course, that's where I'm at.

I scowl as I walk around the car and get into the driver's seat. On top of that, I got nothing out of Buster. I drive to the police station as the vibrator buzzes away on my passenger side floor. It's too far out of my reach to turn it off.

When I park, I reach into the back seat to grab a coat or something to toss over the heinous things all over my floor. I'd never hear the end of it if someone saw my new collection. Boxes and bags fall from my coat since he didn't take the time to throw away any of the packaging the adult products came in. I turn the vibrator off, toss my coat over them, and quickly get out of the car.

Once through the door, I briefly nod at the secretary before zooming on past her to Henry's office. I knock once then push the door open.

"I need everything on the Sandman."

His eyes get wide, then he starts laughing. "I-I take it you had a run-in with him?"

"What?" I stare at him. "What are you laughing about?"

"Go to the bathroom... wait! Before you do that!"

He pulls his phone out, and I realize he's going to snap a picture of me. He's laughing too hard to steady the phone, and I manage to turn around to flee before he can. As I rush through the precinct, eyes turn to me, but I thankfully manage to slip into the bathroom and lock the door before too many get a look. I stare into the mirror and realize that my life accomplishment will be putting the Sandman behind bars.

On the right side of my face, in permanent marker, is a penis, ball hairs and all. On my left cheek is *Love, the Sandman* with a heart like he puts on my notes.

Then I see an arrow running down my neck. I yank my shirt up and look at my chest covered in ink. How long was I out for? And instead of caring about the fact that a human should *not* be unconscious that long, he turned me into a fucking sketch pad. Besides coloring my nipples black, he wrote me a few things.

Call me.

And then a new phone number.

I spend the next ten minutes finding out that getting permanent marker off my face is not an easy feat. When I walk back into Henry's office, my face is bright red from the constant rubbing, and there's still a shadow of a penis on my face.

He's grinning at me like a madman when I walk in.

"I want *everything* you have on him," I growl.

"I can't give you everything."

"I gave you the address to the house, you give me something."

He thinks about it for a moment. "Let me see what else I can find. Are you going to give a statement? I would love to see this man behind bars after what he did to my partner."

"I'll do what I can," I say.

As he goes to gather information, I turn the lights in the office off and search his desk for something to calm my headache. I take what I can find, then close my eyes as I try to tell my brain that it doesn't need to feel like it's being squeezed through a hole the size of a dime.

Henry returns after a few minutes and sets a folder on his desk. "While I can't let you look at it, I can't exactly tell what you're doing while I'm in my meeting. I'll be back in an hour."

"Have fun," I say.

He slips out the door and I go over to his chair and sit down. I flip the folder open and look down at what Henry has supplied me.

The first paper surprises me the most. The first known case involving the Sandman goes back to the early eighties. That kid couldn't have even been born in the early eighties. Probably nineties, if I had to guess. So... a copycat?

I examine the handwriting of the first note and compare it to a later note. Both are pretty sloppy and simplistic. The ones he writes to me are the only ones with more... personality to them.

The second note was found on the body of a governor who was allegedly stealing money.

I record the date of each note. Most are people who have clearly done something wrong or there were rumors they were doing something wrong. It seems like the police only halfheartedly tried to figure out who the Sandman was during the eighties and nineties. That is until ten years ago when he killed Henry's partner, Ted Williams. According to the reports, the man was a dutiful cop, friendly with everyone, and a loving father.

Autopsy reports showed that he didn't go down without a fight, but they couldn't find any DNA of the attacker on him. The fight ended with a bullet in the chest before he bled out. It threw the police force in a frenzy to find the man who killed such an innocent person.

I never knew Williams or much about the case. My focus during that time was military related.

The thing that gets me is that the Sandman's focus had been people who subjectively deserved to die. Granted, he was not a cop or legally allowed to kill them, but he was, in a sense, doing the world a favor. All but Williams.

Was it a mistake?

It looks like there was speculation that Williams accidentally got pulled into something that caused him to wind up dead, but the note the Sandman left on Williams' chest showed it wasn't.

Another end.
-the Sandman

Another end? End of life? End of what?

I still have the graphic novel he gave me. After I'd ended the phone call with the crazed man, I put it into a bag so I could have them run prints on it. But now I have one more thing I can give them: the knowledge that the current Sandman is not the one who'd started this. I could give them what he looks like and I could get Henry on him like a hound dog.

But for some reason, I don't. I can't stop thinking about how, while he was the reason I was knocked out, he didn't leave me there. He kept me safe. But do I owe him anything?

Leland: Have you *ever* seen a more romantic exchange of phone numbers?

Jackson: You *dropped me*? Did you forget to tell me this?

Leland: I mean… what a magnificent meet-cute. Amiright? Tell me any other meet-cute that is better than ours.

Jackson: You *dropped me*.

Leland: Here, I will tell you why. The weight of my love for you was just… so much that my arms couldn't handle it. Not until we came together and carried that love as a couple could I handle the weight.

Jackson: Cute.

Leland: Thank you.

Jackson: *sighs* It's a good thing you *are* cute.

Leland: *grinning* Thank you. You know, the guy at that shop shares a good laugh with me every time I swing by for something new for our sex dungeon.

Jackson: Oh joy.

Leland: He told me he tells everyone who will listen how adorable our romance is.

Jackson: I just... don't even want to know what you told him. And the grin on your face tells me I'm right.

SIX

LELAND

I lean against the wall of the old brick building, my patience slowly diminishing. Waiting is not my strong suit. I prefer to jump in, get shit done, and move on.

I pull out my phone to see how long I've been waiting. When I see that only four minutes have passed since I got here, I quickly put the phone away and pretend like I never checked.

How could only four minutes have passed? It felt like at least ten.

That's when the door swings open and all my prayers have been answered as the handsome man steps out. His clothes look a little disorderly, but they still fit him nicely enough that I can see a line of muscle. He's not overly muscled but clearly takes care of his body. Maybe a runner. I bet he's a runner.

I wonder if he'd run after me.

He shuts the door behind himself as I push off the wall I'd been leaning against right outside the agency.

"Hi, Jackson!" I shout.

He's also amazing at jumping. Clearly, this is a man worth marrying. He's sexy *and* agile.

He leaps to the side, grabbing his heart with one hand and his side with the other. What's he going to do? Shoot me?

"The only thing you can shoot me with is Cupid's arrow," I tell him. I smile at him as I step up and run my fingers over his chest.

He glares at me but doesn't remove his hand from his side. "You're walking on eggshells; the police already have your fingerprints and your picture. They know who you are."

Oh, what a bad liar he is. "I don't believe that. First off, I haven't interacted around you without gloves on. Well, other than as Tommy, but little Tommy never touched anything." I wiggle my gloved fingers in front of his face. "Secondly, there are no cameras here. If there were, you would have probably said something about the night I let myself in and sat in your chair. I even went through your emails."

He scowls like he doesn't appreciate my sneakiness. "What do you want?"

"I thought you'd never ask. Maybe a drink? There's this really cute place that I would love to have a date at."

He shakes his head. Maybe he doesn't like drinks and would prefer a restaurant.

"I'm not... going on a date with you."

"But... you owe me a drink for saving your life. Oh, and did I tell you I got Buster to give me a name? I might even give you another tip. How about a tip for a tip?"

"I don't have a tip..." His face sours as he realizes what kind of tip I was referring to. "You have a name? Then tell me."

"For a drink."

"Do you want to be paid?"

"No, just a drink."

He shifts his weight as he considers whether it's worth it. *But* he's also aware that without me, he'll have no tip at all.

"Fine."

I give him my best smile and hold my gloved hand out to him. He stares at it in confusion.

"What's that?"

"It's a date. We hold hands for a date."

His slightly unkempt eyebrows knit. "This is not a date, and I'm not holding your hand."

I frown even though I'm enjoying every moment of this on the inside. "That's harsh."

"Let's get this over with."

I start walking and he grudgingly steps up beside me. He's a little taller than I originally thought; over six feet. "Are you always so grumpy?"

"I'm not *grumpy*. I have to deal with a serial killer who is tugging me around."

"Want me to tug you around by the nuts?"

"Not at all."

We're quiet for a moment as I think about the words "serial killer." I glance over at him and notice he's watching me. "I'm not a serial killer, by the way."

"I know, but you still kill people."

I nod. "I do. Tell me about yourself, Jackson. What's your life story?"

"Don't have one."

I grab my chest. "Oh no! You have amnesia? Well, Jackson, I'm here to tell you that we actually used to be lovers but after that horrible, horrible waxing accident, you forgot about me."

He raises an eyebrow. "Waxing?"

"I told you it was a bad idea to wax your nuts," I say as I pat his shoulder. I give his arm a little squeeze to see if my muscle hypothesis is right.

It is.

"Waxing your nuts can cause memory loss?" he asks like he's skeptical.

"In special cases," I say.

He shakes his head. "Have you just... never interacted with humans before so you don't actually know how to?"

I grin at him as I bump my hip into his and slide my arm around him. "I really don't get the chance to interact with people much, but I feel like I'm knocking this interaction out of the park."

He pushes me off him as I look down at his phone I'm now holding.

I reach for his hand. "Can I borrow your finger for a second so I can unlock this?"

He yanks his phone from my hands. "Where are we walking to?"

I point. "It's called The Loft. Ever been there?"

He looks over at the place and nods. "Yeah."

"With an ex?"

"My business partner."

"Did you fuck him?"

"Nope."

"Well, then tonight will end differently."

"I'm not fucking you."

"That's to be determined."

When we reach the place, he holds the door open for me before realizing that he's supposed to dislike me and pushes his way through first. I still find it cute and love looking at his ass as he heads up the stairs to the second floor. It's just so round and perfect in those jeans. I feel like he needs to know this.

"Those jeans fit you beautifully."

He looks back at me. "Don't look at my ass."

"That's not fair. Where am I supposed to look, then? The ceiling?"

He shakes his head, clearly also unsure of where I should look.

When we reach the second floor, he looks around before waving to a table near the window. "I'll grab drinks. Preference?"

"Surprise me," I say.

He nods and walks over to the counter. It would be easy for him to call the police and have them here in five minutes. I wonder if he will.

I go over to the small two-person table and glance over at him before sitting down. It's hard to see what he's doing from this angle. He could be calling them at this moment, who knows?

When he returns with two drinks, he sets one in front of me before sitting down.

"Why are you so confident I won't call the police?" he asks curiously.

I pick up the glass and take a sip. Whatever it is, it's strong. Maybe he's planning on getting me drunk and seeing what I'll spill. "Well... even if you did, the police would have nothing on me. It'd be nearly impossible for them to put me behind bars with your words alone. And... I don't think you will."

"Why?"

"I don't know," I admit. "Maybe because you know they'd eat me alive in prison."

"Would they?" he asks with a raised eyebrow.

I grin. "Maybe not. Maybe you want to eat me alive. Which would be fine with me because I sure wouldn't complain."

"What do I call you?"

I lean forward and lick my lip. "Sexy."

He tips his glass up and takes a sip without breaking eye contact. When he sets it down, he says, "But you're not."

I scowl at him. "You're mean. I just want your attention. I've been doing this mating dance and everything for you. Tell me what I'm doing wrong."

The music is low enough that it's just background noise since the place is not as much of a bar or club as a meeting spot. There are a few people here, but most are out of hearing range.

"Who are you targeting?" he asks.

"I was hired to put a bullet through Hardek's brain."

"So you're hired to take jobs?"

"I am."

"Who hired you?"

"Honestly? I don't know. He went through my handler and said he'd prefer to keep his identity quiet."

"So you'll kill anyone you're hired to? If someone hired you to kill me, would you?"

I watch him as a smile plays at my lips. "I'm not here to talk about work or about me. I'm here to talk about you."

"To me, time is wasting when I could be saving these girls. Every minute I spend fucking off, my chances of finding them alive diminish. Do you understand?"

I watch him for a moment, glad to hear that. The thing is, before I trust him, I want to know how far he'll go. "I do."

"Then yes, I want to talk about this."

"Fine, fine. Then you owe me a date after."

"I don't owe you anything."

"I'm going to go to the bathroom, and then we'll have a chat."

He hesitates but nods. As I stand up, I kick my backpack on purpose. To him, it appears that I tripped, but I want to remind him it's there. I want to know what he does while I'm gone. If he searches it for my ID or anything about me, I'm done trusting him.

My heart will be broken, but I'll pick up the pieces and make my escape.

JACKSON

My eyes are adhered to that backpack. Almost every time I've seen him, he's had it with him. There has to be something inside that'll give him away. I glance over at the bathroom, but I can't even see it from here since it's behind the bar.

I pull my phone out and stare at it without really looking at it. Why am I not calling the police? I could have them here and have this man arrested in minutes. I don't believe that once we have him in custody we won't get anything from him. They would get a warrant for his apartment and find something. It wouldn't take much.

So why can't I get myself to call them? I try to tell myself that it's because he could have some information to help me get the girls back, but I don't know that. I don't know anything, yet I'm trusting him in a way by letting him remain free.

By the time he returns, I haven't decided on anything and have lost all opportunity to do something. He looks nothing like the criminals I generally deal with. If anyone saw him on the street, they'd assume he was a college student. A *very* attractive one, but still a college student. He smiles at me and the look pulls me in. If he weren't the *Sandman*, I would probably be trying to figure out how to get him into my bed. I don't have much time for relationships, but I could make time for a night with this man.

His blue eyes are vibrant and pull me in as he gives me a smile. His lips are thin, but they match his pale face.

He slides our glasses to the side before grabbing his chair and dragging it next to mine until it hits. Then he sits down and opens his backpack.

"I'm glad you didn't nose in my backpack," he says before leaning into me. He smells good, and he's already in my personal space, so when he leans in and looks up at me from under those thick eyelashes, my mind goes somewhere it shouldn't. It makes me want to lean into him and breathe him in. Do things I shouldn't.

I forcefully drag my eyes away from his and pretend that my drink is the most interesting thing here. "How do you know I didn't?"

"I watched."

His knee knocks into mine and my eyes instantly go down to it. The thing is, I *know* he's aware he's doing this to me. And he's enjoying every moment of it. "You were watching me?" I ask.

"I was. I'm good at peeping. It's part of my job."

I lean away so I don't have to keep pulling in the smell of his cologne. He reaches down and for a moment, I think he's going to touch my leg, but when he slips his hand into his backpack, I'm disappointed. WHY am I disappointed?

I try to push away all ridiculous thoughts as he takes a notebook out of his bag. He unhooks the pencil from the cover and flips through the notebook until he finds the right page. He's no longer pressing into me; instead, his attention has turned to what he has laid out in front of him.

"So, we have Hardek at the head here," he says as he points to the name at the top. "We know that he's taken at least five girls ages sixteen to twenty from a hundred-mile radius within the past six months. Two girls were found four months ago when they managed to escape."

As he talks, I let my eyes run down his notebook. For some reason, I'm surprised by the amazing detail he has. It's messy as fuck—looks like a stream of consciousness was vomited all over the pages—but he's clearly done his research and seems to understand it perfectly well.

"I tracked Hardek's runners to the house I met you at, but something made them panic and run off before I could question them. So when you distracted Buster for me, I got him to spill where he believes Hardek is. He thinks that a man by the name of Caleb Garvin is guarding him. While I know who he is and know that his job revolves around protecting people with his mini army, I'm not positive where he's at. I believe he's at one of these locations," he says as he circles a couple of addresses. "I'm almost positive he's at this first one." He leans back in his chair and stares at me. "With all that being said, I don't work with a partner."

I pull my eyes away from the notebook. "Okay…"

"But I'd be willing to split my profit with you if you'll work with me. I need someone to distract them as I go in and kill Hardek. Then you can grab the girls or whatever you're hired to do."

"How positive are you that he's there?" I ask.

"I plan to watch the place tonight and see if I can be sure. I won't raid it unless I'm at least ninety percent positive."

When he's not goofing around, he seems to be surprisingly intelligent, which I suppose would make sense. There's no way someone dumb or reckless could have gotten to the point where he's currently at. So why he's given me so much about himself, I don't know.

"Do you want to help or are you going to lone wolf it?" he asks.

"Let's go right now."

"That's fine, but I will *not* invade them tonight."

"Every day we wait—"

"Jackson," he interrupts. "I don't make mistakes. When I shoot a bullet, I hit my mark. I'll not miss him because I rushed something. We'll spend the day verifying everything and then, only when I'm positive, I'll invade."

I don't like waiting, not when we don't know what's happened to the girls, but I know that maybe I'll change his mind later or I'll go in alone.

"Let's go."

"Sounds good."

I take a final sip of my drink before following him outside. We walk back to the office and go around back for my car.

He gets into the passenger seat and looks absolutely gleeful when he sees a dildo roll off. "I see you kept my presents." He reaches out and tips my chin toward him. "And there's still a tiny hint of a penis on your cheek."

I push his hand away as he laughs. The noise makes me want to smile, but I refuse to show him that he has amused me.

He picks up the massive silicone dildo and wiggles it around. "I thought you'd like this one the best. Did you like it?"

"Loved it," I say dryly.

He starts laughing. "Fantastic."

I pull up my GPS. "Address?"

He holds his notebook out and hands it to me. Then he smacks the address with the tip of the dildo. "That one."

"Wait… you said the first one."

"I lied," he says. "I was going to send you on a wild goose chase if you refused to help me."

"Hmm…" Of course he would have. Now that I'm thinking about it, who knows if this is the right one. He's probably taking me to some strip club or something equally ridiculous.

"I want to stop by my car and grab my gun in case something bad goes down. Got it?"

I continue typing the address in until he jabs my face with the silicone tip.

"I asked if you got it."

"I got it."

He grins at me. "Open wide!"

"Get it out of my face."

He jabs me again, and I glare at him. For some reason, I'm startled by the look of pure joy on his face. All of the times I've interacted with him, he's been cocky and almost full of himself. But at this moment, he looks… delighted.

"If you don't knock it off, I'm going to beat you with it," I growl.

"No! Don't beat me with your dildo!"

I stare at him while trying not to smile. "Please stop."

That just makes him laugh harder.

"Where's your car? You said you wanted to stop and get something from it."

He points. "Don't worry, the license plate is fake, you can't track it to me," he says as I drive over to the blue Chevy. It's average in every sense, but I make sure to get a good look at the license plate *just* in case it's not fake. I'll run it later. As he hops out to get what he needs out of the car, I text the license plate to Henry.

> Me: Can you have someone run these plates and tell me the owner? No rush.

After a minute, the young man slides in next to me. "Did you run them?"

"Run what?" I ask as if I have no idea what he's talking about.

"My plates, obviously."

"No."

My phone buzzes where it's tucked between my legs. He looks at it then gives me a grin. "If you didn't, let me see your phone."

"I just want to know your name. I feel like there's this gap between us with me not knowing," I say as I start driving.

"Sandman."

"I'm not calling you *Sandman*."

"We can shorten it to just Man if you want. Or Andman sounds cool."

I start driving. "It does not."

"Analman works too."

"That has... no."

He grins. "There's no pleasing you, is there?"

"Real name."

He seems to get an amazing idea as his eyes go wide. "I want a catchphrase or theme song. Da na na na na Analmannn!"

"You've ruined *Batman* for me for the rest of my life," I say, and he starts laughing again. The sound fills up the car, and for a moment, I forget that he's on a most wanted list. "Fine. I don't need your name. And I'm sticking with Sandman."

"I *suppose* it sounds a little cooler. But if you ever change your mind, I'm open."

"That's okay, I won't."

He leans toward me and smiles. "I've never been on a date before where we sneak off to spy on people. It's kind of fun."

"This isn't a date," I remind him, even though I know it's not worth mentioning.

"I've never worked with anyone before, so you better not fuck this up. If you run ahead and try to blow the mission, I will probably shoot you in the knee. Then maybe I'll take you home and nurse you back to health."

Why my mind flashes over to being cared for by this man, I'll never know. "I... won't."

"Good. You were in the military, right?" he asks.

"Yeah."

"That's neat. I bet I would have been good in the military. Well... I can't always remember to keep my mouth shut, so I would have been *decent* in the military. Like, I think they would have liked my skills but hated me as a human."

"Nah, most aren't as strict in real life as they portray them on TV. Obviously, you have to know when you can and can't crack jokes, but they're people too. So where'd you learn to shoot, then, if you weren't in the military?"

"My daddy was a hunter and loved taking me out to hunt. One day, we were hunting and we killed this momma deer, and her wee little baby had to survive by befriending a rabbit. It was really sad."

"Basically, you shot Bambi's mother?"

He grins at me. "Maybe. I don't think I've ever actually seen *Bambi*, so all of that might not have even happened in it."

"You're not going to tell me anything about you, are you?"

"Probably not."

"You told me you weren't in the military."

"That's true."

"And you don't watch Disney."

"I haven't watched *Bambi*. I love Disney. I relate to the characters, you know? Because Disney kills off the parents in every one."

"Disney killed your parents?"

He solemnly nods. "They couldn't stop watching *Frozen* when it was out. They were addicted to it. I tried saving them, but it didn't work. It was too late. I had to let it go."

"That's... awful. I'm sorry to hear that."

He smiles at me. "Thank you. What about your parents? How are Ava and Lewis?"

Of course he knows my parents' names. "Doing good. They bond over the belief that I should conform to their standards."

"Well, that's good they're bonding."

I grin as I shake my head. My GPS interrupts us by telling me to turn down the next road.

"So, we're getting close to the building. It's a car garage that they work out of, but I believe they're keeping the girls there until they can transport them. After dark, there isn't much movement, so I could be one hundred percent wrong, but I think Hardek might be there as well."

"Where do you want me to park?"

"Drive past it and there's a convenience store. We'll park there, then walk to the place. It's a bigger property with a junkyard out back, so it's hard to get a good assessment of it."

"Okay," I say as I pull into the parking lot he pointed out. I put the car in park and look over at him, but he's out before I can say anything. I quickly grab my binoculars and check my phone.

Henry: Alright, I sent the plate to Keats to run.

I slip my phone into my pocket and look at the back of the man heading away from me. I wonder what Henry would do if he realized that I was feet away from the man who killed his partner. Feet away from the man he wasted months searching for.

I could put a bullet in his back at this very moment. Instead, I follow him as he leads me away from my car. Why am I even trusting him?

I'm doing this just to bring those girls back, right? There's no other reason why I would put myself in this situation.

"Are you coming, Grandpa?" he asks as he looks back at me.

"I'm not a grandpa."

"That's just because no one's chosen to procreate with you. You're sure old enough."

"I'm thirty-nine."

"Ooh…" He visibly cringes. "You might need to get some work done."

I raise an eyebrow.

"I'm just teasing you. Don't take it to heart. You're very handsome. So handsome, I'd let you raid my hole."

"I'm not sure what's worse."

He shakes his head as he snickers. "I like you, Jackson. You're fun."

"Yay." My dry response makes him smile even more and I find that I'm glad he turns away, so he can't see my smile.

"Get up here and walk beside me. It's a date, remember?"

I step up to his side *not* because it's a date, but so that we don't look strange trailing after each other as we had been. When he gets near the garage that's surrounded by a chain-link fence, he heads around the side, following the fence.

"Don't we want to stay back?"

"You can't see anything from out front. That's where the garage is. The offices are in the back," he whispers.

While this sounds reckless, I follow him anyway as he makes his way to the back. When he finds a spot he seems happy with, he sits down in the tall weeds of a neighboring empty lot. I sit beside him as he unzips his bag and pulls out his binoculars.

I'm honestly surprised that he's quiet as we wait. While he fidgets every five seconds, he keeps his mouth shut. He flops to the right and to the left and rocks back then forward, to the point where I'm about to ask him if he has fleas.

"Why are you fidgeting so much?" I whisper.

He lowers his binoculars and looks over at me before grinning. "Why are you watching me so much? Like what you see?"

"No, I just want to know if you're having a seizure or if you have fleas."

He chuckles. "A bit of both."

He returns to fidgeting and watching.

Leland: Let's take a moment to talk about codenames.

Jackson: And how you haven't gotten any better at coming up with them, even after all these years?

Leland: *gasps* Excuse me? Seymour Shhlong—

Jackson: *You* didn't come up with that one.

Leland: *tsks* Yeah, but if I get rid of the person who did, I can claim it was me. No one will ever know the truth.

Jackson: That's a no.

Leland: Fine, fine, I'm amazing enough without claiming that one single thing. So… if you were a badass motherfucker hitman… what would your hitman title be?

Jackson: Oh… I guess I don't know. I've never thought about it. I generally just let you give me some random name.

Leland: No, we need something like Sandman. Hold on… it's coming to me… it's coming… it's almost here… aaaaaand… Can't Climb a Fenceman.

Jackson: No.

Leland: Yum-man because you are looking *Yum*.

Jackson: No.

Leland: I Wanna See You Naked-man because I wanna peruse your naked body with both of my eyeballs.

Jackson: No.

Leland: Tushman because your tush is making me feel like a man.

Jackson: *just stares*

Leland: Jackson, sometimes I feel like you're unnecessarily picky. Okay, okay… it's coming to me… I almost have it… what about… Jackson?

Jackson: That's perfect! I love it.

Leland: Yay… thought so. Glad I could finally please you.

Jackson: *smiles* You took the long way around, but you got there in the end.

Leland: Thanks, Tushman.

SEVEN

LELAND

My brain is screaming inside. I'm tired of sitting and staring and sitting and staring. At least I have a very, *very* handsome man to sit and stare with. While our first few meetings he liked to pretend I was annoying, I'm starting to wonder if he's getting tired of pretending.

That's when a van pulls around back.

"What are they doing?" Jackson asks as he straightens up.

"It's two in the morning; I can't imagine they're up to anything good."

The van has no windows in the back—perfect for transporting things or people.

It pulls up to the back garage door which slides open before they back into the building. I can only see the nose of the van, so I quietly get up and keep moving.

"They might be transporting them. We have to stop them."

As I reach the side, I still can't see what they're transporting, but I can see the huge group of men waiting inside.

Jackson starts to get up, but I grab his arm. "Hold up, I need to find Hardek before we do anything."

Jackson shakes his head. "My priority is the girls."

"This is why I didn't want to bring you. Jackson, we have to worry about Hardek before anything else."

The van's doors shut, and the vehicle begins to move. I see that Jackson is fixated on it like a dog on a hare.

"Can't," he says as he gets up.

"Dammit, Jackson. You could fuck this all up."

"I have to know if those girls are in that van," he says as he takes off running toward the front of the garage.

What the fuck is his plan?

I'm not sure what I should do. I *should* continue on with my main mission to kill Hardek. But maybe I can still keep Jackson from fucking this whole thing up.

I sling my backpack onto my back, grab my case, and take off running after him. He's already at the road running for the car. He clearly plans on following them. Maybe I should leave him to his wild goose chase. I could leave him to do whatever his plan is while I stay here and keep my eyes on the garage.

Fuck.

He gets to the car first and starts it as I reach the passenger door and pull it open.

"You're fucking this up," I remind him.

"No, I'm not," he says as the white van passes in front of us. He quickly pulls out behind the van and follows at an adequate distance.

We trail them through the city, but the issue is that once we get beyond the city limits, it's apparent that we're following them. Even while keeping a good distance, there's no way we can hide the car.

"They've spotted us; they're speeding up to see if you speed up," I point out.

He raises the speed a little but lets them get farther ahead. "There's not much else I can do."

I flip the latch on my gun case open and closed as I watch. I'm not used to letting someone else do things. I want to get behind the wheel and do it my way. If we were doing it my way, I would have stayed behind for Hardek. It's the difference between saving a couple of girls or saving all the girls Hardek would continue to traffic. But I guess Jackson doesn't see it that way.

That's when I notice the window going down and a hand coming out.

"They're going to shoot," I yell a moment before I hear a *ping* on the front of the car and then the car lunges. It jerks to the side as the tire loses air and the car starts to coast.

"Shit. They must have hit something."

"Stop the car, fast."

"But—"

"Stop the fucking car."

He slams on the brakes as I yank my seat belt off, flip the latches on the case and push the car door open. Since the car is turned at an angle, I'm on the wrong side, so I get out and drop down onto the road. I pull my rifle up and look through the scope at the van racing away from us. Once I have a good visual, I lower the gun until I have the tire in my sights and fire.

The hit is perfect, so I switch to the other rear tire and hit it, making the van jerk a little. The driver turns the wheel in an attempt to avoid the hit, but it just gives me a visual of the front tire, which I take out.

"Don't shoot them," Jackson says as the van rolls to a stop.

"What? Why?"

"We're going to arrest them."

"Arrest?" I ask. Clearly, the man's crazy. He's all beauty and no brains. He'll take that suggestion back once they start shooting at us.

Which they almost instantly do.

I climb behind the door to use it for cover and look over at Jackson who is hunkered down next to the steering wheel, his own door also open. "Go on then, arrest them."

He hesitates. "I will."

A bullet hits the window above my head, and I give him a very pointed look. "When?"

"Soon."

Another hits the mirror.

"How soon is soon? Like in a minute or ten minutes or when we're both dead?"

He looks over at me and raises an eyebrow. "One of those."

"I'm going to give you a minute. *One* minute. And if you're dead in that time... then I'm sorry to hear that. I kind of liked your face."

"Fine. Can you stop them from shooting but not kill them?"

I raise an eyebrow. "What do you want me to do? Shoot an ear off?"

"Like... a knee or a—"

"Head?"

"No, not a head."

"But... they don't care if they shoot *our* heads."

"But we're better than them."

"Are we?" I'm not convinced.

"YES!"

I sigh and wait until the guy sticks his arm out to shoot, then I shoot the appendage. I can hear him hollering from here. The other had been working his way around the vehicle, but the shrill scream of his buddy's near demise makes him hesitate. I wait until he inches forward to get a good shot on me to shoot him in the leg.

Then I leave Jackson to do the "arresting," since I'm quite content not dying so some lowlifes can live. He manages to get the men pinned down without any help from me. And I only bother wandering over when he's shouting something like, "Help me!" Men. Can never do anything themselves. Always needing my help.

"What do you want?" I ask as I casually walk over. He has the two on the ground, gun pointed at them.

"Help me tie them up."

"With what?"

"I have cable ties in my car."

"I'll watch them while you do it. If you come back and there's only one, it's not my fault. Sometimes my finger slips on the trigger," I say as I take over his job of aiming a gun at their faces.

He hesitates but probably realizes that I'm going to do whatever I want to do. I catch the other two watching him as he runs off.

"He's cute, isn't he?" I ask.

They look at me like they're confused.

"This is our first date," I tell them. "It's going really well so far. I think he might even kiss me."

If looks could kill they'd have both murdered me as soon as I walked up. They would have murdered my corpse, though, with the look they're currently giving me.

"Fuck off," the one I'd shot the arm of says.

"Well, that's not a very nice thing to say. Or are you jealous? I'd be jealous if I were you too."

"Cocksucker," he hisses.

I lean over and grin. "Who knows, maybe you'd like it too. I could cut your cock off and shove it down your throat and see what you think, if you want? If you don't shut up, that's *definitely* what I'm going to do. And if either of you mention my presence here or anything about me, I'll have my friends in prison take care of you."

He quiets down just in time for Jackson to return, which allows me to pretend like I'm a decent human being.

Jackson watches me for a moment before saying, "I called Henry. He'll have some people down here within five minutes, so you might want to get going."

I'm thoroughly disappointed and make sure it shows on my face. "Aw, but I was having a lot of fun on our date."

"I…" He shakes his head. Clearly, he's submitted to the date idea. "Thank you for your help. Now you need to move on. The next time I see you I *will* have you arrested."

"Oh?" I step into him until our bodies brush. Heat wells up inside me where I can feel him, and I push forward until we're pressed against each other. We're close enough that I have to look up to stare into his eyes. "I would love to have you put me in handcuffs."

"Not like that."

He tries to pull away from me, but I reach up and grab his chin before pointing it in my direction. Then I gently press my lips to his. Even though he doesn't push into the kiss, I feel his lips twitch, like he wants to but knows he can't. I don't want to let go. My body insists that I should keep pressing into him, capture those lips and make them my own.

But I grudgingly pull back so my mouth hovers before his. "It was fun working with you, even if you screwed everything up and created a massive shitstorm for me."

His dark brown eyes focus on mine, but he's not pulling away. Instead, his body remains so close, I can feel his leg brush mine. Oh, how I long to pull him to me, but I know that sometimes, the best things are the ones I'm forced to wait for.

"See ya around," I say, giving his cheek a gentle smack before turning away. Once at his car, I gather my case and my gun, give the seat a once-over for hairs or anything else I left behind, then start walking.

While it *was* fun, I've likely ruined my chances with Hardek. I'll have to start from scratch and tear this city apart looking for him.

My client won't be happy.

So I'm not sure why I have a grin on my face I can't seem to wipe off.

JACKSON

I let him go *again*. At least this time, he did me a favor, so I will do one in exchange. But I could've had Henry and a unit down here in minutes to capture the Sandman, yet I let him walk away.

Again.

With an eye on the men, I pull open the door to the van. Inside are three girls, all late teenagers. They're staring at me with wide eyes, terrified of what will happen next. They're gagged, dirty, and terrified, but they're alive.

I guess saving them was worth letting the Sandman walk away. "It's okay," I tell them. "The police are headed here."

I can almost see a weight being lifted off them by my words. But because I don't want to let my eyes off the men, I don't go in to help the girls. They've been tied up this long, another five minutes won't hurt them.

The sirens come quickly after, and I find myself hoping that the Sandman has gotten away. It's strange, feeling that way when I should *want* him to atone for his wrongdoings. Is it because I've gotten to know him?

I look around, but I have no doubts that he'll easily slip into the background since no one would suspect him if they saw him around.

The first people on the scene take over watching the two men, allowing me to go into the back of the van to help the girls.

"It's okay," I tell them as I reach for the gags.

"Excellent job, Jackson."

I turn to see Henry climbing into the back of the van to help.

"Thank you."

"You shot them?" he asks as he nods at the men being assessed by the EMS team.

Here comes the issue. I could lie, but when they extract the bullets, they're going to be from a rifle which I *really* shouldn't be toting around.

"No."

"Then who did?"

I shake my head. "I called in some help from a buddy."

Henry watches me closely. "Have I met this 'buddy'?"

I shrug. "I'm not sure. Have you?"

He raises an eyebrow. "Sometimes, you do a fantastic job, but you're a pain to legally deal with."

I shrug like I'm innocent. "I did nothing but drive the car and tie up the men. I'm not sure how much of a pain that is."

"Uh-huh. Okay."

But I found the girls. Hopefully, I found them before anything too horrible happened to them.

As Henry continues assisting them, I notice movement by my car. Everyone else is so preoccupied with the girls or the men that no one else notices. I watch as the Sandman retreats from my car, literally ten feet from the nearest cop car, and gives me a huge smile.

What the fuck did he do to my car?

And with that, he casually walks off.

"Excuse me," I say as I jump out of the back of the van. Before I get anywhere, Jeremy, an officer who seems to hate me, stops me.

"You need to stay on scene and explain what happened," he says coldly.

His beliefs are that I should leave this kind of stuff to the police. That I'm working "illegally." He always loves looking for a reason to get me in trouble.

"Yeah, I'll be right there. I need something from my car."

He looks annoyed but doesn't say anything as I move past him.

When I turn back to the car, the Sandman's gone, but I know he took something from it or did something to it. I rush over to my car and pull open the driver's door before looking inside. The extra-large dildo is strapped in with a seat belt in the driver's seat, but besides that, nothing looks out of place.

That's when I realize with horror that they're probably going to use my car as evidence.

And it's filled with dildos, vibrators, and fluffy handcuffs.

Oh, fuck my life.

I have to get rid of them. There is no way I can face these people with all of this shit in my car. I quickly scavenge through my car for any type of bag or box I can put them in, but of course, I have nothing.

That's when I see Henry heading my way. Quickly, I gather them all up and debate where to shove them. In a panic, I stick them inside my shirt, praying my hoodie will hide them and I'll be able to sneak off with them.

"What are you doing?" Henry asks.

With vibrators, dildos, a ball gag, and more safely tucked into my shirt, I stand up and try to look casual like I don't have these weird bulges covering my body.

"Just… you know… *stuff.*"

That's when the ball gag falls from my shirt and rolls right over to Henry's foot. As I stare at it in horror, Henry stoops down and picks it up. "What's this… oh…"

"It's not mine!" I say.

"Oh?"

"No!" I'm going to die. "My sister!"

Now he looks horrified. "It's your sister's?"

"No! God, no! She thought it'd be funny. She put it in my car, and… I didn't want it in the car when they looked it over."

"I… see…"

He hands it to me and I stare at it, unsure of what I'm supposed to do with it now, so I tuck it into my pocket.

"Is that... all you have? Because it looks like you have a massive penis in your shirt."

I look down and realize that my clothes might have been a bit too tight to hide an ultra-large dildo in. "That's just... the way my shirt is shaped."

"Do you want to hide it in my car?"

"I do." It sounds so pitiful.

Henry starts laughing harder than I've ever seen him laugh.

Leland: I want to hear the thought process behind this. So you're faced with a giant schlong that you need to get rid of quickly. Do you: A) Throw it in the ditch—if you roll it just right, no one will see; B) Throw it in someone else's car or *under* their car. No one will know where it came from, and it'll then be their problem; or C) Put it in your too tight shirt and then walk all around in front of half the police force?

Jackson: *refuses to make eye contact* My... what nice weather we are having.

Leland: Think hard on this. Long and hard just like that giant schlong.

Jackson: In... retrospect, there might have been a ditch or two I could have tossed it into. Did I? No. Did I carry it around while you enjoyed my misery... yes, yes I did.

Leland: *grinning* God, I love it. It was so apparent, too! Just like this big-ass dick right there under your shirt. I love it. And I love you. Gosh, this is so much fun. On to the next part!

EIGHT

LELAND

"You told me it would take only a couple days to get Hardek," the man on the other end of the phone says.

"I know I did," I say from my spot on the building's roof. "The police fucked everything up because of those girls. I'll still get him."

"I'm not paying *the police,* I'm paying *you,*" he growls.

Since I've never met the man in person, I like to envision that his face looks like a ninety-year-old's nut sac that was never properly cared for. Like it's hairy *and* smelly.

That's what this man's face *has* to look like.

"You actually haven't paid me anything yet," I say as I zoom in with my binoculars.

I can see the desk clearly from here, but it's currently empty of life. I should have left Tucker, my handler, to deal with this man because my patience is running low. While I'm not necessarily fond of dealing with Tucker, he does get my jobs for me so I don't have to risk my identity.

"Is this a fucking game to you?" he growls.

"Don't think you're free to be cocky just because you think I don't know who you are. My job is finding people and I can *very* easily find you. So let's talk sweetly to me. Yes, I am still on Hardek's trail. If you *want* someone else to do it, I'm more than happy to step down. Understand?"

The man makes some grumbly growling noise as I see someone set a huge vase of flowers on the desk. There are so many flowers, they seem to take up half the desk. "I understand."

"Good, I'm glad. I'll call you when I have something new to report."

I hang up on him, not really thinking he deserves a proper good-bye. These people who expect things done immediately irritate me. While it *has* been a week since the girls were found, I've had better things to do.

Like this.

I see someone enter the room as my excitement grows.

Finally! Someone's there.

I watch as he walks over to the desk, picks up the tag hanging off the vase of flowers and scowls.

Aw! Jackson loves them!

I must buy him more.

Using my burner phone, I call the office. When he picks up the phone, a smile is on my face. He looks very handsome in a dark blue button-up that he really should wear on our next date. I can't keep myself from thinking about unbuttoning that shirt and sliding it off his broad shoulders. Oh, the fun we'd have once I got him naked.

"Wellstone Detective Agency—"

"Hi! My name is Billy, and I was wondering if you could help me find my Willy."

Through my super-awesome binoculars, I can see the expression on his face change. "Are you watching me?" he growls as he looks out the wrong window first. Then he makes a show of pulling a flower out of the vase and popping its head off. How can he even look handsome murdering a flower?

"What a naughty, naughty boy," I say.

"You need to leave me alone."

"Or?"

"I'll call the police."

"Because someone bought you flowers? I didn't know you hated romance."

"This isn't *romance*."

I grin at the handsome man as he glares out the window while trying to find me. There's no way he will. "Yes, it is. I'm courting you, Jackson. I'm showing that I'm an adequate mate."

"All you're showing me is that you've lost your mind."

"Stop with all the flirting. My heart can't take it!"

"What do you want?" He sounds like he's not interested, but I'm positive he's nearly popping a boner just from talking to me.

"Five years ago, there was a huge investigation on a man named Barry Witt. At one point in the investigation, he mentioned dealing with Hardek. He was brought into the police station, but they let him go for some reason. Why was he pulled in? What are his ties to Hardek? And why'd they let him go?"

He hesitates. "I don't… I don't know. I never heard about that. Was it in the reports?"

"I'm guessing someone cut a deal with him. Maybe he said or did something in exchange for them letting him go. I can't find any legal record of it, but I'm sure someone knows something."

"And you want me to figure it out and help you because…?"

"Don't you want to stop him?"

He takes a deep breath. "Fine, I'll snoop around and see what I can do. And then that's it, I'm not dealing with you anymore."

"I heard that the last time, but I think you're too excited after our little kiss."

"What kiss?" he asks dryly.

"Oh, low blow. Not nice. Don't tell me you didn't jerk off to it. Saying, 'Ohh, Sandman. Come visit my dreams.'"

"Is that all?"

"I suppose. Oh, and I like your shirt. It makes you look *very* hand-some. But it'll look even nicer when I rip it off your steaming hot body."

He hangs up, clearly unable to take any more flirting.

JACKSON

In all my research on Hardek, I never came up with anything about this Barry guy coming in for an interview. I call Henry, who doesn't answer, then decide that I'll head over to the station and see what I can pull up.

Before I do that, I look over at the flowers and debate tossing them in the trash. They're not the first thing he's sent me, and I'm sure they won't be the last.

I decide it's not the flowers' fault and leave them.

When I reach the station, I head inside. Henry is out, so I'm trying to figure out who else I can talk into helping me when Jeremy walks up.

"Need something?" he asks, like he'd actually help me if I did.

The thing is, I *do* know he would've been here around that time and might actually know something.

What does it hurt to try? "I was talking to Henry about the time Barry Witt was brought in for questioning, but Henry's not here, so we'll have to talk more about it later."

He raises an eyebrow. "When was that?"

It's clear he knows something by the way he's lowered his voice like he doesn't want others to hear. "About five years ago at this point. I guess he said something about Hardek, so I thought I could look into him."

"Henry... was talking to you about it?"

"Yeah."

He seems suspicious. "Henry wasn't here."

"Oh? But you were."

His eyes narrow. "No... I'm just saying five years ago he was in a different precinct."

"Why was Witt let go? And why are there no records of it?"

Jeremy's upper lip twitches.

I shrug and look around, like I'm planning on finding another person to talk to. "That's okay, I can ask someone else."

"Hold up! Let's... talk."

Clearly, the Sandman was onto something.

The phone barely rings once before he answers.

"Oh? And what did I do to deserve such a wild stallion to call me?"

I regret calling him the moment he answers. "I got your info."

"That was *quick*. I hope you're not that fast in the bedroom."

I rub my head before remembering that I probably could have sent him a text. Why did I call him? "If anything else comes out of your mouth, I'm done."

He chuckles. "I apologize. Go ahead. Let me hear it."

"So they called Witt in, who, at the time, wasn't yet involved in a lot—just petty stuff—and he mentioned that he was working for a man named Dante Wilson who was smuggling drugs for Hardek."

"Oh! I know him. He ended up getting arrested a few years back, but since they barely had anything on him, they only held him for three years. He's 'turned his life around' and is now working out of a bar."

"Yeah, that's the guy. That's all I got for you," I say.

"What about Witt? Where's he?"

"He was shot and killed last year in a drive-by."

"Ah, okay. Let me see what I can get on Wilson. Thanks, sugar plum. I'll buy you something tomorrow if you want. Did you like the chocolate I sent to your work?"

It was delicious. "No. I don't want anything." Who knows what will arrive at the door next? Mason is already getting suspicious.

"I'll do it anyway."

I sigh. "Please don't."

"Dildo or butt plug. Preference?"

"Neither."

"Both?"

"Go away."

And I hang up to the sound of his laughter. Such a joyous fucker. Why does he make me smile?

LELAND

As soon as I hang up with Jackson, my phone rings again. I see that it's my mystery client who is starting to get on my nerves. I lean back on my couch, not sure I'm ready to deal with the many annoyances of this man.

"Hello?" I answer, irritation probably pretty clear in my voice.

"I've found someone else to handle the job. You are relinquished of your duties."

"I found a lead," I say as I set my feet on the coffee table. I'm pretty sure it's close to breaking from me using it as a footrest.

"What kind of lead?"

"Hardek's interaction with a Dante Wilson."

There's a strange silence that fills the phone. "Who gave you that?"

"I figured it out myself, why?"

"Your job is to focus on Hardek. To kill Hardek. Not Wilson."

"I'm not killing Wilson. I'm going to question him." This guy rubs me the wrong way, but he has from the beginning. If I hadn't been pushed toward him by Tucker, I never would have taken the job.

"Fine. And you're meeting up with Wilson tonight?"

"Yes, but if you're done with me—"

"No. Call me in the morning."

Of course he's not done with me now that I have a lead. "Understood."

I hang up on him and start searching for the location and hours of the bar. Even though Wilson owns it, there's no guarantee he'll be there tonight, but it's a place to start. The bar opens at seven, so I'll be ready by then.

Leland: I'm still thinking back on our very first car chase together. You've changed, Jackson, you've really changed.

Jackson: You mean you've tainted me into forgetting how to be a law-abiding citizen?

Leland: No one abides by laws anymore, don't be a fool. I'm…

kind of disappointed that I didn't share with you my car chase song on that very day. I feel like if I had... you'd have asked for my hand in marriage right then and there.

Jackson: Wow... you really think your songs have some powers, don't you?

Leland: You... don't love the car chase song?

Jackson: Honestly, it's different every time I hear it, so refresh my memory. How's it go again?

Leland: Okay... okay... Uh... got it right here in my head... I sure do... *Car chase... car chase... gonna... chase a car... gonna... get a cigar... gonna... eat some rhubarb.* I don't even know what rhubarb tastes like...

Jackson: You're just trying to rhyme things at this point.

Leland: It's because I can't do it on command! I have to be *in* the car chase for the words to bubble and spill out from within me to spin and mix until they ejaculate out in a beautiful harmony. Why don't you try it if it's so easy?

Jackson: Oh, no, no. I don't want to take that from you. Your beautiful words are all I'll ever need.

Leland: Ooh! I could make a sex playlist singing all of my songs!

Jackson: You could title it "How Not to Get Laid."

Leland: Joke's on you because I get laid *plenty*.

NINE

LELAND

The bar is dark as I drive past it. I'm not too far from Jackson's house; I could probably pay him a visit and antagonize him at least a little when I'm finished here.

I pull my thoughts away from Jackson and back to the bar. The windows are covered, but the lights are on, telling me it's open. I find a parking spot about half a block away and get out of my car. With only my handgun hidden beneath my coat, I walk toward the bar. Anything more and I could get stopped and searched by the bouncer who is waiting out front.

I pull my fake ID out as I walk toward the front and hold it out.

"Here alone?" the man asks.

"My friends will be joining. At least I hope they will." I make a show of glancing at my phone.

The man stares at the ID like he's never seen one before. "Are you sure you're over twenty-one? You don't look it."

"Positive. I don't look that young, buddy."

He nods and hands the ID back. "Go ahead inside."

A strangely chatty bouncer... how odd.

I step past him and push against the door. The moment it swings inward, my instincts start screaming that something's up. There's a *reason* he was so chatty. There has to be.

I don't have the time to assess any of that before pain tears into my side, racing up to my chest and down to my hip. The shot throws me back into the door that's almost closing. The bouncer grabs the door and yanks it the rest of the way shut, locking me inside as I look into the eyes of the man who just shot me.

He moves the gun up toward my head since his first bullet didn't do enough. Sure feels like it did enough.

"I think I fucked up," I say as I assess my surroundings.

Five men. All with guns. The bar is empty, telling me that they were waiting for me. They knew I was coming. Only two people knew I was coming here tonight: Jackson and my client. The client was adamant about replacing me until he heard me mention Wilson. The same Wilson who is currently aiming a gun at my head.

Which tells me that Wilson is my client.

With that figured out, I lunge to the right, sliding behind a booth as gunshots fill the bar. They're all silenced, but it doesn't completely quiet them.

My side is throbbing as I look down at it and see the blood coloring my shirt. It was a good hit. A very good hit.

I rarely make mistakes, but boy have I fucked this one up.

"How'd you know it was me and not someone else?" I ask curiously. "Let me guess, you were having the bouncer chat with each person as they came while you listened in. Then you had him turn away anyone who didn't match. Was it my voice?"

"Yes, it was your voice," he says. His voice is familiar as well. I would have realized he was my client the moment I started listening in on him.

"Ah. And why kill me? I was doing a job *for* you."

"Yeah, and when you started sniffing into *my* shit, that meant the end of the road for you," he says confidently.

I hold on to my gun tightly as I inch forward until I can see the mirror behind the bar. Thankfully, my pain isn't too severe at the moment, but it won't be long before the shock fades and my body starts to realize what happened.

Wilson waves a couple of his guys toward me but doesn't realize that I can see them in the mirror. I slide my arm around the corner and fire. The first hit goes wide, but in the mirror, I can see my mistake and shoot a second bullet. This one hits the closest man in the chest. The other man momentarily glances at his partner, and that's all I need to peek around the edge and shoot him.

"Kill him," Wilson growls.

Instead of taking a chance shooting at them again, as they move by the bar, I shoot one of the bottles sitting on the counter. The glass explodes and the man cringes back as it pelts him. That's when I lean forward and catch Wilson's eyes. Well... *eye* once my bullet finds its home right through his left eye socket. He has a startled look on his face as he drops to the ground.

To my left is a bare wall but to my right are the restrooms. While they're distracted, I push myself to my feet and race for the restrooms. A bullet pings off the door as I run by it, but I manage to slide into the bathroom before I get hit. I shove the trashcan under the door and turn around. There's only a small window up high that *might* be big enough for me to fit through. I shoot the glass as I rush over to it. Then I use the butt of my gun to knock the remaining shards away. With my hands tucked into my sleeves, I hoist myself up. Once my front is through, I can't catch myself and end up falling the rest of the way. I slam down on my back and it knocks the air out of me. Pain flares throughout me, making me pause as agony pounds deep inside my body.

Fuck.

I hear someone kick the trash can in and know that I need to keep going. I struggle to my feet and stumble before getting the rest of the way up. The shock my body was in is starting to diminish as pain and weakness take over.

Somehow, I manage to reach my car as I hear a noise behind me. They're not far behind, but all I have to do is start the car and drive. Just drive.

But to where? I can't go to the hospital. Not only would that make it easy for them to find me, but there's a chance I could give something away. They'll try to figure out who shot me, and if the police are called to this place, they'll find my blood. They'll know I killed Wilson.

My fingers are bloody, making it hard to turn the key, but I get the car started and begin to drive.

My only option is Tucker, so I pull out my phone and call him.

I set my hand against the bullet wound and press down on it. The initial adrenaline is starting to diminish, so the moment I make contact, pain shoots up my side.

The phone rings and rings before hitting a voice mailbox that's full.

"Well… fuck…"

This was because I got cocky. I'm always careful, but this time, I didn't research enough. I didn't stay focused. I kept getting distracted. Why did I keep getting distracted by Jackson? If I had gone at it alone, I would have been fine. I would have researched everything and would have known more going in.

I slow for a stop sign and look around.

Why's this area look familiar? Oh yeah, Jackson lives around here. I'll make Jackson save me. Light-headed, I turn onto his street and try to remember which house is his. I might have snooped around it before, but I can't seem to wrap my mind around anything.

That's when I see the house that I'm positive is his. Quickly, I yank on the wheel. I miss the driveway and end up in the yard instead. I press on the brakes, stopping the car inches before a tree. Somehow, I remember to put it in park, and then I lay on the horn.

I'm going to die… this is how I'm going to die.

Why the fuck did the shot have to be so precise? Now I'm going to bleed to death in Jackson's yard.

Suddenly, someone's yanking on the door, but it's still locked. I aim my gun at them and nearly blow their head off before realizing that it's Jackson.

"What the fuck are you doing?" he yells.

Reaching for that unlock button is the hardest thing I think I've ever done. Almost as hard as pressing down on it. He yanks the door open and the look of anger on his handsome face diminishes.

"What the fuck happened?"

"Jackson…"

His look of alarm tells me that I probably don't look very good. "What happened? We need to call an ambulance."

I try to shake my head, but it makes my vision go funky. "No, I can't… I just didn't want to die alone. So let me die here, please. I've been alone for years… I don't want to die alone…"

I don't even know what I'm saying or why I'm saying it.

But even though I don't want to say it…

I know it's the truth.

JACKSON

His head bobs as he starts to dive forward, and I quickly grab him. Instead of wasting time pulling him out of the car, I push him over the middle console and into the passenger seat. I leap into the car that's still running and throw it in reverse.

"Jackson?" he mumbles as he straightens up.

"Hey, it's okay—"

"Don't take me to the hospital. They'll… if they run… my blood will be at the scene. I don't want… I don't want to go to prison."

I'm not sure why he'd rather die because I'm positive he currently has two options. Hospital or death.

Since the road is straight, I use my knee to drive as I reach into the back seat and find a hoodie. Since he's lying against the door, I can slide it behind his back before wrapping it around his midsection. He tries to throw me off him, but at this point, he's barely holding his head up anymore. When I'm at a stoplight, I ball up his shirt at the location of the bullet wound and tie the sleeves of the hoodie over it as tightly as I can so it's putting pressure on it.

He groans and pushes my hand away, leaving blood streaked across my arm.

As soon as I have it tied, he leans into the door and closes his eyes. "I don't think anyone will care if I die."

"I'll care." And I know I will, even though I barely know him.

He shakes his head slowly. "You'll be happy."

"No, I won't. Who will pester me then?"

"I do like pestering you," he mumbles.

I pull out my phone and call the hospital so they're prepared to meet me out front. When I hang up with them, he's still mumbling about something, but I can't hear him.

When I reach the hospital, I drive up to the emergency center, and they're on us almost immediately. They pull the door open, and he almost falls out since he'd been leaning against it.

"What happened?" a woman asks.

"I don't know. I found him. It looks like he was shot in the abdomen."

"Do you know how long ago?"

I shake my head, honestly not knowing. It couldn't have been long before I found him, or I'm positive he'd have bled out by now. "No."

That's when I see a bulge in his pants pocket. Does he have a wallet? Would he be carrying his actual ID? And if he is, can they tie him to what he's actually done? I have no idea if they have the Sandman's DNA, since it's not something Henry would have shared with me.

I rush over to them as they put him on the gurney. "It'll be okay," I say as I reach down and set a hand on him like I'm comforting him. They're too busy rushing around to see me slip my hand into his back pocket and pull the wallet free.

"Sir?" a man asks and for a moment, I think I've been caught.

"Yes?" I ask.

"What's his name?"

I shake my head, wallet heavy in my hand. "I don't know. I found him."

"Where at?"

Fuck.

"Is he going to be okay? I'll talk to the police when they get here."

The man doesn't seem satisfied with that answer, but he hurries off with the young man.

As I stand there in the hallway of the hospital, I can't help but wonder if I just sealed his fate.

Jackson: Leland, why did you pick me that night?

Leland: I don't know.

Jackson: That's it? Don't know?

Leland: *quiet for a moment* I just… I don't know. The thing is, I grew up knowing that I was never able to depend on *anyone*. If I got hurt, my only option was to pick up the pieces and go home. If I lived, I lived; if I died, I died… but I guess… I just… couldn't do it that time. I *wanted* someone to depend on unlike anything I'd ever wanted before.

Jackson: I guess… I'm pretty damn lucky that you went to me, then. I'm glad you can now depend on me anytime you want.

Leland: Yeah… me too. Imagine if someone else showed up at your door. Like Jeremy. Imagine that romance.

Jackson: *laughs* I… don't think it would have turned into a romance. But you know what? I bet he wouldn't have made fun of my fence-climbing skills as much. Or make me wear weird things. Or buy me things that you really shouldn't have.

Leland: Exactly. Think of how *boring* life would be.

Jackson: Sooooo boring. I wonder if we'd do boring things like cuddle on the couch watching TV… go out on normal dates…

Leland: The longer you speak, the worse he sounds!

Jackson: *laughing* Of course he does. Well… I'm just happy that you took a chance on me.

Leland: I didn't take a chance on you; I took *all* of the chances. Then I took my heart and flung it at you too. It was weird but you embraced it.

Jackson: I sure did.

TEN

JACKSON

"When I heard you were the one who found the John Doe, I had to come and see what you're up to," Henry says as he walks into the waiting room that I've been in for over half an hour at this point.

"Yeah…"

"So. What's the story?"

"I already told Jeremy the story. I found him outside the agency," I lie. It just sounds more probable for him to be outside the agency than outside my house. People don't get shot in my neighborhood for no reason. There's a good distance between my house and the neighbors, so it's not like anyone would be out walking their dog or selling drugs. "I never heard a shot. I almost… wonder if the shot was meant for me, you know? With me snooping into Hardek's case? Maybe they thought it was me leaving or someone I was working with. I feel kind of responsible some kid got shot because of me."

Why the fuck am I lying? Henry has given me so much since I started this line of work and here I am, lying to him about the very man he wasted years of his life trying to find.

Henry nods, looking sympathetic since he doesn't know who the man is. "Before he went into surgery, he couldn't remember his name. We'll see if he does once out. If not, we'll run his fingerprints and see if we have a match. I can't tell if he's trying to cover up something or not. He was in pretty rough shape when they were asking him earlier. Once we get his prints, we should have a match within a couple of hours if he's in our system. Hopefully, we don't need to do that."

"Yeah, I agree," I say. I already ran the name that was on his license, but I'm positive at this point that it's fake.

Which reminds me that I'll have to be careful leaving in his car so no one questions me driving a vehicle I had Henry run the plates on.

"I'm surprised you're still here."

I am too. "I… guess I was hoping they'd find a family member or something and then I'd leave. When I found him, he was really scared about being alone, and… I just felt like I needed to stay."

Henry sets a hand on my shoulder and gently squeezes it. "Alright. We'll see what we can find when he wakes up."

I nod, praying that the man is smart enough not to talk when he wakes so our stories won't be wildly different. All I know at the moment is that he's still in surgery. He might not even make it out, but I feel like I should be here in case he does.

Henry leaves after a bit, and then I'm left sitting in the waiting room for another two hours before a nurse comes and gets me.

"Do you want to come back to see him?" she asks.

"Yes, please," I say as I stand up and follow her. She takes me to the ICU where all the patients are separated by only a row of curtains. As I walk with her, my mind is a whirlwind of thoughts. I shouldn't be doing this. I shouldn't be protecting his identity. I've known Henry for years and should be loyal to him, *especially* when dealing with the man who killed his partner.

She waves me inside, and I find him lying in the bed, face paler than normal, dark hair messy and plastered to the side of his head. I take a seat and the nurse gives me a smile before hurrying away.

"Dicklicker," he groans.

"I see you're awake," I say, even though his eyes are barely open.

"Shush. They believe that I have short-term memory loss. Must have hit my head, but weirdly, my head shows no trauma. They've taken my fingerprints to try to track down my identity since I don't know my name. I need to get out of here. If you'd be so kind as to please strip and streak a bit. They'll be so distracted by your mighty penis that they won't see my epic escape."

"You can't even lift your head."

His eyes open and close like there are weights on them. "Yes, I can... Watch me."

He doesn't even lift it a quarter of an inch off the pillow.

"Did you see it?"

"No."

He sighs. "Huh... fuck... what are you still doing here?"

"You said you didn't want to die alone."

His eyebrows rise a little. "I'd never say anything so stupid."

And then he's out.

The thing is, at that moment when he thought he was dying, he was being more truthful than he's ever been with me. And I know how hard it is being left alone when you feel like there's no one left. I don't want him to feel that way.

About an hour later, my phone beeps, and I glance down at it.

Henry: Got a match on his fingerprints.

I'm up in an instant and rushing from the room. A match? Will they know he's the Sandman? Will Henry realize that I've been involved with the Sandman and haven't told anyone? I could play naive, but I still feel guilty.

I call him as soon as I'm outside the ICU, and he answers almost immediately. "What's his name?"

"That was fast. Maybe I'm not supposed to—"

I'm tired of playing the "you're not supposed to know" game. "Name, Henry."

"Leland Clarke. Twenty-seven years old."

"What's he in the system for?"

"Running from a foster home at thirteen. He was removed from the missing children list when he applied for a driver's license at eighteen."

"Do you have any information on what happened to him?"

"Just a runaway. By the time he hit eighteen and made himself known, it wasn't something worth looking into anymore."

"No criminal record?"

"No."

"What'd the foster family have to say?"

"I'll have to look into it."

"Can you send me everything on him?"

"Jackson, this isn't a case. You don't need to investigate *everything* all the time."

But I do. I *need* to prove that I shouldn't turn him in. That I'm making the right choice letting him walk out of here. "Henry, please."

"Fine. I'm going to get my ass fired one of these days for sharing shit with you."

"No one's going to know," I assure him.

"Alright. I'll email it now."

As soon as the call ends, I walk back to the room, but he's still asleep. Lying in the bed, he looks strangely innocent and small, like he needs someone to protect him. Or maybe I want to protect him, but I don't know why. Especially when I'm positive he could kick my ass.

Maybe not at this moment, but any other.

I sink down in my chair and pull open my email so I can start reading. He ran away at thirteen. The foster family didn't alert the authorities; instead, the school did. They found out he'd been gone almost a week, yet no one had contacted them. He'd run away a few other times, so they didn't suspect foul play, but they still removed fostering privileges from the family.

Now, what happened to his parents?

"What's so interesting over there? Did you find my nudes?" he asks.

"Something better, *Leland.*"

He snorts before a tired smile takes over his face. "So, you know who I am."

"I do."

"When are the police coming?" he asks.

"I don't know yet."

He gives me a soft smile. "How about… you tell me before they do. Give me a five-minute head start. I've always loved a game of cat and mouse."

"Deal. But first, tell me how you got shot."

He thinks about it for a moment before telling me everything that happened between him and Wilson.

LELAND

I'm starting to understand why all the people I've shot cry so much. It kind of fucking hurts. At least the drugs are good.

"Jackson? Jackson? Jackson?" I call.

Jackson groans, like he's annoyed by me, but he's still here. Even after they've moved me to a room. "What?" he asks from his spot in the chair facing my bed.

"Do I look sexy half-dead?"

"Breathtaking," he says dryly.

I laugh, but then it hurts, so I quickly stop. "You're funny."

"Thanks."

"You know you can go, right? People are going to start thinking I'm like your sex slave or something and you're scared I'm going to escape." He watches me with his dark brown eyes. The room is mostly dark since the only light on is above my head, but I can see him in the little light that's coming through the curtains.

He shakes his head. "The moment I leave, you're going to slip out of here."

Probably. "No, not at all," I say. "I like the food too much. Look at that green mush." I point at the tray that I barely touched. "Five-star dining."

"Definitely."

"So? Are you going to leave?" I ask.

He leans back in his chair. "I will only leave when they come in with handcuffs."

"Ooh. You bought me a stripper for a get-well present? You're so sweet. When's he coming?"

"No."

I make sure to look disappointed. "No, he's not coming or no, you're not sweet?"

"Both."

"That's sad."

"I know."

I grab for my stomach. "Oh, it hurts. I'm wounded. Basically dying. This could be my last wish."

He raises an eyebrow like he's not at all amused. "Your last wish is for a stripper?"

"No, my last wish is for you to treat me with sweetness and pure kindness."

"That sounds awful."

I chuckle. "I like you, Jackson. You're a nice guy."

"Am I? I have them prepared to arrest you."

"You're kind of like the boy who cried wolf. You keep saying it, but it doesn't happen. I'm starting to think you just like the attention."

"I haven't called them *yet*. I'm giving you one last day of freedom to do anything you want."

"Ah, makes sense. Anything?" I'm very hopeful that he'll say yes.

"Anything."

"Can I touch your willy?"

"Besides that."

"Can I look at your willy?"

"Besides that."

"So not actually anything," I realize.

"Anything else."

"Can you show me your nipple?"

He sighs and lifts his shirt like it's the hardest thing he's ever done. The look on his face while he does it has me laughing, which sends pain coursing through my body. I can't even focus on my joy of seeing his bare chest and tiny nipple because I'm laughing and cringing too hard at everything else.

While holding my stomach, I smile at him. "I feel like in a different life, you and I would have been soul mates."

"I wouldn't go that far. Acquaintances at the very most."

"We're already past that part. Remember? You showed me your

butthole, I bled all over you and said things that I'm hoping you'll erase from your memory. I honestly don't know how much closer we could get. So when you eventually give in and have them arrest me, will you visit me in prison?"

"I might."

"Show me your nipple through the foggy glass window."

He's trying really hard not to grin at this point. "If you insist."

"I will. I'll make sure my harem of men isn't jealous."

"Alright... you do that."

I shift in the bed and the sheets crinkle like they're made of paper. "I think I'm going to take a nap."

"You have one day left of freedom and napping is what you're going to choose to do?"

I stifle a yawn. "Yep. Show me your nip again so I can have dreams about it."

"That's all I've got."

"That's no fun. I'll just have to try to remember what it looks like. Was it hairy? I can't remember. Like... really curly hairs, right? Gray, I think. You are getting up there in age."

He shakes his head like he's disappointed in me. "Take your nap."

I grin at him before closing my eyes and lying in silence for a moment. "Oh, Jackson... what big nipples you have."

He sighs which makes me grin again. Of course, I'm not *actually* tired—I already did the world record of sleeping for one day—but *he* hasn't slept, and I'm hoping he'll nod off. While he hasn't called the police yet, it's not promising that he won't leave. And who knows when he'll decide to call them. Honestly, I have no idea why he hasn't yet. I'm not *that* charming. And he owes me nothing.

When I peek at him after fifteen minutes, I find him in his chair, head hanging down as he snoozes away.

That did *not* take as long as I thought it would. Now I have two options: sneak out when he goes to the bathroom or sneak out when he's in the room with me. Another issue is that I also have the monitor on my finger to worry about. If I sneak out while he's in the bathroom, he'll find out in minutes or the nurse will notice the monitor. But if I put the monitor on him, he'll keep it running nice and smoothly.

The first thing I do is pull up the edge of the tape holding the IV line in place. I pull the needle out and set it to the side before quietly pushing my blankets off. He's still out, so I slowly sit up. It causes slight pain in my abdomen from where they'd cut me open to fix the internal damage the bullet caused, but nothing I can't handle with the drugs they have me on. I lean into him before pulling the little monitor clip off my finger and sliding it onto his. There wasn't even time for the machine to get angry. And as I stare at him, his expression never changes.

Then I push myself up on my socked feet and walk quietly toward the door. Of course I'm decked out in hospital wear, but patients get up and walk all the time. I'll just have to be sneaky about slipping into the elevator or down the stairs. As I walk, it pulls at the sutures, but with the drugs running through me, it doesn't hurt too badly.

"I'll make a deal with you."

I freeze with my hand on the doorknob. When I turn around, Jackson is staring at me from the chair. "What kind of deal?"

"I won't report you if you promise you're done."

"Done?" I ask, confused about what he's referring to.

"Yes. Done with all of this." He waves a hand. "Done with being a hitman. You'll stay with me for a while so I can watch you. And when I trust you, I'll let you go back to your own home. You'll stop killing people and go to school or find a real job. I think deep down, you're a good person. I don't want to see you rot for life in prison, but I also can't let you go."

He's such a strange man. He thinks I'm a good person? He's the saintly one. "So... you're going to babysit me?"

"Yes."

Why does this man even care what happens to me? No one else ever has. "Why?"

He's quiet for a moment, eyes searching mine. "I don't know. I just want to give you a chance."

So all I have to do is pretend to give this up, stay in his house for a few days, then leave when I'm healed? I'll probably move to a new area. I'm sure I can pick up my life elsewhere, and I have plenty of money to keep myself going until I get some good clients.

"Okay," I say.

He nods. "Good. Now sit back down; I'll page the nurse and tell her you accidentally tore the line out while flopping around."

"Are you lying?" I ask as I start walking toward him.

"No."

I stop when I'm standing in front of him. My brain is on overdrive as I look down at him and he stares up at me. "I'm honestly nervous to trust you... I never expect anything out of anyone because I've learned that people only care about themselves, and they'll hurt you to get what they want."

"I'm sorry you feel like that, and I can't promise you much, but if you listen to me, I assure you that I won't turn you in."

I nod. "I can handle that. Now that we got that out of the way, I'm SO excited to move in!"

He scowls at me like he also can't contain his excitement.

Jackson: So now that you hooked me... what's your last wish?

Leland: Oooh... real or goofy?

Jackson: Both.

Leland: Okay, okay. My last wish would be for you to spend the whole day naked, like everywhere we go it's all out so everyone can ooh and ahhh when they see you. And then you're going to pull out your mighty sword and be like "Back off, you lowly fuckers, for I already have met my one true love!" and then you'd strut right up to the love of your life and would kiss that love so hard... but maybe not too hard because we don't want you to get splinters.

Jackson: In this scenario... I've married The Fence?

Leland: Maybe. What about you?

Jackson: My last wish... would be for a flamethrower. And as I'm breathing my last breath, I am torching that fence.

Leland: Ooh, that's hot. Literally.

Jackson: Thanks.

Leland: It's fitting. I feel like it makes sense for The Fence to die with us. OH MY GOD. We'll have it buried with us!

Jackson: Yay… so glad we will eternally be together with a fence. Now serious wish.

Leland: That one's easy. That we grow super old together. Bam, done.

Jackson: That was a pretty easy one. I also hope we grow super old together and I want us to stay just like this. You out there beating up men with your walker.

Leland: I've killed a man with a walker.

Jackson: Of course you have.

ELEVEN

LELAND

"Oh my god. If I have to be in this room for one more minute, I'm going to break my resolution and just start shooting shit," I say as I refrain from kicking my feet while having a tantrum.

"You'll have broken your agreement in less than twelve hours."

"It's only been twelve hours? Heaven have mercy. How long does it take to get the papers around to let me leave?" I ask in annoyance. "Let me get dressed. You brought me clothes, right? At least then I can run as soon as they're here."

"Okay," he says as he grabs a bag he'd brought back with him from his home. I think he might have been a little surprised that I was still here when he returned. Clearly, he has zero faith in me.

Then again, I was honestly just as surprised.

"Still no call about the shoot-out at the bar? I mean... I killed Wilson," I ask as he stands up.

"No, they must be covering it up for some reason. I had my business partner drive by, and he said that there's a sign out front stating that it's closed but no one's called it in."

"Interesting. I wonder what Wilson was doing. Clearly, something illegal enough they're just going to make him disappear."

Jackson shakes his head. "I don't know. I didn't think he was up to anything after he'd gotten out of jail. At least, there were no more police reports on him."

"That's good… I don't need them to find my blood at the scene now that the police are snooping in my business. They know I was involved in something; I don't need them thinking that it's anything more than a drive-by like we're pretending it is."

He sets the bag on the bed as I sit on the edge of it. He unzips it and pulls out a shirt. I quickly untie the stupid gown and drop it onto the bed so I'm only wearing the socks as well as the fancy underwear they'd given me.

I notice his eyes flicker down to it before quickly looking away. "Do you like my underwear?"

"Very sexy."

"They tear easily so you can quickly get to the prize beneath. Wanna try it out?"

"No, I'm not going to tear your underwear off in the middle of a hospital after you got done nearly bleeding to death."

I grin at him. "I can ask for some spare pairs for when we get home. We'll be like newlyweds."

"You are aware that we're going to my home so I can watch you, not… *that*."

"I'm pretty sure that was part of the rules, right? A daily fucking?"

"No. Keep your perversions to yourself."

I grin at him. "You're no fun. Now dress me."

He stares at me, like he's not sure whether or not I can actually dress myself. But, like the kind-hearted sucker he is, he helps me into the button-up, then promptly begins buttoning it for me. It's utterly adorable.

"Oh my god. You're going to be so good with our children," I say.

His eyebrows rise as he stares at me. "No."

"I think you will. Look how gently you're dressing me."

"We're not having children. We're not… I'm not moving you into my house for good. This is just to watch you… so I can help you."

"I can already hear wedding bells. The angels are singing our names. Jackson and Leland, together forever."

"I'm starting to wonder if this was a really bad idea."

I start laughing. "It might have been. I've never even had a sleepover before, so I'm excited about this. I'm overly excited about all the things we're going to be doing. Like…" I think about it for a moment. "We could braid our hair and have a pillow fight and measure each other's penises."

His eyebrows knit as his head tilts. "I… I'm not sure that's what *anyone* does at a sleepover. At least none of the sleepovers I've been to."

I grin. "Well, that's disappointing."

He smiles as he shakes his head. "You have some of the most ludicrous thoughts sometimes."

"I feel like it stems from me not interacting with humans too often so when I do, I get really excited and just blurt out everything I'm thinking. It gets worse. Like I feel like I'm kind of holding back at this moment. I can be naughtier if you want."

"Please don't."

"Like the nurse? Look at how far her scrubs are up her ass crack. Like what'd her butthole do? Suck it in there?"

He cringes. "No… please."

"Then what about—"

"Shush, the nurse is coming."

"Tell her that her scrubs are trying to find Narnia. Maybe she doesn't know."

He gives me a quick shake of his head as the nurse walks in and smiles at me.

"We've got your paperwork ready. I have an aide bringing you a wheelchair. You're all ready to go!"

I look at her in horror. "I don't need a wheelchair."

"Not an option," she says.

Clearly, neither is pulling her scrubs out of her butt crack. Once the wheelchair is there, I grudgingly get in it and let them wheel me down to the first floor as Jackson brings up his car. I'll need to talk to him about what he did with mine.

He's waiting out front and even rushes around to open the car door for me. Clearly, he's forgotten that he's supposed to be evil and dislike me. As she heads away with the wheelchair and I get into the passenger seat, I notice him looking back at the lady.

"Checking out her butt crack?" I joke.

"No... but it really is up there, isn't it?"

I grin as I reach back for my seat belt. "I'm actually not sure where it's going to. Maybe her butthole is eating it."

"Gross."

He goes around and gets into the driver's seat. "Now don't make me regret this."

"I thought you were already regretting it?"

"I am... but don't make me regret it even *more*."

"I'll think about it."

He sighs and starts driving. The first bump he hits makes me question everything as it makes my stomach ache.

"Are you driving me off to prison?" I ask curiously.

"Not yet. I don't want to go to jail for being an accomplice."

"They don't need to know you know who I am. You can always tell them you had no idea. I was tricking your tiny brain into thinking I was sweet, innocent, and so fucking sexy. Do you dream about me?"

"No."

"Think of me when you're beating your meat?"

He nonchalantly shakes his head. "Not once."

I sigh like what he told me was devastating. "That's not very nice. I think about you every time I do it."

"I... don't need to know about it."

I smugly grin as he continues to chauffeur me to his house. It would be nice, if it weren't for the pain every time he hits a bump in the road. I try to distract myself by annoying him, but so far it isn't helping a lot.

"Oh..." He looks over at me. "I suppose I should have asked if you needed anything from your house."

"No, I'll just wear your clothes. I like them. It makes me feel like I'm wrapped in your embrace. You do have my gun, though."

"I do."

"I'd like that."

"What part of you quitting do you not get? You don't need a gun if you're quitting."

This man can't be serious. "What if I'm attacked? I still need to know where a gun is, at the very least."

"That's not the deal."

"But…"

He looks over at me. "If you were a good enough hitman, you wouldn't need a gun."

I nod like I actually agree. "You're right. My spoon-maiming skills are astounding."

He grins. "You'll be fine without a gun. I know where all the guns are, so you'll be safe."

I have my doubts, but if he wants to play knight in shining armor, then I'll allow him to. As long as he penetrates the princess at the end of the fairy tale, we'll both be happy.

When he pulls into the driveway, I look at the huge ruts my car left in his yard. I must have been *really* close to hitting that tree.

"What happened to your yard? Who tore it up so badly?" I ask in mock horror.

"That would be you."

"I would never do that. Where *is* my car?"

"In my garage."

"Ooh. I want you to park your car in *my* garage."

He shuts the car off and quickly leaves. For a moment, I'm positive he's leaving for good, but he grudgingly comes around and pulls my door open. I release my seat belt and slide out of the car as my scowling prince awaits me. Instead of carrying me like a virgin bride, he chooses to lead me up to the front door of the small, one-story home. He has an adequate yard, though he should do something about those ruts, and a couple of nice trees.

While I knew where he lived, I hadn't nosed around his house yet, so stepping inside is my first experience. He kicks his shoes off at the door, so I mimic him before slowly walking in. It's an open concept home with the living room to the right and the kitchen to the left. It looks like a hall on the other side leads to the bedrooms.

"I'll set you up on the couch. Do you want to lie down or sit up for now?" he asks.

"I can sit up. I'm fine," I assure him.

He waves to the couch, so I walk over to it and sit on one end while curiously looking around. It looks lived in, unlike my place. It's filled with character, defined by the photographs of him and family members hanging on the wall. The walls are painted light tan with a red accent wall. It's clean but clearly lived in.

I like it.

"Need anything?" he asks.

"My gun?"

"Need anything that I'll actually get you?"

"My... gun?"

"I'm going to take a shower. If you need me, holler. And if you walk out that door, I'm calling Henry and telling him all about you."

"Why do you trust that I won't kill you?" I ask curiously.

He stops walking and turns a little to look back at me. "You don't kill innocent people, do you, Leland?"

I'm surprised by that. I thought he'd say something about knowing he could take me on or protect himself from me. Which would be horribly wrong. I'm positive I could take him just because he's so open to me. He doesn't leave any guards up. "No... I suppose I don't. But I can always start somewhere."

"I'm not concerned. As long as you stay in this house and listen to my rules, we'll be fine. Understand?"

"Understood. I like it when you boss me around and force me to listen. Will you spank me if I don't?"

He walks away without saying "no," so I assume that means "yes." I always knew he was a bit kinky. I mean, our first meeting was him mooning me. Who else makes a first impression like that?

I grab the remote and turn the TV on before absentmindedly flipping through it. When I find a movie starting, I select it and wait for Jackson to return so I can pester him some more. It doesn't take him long before he comes back and sits in the recliner next to the couch.

"I missed you," I inform him.

"I bet you did."

"It was lonely."

"That's too bad."

My mouth feels dry. Probably from something they'd been giving me. So I sit up and swing my legs off the footrest.

"What are you doing?" Jackson asks before I have a chance to stand up.

"Getting water. What, did you think I was already running?"

He shakes his head. "Sit. I'll get it for you since you're not supposed to be getting up. You should be resting, remember?"

I watch him in near amazement as he stands. I'm so dumbfounded that I can't even think of an appropriate joke.

"Just water?"

"Yeah."

Why does it strike me as strange that he's getting me water? I suppose it's because no one ever gets things for me. I grew up learning that the only person I could depend on was myself. And I still live by that rule.

He returns with a cup. "Are you hungry? Need anything else?"

"No, I'm fine… thank you."

"You're welcome," he says as he sits back down.

What a strange man.

I stare at him as I try to determine what his angle is. Clearly, he wants something—why else would he get water for me? But what? Sex? I can handle sex. Maybe not when my intestines feel like they're wanting to crawl through the hole in my side, but my hand still works.

If he wanted sex, wouldn't he have tried a little harder?

"What are you staring at me for?" he asks as he raises an eyebrow.

"I'm trying to figure out what you are."

The eyebrow manages to go even higher. "What's that mean?"

"What do you want?"

"Um… like right now?"

"Yes."

"To… sit here? I'm kind of tired after not sleeping all night."

I narrow my eyes. "Hmm. Sounds suspicious."

He slowly shakes his head. "Do you have a concussion?"

"No. My head is fine. Unless you want to check it?"

"No."

I stare at him some more, like I'll be able to figure out what's wrong with him by scrutinizing everything he does. While he's fun to look at, I eventually get bored of staring and move on. I turn my attention back to the movie, but my eyes are too heavy to watch it. I fight to stay awake for a couple more minutes before letting sleep begin to pull me under.

Just as I'm nodding off, I feel something touch me. Startled, I jerk awake and look up at Jackson.

"I didn't mean to wake you," he says.

For a moment, I'm confused about what he's doing standing over me before realizing that he had laid a blanket on me.

"Were you going to smother me?" I ask.

"W-What?" he asks with clear confusion on his face.

"That's why you put a blanket on me, right? You were going to wrap it around my face and choke me out."

"Or… I know this might be strange, but *maybe* I wanted you warm."

I eye him. "You're up to something."

"Up to something *or* I'm being nice."

"Oh." I look down at the blanket. "You were just… being nice." I reach down and squeeze the blanket in my hand. "Thank you."

"You're welcome, even though you were convinced I was strangling you with a blanket… what kind of friends do you have?" he asks.

"I don't have friends… This," I say as I wave around me and then motion to the blanket, "I've never had this. I don't understand this. These pain pills are weird. I'm on drugs. That's all this is."

"Would you have preferred if I was strangling you?" he asks.

I grin. "Maybe."

He pulls the blanket up and holds it against my neck. "Ready?"

I start laughing. "Yes, this feels normal. This feels right."

"I'm only going to do a half-hearted strangle because I don't want you to tear anything open, alright?"

"I can handle that."

He throws the blanket over my head. "Take a nap."

I pull the blanket down. "I'm all horny now. Strangling makes me horny."

"Fuck off," he says. "I'm taking a nap in my bedroom. If you need me, call. I threw a pillow down if you want to lie down."

"Thanks, sugar muffin."

He snorts and leaves the room, and I can't help but smile.

Leland: And that was the moment that I began to question if you were really the villain of the story.

Jackson: Because I… covered you with a blanket?

Leland: You ripped my beautiful babies away from me and kept them hidden away!

Jackson: Oh, your gun. You know… it's a wonder you survived. Like how many guns do you usually keep on you at a time?

Leland: Like right now? I have three guns, two knives, and a peanut butter cup.

Jackson: What's the peanut butter cup for?

Leland: In case someone's allergic to peanut butter.

Jackson: Ah… I see.

Leland: But back then you were *mean*.

Jackson: Was it mean to keep a literal weapon away from a hitman I didn't really know or trust?

Leland: Horribly mean. And I'm sure you didn't treat Wandaleigh with the love and respect she deserved.

Jackson: Is that the gun's name?

Leland: Sure is.

Jackson: Well, I'm sorry, but I feel like I have now more than made up for it. Think of how many I let you keep in the house now.

Leland: It's never enough.

Jackson: I'm literally *drowning* in them.

Leland: Well, good thing I have plenty of guns to save your ass with, then.

TWELVE

JACKSON

And I've lost my mind.

What am I doing?

This entire thing is clearly stupid of me, but no matter how many times I remind myself of that, he's still in my living room, covered up with a blanket that I put over him.

Clearly, my brain needs to be checked. I feel like I should handcuff him or sleep in the living room or something to keep him from escaping. But at this moment, I think being as far from him as I can is ideal.

When I reach my bedroom, I toss my clothes in a hamper and crawl onto my bed with just my underwear on in case I need to deal with Leland. I can only imagine the harassment I would get if I had to quickly come out in the nude. He won't let me live down seeing my ass; there's no way he'd let me live down seeing the rest of me.

I need sleep, but my mind is racing.

What have I done? I've brought a wanted hitman into my house. Not only did I *not* report him, I was all, "Hey, come move in! Join my household! Let me tuck you in!"

I pick up my phone and stare at it. All I need to do is call Henry. Tell him I just figured it out with my superior detective skills.

What a load of shit.

I burrow under the blanket and lie awake for hours.

I must eventually fall asleep because I wake up when my phone beeps. When I look at it, I realize it's my mom.

> Mom: Just wondering if you still knew who I was. You've ignored me for years, it seems.

> Me: I called you two days ago.

> Mom: Years.

> Me: Work has been busy.

> Mom: Do you even remember what I look like?

> Me: I'm trying to forget.

> Mom: Don't be a brat. Do you want to have supper?

> Me: Can't tonight.

> Mom: Date?

> Me: Case.

> Mom: Is that her name? I like it.

I sigh and tug the blankets closer. She knows I'm gay, but she refuses to let go of the idea that I *might* change my mind.

> Me: I was taking a lovely nap until you annoyed me.

Mom: I'll see you at Christmas.

Me: Stop being dramatic. I'll see you on Sunday.

Mom: You'll have forgotten my face by then.

I toss the phone onto the bed and groan. I really don't feel like getting up, but I should probably confirm that Leland hasn't run away or destroyed the house in any way.

Once up and dressed, I walk into the living room where Leland is still on the couch. He's on his side, facing the back, blanket pulled up to his chin.

When he's not harassing me or doing something stupid, I can appreciate how attractive he is. Who am I kidding? He's always attractive. His narrow face is paler than usual, even though he's very pale to begin with. The amount of blood he lost is more than enough reason for that.

I tear my eyes away from him and go into the kitchen. Since we haven't had a proper meal in a while, I pull open the fridge and take out some chicken. I'm not used to cooking for others since my mom prefers to cook when we eat together. But for once, I have an excuse to cook. I season the chicken then stick it in the oven.

While it bakes, I pull out my laptop and do more research on Leland, but there isn't anything I haven't already seen. I end up just going in circles before giving up and checking my email.

When the chicken is close to being finished, I toss some broccoli in the microwave and set out plates.

"I must be in heaven," Leland says as he sits up and looks at me. The smile that forms on his face tells me that I should be worried about what he's going to say. "Or maybe it's hell because it looks like an incubus has come to taste my seed."

"Because of that comment, I'm going to eat all this food by myself, and you're going to watch."

He starts laughing, and I realize that he always does so easily. "No! I'll starve to death. You wouldn't want that, would you?"

"It would actually solve all my problems and relieve my stress."

"But I'm too handsome to starve," he cries.

"What, you think it's okay for ugly people to starve?" I ask as I try not to grin.

"You said it, not me."

"Do you want to eat on the couch?"

"No, I want to sit at the table like I'm sophisticated."

"Where do you usually eat?"

He leans against the back of the couch, setting his chin on it. "I don't even own a table."

"Seems fitting."

"Before that, where's the bathroom?"

"Down that hallway," I say as I point.

He slowly gets up and walks toward the bathroom as I watch him. He stops halfway there and looks back at me. "Are you watching my ass?"

My eyes drop down to it. Since he's wearing my sweatpants, they hang on him. "No."

"Why not?" he teases.

"Do you even have an ass? I can't see it in those sweats."

He hikes them up so they ride up his ass crack. "What about now?"

"Oh, gorgeous."

He chuckles as he disappears into the bathroom, and I'm left shaking my head with a grin on my face. Which I *shouldn't* have. He's the freaking Sandman, for heaven's sake.

I sigh.

I set the table, get us both water to drink, and am putting food on the plates as he returns. He looks oddly delighted.

"You even set the table."

"I did..."

"It's like we're already a married couple. I love it."

"We're not married."

"Not yet, but I'm ready whenever you are."

"Which will likely be never."

"Now that's a bit harsh, but I'll win you over. I mean, you've already asked me to move in with you—who knows what you'll ask next?"

Maybe I should have kept him chained up so he understood this was more of a... what? Hostage situation? He'd just think it was kinky foreplay.

He takes a bite and looks surprised. "It's actually good!"

"Why wouldn't it be?" I ask, secretly delighted that he enjoys my food.

"You don't look like much of a househusband. You look like a worn-out detective who should be getting gray soon from all the worrying and scowling you do."

"Do you ever think that I only do those two things when I'm trying to deal with you?" I ask as I cut into the chicken.

"Never thought that at all, honestly. I assumed you loved dealing with me. I always seem to bring a smile to your face," he says as he gives me that charming grin.

Why does it make me want to smile back?

Instead, I stuff a piece of chicken in my mouth so I'm not tempted to do anything else.

"What's next on your househusband agenda? Are you going to give me a bath?" His eyes get wide. "I want you to give me a bath."

"No."

"What else could we do?"

"Watch TV. Read a book. Question why I'm letting you in my house."

"That," he says as he points his fork at me, "is a good question that I don't have an answer to. The only thing I can think of is that we're soul mates and you're drawn to me. Fated mates."

"I definitely don't think that's it."

When we're finished eating, I reach for his plate.

"I can get it," he says.

I wave him off. "Go rest."

"I'm going to start growing mold if I just sit on the couch all day."

"You'll heal faster by resting."

"Okay..." He's giving me that suspicious look again like *I'm* the strange one in this duo.

He stays at the table and watches me as I clean up. I'm surprised he's managed to stay quiet for as long as it takes me to put everything away. "Do you need anything else?" I ask.

"No... thanks."

"Want to watch something?" I ask. "Other than me, that is?"

He smiles at me. "Sure," he says as he gets up and follows me back into the living room.

Leland: You thought I was cute!

Jackson: You're not bothered it was only when you were being silent?

Leland: Cute! Gosh, Jackson, *you're* cute too. You were already the best househusband one could ask for. Looking after me. Pampering me. Telling me that it was love at first sight.

Jackson: I feel like your comprehension of past events is wildly different than mine.

Leland: Maybe, but you still made me feel like a prince. I was like royalty. You were getting things for me. I'd just *look* like I'd want something, and you'd run off to get it. I mean... you ask why I was willing to give up so much... and maybe it was because there was something worth giving it up for. It was... shockingly nice.

Jackson: I'm glad I could do that for you. It didn't seem like that much at the time, but I guess if you'd never had anyone do things like that for you before, I can see why it seemed like a lot.

Leland: It was a lot... more than you'll ever imagine. Gosh, this is disgustingly sweet, and I've got hives from it. HIVES, JACK-SON. Yuck. Let's get to some murder.

Jackson: I... I don't think there's murder right away...

Leland: *tsks* We can change that.

THIRTEEN

LELAND

It's already been a day since I moved in, and I'm strangely enjoying it. I've been hurt before on the job, like the time where I suffered a severe concussion and lay on my bathroom floor for hours before even realizing I'd made it home. Or the time I'd been stabbed and was told that it would eventually heal.

But here, anything I need is instantly given to me. Even if I don't need it, he's there with it.

"I'm going to run into the office," Jackson says as he sets an ice pack down.

Since I don't "properly apply it," he yanks my blanket back and sets it against my abdomen.

"Do not leave or I'll call them." He's awful at threats.

They almost just make me grin. "Yeah, yeah, I heard it yesterday. Why would I ever leave? I get treated like a princess here."

He gives me a nice cheek pat for that one. "Do you need me to swing by your apartment and pick up anything?"

"That… actually would be amazing. I'll text you the address. If you don't mind, I'd like underwear and clothes that show off my ass. And my laptop. I'll make you a list. Do you want me to go with you and grab the stuff?"

"No, you're resting."

"Yeah… but I can go. My legs haven't been hacked off."

"Rest. Make a list of what you want and where it's at, and I'll grab what I can."

"Thank you, love."

He hands me a piece of paper, so I jot down everything I need as he gets ready. When he returns, I hold the list out and he scans it. "Clothes, laptop, charger, butt plug, handcuffs…" He looks over at me like he's not amused. Clearly, he is.

"Keep reading," I urge.

He sighs as his eyes drop down to the list. "Nipple clamps. Sex swing." He looks up. "And where's that going to fit in my car?"

I laugh as I shake my head. "I don't know. Strap it on top."

"And… 'Super-Secret Stash of Illegal Stuff.' That's what I'm supposed to grab?"

"Yes, it's in a box under the bed labeled like that. Oh, and don't forget Blow-Up Randy. He's in my bed."

He sighs as he tucks the list in his pocket. "Where are your apartment keys?"

"They're attached to the car keys."

"Alright, I'll be back in a couple of hours. Maybe more, depending on how hard it is to disassemble the sex swing."

I laugh, which makes him grin at me. He tries to hide it by quickly turning around and heading out to the garage. I wait about twenty minutes before throwing back the blanket. Honestly, I don't have the capability to wait any longer. While I'm still sore, the pain is manageable unless I accidentally pull on the stitches. And I'm definitely not too sore to snoop, especially with the pain pills and as long as I don't stay on my feet for too long.

I set the ice pack aside before getting up and heading toward the back of the house. While I should probably be considerate of the man allowing me to stay in his house, I also feel like he's up to something. Why else would he be this nice?

I find Jackson's laptop in his bedroom and open it up. With the angle he'd been sitting on the couch earlier today, I was able to see the four numbers he entered for his password. Without a smidge of guilt, I easily type them in. The first thing that's up on the screen is a Word document.

`Get off my laptop, you nosy bastard.`

I grin at the screen. How the hell does he know me so well? Clearly, he knows me better in the limited time I've known him than most do.

I decide that there's really no sense in keeping it a secret that I was on his laptop. I'm sure he's already figured it out.

`I like your butt. How about you show it to me again like you did during our first meeting?`

When I pull up his browser, I see that he only has one tab open and start laughing when I read it. It's a Google search for "What do I do when my roommate is a nosy bastard?" Besides that, he's wiped all of his history and has no tabs open. What an asshole. I just wanted to nose a little. When I don't find anything of interest on the browser, I start opening files. Quite a few documents are password protected, but my attention gets drawn over to the pictures on the computer. So many pictures of him and his family smiling and enjoying life. I make one bigger and look down at the picture of him hoisting a toddler into the air as the child laughs.

Then I switch to the next, and soon I'm looking at every picture he has on his computer while wondering how our lives can be so extremely different.

JACKSON

Since I'm sure he's tearing my house apart, I decide that it isn't completely immoral of me to do the same to his home. Honestly, I'm surprised at how bare it is. But I suppose when you live like him and want to remain inconspicuous, it makes sense to stay in a place like this. Or maybe he really doesn't have the money for a nicer place. I'm not sure what he charges, if anything. And then maybe he blows it on stupid things, like all those sex toys he left in my car that I threw away as soon as I got them out of Henry's car.

I go over to the coffee table and grab the laptop that's sitting on it before winding up the charger and slipping it into the backpack he carries with him everywhere. If it weren't password protected, I would get on it, but I'm not tech savvy enough to figure it out without help. What I do pull out is his notebook before sitting on the couch. I begin going through it, looking at the absolute detail he has on his cases. There are even leads that the police know nothing about.

He must be pretty damn cocky to carry this around with him. Or is he that confident he'll never get caught? This notebook alone could connect him to multiple cases. It almost seems out of character for him when he's so meticulous with everything else. Maybe it's because he's cocky, or maybe there's another reason for it.

I put the notebook away and turn back to snooping. The front of the apartment is pretty bare, so I go into his bedroom and start digging through things. Since he doesn't own much, it saves me a lot of time. His bedroom is messier than the living room, with clothes strewn about, but it's still clean. I search his drawers before dropping to the floor and reaching under the bed.

I'm worried about what I'll find, but besides a lot of junk that'd probably been absentmindedly shoved under there, I find the box he's talking about.

The cardboard box doesn't actually say anything on it but is pretty heavy. I pull it out and stare at it apprehensively. I'm worried about what I might find inside. Ball gag? Anal beads? Who fucking knows?

I flip it open. On top is an ID. I pick it up and realize that it's his *real* ID. The next thing is a birth certificate, so I figure out that this box might actually be personal stuff. And it makes me feel strange going through it. Even though I'm sure he's going through all my personal stuff without a care in the world.

I grab the box, then head to his dresser and start filling a bag with clothes and necessities. Once I have everything on his list that isn't something perverted, I carry the bags out to the car. I drive home, wondering if I'll find him wrapped up in a blanket with my laptop open on his lap.

But when I walk inside, he's sitting on the couch. He looks at me, a huge smile on his gorgeous face. There's something else there that just *tells* me he snooped more than he needed to, and he had fun doing it.

"Oh, thank god, you're back. I was so bored," he whines. "Quick! Entertain me!"

"No," I say as dryly as I can.

An actual pout fills his face. And somehow, it still looks handsome on him. "Please? Do a little dance. Moon me again! That one! Please!"

I try not to grin. "Fuck off."

"I laughed so hard when that happened."

Why will I never be able to live down the most embarrassing moment of my life? Why will it always haunt me?

"This time, can I stick my finger in your butthole?"

Why I'm even surprised by his request is beyond me. "No."

He holds out a finger and wiggles it in a come-hither motion. "You know you want to."

"You want me to walk over and just bend over? What is it? A prostate exam?" I ask.

He starts laughing. "You're getting older, so I bet you've had one of those before."

I kick my shoes off in the corner before walking over to the couch. "I'm *not* older."

"Oh… I thought you were like seventy or eighty at this point. At least that's your current sex drive."

I swing his backpack off my back and set it on the couch next to him. "I brought your stuff."

"Did you bring me Blow-Up Larry?"

"I thought it was Randy."

He shrugs. "I have so many sex dolls it's hard to keep track of them. I tried finding yours. No luck."

"Sorry, I'm not that desperate."

"*Yet.*"

"Yet," I agree. "Did you get on my laptop?"

His eyes get wide like he couldn't fathom doing something so heinous. "No. I would never do that. What am I? A heathen? God, no. Do I look like that type of person?"

"One hundred percent."

"Alright. I just want to get it out there that I *did* nose around your house. I looked everywhere and it was really boring. It was almost *sad* how boring it was."

"Thanks."

He gives me a charming smile that lights up his gorgeous face. "You're welcome. Did you nose in my apartment?"

"I did."

"What'd you see?"

"Nothing under the filth of your bedroom."

"My bedroom is not that filthy."

"It's like your dresser exploded."

"My dresser is small and not everything fits into it! Especially with my strap-on collection in there."

"What do you need strap-ons for?"

"Haven't you ever wondered what it'd feel like to have *two* penises?"

"Never."

"Well… if you ever wonder, I gotchu."

I shake my head. "Thank you."

I set the rest of his stuff next to the couch and pull his laptop out for him so he doesn't have to reach into the bag to grab it.

"Do you need anything?" I ask as I pick up his water and check to see if it needs to be refilled.

"No," he says as he watches me carry the cup into the kitchen and fill it with ice and water.

I've noticed that whenever I do anything kind, he stares at me suspiciously.

When he's situated, I head back to my bedroom and open my laptop. I type the passcode in and look down at what he wrote on the Word document.

`I like your butt. How about you show it to me`
`again like you did during our first meeting? I`

```
just looked through all your pictures. You're
going to be such a good daddy for our children. I
want at least two.
```

And when I pull up the browser, the search has turned to "how do I tell my roommate that I want to lick his balls?"

LELAND

As Jackson's off looking through what I did to his computer, I go through what he grabbed for me. He did a pretty good job finding everything I asked for. When he returns, I smile at him. For some reason, I'm compelled to see what else he'll do for me. I mean... he *knows* I snooped around in his stuff, but the first thing he does is refill my water?

"I feel really dirty. I want to take a shower, but they didn't want me to. Will you give me a sponge bath?" I ask.

"No, but if you want me to wash your hair, I can."

This man *can't* be real. "Really?"

"Yeah. You probably shouldn't reach up and wash it."

Even though I'm positive I can wash my own hair, I quickly follow him into the bathroom.

He looks over at me. "Do you want a bath? I can fill it up and you can wash up that way. Just don't soak the sutures."

"Sure."

He starts the water and gets a washcloth and towel as I watch him. Even as he plugs the drain, I can't look away.

"Why do you stare at me so intently when I do things for you?" he asks.

"I'm trying to figure out what's wrong with you."

"What's that mean?"

"My dad left me to my own devices. Like I'm not sure he ever helped me a day in my life. I popped out of my mom's vagina, and he said, 'good luck, feed yourself.' And the guy I lived with later treated me like a mini machine. So yeah... it's strange. And I love it. I'm going to pretend to be in pain for weeks, maybe even months. You'll help me forever."

"I have my doubts."

"But Jackson, I can't push my pants down."

Without hesitation, he steps up to me and grabs my sweats but holds on to them as he stares down into my eyes. "I know how long a wound takes to heal. You're not pulling one over on me, but I *will* help you until you are healed."

He pushes them down my hips and lets them pool at my feet, so I kick them off. As he starts unbuttoning my shirt, I continue to stare at him.

Is this what it would be like to be in a relationship? To not cut everyone off and kill people for a living? Who am I kidding, this isn't how someone like me lives. This is for other people. People in books or movies.

He reaches up to my shoulders to push my shirt off as his eyes stay focused on my chest.

"You like my nipples?" I ask.

"Your chest is so blindingly white I actually can't even look at them. Have you ever seen the sun?"

"I'm the sun and you revolve around me."

He snorts as he shuts the water off.

"I can't get in with underwear on."

Without hesitation, he grabs the underwear and pulls them down. He doesn't even act like there's anything interesting that he's revealing. Like… not even a peek. Even *I* peek at it, and I know exactly what my cock looks like.

"Oh my god," I say, like I'm horrified.

"What?"

"You're not gay. I thought you were gay but you're not. And now I realize that I just made that assumption because I wanted your peepee."

"You're right, that was an assumption."

I point down at my groin. "Look at it."

He shakes his head. Clearly, my command was not properly understood.

"Get in the bathtub," he says.

"I want you to look at it, and I want to see your reaction so I can judge for myself. Like if you're all, 'wow,' I'll know you want me. Wait… maybe you're an ass man."

I turn around and smack my ass cheek while watching him.

He doesn't do anything but give me a hint of a smile, which he's trying his hardest to hide. "Get in the tub."

"I can't. I need your manly muscles to help me."

"Figure it out."

I start to lift my foot then make a show of dramatically stumbling. "Oh no! The pain!" I cry as I fall into him. He instinctively grabs onto me.

I look up at him as he stares down at me with a raised eyebrow. "Your manly arms caught me in my moment of peril."

"Get your ass in the tub."

"Tell me you like my ass."

"Get your scrawny, flat ass in the tub."

"The thing is… that's *exactly* how I would describe my ass, so I'm pleased that you looked at it. Hold me tighter, prince. Kiss me awake."

"Are you always this dramatic?"

"Probably," I admit as I stand up. "You do bring out the worst in me, though. Before I get into the tub, I do want to know…"—I run a finger down his chest—"is your chest as hairy as your ass crack?"

"My ass isn't hairy."

"Maybe I need another look to verify because I feel like it was hairy. I won't be able to think otherwise unless I see it again."

He gives me a gentle push. "Get in the bathtub."

I grudgingly climb in and sit in the shallow water. I make sure my groin is easily noticeable, but he never seems to glance down. Instead, he pulls the showerhead down and kneels next to the tub.

"I feel like a dog you're giving a bath to. I want a dog. Will you get me a dog?"

"I would like to get one thing straight: this is a prisoner situation. I'm not your husband or your partner or whatever else you want."

"Daddy?"

"*Not* your daddy."

"*Fine*, I'll be your doggy."

"Has your brain always been this damaged?" he asks as he tilts my chin up.

"I think so. There were a couple of times I had a lack of oxygen to my brain as well as some severe hits and falls. I feel like it's given me some character, but maybe I've actually lost my mind."

"You have."

He runs the water over my head as I close my eyes, disappointed he won't even bother fondling me a little. Even an eye fondle would have been better than nothing. Instead, I feel like I'm at a barber's getting my hair professionally washed.

Even so, I keep my eyes closed and enjoy every moment of him scrubbing my hair with shampoo. With the warm water licking my thighs and his hands on my head, I feel like I'm in ultimate bliss.

I'm really going to miss this when I leave.

He rinses the shampoo out, and I realize that I feel disappointment that he's done. He runs his fingers through my hair one last time, and I find myself leaning into him.

"I can't wash my body; it hurts too much."

"You can figure it out."

"My back is dirty; I need it washed."

He grabs the washcloth and starts running it over my back. Feeling the brush of his fingers makes my cock start to harden. I want to push into him, but I also don't want to thank him with an erection he clearly doesn't want. The washcloth runs down my back, almost to my ass, and I want to beg him to move it down just a few more inches.

"There," he says, and I'm kind of glad since any more and I would have been at half-mast.

"Thank you, doll."

He grunts unattractively, like he's not very fond of his pet name. I can't fathom why. "I'll leave you to it."

And then he leaves. He could have at least *pretended* to be interested.

I lean back but the faucet cuts into my back, since if I'd have sat the other way, he wouldn't have been able to reach me with the hose.

I groan as I lean against the tub wall, wishing I could get my mind to return.

Clearly, I need to stay focused and stop getting distracted by his nurturing charm and ridiculously good looks.

Leland: That would have been a real bummer if you were straight.

Jackson: Our tale would have turned into one of horror.

Leland: Why? Because you couldn't love me because of my peepee?

Jackson: No, because there'd be some strange man running around, "flirting"—and I say that with *thick* quotation marks—and shooting at me! You know what... it really doesn't sound romantic when I sum it up!

Leland: You're so sassy. It was horribly romantic! It was dripping with romance juice!

Jackson: No wonder it seemed so creepy.

Leland: *sighs* You're being dramatic again. I really am glad you liked me, though. That would have been *awkward*.

Jackson: Just a little bit.

FOURTEEN

JACKSON

I hear the door hinge squeak as it slides open. I've been in bed for about half an hour but had just set my phone aside to drift off to sleep. Instead of finding sleep, I find an annoyance letting himself in.

"What are you doing?"

"Shh, it's just the Sandman coming to penetrate your dreams," he whispers.

"Go to bed."

"The couch is lumpy, and it's making my wound hurt."

"How the hell is the couch making your stomach hurt?"

"It is," he says as he pulls back the covers before I can pin them down.

I can see him in the minimal light coming through the window and stare at him in disbelief as he climbs right under them.

"Go back to the couch."

"Why?" he asks, making it sound pitiful. Like how horrible of me to kick out a wounded person. What a conniving man.

"Because I don't want you in my bed," I say, but he's already aware he's won. For some reason, I seem to let him get away with anything he wants.

"I'll be good."

I sigh like I'm dreading the attractive man in my bed. "Fine, as long as you stay on your side."

"Okay."

Turning so my back is to him, I try to pretend he's not there. Honestly, I'm shocked when he stays on his side. Maybe this will be alright after all.

I close my eyes, and just as I'm starting to relax, I feel the bed move. Then I feel his hand snake under my shirt and I nearly crawl out of my skin. I can*not* handle this right now. He's been trying my ability to resist him again and again, but I'm a strong man and I can ignore him.

"Get off me." It almost comes out like a plea.

"I'm used to sleeping against a wall, and it feels really weird being out in the open," he says as he pushes his hips forward until I feel his groin against my ass. My dick is instantly into whatever this is while my mind chastises me. I want to push him away, but I know I have to be careful not to hurt him.

Ignore him. Ignore him. He's *not* attractive. Especially with that attitude. And with his... oh god... I can feel it. His cock is touching me.

"You need to stay on your side of the bed," I growl.

"Is it because you're the little spoon? I can be the little spoon."

"No, it's because of your erection digging into my ass."

"But... that's just a natural reaction when I'm with a handsome man such as yourself."

"Nope," I say, carefully pulling away because I'm afraid I'm going to hurt him or show him that I'm not as indifferent as I'm pretending to be.

No matter what he does or says, I *cannot* have sex with him. I can't get involved with him any more than I already am. If I became attached, if I slept with him and started to fall for that outgoing personality of his, I wouldn't be able to turn him in if I had to.

His arms tighten around me. He smells good from his bath, and suddenly I'm thinking about the peek of his dick I'd gotten when he hadn't noticed.

"Leland!" I snap.

He freezes. "What?"

"Get off me."

He quickly retreats. "I'm sorry."

For some reason, I now feel guilty. "It's... I didn't mean to snap. But... we can't, alright?"

"Okay."

Oh, but I want to. More than anything, I want to lean over and grab him. Claim his lips and leave him panting for breath. God, I fucking want to. I've already done everything else wrong, would it matter if I do one more thing?

I roll over as if my body is possessed and climb onto him in a way that I'm not touching him at all. He looks up at me as I lean over him, my legs on each side of his hips, unsure of what I'm doing. I know what I *want* to do, but I also know what I shouldn't do.

He's quiet as he looks up at me, dark hair splayed out on the pillow, gorgeous blue eyes watching me. His lips part slightly, and my eyes are drawn to them. He's not saying a word, but he doesn't need to. I'm already mesmerized by him.

I reach down and cup his chin and he tilts his head into me while his lips turn up, like he's smirking at me. He knows I've given in.

I lean down until he starts to lift into me. With the hand cupping his smooth cheek, I run my thumb over his lips. "I will not fall into your trap and grow to like you enough that I won't turn you in."

His smirk turns into a smile that takes over his face. "You can't blame a man for trying."

"Well, guess what? It's not going to happen," I say as I dip down close enough I brush his lips. It takes everything in my willpower to not dive into him, especially when I can feel his breath.

"No? But... I promise you'll enjoy it," he says as his fingers trail up my bare leg. Thankfully, I'd worn shorts to bed, or I wouldn't have been able to hide the start of my erection as well as I'm currently hiding it. Especially as his fingers draw the side of my shorts up until his fingers run over my bare thigh.

I squeeze his face in my hand. "I don't need any of the enjoyment you're offering," I say as I slide off him and put my feet onto the floor. "I'm getting some water. Want anything?"

"Your dick…" he says in a very pitiful voice.

I try not to laugh as I leave the room.

Of course I don't *need* water. What I need is to get away from the incubus in my bed. How the hell am I supposed to go back in there and sleep?

I try to think about *other* things as my cock tries to make me think about only *one* thing. One very handsome thing.

When I reach the kitchen, I chug a large glass of water while trying to distract my mind. This is not good. Not good at all.

Thankfully, when I crawl into bed, he doesn't try to touch me again and I manage to keep my body aimed away from him, but sleep takes a while to come.

LELAND

What a tease.

Oh, what an evil tease Jackson is.

Last night he refused to fall into my trap and this morning he wanted nothing to do with cuddling against me. Too bad I didn't wake before him or I would have made sure I'd snuggled up against him.

Jackson stops in front of the couch I'm sitting on. "I'm going to work. I have a camera aimed at you, and I will check it throughout the day to make sure you haven't left," he says as he points to it.

"Oh, you naughty, naughty boy. You want a sex tape, is that it?" I ask.

He looks taken aback. "No."

"Is it recording? When do I start jerking off?"

He sighs, quickly figuring out this was a bad idea. "None of the time."

"But… what if I go to the bathroom?"

"I don't care. I'm just going to notice if you're gone for more than fifteen minutes. Got it?"

"That's not enough time to jerk off in your bed, though. I like to take it slow."

"Don't jerk off on my bed."

"Spritz my spunk on your pillow, maybe."

"I wish you'd have gone to jail."

I start laughing. "I'll be good as long as you give me a goodbye kiss," I say as I pucker my lips.

He barely glances down before scowling. "No thanks."

"Love me."

"No."

"I don't want to be in a loveless marriage, Jackson! Love me."

"I don't even know you! I didn't even know your name until a week ago!"

"Sandman."

"Shut it."

"I wanna come in your dreams."

"Fuck off. Don't do anything stupid."

"I will."

Jackson sighs, but I can't understand why.

Hesitantly, he walks out the door with one last look at me.

"Are you trying to memorize the look of my face to help you get through the day?" I ask.

He wrinkles his nose and slips out the door. It's the first day he's gone back to work for a full day since I arrived. I think he was too afraid I'd set his house on fire or something. But maybe after nearly ravishing him last night, he's decided that he needs to get a good distance away from me. What he doesn't know is that he can never escape my charms.

As soon as he's gone, I try to entertain myself for a few minutes before deciding that maybe I'll let Tucker know I'm alive.

Since I don't have my burner phone, I decide to send an email. So I pull up the email and type:

Pencildick. I'm alive.

The reply is almost immediate.

Dammit.

Well, all is well there. Now, what do I do? Hmm…. Hmm…

I turn the TV on and flip through the channels, but at nine in the morning on a Monday, there isn't much.

Then I decide that maybe I'll hook my computer up to the printer. Once that's set, I find a very detailed picture of a vagina and print it out. With that complete, I make it a little easel so it'll stand on its own and stick it in front of the camera.

Well… that was fun. Now I just have to wait.

It takes five minutes before my phone starts ringing.

"Hello?" I call.

"Burn that," Jackson growls.

"What?"

"That picture."

I play the innocent card. "The picture of what?"

"The picture in front of the camera."

"I don't know what you're talking about."

"Burn the picture of the vagina."

"Oh! Is that what that is?" I ask while trying to sound surprised. "I've never seen one, so I thought it was like a little sea creature."

I pull the picture away and stuff my face in front of the camera. "I have this nose hair I can't seem to get. Can you see it?" I ask as I aim the camera up my nose.

"You are the least attractive human ever."

"Am I? That feels like an accomplishment," I say as I turn around. "I feel like since I've seen your ass, you should see mine."

And then I pull my pants down.

"Just as flat as when you have pants on."

I look back at my ass. "What? My butt's not flat."

"Yes, it is. Did you not know that?"

"No…" I say while trying to sound like my heart is broken. I even have a little quiver to my voice.

"It is."

"That makes me really sad."

"I'm sure. Now be good."

"Which means… you want to see my balls?"

"No! Just… sit on the couch."

I chuckle. "You're no fun."

"I know. Be good."

And he hangs up.

I should leave. I'm healed enough at this point that I would be fine going home, gathering my things, and running. I might not even need to run. I doubt he'd find me in this city again. Maybe I'll just lay low for a while. See if Tucker has anything of interest for me. I'll leave Hardek to the police until I find something solid on him, especially since I won't be paid for the job.

I sink back onto the couch and squeeze the blanket Jackson had covered me with. One more day won't hurt, right? Just one more day before I leave.

I pull the blanket over me and burrow under it. If I have to, I can make it one more day here. Maybe he'll fall in love with me in that extra day and not call the police.

One more day.

Leland: You willingly let a strange man climb right into your bed and snuggle with you.

Jackson: I don't think I'd call that snuggling. And you were definitely "strange," but not in the way you're implying.

Leland: You were so close to caving, weren't you?

Jackson: Unbelievably close. But imagine if I did and then you were arrested or ran away or something like that?

Leland: This ass can never be tamed, Jackson. You don't have to worry about me. No prison could hold me.

Jackson: I… am wildly skeptical about that.

Leland: This one time, I was abducted by this guy who created a wild maze for me to escape from. It was his "thing," you know? He'd abduct people and then set them loose and if they made it out alive… he'd let them go free, but if not, he'd murder them. So I dragged him in with me and I hunted his ass down with a feather duster and a deck of cards.

Jackson: This story started out fascinating… until the end.

Leland: What the hell, Jackson? How's that not more fascinating? I bet you wish you could go back in time and snuggle my ass that night you turned me down, don't you?

Jackson: How do you kill someone with a feather duster?

Leland: You dust them to death, obviously.

Jackson: And the deck of cards?

Leland: You deck them to death.

Jackson: You're literally just using alliteration to try to sound cool.

Leland: Jealous Jackson, just turn the page and join me in this journey of jove.

Jackson: What is jove?

Leland: It's love but with a J.

Jackson: I jee.

Leland: ha ha ha you're the man for je.

FIFTEEN

JACKSON

When I get home, I'm honestly surprised he's still here. I'd checked on the camera throughout the day, but after he hadn't left the couch most of the morning, I had stopped worrying about it.

When I walk in, he smiles at me from where he's lying.

"Snuggleberry!" he calls. "Welcome home! I was going to have a feast prepared, but then I started watching this vet show and there was this dog that was trying to die, and I had to know if it lived. It did."

"That's… good."

"It is, isn't it?" he says as he gets up and walks up to me. Saunters is more like it. "Let me get your coat."

He starts unzipping my coat as I stare at the strange creature. "What do you want?" I ask warily.

"It's like unzipping a Christmas present," he says as his hands drop to my pants zipper and yank it down. "Whoops."

"Whoops my ass," I say as I try to shoo him away.

"You want me to whoop your ass?" he asks before smacking my ass cheek. "There ya go!"

I glare at him.

He shrugs. "What? I thought that's what you wanted!"

"It wasn't!"

"Oh… sorry. I'll rub it to make it better," he says as he tries rubbing me.

I grab his hands, but because I have to be mindful of his wound, I can't give him a good shake to see if I can knock his brain into position. "No."

He grins at me and I realize that even though I'm saying "no," my body is saying "yes" to anything he's prepared to give me or let me do. I let go of him, but he's still grinning at me, telling me he's planning something.

"Boop," he says and pokes my penis before stepping back.

He's going to be the death of me. The absolute death of me.

I decide that while my balls have begun to hate me, I *will* remain strong.

He turns around and sinks back onto the couch. "Feed me, Seymour!" he says, and his reference to *Little Shop of Horrors* even turns me on.

"I saw that in the theater once."

"You did?" he asks. "I love that movie. I want to see it in the theater. Take me!"

"No, I'm not taking you places. This is like… house arrest, alright?"

"It is?" he asks. "You've pampered me, washed my hair, fed me, clothed me, covered me with blankets… is this anything like house arrest?"

"I do sound like your mother, don't I?" I ask in horror.

He laughs as he watches me walk into the living room. "That's okay. I've really appreciated it. I can make supper, though," he says as he gets up. "Does it matter what I make?"

"No. I can do it."

"Nah, if I can't get you to love me through your penis, let me try through your hole. Not that hole, you dirty boy. Your mouth hole."

"I was not… thinking… Yeah. Mouth hole works," I say. "I'm going to get a shower. Don't burn the house down."

"Can I wash your willy?"

"No."

"What if I just watch through the curtain?"

"No! You're like a little creep."

"I know," he says with a grin.

I sigh and go into my bedroom before gathering some sweats and a hoodie. Then I head into the bathroom and start my shower. Sadly, my bathroom door doesn't lock, so there's only a matter of time before he lets himself in.

I undress and step into the hot water. After adjusting it, I sink into it and close my eyes. The day felt long and unproductive since I really didn't get much done. My mind couldn't focus because I spent half of my time wondering if Leland was gone. And the other half wondering what I would do *if* he was gone.

This is why no one should ever get close to someone they might have to seal the fate of.

There's a knock on the door a moment before I hear it slam open. I wouldn't be surprised if the handle punched a hole in the wall.

"It's okay! I have my face covered so I can't see anything," Leland announces.

I pull the curtain back enough to see him wandering around with a shirt over his eyes. He pats the sink counter and climbs onto it. "What are you doing?" I ask.

"Honestly, I was feeling lonely, so I came in to spend time with you."

"I thought you were making supper."

"It's marinating."

"In what?"

"My own concoction of arsenic and rat poison. You're gonna *love* it."

"Love it to death?" I supply.

His laughter fills the small room, and I find myself having to let go of the curtain so I'll stop staring at him. "That's a good one. No, this soy sauce stuff. It's good, I promise."

"Okay, I'll trust you."

"Have you had a long-term boyfriend before?" he asks curiously.

"Like one that's moved in with me?"

"Yeah."

"No. While I was in the military, my focus was on that. Then once I was out, I dated some. But like a couple of months or so."

"Ooh! I'm the first boyfriend you've ever asked to move in!"

I sigh as I grab the shampoo, knowing I'm not going to win this. "Yep."

Agreeing with Leland results in more laughing. "Hey! I don't know what to say when you agree with me!"

"I know." I rub it into my hair before stepping under the water to wash it out. "What about you?"

"I was never good at living with others. Or maybe they weren't good at living with me. Whatever the case was, I was always happiest alone… at least I thought I was," he says.

The last part is almost a mumble, but the beating of the water doesn't hide his words from me. I don't know why it makes me feel so good to hear his honesty, but I find myself leaning toward the curtain to hear him better.

I look out at him as he remains seated on the sink. He smiles as he says, "And then I realized what it was like to have a slave who does everything for you! I *love* it."

And… he ruined it. "I'm not your *slave*."

"You get me water, bathe me, clothe me, and I don't pay you in any way. If that's not a slave or a husband, I'm not sure what it is."

"I'm neither of those things."

"But you will be soon. The issue is… do you want to take my last name, or do you want me to take yours? I should probably take yours since I'm being all sneaky-sneaky, but that's up to you."

"I think the meat is marinated."

"Not yet. I have another twenty minutes or so to spend with you. Do you want me to wash your hair since you washed mine? That sounds like a good idea."

"Nope."

"Here I come!" he says.

I pull back the curtain as he blindly comes at me, arms outstretched, a grin showing on what little of his face I can see.

For some reason, I stand still and let him run into me, palms smacking against my wet chest.

"Ooh. I found you. Now to wash your hair," he says as his hands start dropping.

"*Nope*," I say as I grab his hands.

"But I'm just trying to find your head. I'm blindfolded, so I'm confused."

"You forgot the general layout of the body because you're blinded?"

"Yes!"

I hold his wrists captive as my body degrades my mind. Just another foot and he would have found a different head. I should have given him another foot.

I need to stay focused. "I really think the meat is marinated."

"I don't tell you how to cook when you're cooking," he says.

His bound hands begin to move, fingers wiggling as if he's aching to reach me. Just then, the shirt wrapped around his face falls. There isn't even a moment's hesitation before his eyes drop straight down to my groin.

"Oh... *OH*." While the smile on his face pleases me, I know I can't give in. "Well, hello there. I don't believe we've met."

"Don't... stop looking down there."

"I can't look away," Leland says as his grin widens.

I give him a gentle push back and yank the curtain closed before my cock betrays me and shows just how turned on I am from him just *staring* at me. For fuck's sake, am I fifteen again?

"Oh? Is he shy?" he asks.

"Put your shirt mask on and leave."

"I can't find it."

"I bet you can."

"I really can't. It must be gone."

"That's so strange. Maybe it's in the kitchen?"

He laughs. "I've got my eyes closed. You can come out. I promise I won't peek at your willy."

"Thanks," I say dryly, knowing full well that he's going to peek. He can look all he wants, but he's getting none of it because he is the Sandman, and I'm *watching* him.

I turn the water off and pull back the curtain. To my surprise, his eyes are closed as he sits on the sink and kicks his legs like a toddler. Even though it's clear he hasn't done anything with his hair and is still wearing sweatpants, he stands out. For a man wishing to blend in, he was dealt cards that didn't allow it. But it's the smile he almost always wears that really pulls me in.

As I dry off, I can tell he's starting to get impatient. He fiddles around and sighs. "How long does it take to dry off? You won't melt if you have water left behind your balls."

"Have patience."

"I've never had patience," he says as I slide my sweats on.

"There, you can open them."

He quickly does. "Ooh, I get to see your nips then," he says as he reaches out and jabs me in the nipple.

"Is this how you interact with people? Just... poking them in strange places?"

"Do you think that's why I don't have any friends?" he asks, like it's a real concern.

"Almost positive."

"Almost is not completely positive, so I say that must not be the reason. Well... now that you're clothed, I bet the marinade is done," he says and heads off.

At least I can now finish getting ready in peace. Once I'm dressed and done in the bathroom, I find Leland busy at work in the kitchen. He has some pork chops on the stove, brushing something on them. The kitchen smells wonderful as I sit at the table and pull out my laptop.

Instead of working on what I'm supposed to be working on, I find myself watching him busy himself. He always acts highly distracted and goofy, but when he's focused on something, it's clear.

By the time he has supper ready, I've barely done anything else but watch.

I watch him as he eagerly cuts into the pork. "What'd you do today?" he asks. "Hunt down bad guys? Kinky peep show?"

"Not... either of those. I dealt with a woman who is convinced her husband cheated on her."

He cringes. "Oh. Sounds boring."

"That's what pays the bills."

"Then be poor."

"I don't want to be poor. It makes it all worth it when a big case comes along."

He cuts into the pork and examines it. "Yeah but... cheating husbands... do you get to taser them or anything? Spray them with pepper spray?"

"No," I say as I stick a piece of pork in my mouth and find it surprisingly delicious.

"That's disappointing. The pepper spray thing is tricky, though. This guy tried shooting me with it once and he didn't realize how easily that stuff moves through the air. He sprayed it right into the breeze. The poor guy rolled around on the ground, gagging, coughing, and crying for quite a while. It was so funny that I couldn't even beat him up. I almost felt sorry for the stupid fucker, ya know?"

"I've been sprayed with it. It's not a fun experience."

"No, it's not. But spray the cheaters next time. It'll make it fun."

"I'll... keep that in mind."

"Good," he says. "Then again, I feel like I'm much more evil than you."

"That you are."

He smiles like he's proud of that fact.

Leland: So... when I first heard about your PI business... I'm going to admit, it seemed a bit boring with all of the cheating spouse cases. What if we came up with a way to make them more exciting?

Jackson: I'm... not going to lie, I wouldn't mind a bit more excitement.

Leland: What if we gave both people tasers and set them loose in an arena? The cheater will have to eventually cave, right?

Jackson: Why would we give it to both of them?

Leland: I don't know. Twice the fun. Ooh, we could toss in the person they're cheating with. But then the women would meet each other, and they'd realize that they were both being fooled by this horrible, horrible man and they'd look into each other's eyes and sparks would fly—obviously, they're both holding tasers. They would realize that he wasn't the one for them all along and that they were, instead, meant to dig a hole to bury him in together.

Jackson: I really thought that was going to turn into a love story.

Leland: They can make love after they're done burying him. Don't restrict them.

Jackson: Maybe I'll just keep doing the cases my way, alright?

Leland: I'm just saying that giving at least one of them a taser can't hurt anything.

SIXTEEN

LELAND

I wake when Jackson gets out of bed, but I don't let him know. Instead, I slide my hand over to his side of the bed and feel the warmth his body left behind. I really should have tried harder to fuck him on my final night here, but that felt like it bordered too far on the side of wrong. Instead, I taunted, teased, and relentlessly annoyed him until he fell asleep.

Now I wait for him to go to work. Once he leaves the room, I still wait until I hear the front door open and close. Only then do I get up and start gathering my things together. I put them all into my back-pack before sitting down at the table.

It was fun eating meals here, but I'm not just going to rot in this man's house doing nothing with my life.

I write him a note and leave it in his spot before grabbing my back-pack and heading out to my car.

The car is a mess with blood everywhere, but he left the keys behind, so I start it and back out of the driveway.

Once on the street, my phone rings.

I flip it over and see that it's Jackson calling me. Hoping he hasn't already noticed my escape, I answer it. "Hello?"

"Hey, I started a load of clothes in the washer. Can you throw them in the dryer for me when they're done?" he asks.

I slow the car at a stop sign. "Yeah…"

"Okay. I'm just going to bring Chinese home for supper tonight. Do you like Chinese?"

"I love Chinese," I say.

I do.

"What do you want?"

"Lo mein, please."

"Got it."

"Thank you," I whisper.

"Is something wrong?" Jackson asks.

Of course not. Everything is fine. Everything is perfect. "No, I just woke up."

"Did I wake you up?"

"No, I was awake."

"Okay. I'll see you around five. Have a good day."

"Thanks. You too."

I could turn around. He doesn't know I'm gone yet. I could turn around and eat Chinese food and pretend I'm normal. I could sit in his house and be a good person. I could stop killing people and live a normal life. Would he grow to like me? Love me? Would he let me stay?

I slow at another stop sign and beat my hands against the steering wheel.

"*Fuuuck*," I cry.

I can't. I can't go back. What would I do if I went back? Be a stay-at-home leech? He wouldn't let me do my job. I'd be stuck watching TV every day all day while he's at work until he makes me get a job. I have no skills. I didn't finish high school. What the fuck would I do? Yes, I have money, but what would I do with it?

Just drive on. That's all I can do.

I push Jackson to the back of my mind and drive across town to Tucker's bar. I park out back by his car and force myself out. He's there, since he lives in an apartment above it. So I beat on the door until he comes down the stairs looking pissed. He's wearing a stained white T-shirt pulled over his beer gut and his underwear, which look like he's worn them for half his life. They hang off him, or maybe his balls are just hanging that low which makes it look like that.

"I was sleeping," he growls.

"It's going to take more than sleep for you to look decent. Why don't you let me in?"

He scowls at me like he doesn't love my charm. But he must love it enough to unlock the door and let me inside. "I see you're not dead."

"Not yet."

"Thought you might have been after not hearing your nagging voice for a bit."

"I got shot."

He raises an eyebrow. "You alright?"

I pull up my shirt revealing the reddened skin from the surgery. "I'll live."

"You were admitted?"

"I was, and they identified me."

He looks shocked. "No shit?"

"I tried playing dumb because I had a plan to just slip out, but they fingerprinted me before I could. So far everything is alright, though. But I need a place to stay for a couple of days."

"Hmm… if you do a job for me, I'll let you stay."

Oh, Tucker. Always wanting something out of everyone.

"What kind of job?"

"Parents want the man who killed their daughter to confess or die. Our choice."

"How positive are we that it's him?"

He shrugs. "That's your job, not mine."

"Fine. I'll start the job tomorrow."

He scratches at his groin, which makes me grimace. "Alright. You can sleep in the break room for the time being."

"I can't sleep in your apartment?"

"My daughter's up there."

"So?"

"I don't need you around her."

I sigh, but the breakroom is better than nothing.

JACKSON

By eleven o'clock, it was apparent he'd left. I still drove home just to check, but as soon as I walk into the quiet house, I know he's gone.

I'm pissed as I walk into the house and rush to the bedroom. The bed is made but empty. His bag is gone and all of his possessions with it.

He took my trust and destroyed it. That's what I'm angry about, right?

I walk into the kitchen and notice a paper sitting on the table.

Thank you,
Love, the Sandman

Out of irritation, I throw the paper to the floor and pick up my phone. He deserves this for going against my trust.

I call Henry and listen to the ringing.

"Hello?"

"Henry..."

"Yeah?"

I know who the Sandman is.

"Jackson? Is something wrong?" Henry asks.

"Sorry, I hit your number by accident."

He chuckles. "Oh, did you miss me?"

"Subconsciously, I must have," I say.

Henry hesitates. "Are you sure nothing's wrong?"

"Positive," I lie. God, I'm lying so much. Right now, it feels like a lot of shit is wrong, and at the top is anger at Leland as well as anger at myself for not reporting him.

What if I report him if he shows himself again? That's what I'll do. He's been warned. This time, he's not going to get a second chance.

Jackson: And so you left me.

Leland: Accidentally.

Jackson: You left a note.

Leland: I was just thanking you for passing the salt the night before. Not for like... anything sentimental, you know?

Jackson: You can't fool me.

Leland: I... made a dumb decision, okay? But you have to understand how hard it is to give up everything for someone... when I didn't even know how to trust anyone, you know? Yet I did it... I was a brave man, all for you.

Jackson: You were.

Leland: And it was worth it. Everything from the moment I met you, to now... it was worth it.

Jackson: I'm... I'm having terrifying flashbacks... oh... no... moments of... is that Bigfoot? And... urgh... a porn studio... and... no... am I... am I a stripper?

Leland: Shhh, just forget all of those things, baby. By the time that stuff happens, I have you hooked. A ring around the finger. You aren't going anywhere.

Jackson: Besides that... it was worth it.

Leland: You loved all of that. Don't deny it.

Jackson: I will never cave! You can't make me!

Leland: You will, you will! Let me tell you a secret, Jackson... you already have.

SEVENTEEN

LELAND

I wake on the couch that smells like beer and cigarettes. Slowly, I push myself up and look around for what woke me. It's been two days since I left Jackson's place, and I've just felt... weird. Strange.

Clearly, I got used to being waited on and want someone to wait on me some more. That's the only reason why I'd go back. Can't blame me for enjoying my time as a prince.

I sigh and go over to my bag for my clothes. The last two days I've spent watching Rick Berg, the man who apparently killed the teenager, Natasha Gibbs. He's the Gibbs' next-door neighbor who had allegedly been creeping on her. The police took Rick in after Natasha went missing one night, but they couldn't get anything on him and promptly let him go.

There was a missing person case opened on her until they found Natasha buried in a wooded area two miles from Rick's house. She'd been missing ten days at that point when a search and rescue worker found the mound of fresh dirt. She'd suffered from a bullet wound to the head which had killed her, but her body also showed bruising from being hit multiple times.

During the last few days, I've learned that Mr. Rick Berg goes to work every day at three p.m. and returns home around eleven. Today, I decide that I'll entertain myself by sneaking around his house. Since I have an hour to kill before he leaves for work, I pack up my stuff and head out to my car. I honestly can't stand any more time in this bar than I have to.

As I get in my car, my mind wanders to Jackson. Clearly, his threat was empty, as I had guessed. The police aren't tearing the city apart for me. No one is. No one cares because Jackson has kept his mouth shut.

But why?

I drive to Berg's neighborhood and watch his house until he comes out, as he does every day. He looks over at the Gibbs' house, as he does every time he leaves his home. It's almost like he's still looking for her.

I watch him as he walks. He's an average-looking man who works in a factory. Nothing strange in his record or appearance. But he still looks at that house every single day.

He could be doing it just because they're currently out to get him, but there's something more to that look. Something the police didn't notice.

When he gets in his truck and drives away, I get out of my car. The blanket I'd bought to cover my seats gets pulled partly off, so I toss it back over to hide the blood stains.

Then I walk up to the house like I know what I'm doing. I'm wearing my hood so if anyone notices me, they won't get a good look at me, but I still look casual enough to not come across as suspicious. I walk around to the back door where I'll have more privacy, even though I'm pretty sure the Gibbs aren't home.

As I step up to the door, I pull my lockpick kit out and find what I need. I slide the picks inside and move them around until the lock gives and the doorknob turns. Now, I just have to head inside.

I walk in and find the house very messy. I know I'm not the best at keeping things neat and orderly, but the place is nearly trashed with boxes and clutter. He looks like he's the ultimate hoarder, so it makes it hard to find anything when he has so much of everything.

Wandering around the house, I pay attention to the windows that look over at the neighbors' house. Most have too much junk stacked in front to look out through.

I head up the stairs and find his bedroom to be comparable to the rest of the house. The only difference is how easy it is to access the window. There's nothing in front of it but a box that has a divot on it, like he has repeatedly sat on it. I open the box and find that it's filled with clothes, which keep the box from collapsing under his weight.

I flip through the clothes, curious if there's anything else inside, but there isn't. From what I can figure out about the neighbor's house, the window looks right into her bedroom.

Clearly, the creep was peeping in on her.

I go over to his bed and see a book lying on his nightstand. When I pick the book up, I realize there's a photograph sticking out of it. Careful not to lose his page, I flip it open and look inside, where I find a photograph of the teenage girl wearing her cheerleading outfit in the front yard with her friends.

I slide it back into place and shut the book.

Well... that's more than enough for me to question him.

I head back out to my car, where I'll have to wait until tonight for him to show. Once I have him, I'll get him to admit everything.

Instead of waiting at the house, I leave and wander the city to kill some time. A part of me wants to go to Jackson's detective agency and pester him, but I know that fun is over with. I need to stay as far away from Jackson as I can.

Honestly, I thought pouring myself into this case would help, but instead, I find myself dreading it. There's that excitement that I love. When I broke into his house and went through his belongings, I was loving it. When I found the photograph the police never found, my attention was absorbed, but the moment I left, my mind wandered back to Jackson. I don't know why. I barely know the man except for the week and a half I spent with him and the pestering I'd done before.

Once back at Rick's place, I leave my car along the street, now that it's dark, and head up to the house so I can catch Rick before he goes inside.

I sit in the darkness of the yard, trying to keep my attention on Rick and the case, but it keeps wandering. I know I should never be in the middle of a case while my mind is elsewhere, but I can't keep it from continually crawling back to Jackson.

When Rick's truck pulls up, I drag my mind away from those thoughts and turn my attention to the man getting out of his truck. His porch light is off, so as soon as the truck's headlights diminish, we're immersed in darkness. He walks right past my spot by his trash can and never notices when I step up behind him. I loop a rope over his neck and pull it tight.

He's bigger than me, but it doesn't take much to choke a man. He thrashes and fights, but I've done it enough that it isn't long before he sinks into my arms. It was never a fair fight, but his movement jerked my side and caused pain to creep up it.

Pain emanates from my side as I drag his limp body back to his truck and help him into the passenger seat. I pull his arms together and use a cable tie to keep them there. Then I do the same to his feet before attaching his hands to the door. Next I open up a plastic table cover, which I tuck over the driver's seat so I don't end up leaving anything on it that could be tied to me. It's not foolproof, but it'll be enough. I have a hat and a hood on, and my clothes are clean and new.

I start driving as his head rolls around in the passenger seat. About halfway to the cemetery, he starts to come to. At first, he seems confused, then he jerks back and looks at me in alarm. I have duct tape over his mouth, so all he can do is mumble and jerk against his binds.

"Stop moving or I'll shoot you," I warn as I aim my gun at him. It's not my *favorite* gun since Jackson is keeping that hostage, but it still shoots bullets quite well.

He sinks into his chair with wide eyes and continues mumbling something that I can't make out. But as long as that's all he's doing, we'll be fine.

When I reach the cemetery, I park the truck and get out. I come around to his side as he frantically looks around for something to aid him. When I pull the door open and free him from the handle, he lunges at me, planning on body slamming me to the ground.

I easily step out of his path and watch him hit the ground. He flops around like a fish out of water while I stand just out of reach. "Are you done?" I ask curiously.

He stills and looks up at me with wide eyes. There's so much fear in his expression. I wonder if he enjoyed the fear on Natasha's face when he took her out into the woods and shot her?

I leer down at him, a grin on my face. It makes him shake on the ground. "Now, I'm going to cut your feet free and if you run, I'm going to blow a hole through your kneecap, understood?"

He continues to stare at me, so I give him a little tap with my foot. "Understood?"

He nods, so I pull my knife out and slide it between his binds. I cut it, then stand up and wave for him to get to his feet. He does and I can see his eyes frantically looking for where to go, but he stays still.

"Let's go visit Natasha's grave. I'm sure you know where it is. Go on."

He hesitates but starts walking, showing me that I'm right and he knows exactly where it is. Her plot isn't too far from my car and he takes me straight to it. Once in front of it, I reach up and tear the tape from his lips.

"Now, Rick, did you kill her?" I ask.

He shakes his head as fast as it can go. "No!"

"Who did?"

"I don't know!" he says, and it comes out almost like a plea.

"Tell me something."

He shakes his head, so I switch my gun to my left hand and punch him in the face with my right.

"Want to try again?"

"I don't know!" he yells.

I punch him again, this time my fist connecting with his cheek and nose.

He puts his hands up to protect his face, but he's a fool if he thinks that'll stop me. I give him a moment to think it over as I watch the blood run from his nose in the light of a lamp. "Want to try again?"

He's nearly sobbing now. "Please! Stop!"

I drive my fist right through his weak block, striking the side of his head in a hit that sends him stumbling. It also makes my side ache, but I ignore it.

"Stop! I don't know!"

"Did you watch her from your window? You have her photograph in your bedroom. Clearly, you know something you're not telling anyone."

"She…" He shakes his head.

I raise my fist again, but before I can hit him, he drops to his knees. This time he curls up, protecting his face and sobbing. I give him a minute because he's close to breaking. He just needs a little more push.

"We would talk," he whispers.

"About?"

"It started off just… she put a sign in her window. It just said, 'hi.' She was a pretty girl. I didn't know she was underage. I said 'hi' back. Then it grew from there. We would put little notes up for each other until we started talking over the summer while her parents were at work. She made me believe she was in college. It wasn't until much later that I found out she was underage. But her parents were strict, especially her father. He'd hit her if she didn't do good enough. She'd tell me about feeling like she could never live up to what he wanted.

"Her mom was a good person, but she stayed with him just because… I guess she felt like she had nowhere else to go. She was very religious. Didn't believe in divorce; at least that's what Natasha said was keeping them together."

He takes a deep breath. "Natasha… I loved her… I didn't hurt her. I promise. Every bruise and hit came from her father. One day, she asked me to take her away, and I told her we couldn't. She was sixteen. I'm thirty… She was so upset with me, but I thought she'd get over it. I got home from work and found a note she'd left me on the kitchen table. It seemed like a farewell. Something about always loving me, but now she wanted to be in our favorite spot forever.

"I knew she meant the woods, so I ran out there. And when I got there… I found her dead. She'd shot herself."

"Why didn't you call the police? Let someone else deal with that?"

"I don't know… a few reasons. In her note, she asked me to leave her in our favorite spot. I knew they'd take her away, and I felt like… I felt like it was the least I could do. I felt like if I'd have just…" A sob escapes him. "If I'd have just… taken her somewhere, she'd still be alive. I could bury here there, I could do that for her."

"Once they found the body, why not confess then?"

His sobs sound awful. I'm not used to someone who isn't crying for themselves. This man is not. He's crying for the love he lost. "I don't know. I was scared I'd go to jail… another part of me was glad her mother didn't know she killed herself. Natasha had talked about suicide before… but she said her family was very religious. That to commit suicide was to go to hell."

I snort at the thought. "It's not that easy to fall into hell," I say. "You might have wanted to keep it quiet, but they need to know, otherwise they won't stop until you go to prison for it." I think about what I want to do, but there's only one thing that feels right. "Let's go."

"Where?" he asks hesitantly.

"Get up."

He slowly gets up and starts walking back to the truck. Once inside it, I tie him back to the door, then I slide into the driver's seat and begin driving.

He looks over at me and stares at me for a moment before saying, "Thank you for believing me."

"I've gotten good at interpreting lies." A man does not sob like that for himself. This is someone who has lost a part of himself.

I drive to the police station and park in front of it. "If you don't tell them the truth, you'll be seeing me again, understood?"

He nods, tears and blood wet on his face.

I get out of the car and call the station. A man answers.

"Good evening. I have Mr. Rick Berg sitting in his truck in the parking lot and he'd love to talk to you guys about what happened to Natasha Gibbs."

"Who is this?"

I hang up the phone and continue walking. It'll be a long trek out to my car, so I decide to try to find a spot where someone will give me a ride.

But now that my mind isn't occupied by Rick and Natasha, I find myself feeling the weight of the darkness. My entire life, I never had anyone to care for me. No one *ever* cared whether I came home or not. Yes, the man who taught me how to shoot noticed me, but I was a dog he was training to hunt. When I came home, I didn't become the family pet. I was set to the side until the next hunt.

I barely even know Jackson, but he showed me more stability, care, and support in the week and a half I was with him than I've ever seen my entire life.

But to go back to him, I would have to give up so much of myself. I would have to give up what I trained for. What I fought for. Everything.

And what would I become?

It's a scary thought.

Much scarier than any gun.

Jackson: Hey, Leland, do you ever get scared or worried when you do things like this?

Leland: Like... jobs?

Jackson: Yeah, I guess. You're always so confident... but like... are you ever worried that it's going to go wrong?

Leland: I get much more worried now that you go with me, but at that point in time? No. I mean... growing up, I did. I... learned at a young age that it wasn't good to be cocky. I learned that people are unpredictable. And that even if you think you're better than someone, it sure as fuck doesn't mean you are. I think... I forgot how to fear, you know? Does that make sense? With a case like this, I wasn't worried. The guy clearly wasn't a professional, but times when I was up against people who knew what they were doing, I'd just go in knowing either they were going to die or I was. And it happened so many times that I forgot how to fear it... until I met you.

Jackson: Is that... a good thing? I don't want to be the reason you make a mistake.

Leland: Jackson, you're the reason I don't run into a situation. You're the reason I make it home every job because I know there's someone waiting for me. Someone who loves me with his whole heart. Someone... that I would be fucking *devastated* knowing I hurt.

Jackson: *squeezes Leland's hand* I'm... extremely lucky to be that person.

Leland: I mean, think of how upset you'd be if you didn't have someone to remind you of your fence-clambering skills every five minutes.

Jackson: *dryly* Oh no, sounds awful.

EIGHTEEN

JACKSON

"Jackson!"

I jump and look over at Mason. "What?"

"You know this business can't run if we *both* don't work," he says as he walks over to my desk. "What's going on with you?"

"Nothing. Just lost in thought," I say as I turn my attention back to my computer screen. He looks down at me as he leans against my desk.

"Can't talk about it?"

I think about it for a moment before realizing that it probably wouldn't hurt to tell him a little something. "I was helping an acquaintance out for a bit as long as they promised to not go back to what they were doing before… and of course, they went back."

"Abusive boyfriend or something?"

I hesitate. "Something like that."

Mason sinks down in his chair, making it groan against his weight because he chose to buy the cheapest chair he could find. "Hmm… That's a tough one. Sometimes… I think they feel like they don't know how to function away from what they're used to. That's the norm for them, and they begin to feel like that. Then when you take it all away, it's too much at once. Maybe try weaning them away. See if that helps."

"I could try," I say, although I know I'll never run into him again.

That's when my phone rings, and I see that it's Henry. "Hello?"

"You'll never believe what happened last night," he says.

"The Sandman," I say without wasting a thought. Please let me be wrong. Please let me be wrong.

"I think it was. He didn't leave a note, though…"

My grip tightens on my phone. "What happened? I'm coming down."

"You don't even know if you *need* to come down," Henry says, but I'm already motioning to Mason that I have to go while rushing for the door. When I reach it, I slip through and head down the stairs, taking the steps two at a time.

He sighs. "Just calm yourself, and I'll explain. So the station gets a call. A direct call, not a 911 call. The man says that he has Rick Berg out in the truck ready to confess."

Rick Berg? "Who's that?"

"Where the hell have you been? You haven't heard about Natasha Gibbs' murder?"

Have I? God, I've been so consumed by Leland that I haven't really paid attention to anything else. "No…"

"She was gone for over a week and then turned up dead. Parents suspected the neighbor, Rick Berg. Homicide pulled him in and questioned him, but they got nothing on him. Well, so we get this call that he's in the parking lot. My guy goes out there, Berg's covered in blood, beat up, ready to confess. In an instant, he tells us everything."

"Did he kill the girl?"

"No, he claims the girl shot herself."

"You guys didn't get any gunshot residue on her hands during the autopsy?" I ask. It's generally a good way to tell who fired a weapon when no one is willing or able to talk. Every time someone shoots a gun, there's residue left on their hands. It helps the police identify who shot the gun.

"No. Nothing. We asked him that, and he said she'd been wearing gloves which he'd taken off her because he wanted to keep them. Explained that her father had been the one beating her. She couldn't stand it anymore and killed herself."

I slow as I step outside. "Do you think he's telling the truth?"

"It's still homicide's case at the moment, but they're starting to think he's right."

"Well, shit."

"I thought you'd be curious since I think it was the Sandman who brought him in."

"Will I be able to look into the case?"

"No, you're not supposed to know about it."

I sigh as I look over at my car I'd been more than eager to jump into.

"If you wanted to know more, you should have joined the force," he says almost teasingly. It isn't the first time he's suggested I join.

"I'll figure out more on my own."

"If you do, let me know."

"I will."

I spend the day fixated on it but find nothing because no one wants to let me play with them. Around seven, I end up going back home while wondering why I spent the entire day caring about who brought the guy in. If it *was* Leland, it doesn't matter. He didn't kill anyone this time.

If it *wasn't*, it *definitely* doesn't matter.

I let myself into the quiet house before walking over to the fridge and pulling it open. It isn't worth making anything for myself, so I slam it shut and head toward the bedroom.

That's when the doorbell rings.

It's probably my mother ready to skin me alive for skipping *two* family meals with them. She probably has a potato peeler in one hand and a knife in the other. But when I reach the door and pull it open, I see that there's no one there.

There's not even a car in the driveway or anyone out on the street. I step out to get a better look, but I'm either hearing things or a kid is fucking with me.

When I turn around, I nearly crawl out of my skin, I jump so badly. Leland is standing in the kitchen with a KFC bag in his hand.

"I'm sorry it took so long. The line at KFC was *outrageous*," he says.

I stare at him as he watches me closely like he's trying to anticipate what I'll do. "What are you doing here?"

"You asked me to move in with you," he says innocently.

"You *left*."

He sets the bag on the table. "I did… and I want to come back… if you'll have me. I don't even know why. I *wanted* to leave. I *had* to leave, but as soon as I left, all I wanted was to come back. It's really stupid. I know it is, because I barely know you. Most of the things I know about you, I learned while stalking you. But I'm tired of being the only one who cares whether I live or die. I'm tired of walking in the shadows, pretending like I'm no one and nothing. Please… please let me come back."

He honestly wants to come back? "Why should I trust you? I asked you to give me your trust, and you broke all of it by leaving and going out and doing what you did last night."

He looks devastated and I find that it's such a strange look on him.

"I know! But I needed to… I needed to show myself that maybe that lifestyle is not worth it because… while I was doing it, I was one hundred percent in it, but the moment I stopped… I wanted to come back here. I didn't want to eat alone with no one to talk to and no one to care."

I hesitate as I think about what he's saying. "What if I can't care?" I know it's a lie. I already care too much. "I barely know you."

"We can try?" he asks hopefully. "Like before. We don't have to *be* anything. I just want someone who cares if I die. At my funeral, I just want at least one person there."

"You'd give up your gun and everything?"

He nods, but he doesn't need to. The look on his face is enough to tell me he would. "Everything."

"And you'll tell me the truth about all of it?"

"Every moment of it."

I nod, even though I'm not sure if I should go along with this. But something tells me that I need to give him at least one more chance. "Okay."

"Want to talk while we eat?"

"Let me get plates," I say as I head to the counter.

LELAND

This feels… right.

Sitting down across from him like we're old friends.

"You didn't push yourself?" Jackson asks as he sits down across from me at the small round table in his kitchen.

"No. I'm fine."

"You could have torn something, fucking around with that guy."

See? He already cares whether I hurt myself or not. No one ever cared to ask me that. "I know… but it was a deal I made with someone for letting me stay with them." It makes me feel strangely warm inside.

I start filling my plate with chicken, potatoes, and green beans, but I end up slopping the gravy on the table because I keep looking up at Jackson to see his expression.

"Tell me everything from the beginning," he says.

I really don't want to, but I know that I need to. "It's a long story."

"I have all night."

I take a tiny bite of the potatoes and nod. I've never told anyone my story. It's always been just *my* story, so I feel strange sharing it. "Well… I guess I'll start from the foster home. From around twelve to thirteen, I was bounced from foster home to foster home. I wasn't the best kid. I grew up with a shitty father who never bothered to take care of me or notice me. I always had to be *doing* something to take care of myself. It was the only way to survive, so that's what I did. Well, once I was moved into foster care, my foster families weren't always fond of that. I liked to hide things… I wasn't used to always having food, so when I would arrive at a new foster home, I would steal the food and hide it for when we'd run out. I would take things that didn't belong to me so that when the time came that we had nothing, I always had something.

"The second family I moved in with was almost worse than my

father's home. The man who was supposed to 'take care of me' treated me like shit. He was always yelling at me for doing things wrong, and he just... he creeped me out. I swear he was a pedophile. I was scared to take showers alone and would only take one when his wife was in the adjoining room. I was terrified to do anything when he was in the house. He loved to pin me against the wall, and just whisper exactly what I did wrong so I could just barely hear it, but it would make me feel unbelievably defenseless. I couldn't do anything when he got into one of his... moods. There was just... something inside me that told me if I hung around, he would take all of me and never give any back. So one day, he pushed me too far and I ran away.

"I was a stupid kid. I should have told the child services lady, but I was convinced that I was the only one who would care for me or do anything about it. I thought I could keep anyone from hurting me as long as I was no longer in that house.

"It was naive, I know. The streets weren't a place for a thirteen-year-old kid. Even so, I roughed it for a while. I grew up knowing how to stay out of the way of people out to hurt me. But it's hard to get money or food without stealing it when you're not old enough to work. Well, work that I *wanted* to do. I found my saving grace one day when this baker flagged me down. He would give me things they baked for the day but couldn't sell the following day at full price. Breads, cupcakes, almost anything he made. They were so delicious." I sigh and take a sip of my water. "I started becoming dependent on him, so when he invited me inside one day, I didn't even hesitate. I can still remember how happy I was to get inside because winter had come, and my fingers hurt so badly. When I came out of the bathroom, he had my food waiting in a booth. I slid into it, nearly starving. But when he sat down beside me, pinning me in the booth, I knew something was wrong. That was the moment I got those... vibes from him. The ones that made me feel like prey and he was a predator. I knew he was going to hurt me; he was no different than the man at the foster home."

Jackson is watching me in concern. He has stopped eating, so I point at his chicken with my fork. The look on his face is enough to make me realize he cares—that he isn't just going to look the other way like everyone else always has—and it makes me feel so many emotions.

"Your food is getting cold," I say, wanting to focus on something else for just a moment.

He looks down at it, but it seems like he doesn't even register that it's there. "Are you alright?" he asks, concern coating his words, and again I'm reminded why I returned.

I give him a smile. "I'm fine, honestly. It was many years ago. And he didn't get very far. It was just... knowing he was going to, you know? It was feeling defenseless and alone. But he'd given me a fork and a knife. I still don't even know what the knife was for. Maybe it was just a habit to grab a napkin, fork, and knife. But as soon as I felt his hand on me, I knew I only had two options. Give him a part of myself or take a part of him. So... I stabbed him in the chest with the knife. I don't know how I got lucky enough to hit anything vital. I knew nothing about killing then and the stab was in a moment of panic. But he dropped from the booth and began convulsing.

"That's when I noticed I wasn't alone. There was someone else there. Maybe he forgot to lock the door, I don't know. I don't think the baker knew he was there, or I doubt he would have done what he did. But here I was, staring down at the dying man. I didn't... It didn't register that I'd killed him, you know? I just knew that this man... this man was going to hurt me, and I stopped him. But the other man goes, 'You killed him.' And I remember shaking my head because I didn't! I just stopped him from hurting me. And the man walked up to me and grabbed my face. His eyes were so cold that I should have realized he was a monster. Just another breed of monster. He told me that I was going to go to prison. That I would live and die in prison. I was a kid, of course I believed him, but he told me that if I went with him, he'd protect me. He'd make the baker and the death disappear. Just like that. And... I believed him. Because when you realize you've just killed a man for the first time you feel... numb like you can't understand. It's such a... strange feeling."

"I know that feeling," he says, voice grave. It makes me question who his first kill was. It also makes me want to know his story. I want to know everything about him.

"Yeah… I bet you do," I say quietly.

"So he was the original Sandman? The man who did this before you?"

I nod. "He was. I'm hungry. Let's continue this story some other time, alright? I shared enough to stay, at least for the night, right?"

"I have to know one more answer."

"Okay?"

"Why'd you kill Williams? Henry's partner."

I shake my head. "The Sandman did."

"The other Sandman?"

I nod. "Is that enough?"

He looks directly into my eyes before inclining his head. "Yes."

I smile at him. "Thank you."

"You don't need to thank me."

"I promise I won't let you down. I'll be on my best behavior. Better than I've been. I'll be so well-behaved you'll start calling me Saint Leland."

He gives me a soft smile. "No."

"Tossing rose petals at my feet as I walk."

"Why would I do that?"

I watch him closely, glad his expression has changed. "Because that's how saintly I'm going to be."

"I don't know why, but I have a *very* hard time believing that," he says. "You're still staying here so I can watch you."

"I wouldn't want it any other way."

"Of course not."

I grin, happy for the distraction. There's nothing I like less than talking about my past. I grab a scoop of potatoes and lean against the table. "Open wide!"

"I don't want your potatoes. Who knows what germs you have?"

"Cooties, not germs," I say as I zoom the spoon toward his mouth. "Open for the choo choo!" I bump the spoon against his lips as he stares at me. Then continue bumping the spoon into them repeatedly until he opens his mouth and I slip the spoon inside. "Choo choo is what I call my penis," I inform him.

He shakes his head like I've said something else he can't believe. Honestly, he seems surprised by quite a few of the things I say. Why stop now?

"I'm already regretting this."

I start laughing which makes him grin, even though he's using his napkin to try and hide it. "No, you love it! When I came back, you welcomed me with open arms."

He gives me a pointed look. "Don't think things are going to be different. You're still not violating me, cuddling with me, or staring at me in the shower."

"When you tell me I *can't* do something, it makes me want to do it even more," I warn him.

"I'm not joking."

"Of *course* you aren't joking. How would you like to be violated today?" I ask.

"Just finish eating."

"So I can get to the violating sooner?"

"No! Because supper is getting cold!"

I love this. I love every moment of this. "That's no fun."

"I should probably set up a room for you so I don't have to deal with you. Maybe I'll put a padlock on it after eight."

I stare at him in disappointment. "But... I want to snuggle."

"You can't." He's quiet for a moment, telling me he's thinking about something serious again. "Are you positive you left nothing at the Gibbs' scene? I mean, how cocky do you have to be to drive the guy to the police department? It's like you *wanted* to get caught."

"No, I just knew I *wouldn't* get caught."

"Why?"

I shrug. "It's fun. And if I was like, 'dude, go turn yourself in,' what do you think he'd have done?"

"I understand, but..."

"I'm a simple escort."

It's clear at this point that he isn't going to win, so he just sighs again—clearly, it's his favorite thing to do.

We clear off the table when we're finished, and I head to the bathroom to get a shower. I almost can't stop smiling as I climb inside.

JACKSON

I'm on the couch watching TV when Leland returns. I try not to smile when he walks in because then he'll realize that I enjoy his company.

"I was expecting you to join me, maybe even wash my back again," Leland says as he leans over the back of the couch and stares at me.

His face is too close, and my eyes instantly drop to his lips. I could easily push myself into him, but I can't. I'm still "mad" at him for leaving. If he thinks I forgive that easily, then he'll never learn. Clearly, he's lucky *and* cocky and, I suppose, talented. If only he would be *good* as well and stop this lifestyle.

I pray he does.

"I'm not washing your back."

He's not deterred. "What about my hair?"

"No."

"Between my toes?"

He's leaning on my shoulder now. Everywhere he touches makes me even more conscious of his presence.

I know I need to lean away from him, but I can't. "No."

"Will you braid my hair?" Leland asks with a grin.

"No."

"My butt hair?"

"No!"

The grin has returned to his lips. "I already saw your butt hair."

"You did not!"

"You have two moles on your butt cheek."

"I do not!"

"How do you know? Were you checking out your own ass? How naughty," he says before planting a kiss right on my forehead like he's my grandma or some other elderly being who doesn't associate me with sex.

He climbs onto the couch and lies down with his head on my lap.

When he smiles up at me, mouth inches from my dick, I'm not sure if the heavens have made me lucky or unlucky.

Maybe a bit of both.

What I do know is that I have to remain indifferent and not jab him in the eyeball with an erection or he might see through my lies.

"I missed you so much," he says. "It's clear you missed me." He sets his hand against my chest. "Did your heart hurt while I was gone?"

"No, I was in perfect health. Actually, I think I was doing *better* when you weren't here."

"That's not what I meant. Although, you *do* look in good health. I bet I could do a better physical assessment if you climbed another fence for me."

"Forget the fence."

"But… but… what will I tell our children when they ask how we met? Some boring story? Hell, no. I'll go, 'I met your daddy when he was trying to climb a fence. At first, I was like wow! Look at that sexy man, but as soon as he started clambering over it, his pants got stuck and he hung from it with his ass out for all to see. It was love at first sight.'"

"You will not share that story with our imaginary children."

"Oh shit… I forgot that you can't say ass to children. 'He hung from it with his bottom and testicles out for all to see.'"

"Why would ass not be alright, but testicles would?"

"My children aren't going to grow up calling the penis their 'wiggle worm' and their balls 'dingly dangles.' They're going to use the real words. Vulva, testicles, anus—"

I groan. "Please stop."

"Are we already having our first dispute?"

"No, our first dispute was you being a hitman and me wanting you to be a good person."

He grins at me. "We should have had make-up sex after."

"No make-up sex needed. We didn't make up because I haven't forgiven you yet."

The look on Leland's face tells me that he thinks otherwise. "I have been forgiven. The moment you saw my face, you forgave me."

I might have. "No, I didn't."

"Just admit it. Your heart beats just for me."

"So basically my heart has no purpose but to… work for you, a man I barely know."

"We're soul mates. We were destined since birth."

"You weren't born for at least eleven years after I was."

"That's because I'm so awesome that it took God even longer to finish creating me. Perfection takes a long time to create."

I snort, really wondering how he comes up with the things he says. It has to be a talent of some kind.

"You're turned on at this moment, aren't you?" he asks.

"No."

"I can see it with my eyeballs."

I reach down and cup my hand over his eyes, covering the piercing stare he's giving me. It just makes his grin widen into a full smile. "You can't disappoint me, Leland. You can't go back. You can't sneak out. You can't lie to me, understand?"

His smile falls, and he's silent for a moment. "I won't. I don't want to. I don't regret anything I've done—those people deserved to die— but for once I want to live for myself, not someone else."

I let my fingers fall off his face. "Okay."

His blue eyes cut into mine as he stares at me, all signs of joking gone. The moment must be too serious and intense for him, so he pulls his eyes from me and turns onto his side so he faces the TV. His hand rests on my knee, squeezing it tightly. I reach for his face, wanting to turn him back to me so I can see more of his eyes, more of his expressions, but instead, I set my hand on his shoulder. I run my fingers down his arm and it's almost like I can feel the tension leaving him.

"I like this," he whispers, like he's embarrassed to say it out loud.

"Basically, it's like getting a house cat," I realize. "You come in, eat my food, sleep wherever you want, whenever you want, and refuse to listen…"

He starts laughing. "I'm not like a house cat. House cats are assholes. They only want to be petted when *they* want to be. I want petting all the time."

"Not all house cats are like that. They're basically like you."

"Fine, I'll be a pussy for you if I *have* to. Now pet your pussy."

I should have known this would happen. "No."

"Pet your pussy, Jackson!"

"Fuck off."

"Stroke it, Jackson!"

I clamp my hand over his mouth, wishing I had invested in some duct tape.

Jackson: Why KFC?

Leland: I once killed a man with a bucket of chicken.

Jackson: What?

Leland: He was all like "I'm gonna kill your ass. Bang. Bang." And I was like "You better cole your slaw because I'm gonna potato wedge your ass into the bucket."

Jackson: That joke hurt me to hear it.

Leland: It hurt me worse to say it.

Jackson: *laughs* You are ridiculous.

Leland: Thank you. Honestly? I was driving past it and thinking "What should I do to make Jackson less mad at me?" and then I was like… "What if I bribe him with food?" But I was too impatient to wait for good food to be made, so I couldn't go to like a steak house or something because what if you moved on in that time?

Jackson: I promise that I wasn't planning on moving on.

Leland: Good, because if you did… I would put your new spouse in a room—

Jackson: You'd kill him?

Leland: I wasn't done yet! I'd put him in a room. In one corner of the room would be a fence with you draped over it, ass on display, and then in another corner would be a suitcase with one million dollars. Your new lover can only pick one and his choice would determine how much he actually likes you. But if he goes for the money, he's going to find out it's all fake. That way, when he goes crawling back to you, groveling at your feet, you can see how weak of a man he really is.

Jackson: I'm... glad I didn't have to go through all that. That sounds rough.

Leland: I gotchu, boo.

NINETEEN

LELAND

Clearly, I'm still not to the level of being trusted. Instead of giving me a farewell kiss and a proclamation of how much he loves me, he aims his camera at me.

"If you are gone from the room for more than ten minutes…"

"You'll…?" Poor Jackson doesn't realize that if he never goes through with *any* of his threats, I'll start to think they're not threats at all.

"If you're good, I'll take you with me to my mom's for brunch."

My interest is instantly piqued. Maybe he *does* understand. "Seriously?"

"Yes."

"I'm so excited. Can I call her Mommy?"

"No."

"Momma?"

"No."

"Ma?"

Jackson grabs his bag, stuffs his shoes on, and quickly leaves the house. He must be satisfied with "Ma."

I go over to the couch and sink onto it. And instantly remember why I left. It's so *boring*. Am I really going to be able to do this?

Taking a deep breath, I grab the remote.

I will. I'll just have to find something to do. I mean, normal people live like this. They… read books or… god, what do they do? There are only so many times in a day one can jerk off.

With the TV on in the background for noise, I grab my laptop. Instead of looking up female genitalia, I find a huge penis and print it off before parking it in front of the camera.

The call doesn't take long to come in and I'm grinning like a fiend when it does. "Hello?" I purr.

"Remove the penis."

"NO! I don't want to be a woman! Why would I have to remove my penis?"

"From in front of the camera."

"Oh! That penis."

I go over to the camera and kneel in front of it. Then I grab the paper penis and make it do a little jig. "Hi, Jackson! My name is Hole Seeker! I'm seeking a ring of fire. That's what you call it when you eat too much spicy food."

"Please don't give the penis a voice."

I slide the penis to the side so Jackson can get a good look at my face as well. "Why? You don't like my penis theater? Is this better?" Then I run my tongue all the way up the paper penis. "Do you like that better?"

He's silent.

I can't tell if he hated it or absolutely loved it, so I decide to keep going with the act. I stuff the tip in my mouth, careful about papercuts, before pulling it out and looking at the screen. "Didja like that?"

"No." Simple yet effective.

I stuff the paper cock back in my mouth and bite down before tearing it in half. I spit it out and glare at the camera. "That's what will happen to you if you don't straighten the fuck up."

"You'll tear more paper cocks in half?"

"I will. Want to see it again?"

"Maybe."

"Oh?" I hold up what's left of the paper penis, which is about two inches long. "I can keep licking it. It's more your size now. Or do you want to see a real penis?" I ask as I stand up and grab my groin.

He's silent again.

Clearly, he's loving it.

I push my sweatpants down until just the base of my cock is showing. "Is this what you want?" I run my fingers down both sides of it, *wishing* I could see his face or expression as I do it. "Or would you prefer me to print off some paper balls?" I joke.

"Hmm… let me see your balls."

For a moment, I'm not sure if I've heard him right or at all. "Oh?" I ask, interest piqued. Clearly, he's planning on something mean or torturous because there's no way he'd *actually* ask me to go through with that. But I've never been one who wants to displease, so I push my pants down a little more. "Is this what you want?"

"Step back a little."

I step back as I reach into my pants and pull my cock free but keep it cupped in my hand.

"Take your hand off."

I draw my hand away as I stare at the camera, wishing more than anything that I could see his face. "What now?"

"Am I making you hard?" he asks, voice low and deep in my ear.

"You're making me confused. Who took over your body? What did they do to you? Did aliens probe you? No fair! I want to probe you!"

He sighs. "You're ruining the moment."

"I could never ruin a moment talking about alien probing."

JACKSON

What the fuck am I doing?

Maybe I *was* probed by an alien. That can be the only explanation for me hiding in the bathroom, even though Mason isn't even here, with my laptop on my lap and a hard-on.

Even so, there is nothing sexier than Leland standing in front of the camera, staring at it with a smirk on his face, hand on his cock.

"I wanna probe you," he says, trying really hard to ruin the moment even more.

"Shut up with the probing," I say with a growl. "Touch yourself."

His smirk widens into a grin. "How?"

"What? With your hand!"

He sighs. "No shit, Sherlock. Like… *how*."

Oh… sexy talk. I'm not sure I can do sexy talk, but I'll try. "Stroke your cock," I order.

He slides his lithe fingers down his cock, and I'm mesmerized by it. When he reaches the head, his fingers move back up.

"Do you like that?" I ask.

"I do," he says.

My cock is aching in my pants, but I can't imagine jerking off at work. It's bad enough I'm doing this—am I going to just sit on the toilet jerking it with one hand and balancing my computer with the other?

"Are you touching your cock, Jackson?" he asks, voice low in my ear.

It makes me want to pull my cock out so badly. "You worry about yourself, Leland. Rub the head of your cock," I order as my hand slides to my pants. I unbutton them and pull my cock out, glad to be free of the constraint.

I watch as his thumb rubs over the head before sliding back down. Why the hell am I so damn horny after just *watching* him? I don't know if it's the added secrecy of doing it in the bathroom at work, or just because Leland is the sexiest person I've ever met, but my cock is aching to be touched.

I grab my length as I watch him touch himself. And when his free hand slides between his legs back to his hole and he moans, I have the desire to drive home and fuck him until he can't take anymore. Sadly, I can't see his hole from this position, but just knowing that he's rubbing himself has me unbelievably turned on.

"I wish I could see you," he says as he watches the camera with half-lidded eyes. "It's not very fair that I have to touch myself all alone while you're off being prodded by aliens."

"Drop the aliens," I beg, but the grin on his face makes me realize that he can say anything he wants and I'll probably continue to go along with it just to see that expression.

"Are you touching yourself?" he asks.

"Yes."

"You're so naughty. Is Mason helping?"

"Don't talk about Mason while I'm jerking off."

He grins as he gets closer to the camera. "You just want all your focus on me?" he asks playfully.

I do.

And then he's gone. I'm left jerking off to my empty living room as I sit in mild confusion.

"Where are you going?"

"Hold your horses, you mighty stallion."

Then the camera slides to the side so it's focused on the couch. He backs up until his legs hit the armrest before melting over it and spreading his legs.

"Is that a better view?" he asks.

I can see his asshole, balls, and cock. It's a mighty fine view. "I suppose it'll do."

He starts laughing. "You're so hard to please. Or are you just *hard*?"

"I'll admit that I'm hard," I say as he pops open some lube he must have grabbed. Then, as one hand rubs his cock, his other slides between his legs. He rubs his finger over his hole as he arches his back and stares right into the camera. It's like he's looking at me. My hand quickens on my cock as I hear a moan leave his lips.

"Do you like to watch me touch myself?" he asks, almost breathless.

"I want your finger inside you."

He presses his finger against his hole, pushing inside as his hand slides up and down his cock. Oh, but the look on his face nearly sends me over the edge. How can he look like that?

"Another finger," I order.

"Now you're getting greedy," he says, but he pushes a second finger in with the first. Greedy or not, he seems to be enjoying it. Especially when his body tenses as he gets closer to his orgasm. I'm enthralled by it and my own pace quickens.

All it takes is seeing him coming to realize I won't be able to last much longer. And at the very last moment when my brain is still working, I grab a paper towel to come into so I don't have to wipe cum off my keyboard. There's nothing sexier than watching him lie there, chest rising and falling quickly as my own orgasm surfaces. I groan as I come into the paper towel, wishing I could touch him or be with him.

"I think I might start liking this camera," Leland says.

I hear the door to the agency slam shut and I jump. "Shit, I have to go."

And I hang up on him. He can chastise me later, but for now, I need to make sure there's no evidence left behind. When I come out of the bathroom, laptop in hand, I catch Mason's eyes.

"What were you doing with your laptop in there?" he asks with a wicked grin.

I glare at him like "how could you possibly believe I was doing anything dirty" and he just laughs. "I was taking a shit and needed something to read," I say.

"Ah, of course."

Leland: I was so bored! I hate reliving how bored I was!

Jackson: You were fine.

Leland: Boredom consumed my very soul.

Jackson: I'm sorry being with me was so torturous.

Leland: You were the only shining light left in my life. My babies had been ripped away from me, my fun had been stomped out—

Jackson: Please, stop! I sound like a horrible person! I was doing it to protect you and myself. But in your retelling, I seem almost… disgusting! Heinous!

Leland: Aww, no. You weren't disgusting. You were just evil. You'd make a cute supervillain. I'd be all "Oh, villain, I hope you don't try to dominate my booty when you're done with your world domination." And you'd be all "I will rid the world of all your beautiful guns and then the only thing you will have left to do is peruse me with your luscious eyeballs."

Jackson: Is... luscious really the word that's best to describe eyeballs?

Leland: Hands down.

Jackson: Okay... I mean... why not? I'm so glad you laid your luscious eyeballs on me.

Leland: Me too. Me too.

TWENTY

LELAND

"I feel like I should leave you here," Jackson says, like the savage he is.

"Why?" I ask in horror. "I'm all dressed and ready to impress. Look at my ass in these jeans."

I turn so he can see. He barely glances at it. Like if I showed him my ass or an earthworm, I feel like he'd be equally impressed with both.

He sighs for some reason. "My parents are kind of… strict, okay? So please don't talk about anything improper. Nothing that has to do with how you met me. They tolerate that I'm gay, but they don't… want to see it flaunted. Got it?"

I stare at him like I'm suspicious. "Your mom's going to love me."

"I hope so, because otherwise, this could be disastrous."

"Disaster is my middle name," I assure him.

"That's… what I'm afraid of."

How he could possibly be afraid of me doing *anything*, I don't know. The thing is, I know how to act to fit the crowd. I'm phenomenal at doing what people want me to do; that's how I get them to trust me before I kill them. Not that I'm going to kill his mom. At least, not unless he needs me to.

"Do you want me to change?" I ask as I look down at what I'm wearing. The pants *are* a bit tight.

"No, it's fine. Are you ready?"

I nod and put my shoes on before following him out to the car. "Are you going to give me any insider information so I know how to butter them up?"

"None at all."

"That's okay, I didn't need anything to worm my way into your heart. Besides my overwhelmingly amazing personality. I'm like a peacock. I just flashed my pretty feathers and you were eager to become my mate."

"We're not… mates."

"What are we, then?" I ask as I slide into the passenger seat.

"Acquaintances at best."

"But you made me touch myself. Do you make all of your acquaintances touch themselves?"

He scowls as he starts the car. "No."

"Really?"

"Yes."

I grin at him. "Just me? See? We *are* mates."

"I'm not going to win, am I?"

I shake my head as he backs out of the driveway. "Probably not."

"I didn't think so."

He drives to his parents' house, which is about fifteen minutes from his place. I love that he's so easy to talk to as he drives. He *acts* like some of the things I say are cringeworthy, but then I always see him trying to hide a grin. He pulls into the driveway, which is already nearly filled with cars.

"Ready?" he asks as he grabs his container of cookies out of the back seat.

"Yup," I say as I open the passenger door and follow him up to the house. He keeps nervously looking at me, so I put a manic smile on my face that hopefully makes it look like I've lost my mind. He gets one look at me and starts laughing.

"Please don't look like that."

I make sure to keep the look on my face as I make my eyes wide. "Don't look like what? Are you saying I'm ugly?"

"I'm terrified of you. I'm actually more terrified of you at this moment than I've ever been."

"What? Why? I reek of innocence."

"You reek of something alright, but it's not innocence."

I start laughing as he reaches the door and pulls it open. He holds it open for me like he's pretending he's a gentleman, and I realize that I really do like this guy.

JACKSON

Here goes nothing.

Inside, I kick off my shoes and Leland follows suit. He really does look unbelievably nice in those pants. Especially when he bends over to straighten his shoes. I get a sudden impulse to smack his ass. While I'm sure he'd think it was hilarious, my mom would murder me if she caught me doing that.

Speaking of my mom, she comes around the corner and smiles, making me *really* thankful I didn't go through with my impulse.

"Jackson! I'm glad you finally made it. I was starting to wonder if you thought midnight when I said twelve."

"It's five after."

She raises an eyebrow like five minutes late is inexcusable. That's when she notices Leland and cocks her head like she's never seen a male human before. It's not a very pleased look she's wearing, and I wonder if I should have warned her. "Oh? Who is this?"

"I told you I was bringing someone."

"Yeah, but I assumed Mason decided to tag along again."

"Nope. This is Leland."

Leland gives her a soft smile as he holds his hand out. "It's nice to meet you, ma'am."

Ma'am? *Ma'am*? This is the same person he was wanting to call Momma.

But my mom nods, mistakenly believing him to be a mature, good-natured person. She's not aware that she's being horribly lied to.

"It's… good to meet you too. My name's Ava."

She's being surprisingly civil when I know she has a problem that I'm gay. But maybe she's going to be good and understanding for once.

Mom leads us into the kitchen where Dad is talking to my sister Ella. They both look to the newcomer with apparent interest. Clearly, their original conversation wasn't very entertaining because they drop it as they turn to us.

"This is Leland," I announce. Or a strange variation of him.

"Oh?" Ella asks, like he's a mystical being. Or maybe it's because I haven't brought a guy home in years. The last guy was very touchy-feely and my parents just stared at me with wide eyes and a look of horror. I felt like I would never hear the end of it once my mom got on the subject.

"Leland, this is my sister Ella and my father Lewis."

Leland almost shyly reaches out to my father and shakes his hand. "Good evening, sir. Thank you so much for having me."

What the fuck is he planning? Clearly, his brain is shorting out. *Or is he doing this because I told him to be careful around my parents since they're borderline strict?*

"Why didn't you tell me you were bringing someone?" Ella asks.

Because I'd been planning on backing out.

"Just didn't think about it. Is Grandma still coming?" I ask in hopes of getting the attention off me and my strange and innocent Leland.

"Yeah, she should be here soon," Mom says.

"You didn't tell me I get to meet your grandma too!" Leland says like it's actually exciting.

"Um…"

He turns back to my parents. "You guys have such a lovely home. It smells delicious in here. Oh! Jackson, did you show them the cookies you made?"

He's clearly lost his mind. Full on, lost it.

"No…"

Before anything more can be said, my grandma pulls into the driveway.

"Should we help her carry anything in?" Leland asks as he notices the car. "I'll at least get the door."

I'm no longer the only one staring at the man in confusion. Especially now that he's rushing for the front door like he's a gentleman. The man who broke into my car, shot at me, and refuses to stop talking about my ass is going to pretend he's a gentleman?

How bizarre.

Clearly, I need to stop him. This *has* to be a horrible joke that's going to force my family to disown me for life.

"He seems nice," Ella says.

"It's all a lie!" I blurt before chasing after him.

Leland, who obviously heard my declaration, is staring at me. "What the hell?"

"What?" I whisper.

"I'm like killing it out there and then you tell them I'm *lying*?"

"I panicked. You're acting so strange," I hiss.

"You told me to act well-behaved," he says in a hushed whisper.

"Yeah, like… be good, not be a completely different person."

Mom comes around the corner and stares at our whisper battle. "Is everything alright?"

"Perfect!" I shout as I grab the door and yank it open a bit too vigorously. It slams right into Leland's toe.

"Mother*fucker*," he yelps right into my grandma's face. "Did you not see me standing there, Jackson?"

I grimace. "I did, but I still seem to have forgotten."

"My *foot*." He picks his foot up in the air and tries shoving it in my vicinity. "Kiss my foot, Jackson!"

The gig is up. There's no way Leland, with his foot in my face, can be seen as normal.

I push his foot down and turn to my grandma, who is clearly confused.

Leland seems to remember that he was trying to be sweet and quickly covers his mouth. "Oh my goodness! I'm so sorry! I usually don't have such a potty mouth."

"Stop the act," I say. "I'm not going to have my parents like a fake you."

He grins at me. "Why? Afraid they'll love me more?"

"Yes, that's what I'm afraid of," I say dryly.

He starts laughing before turning to my grandma, who has no idea what's going on.

"Hi, I'm Leland. You must be G-Ma."

I don't know if it's the look she's giving him, the confusion on my family's faces, or the ridiculousness of his name for her, but I start laughing. "Don't make my grandma sound like a gangster!"

"Maybe I like sounding like a gangster," Grandma says. "I always thought the name 'Grandma' made me sound too old."

"I like her," Leland decides.

"This your boy friend or boyfriend?" she asks.

"What?" I ask.

"She means like boy friend or *boyfriend*. We're actually soul mates," Leland says. "His soul has mated with mine."

"No, it has not!"

Ella starts laughing now, and I want to tell her to stop because he's like a child. Laughter just encourages him.

"How about we eat?" Dad says, but he says it in a way where I can't tell if he wants to disown me or if he's really just that fucking hungry. My vote is on the disowning.

We shuffle into the dining room. Leland moves to sit next to my mom, but I grab his wrist and sit him between Ella and me since I feel like she'll be the safest bet. My mom's original tolerance for Leland has turned to justified confusion.

"Do you guys get together as a family like this often?" Leland asks.

"Once a week. Or at least, we try to. Sometimes Jackson pretends like he's never heard of us," Mom says.

"I missed two weekends."

"This month."

"It was Leland's fault, blame him."

"You could have brought me along," he says. "I would've loved to have met you last week. If we had, you would already love me at this point."

Mom passes me the plate of chicken, so I slide a piece onto my plate. "Breast or thigh?"

Leland looks over at me. "I'm more of a butt guy, personally."

"Me too," Dad says, and I look at him in shock.

Mom does too, but he just shrugs.

Instead of letting Leland get any of the chicken, I try to pass it to my sister, but he snatches a breast.

"How'd you two meet?" Dad asks.

Leland stops from where he'd been reaching for the potatoes. "It's a really cute story!"

I give him a look, which makes Leland nod. The look clearly meant "do not tell that story," so I have no idea why he's nodding.

"So I was watching *The Bachelor,* which is awful by the way, but I had no choice really."

Good, he's making up a story.

"So as I was watching it, I look up and see this handsome yet slightly mysterious man. He was wearing dark clothes, which made me look at him and wonder what he was doing. And then he jumps up into the air—"

"No!" I say. "I gave you a look that said, 'don't tell that story' and you nodded like you understood."

"I wasn't going to tell that story, in my rendition of it you were jumping up to save a kitten from a tree, but now I have to tell your parents the truth or they'll think I'm a liar," he says.

I invited him here. I should have known better.

"What happened?" Ella asks eagerly.

"So he jumps up and grabs onto the top of this tall wooden fence. And I'm wondering what the heck he's doing when his foot slips and he dives over the other side. The issue is that his pants catch, yanking them down until all I can see is his bare butt as he hangs from the fence. And he's just *flailing.*"

I'm not sure I've ever heard my family laugh so hard. While they laugh and stare at me, I glare at Leland.

"That was my first impression of him. Usually, I want at least a date before someone shows me their butt, but he's a risk taker."

"Whose fence were you climbing?" Dad asks.

"It was stupid. Just let me forget it, please?" I beg.

Leland sets his hand on my thigh, and for some reason, it fills me with warmth. Instead of pushing him away, like I should for making my life even harder, I set my hand on top of his.

Whatever he was going to say, he falters, and his smirk falls away. He gives me an honest smile and runs his thumb over my thigh before I let his hand go and return to supper.

"How old are you, Leland?" Mom asks.

Leland stuffs a spoonful of potatoes in his mouth as he watches my mom with that confident look in his eyes. He knows my mom is trying to get under his skin, but I doubt Leland allows much to affect him. "Twenty-seven. You?"

"Aren't you a little young?"

"I'm like an old twenty-seven. Like an... I've done it all twenty-seven, so I'm now ready to settle down. Have fifteen children, at least ten dogs, and five cats."

Mom stares at him, and I want to warn Leland that he needs to tone it down with my mother.

A soft smile forms on Leland's face. "Honestly? I don't care if Jackson is forty, fifty, or sixty. I don't care if he's poor, has fifteen toes, and three arms. All I know is that he's made me feel like I can have a family... that I don't have to live alone. I've not exactly had the best upbringing, but Jackson has made me feel like I have a purpose."

"You'd better not be using him," Dad says.

"For what? Money?" Leland asks, then cackles.

I raise an eyebrow, curious why talking about money was so funny. "What's that mean?" I ask.

Leland gives me a look of innocence, even though it's clearly not. "What? Nothing..."

I can't help but wonder how much money he really has.

Thankfully, he doesn't go *too* extreme and seems to tone it down slightly. Even so, I'm honestly pleased with how my parents are acting. My father is kind of quiet; he's never really been fond of my being gay, but he's never been a bad parent. My mother, on the other hand, won't like Leland and will make sure he's aware of that. She'll wait to see if it's serious before sinking her claws in, or at least she did the last time. Hopefully, this time it'll be different. But I'm thirty-nine at this point, so I think it's about time I stop caring what others think and live for myself.

"What do you do for a living, Leland?" Mom asks.

"I'm a hitman," he says.

Maybe I should have brought Mason.

Thankfully, they think he's joking.

Leland: And that is the moment our story turned from an action comedy to a horror.

Jackson: My mom didn't make our story into a horror!

Leland: Psychological thriller.

Jackson: No!

Leland: A tale about Satan's spawn's rise to power.

Jackson: You are *far* too dramatic.

Leland: Once upon a time, there were two lovely men, the sweetest of men who did no wrong. And while they were being perfect as perfect could be, this demon rushed onto the scene with her wicked claws and fangs. But she didn't use the claws and fangs; instead, her ability was sucking the life out of her victims. She ate away the fun and feasted off misery, and one simple look from her eyes would destroy the PI's sweet soul.

Jackson: You done?

Leland: Not quite! *clears his throat to continue the tale* And as the hitman hovered over the body of his beloved man, he tried to breathe life back into him by whispering sweet nothings into his ear.

Jackson: Do you think that the PI might have been playing dead at this point?

Leland: No! He opened his eyes and with his hoarse voice, he whispered, "Leland, my love, the reason I live and breathe. You must vanquish this monster who is my mother!"

Jackson: She's not *that* bad.

Leland: And the hitman splashed some holy water into her face and gave her some cool cement booties for the next time she goes swimming.

Jackson: You're drowning my mother?

Leland: Huh? What? No. I would never! Gosh!

Jackson: And did they live happily ever after?

Leland: Yep!

Jackson: What about my mother?

Leland: Yep!

Jackson: Your "Yep" doesn't reassure me in the slightest.

Leland: Yep!

Jackson: Yep...

TWENTY-ONE

LELAND

Since it's clear I don't need my apartment, I decided that I might as well move everything out of it and into Jackson's house. I canceled the lease on it, so I have to have everything moved out by the end of the month. Since that's this weekend, I decided that I should get started. I told Jackson I could clean everything out myself, but he was adamant about helping me.

When I walk into my apartment with Jackson by my side, I get this strange feeling. It's not exactly anxiety, more borderline panic. Like… what am I doing?

"Are you alright?" Jackson asks.

I'm surprised he even noticed. Hell, I barely noticed, but he always seems to see everything. It's like he's always watching me and understanding me better than I understand myself. I look over at him and the panic begins to dissipate. He's the reason I'm doing this. I can make it through this because of him. Slowly, I nod. "Yeah… you have to be patient with me."

"*I* have to be patient? You're literally the one who's never heard of the word. I didn't even know you knew the definition."

I grin at him, and suddenly it seems silly that I was concerned about any of this. Did I really want to go back to living alone, fixated on case after case, never living for myself? "I know what patience is. I've been very patient with your desire to not have sex until we're married. I'm hoping you propose soon, but I will try my hardest to hold out."

He sighs like he doesn't find me utterly hilarious. "So where do you want to start?"

"Living room works. We can leave the couch here as soon as I pull my baggies of cocaine out of it."

"What?" he asks.

"A joke. There's only one baggie and it's not mine. Well, it is mine since I bought it, but I'm not *snorting* it, nor have I ever snorted it. It's a good… ice breaker."

"Ice breaker?" he asks. "Hi! My name is Leland! Want some coke?"

I start laughing as I point at him. "Exactly how I do it. We'll flush it, unless you want it?"

"No!"

"Well, you seem to be slightly awkward, so I didn't know if you wanted to try it as an ice breaker as well," I say as I go over to the couch and reach under it. I grab the baggie that I'd hid inside it then throw it to Jackson.

"Catch!"

Startled, he grabs it out of the air. "Oh my god! I don't want to touch this! Now my fingerprints are all over it!"

"Go flush it."

As he does that, I retrieve my guns from their hidden positions around the apartment. Of course, this collection doesn't contain *all* of my guns; no, those are dispersed in different storage units around multiple cities. But as I look at the weaponry laid out on the couch and coffee table, I realize that I have a bit of a problem. I just kept buying more because the new one looked so much nicer. Kneeling in front of them, I stare at them, slightly unsure what to do now.

"Holy fuck," Jackson says, eyes bulging from his head like he's never seen a gun before. "You had all of this in your apartment? What if you got searched?"

"They were all hidden."

"Why so many?"

"I... really didn't realize I had so many. I thought I had like two or three in here."

"There are, at *least*, fifteen guns here."

"I know. And they're all so pretty. I love them so much. Do you think we can turn your office room into a gun shrine for all my guns?"

"You're not bringing those guns into my house."

"What?" I ask. Clearly, I have misheard the man. "No... Are you serious?"

"Leland... you haven't necessarily gained my trust back yet."

"What are you talking about? I've been amazing."

"You've been back with me for a week *after* you left, abducted some man, and tossed him in front of the police station."

"I don't remember any of that," I say.

"Convenient."

"All I can remember is your handsome face even when you're not around. I close my eyes and there you are, smiling at me like an angel from heaven. And all I can think about is how blessed I am to be in the presence of one as great and manly as you—"

He shakes his head. "That's the biggest line of bullshit that's ever come out of your mouth."

I grin. "Really? You think that one was? I've said some pretty stupid things, and you think that tops it?"

"I do."

"But it was all spoken in truth," I say as I look up from where I'm still kneeling.

He raises an eyebrow like my confession is slightly farfetched.

"Gosh, all I do is try to love you."

"This isn't about you *loving* me. This is about you wanting to bring fifteen guns into my house. At least five are *illegal* guns that could get me thrown in *prison*."

I look at him in shock. "But they're shiny."

"No!"

I glare at him. "So this relationship is all going to be about you, is it? I get it now."

"It's about me because I don't want to go to prison."

"I just like shiny things that go bang."

"One gun. You can bring one *legal* gun into my house and keep it locked in a gun case."

"What's a... *gun case*?" I ask. "Is that like a cage? For my precious?"

He sighs. "Want me to help you pick?"

"No. *But* you could give me a kiss since you're being mean to me."

"How am I mean?" he asks, like telling me that I can only have one gun is not being mean.

I reach up to him. "Give me a kiss and I'll forgive you."

He walks over to me and looks down. Then he kisses his hand and rubs it over my lips. "I didn't wash my hands after taking a piss."

"Liar. There's no way you were pouring cocaine and forgot to wash your hands. Now give me a real kiss. One that makes my heart go pitter patter."

"You have a heart?" he asks as he tries walking past me. I grab his leg and yank it toward me. He stumbles then looks back at me with a raised eyebrow. "I'm trying to help you pack."

I do a fake karate chop to the back of his knee since I want him down on the ground with me. When he doesn't willingly fall to his knees, I reach up and grab his arm before yanking him down. He eventually submits and kneels in front of me.

"What am I kneeling for?"

I grab his face in my hands. "Can I have at least ten guns?" I ask.

"One."

I push myself forward until I'm pressed against his body, then I drape my arms over his neck. "But... please?" I pout.

"I'm not easily persuaded," he says, but the hint of a grin says otherwise. I give him a gentle shove and he drops to his ass. I climb onto his lap and keep pushing until he willingly goes onto his back.

"Well, aren't you difficult?" I ask as I look down at him. I rock my hips, and even though he tries to pretend that he doesn't notice or care, I can feel his body tense.

I lean down, placing my arms on both sides of his head so my own is inches above him.

"I've never been difficult a day in my life," he says, hands on the floor like he's afraid to touch me.

My eyes never leaving his, I move lower until I can feel his breath on my lips. "You're also a liar."

"I've never lied a day in my life."

My eyes drop to his lips as they move. The upper lip is a little thin, but when he smiles at me, he doesn't have a single imperfection. How sappy. What have I become to think that? It's just lust, right?

I run my tongue over his lips, wishing they'd part for me. Why does he resist so much? I grab his bottom lip between mine and pull on it, but he acts like I'm merely a fly buzzing around him.

Oh, but I can feel his cock hardening beneath me.

I let go of his lip and smile at him. "Don't you want to know what it'd feel like to have your nice thick cock between my ass cheeks?"

He says nothing, and I hope that means he's struggling to come up with a better excuse. I run my lips down his cheek to his neck, which I nip gently. He's driving me mad and he isn't even touching me. It's like I'm making out with a fucking couch. A couch with a hard lump in the middle, but still a couch.

"What about your cock pushing into me?" I taunt before sucking on the reddened spot on his neck. "You can watch your tip slide right in as I beg you for more. I'll be all, 'Oh! Jackson! I want your jackhammer in my pothole.'"

His eyes narrow. "I can feel my dick deflating."

I wiggle my ass on his groin. "You still feel pretty hard to me."

"One gun."

"Are you serious? I just dirty talked you, licked you, *and* sucked you, and I still only get one gun?"

"Yep."

"Why did we ever decide that we're going to your house? Maybe I'll handcuff you to my bedpost and leave you in *my* apartment where I make the rules."

He snorts. "That's not going to happen."

"Want to make a bet?" I ask. "If I can get you handcuffed to my bedpost, I get to bring at least two guns and a grenade launcher."

"Please don't tell me you have a grenade launcher."

"I don't. But if I get one, we'll be putting it right above the mantle."

"I don't have a mantle."

"Well, we'll build one so I can put it there. Then on the other side is going to be my dildo collection. They'll be mounted up like those animal trophies."

"No! No more guns. No dildo trophies."

I grab his arm and pull on it as I slide my leg under his. Then I flip him onto his stomach. He tries to push me off, but I pull his arm up and lie on top of him. "Give me my dildo trophy!"

"No!" he says as he tries to figure out how to get me off his back, but there's no way he's budging me.

"Three guns and a dildo trophy!"

"What is wrong with you? And why the fuck can't I get you off me? I can't even move!"

He flails around some, which I think is really cute. Instead of giving in, I grab onto his earlobe with my lips and pull on it.

"I'll suck your jackhammer."

"No! Stop tempting me!"

Now he's trying to crawl out from under me, but I'm just riding on his back as he goes.

"Please?" I whisper into his ear. "Just for me?"

"Two guns, happy?"

I roll off him, onto my back. "I am."

He looks over at me, like he's not yet done wallowing around on the floor. I reach out to him and he takes my hand, so I pull him on top of me. He gently sits on my thighs since he's worried about my wound even though it's completely healed, or at least enough for me to function normally. He looks down at me but doesn't do anything more. Of course he doesn't. He never does.

"Why don't you want to kiss me or touch me?" I ask in seriousness.

He reaches out and runs a finger over my lips. "I do... but you feel like a flighty bird. If I make the wrong move, you'll fly away. If you're caught, you'll be pulled away. If I have sex with you, we'll just become that much closer. And then what do I do when you disappear?"

I'm honestly surprised with what he's saying and unsure how to understand it. "You... think I'll disappear? Jackson, I came back! If I was going to just disappear, why would I have come back?"

"What happens when the police trace something back to you?"

"I'm extremely careful, Jackson. I've done this for ten years and I haven't been caught. I promise, nothing is going to happen to me." Why does it mean so much that he's concerned? The man who took me in would send me out and barely bat an eye when I came back. But this man already cares? "I don't want to go anywhere, Jackson. I want to stay right here beside you every day."

He leans into me and presses his lips against mine. I've waited so long to feel them, and I never imagined they'd feel so wonderful. The first kiss is soft, gentle, and sweet. It means so much, like telling me that he cares isn't enough, he has to show me. I lean into him and open my mouth. His tongue slides in and brushes against mine as I wrap my arms around him and pull him closer.

"Are you going to fuck me or chicken out?" I ask teasingly.

"Are you going to ruin the sweetness of the moment?"

I grin at him, which makes his kisses rougher for some reason. "Maybe," I mumble against his mouth. "I can't handle too much sweetness. It makes me feel funny." I push my shirt up to my neck. "Tell me you like my nipples and everything will go back to normal."

"They're very round."

"What else do you like about them?" I ask.

He glances down at them again like he's honestly contemplating it. "I like the one long hair."

"Do you? That's my nipple's beard."

"Oh?"

He reaches down and of course I think he's going to touch my nipples, but instead, he grabs the not-so-imaginary hair and tugs it.

"Oh my god! I thought you were joking about there being a hair there! That hurt!"

"I was just trying to make it less sweet. I thought maybe you wanted a bit of kink."

"Kink? That was abuse."

He shakes his head. "One little hair? You *shot* at me, and me not even pulling out a hair on your chest is abuse? I didn't know you were so *dramatic*."

"Dramatic is my middle name. Now carry me to my bed and fuck me like it's our wedding night."

He's trying not to laugh. "As you wish, my virgin bride."

He stands up and looks down at me as I hold my arms up like a stubborn toddler. "Oh, you're serious."

"Of course I am."

He reaches down and grabs my wrist in one hand and my ankle in the other. Since he can't exactly hoist me up this way, he starts dragging me toward my room.

"Come my precious, let me show you a good time," he says with the creepiest voice I've ever heard.

"Oh no... I've ruined the sweetness of this moment," I cry as I'm dragged across the carpet. "Bring back the sexy and the sweet!"

"You weren't happy with that," he reminds me as he reaches the doorframe before realizing that my body won't go sideways through it. Instead of letting go of me at that point, he keeps pulling so I'm smashed into the doorframe and wall.

"You're going to murder me!"

"Bend your body!"

"I'm trying to be romantic!"

Jackson lets go of my arm and leg and stoops over. "Is that what we're going for?"

"Yes," I say while trying to pretend I wasn't the one who told him to lug me around.

He grabs my hand and pulls me to my feet, then he draws me against him. His hands slide around my waist as he looks down at me. "You're gorgeous. How did I find someone as gorgeous as you?"

"It's probably my less-than-ideal personality."

Jackson smiles at me. "You're a fool if you think that I'm only attracted to your looks."

His comment makes me hesitate. I was planning on making another joke, but his words have stilled me. "What... there's really nothing else to like about me."

He grabs my shoulders and pushes me back like he's trying to get a better look at me. "Are you serious?"

I feel like I've ruined the moment again. "What? We're just... ha ha! We're joking. Now show me your penis." That should be a good way to get back on topic. When he asks me a serious question like that, I don't like it. It's like he expects a serious answer when I honestly don't know what to say.

"Leland... I'm not drawn to your looks. I mean, of course I think you're gorgeous, but do you really think I would keep you from going to prison—from turning you in, as I should have—just because of your looks?"

I honestly don't know why he didn't turn me in, so I don't even know how I can answer that.

His eyebrows knit, like he's faced with a difficult question. "Leland, you're funny—you make me laugh every day. You're nice and caring, even if you act like you're not. There's a lot more to you than a pretty face. I could put a bag over your head and still like you. I might even like you better."

I can't even understand the emotions rushing through me as his words absorb into my semi-defiant brain. "You don't think I'm annoying?"

"No, not at all."

"Really? Even when I say stupid things? And ask to see your willy?"

"Even then."

I don't even know what to say, so instead of saying anything, I step into him. "Thank you."

"You don't need to thank me."

My chest almost *aches*, and I have this weird feeling in my stomach. It's not a bad feeling, but it's a strange one. One I don't seem to know how to understand. I slide my arms around him and press myself to him so I can tuck my face against his neck.

"I don't know why this makes me feel so weird," I mumble.

"A good weird or a bad weird?" he asks as he slides his hand under my shirt and gently runs his fingers over my back.

"A good weird. Stop! I can't take any more of this! My body doesn't know how to respond. I think it's shutting down. I think I'm dying, Jackson. Is that what this feeling is?"

He shakes his head as he chuckles. "You're not dying."

He reaches down and grabs my waist before pulling me into the air. I grab onto him as he carries me over to the bed and gently lays me onto it. He follows me onto the bed, straddling me as he lowers himself to me. His lips softly press into mine, and I realize that I've never done anything sexual with someone I cared about. I wasn't allowed to have emotional ties to people, so when I had sex with anyone, it was generally someone I barely knew and just for the pleasure of sex. Not someone I had an attachment to.

I slip my fingers under his shirt and run them over his sides before pushing his shirt up. He grudgingly breaks from my lips to pull the shirt the rest of the way off.

"Ooh, am I allowed to look at your chest this time?"

"I'll allow it this once," he jokes.

I grin as I set my fingers against his skin. "Your nipples are adorable."

"What?"

I pinch one which makes him grab my hands and pin them on each side of my head. "You don't like your nip-nips pinched?" I innocently ask.

His fingers intertwine with mine as he holds them there, making it feel much more intimate. "Hmm... I just get nervous every time you're allowed to do anything to me," he says.

I chuckle as he lets go of my hands and slides his hand under my shirt. Just the pads of his fingers brush over my stomach, making me shiver and ache for more. He pulls my shirt up and over my head before tossing it. Now that my hands are free, I unbutton his pants and push them down.

He backs up to pull his pants off, sliding them and his underwear down and freeing his hardening cock. As he turns to set the clothes on the ground, I get a good look at his ass.

"Hello, old friend," I say.

He looks at me and shakes his head. "No."

"Shush. Don't be jealous."

"I'm not," he says as he climbs back on top of me.

I reach for him and grab his perfect ass in my hands, squeezing the globes tightly.

His lips move from my mouth to my neck, tracing a line down as my fingers brush and explore over his ass and up his back. Soon, he's too far out of my reach as his mouth continues down my chest, kissing and sucking as my hands are left to his upper back and then his hair. My cock is aching as he unbuttons my pants and slides them down my hips. When he finally frees my length, he looks up at me.

"You have lube and a condom?"

I turn so I can reach into the bedside table and grab the stuff. As soon as they're in my hand, he drags me back to him.

He slides his fingers over my cock as he kisses a line down to my waistline, stopping to brush a tender kiss over my mostly healed wound along the way. As I watch him, he lifts my cock up to his lips before his eyes catch mine. His tongue slips between his lips and twirls around the head as I'm mesmerized by him. I'm not sure what drives me crazier, the feeling of his tongue, or him looking me in the eyes as he does it. He pushes my cock up and runs his tongue up it as he pops open the lube. He moves his hand between my legs until his wet finger finds my hole. I spread my legs as I moan, eager to feel him inside me.

He takes the head of my cock into his mouth as his finger swirls and rubs before pushing inside me. It's been a while, but even so, I've never been this excited. My cock feels like it's never been so hard and my body's never been so eager. I've never desired a man like I do Jackson. I would eagerly give him every ounce of me. He could take all of me, and I would willingly hand it over to him. When a second finger joins the first, I moan. I want more of him. Even as his fingers rub and stretch me, I want to feel his hard cock that's dripping with precum.

"I want you inside me," I say as I reach for him.

He pulls his mouth from my cock and raises an eyebrow. "Remember me saying you don't have patience?"

"Nope."

"Well, have some patience."

"I have all the patience in the world," I say as I sink my fingers into his hair and grab a good handful of it.

"You do not!" he says as I tug on his hair in an attempt to pull him to me. "Stop it!"

"Your penis is too far away! I want your penis!"

"Let me pleasure you!"

It *does* feel good. But I also really want his cock inside me. Such a difficult decision. But when his mouth slides down me, I decide to give in a little longer. It *will* make the end result so much better when I'm left waiting and aching for more.

He pulls his fingers from me as his mouth leaves my cock and I'm able to drag him back to me. I press his mouth to mine as I fumble with the condom wrapper like I've never opened anything in my life.

I pull back so I can actually see what I'm doing. "How have you betrayed me?" I growl at my fingers.

Jackson grabs it to help, but all he manages to do is wipe lube all over it and make it slippery as fuck.

"Thanks for not helping at all," I say.

He grins at me before kissing my forehead. "You're welcome."

"Please come out."

"Are you going to plead it free?"

"I'm trying all angles here," I say as I wipe it off on the bedsheets before finally managing to tear it open. "I have prevailed! Now sheath your mighty sword and plunge it into my cave."

He sighs, so I decide to take matters into my own hands. With the condom in one hand, I grab his cock with the other and let my fingers gently run over it. I press my thumb against the precum, smearing it over the head before sliding my fingers down to the base. Then I set the condom against the head of his cock before rolling it down and grabbing the lubricant. I rub it over him with one hand as my other slides down his back to his ass that I really seem to love.

He settles between my legs before looking up at me. "Are you good?"

"More than good."

So much more. I've never wanted anyone inside me as much as I want him. I want to feel that level of connection to him, to bare everything. He presses his cock against my hole before pushing gently. He always does everything very gently and carefully. He should know that out of anyone, he shouldn't have to be careful with me, but I appreciate it. It makes me feel cared for. It makes me feel like he wants the best for me.

He keeps pushing, opening me up until his thick cock is sliding inside me. It feels tight, since it's been so long, but it sends pleasure rushing through me. I moan as I grab onto him, digging my fingers into his back.

Once he's buried deep inside me, he stops and gives me gentle kisses that make me grab onto him even harder. Why is he this kind and caring?

"Are you good?" he asks.

I nod, not sure if I could trust my voice.

He rocks his hips slightly before pulling back a little more and pushing in. The sound of his moans excites me. It's like I care more about how he's feeling than myself, and I've *definitely* never felt that way before. His hand finds my cock and strokes me as I do nothing but cling onto him. I know I'm not giving him much room to move, but I don't want us to be apart from each other. I want his bare skin to rub against mine. I want to feel every part of him.

He continues to rock his hips inside me until the pleasure pushes away all my wild thoughts. Until I can only focus on his movement as my cock aches and feels unbelievably hard. Have I really been missing out on sex this good my entire life? Is it because I care about him that it feels so different?

I could never lose this man. I could never lose any of this. Without a doubt, I would give up everything for him.

The pleasure makes me moan as I arch into him and he squeezes the base of my cock. "There," I moan, but if he continues to hit "there," I'm not sure how much more I can take.

I throw my head back and his mouth captures mine as his thrusts quicken. He's driving me crazy. I hook his hips and pull him into me as my balls tighten and my toes curl. He keeps stroking me as pleasure consumes my body and my arms feel weak from clutching onto him tightly. I moan as cum hits his stomach and he buries himself into me. He groans as he comes inside me, tucking his face against my neck, cock deep inside me. Instead of pulling out of me, he covers me with kisses that run from my neck to my lips. And only when I'm coated in them, does he pull out.

He acts like he's going to get up, probably to clean us up, but I refuse to let him go and drag him down beside me. I roll into him, pressing myself to him.

"Don't ever leave me," I whisper.

His hands tighten behind my back. "I won't."

"I'm a mean motherfucker when you piss me off. You will *not* be safe from me if you make me mad."

"So no mustard on your sandwiches, or you'll hunt me down, got it."

I smile, glad for the break from the emotions and seriousness. Fuck, I don't even know how to interpret that shit half of the time.

"Please tell me if I get to be too much. I'm greedy because I've never had this stuff. I never knew how much I needed it. Jackson, I want things. A lot of things. I want to go on dates. I want to wake up Christmas morning with a fucking tree decorated with those stupid little lights. I want your family to love me. I want you to love me. Not now! God no, we're not there yet. But that's what I want."

The smile that forms on his face tells me that he wants them too. "I will gladly give you all of that as long as you stay beside me."

"I won't run away again."

"You can't leave me."

"I won't."

And I will do everything I can to make sure that stays true.

Leland: You were so cute back then. Back when you thought you could limit me from bringing more than two guns into the house.

Jackson: I think naïve is the word you want to use here.

Leland: Back when a "gun shrine" was just a hopeful idea.

Jackson: Now I find weapons everywhere. I found a shuriken in the bread box yesterday. A *shuriken*.

Leland: Just in case you wanted to cut a piece of bread in half.

If you ask me, it's a handy device. Cut bread one minute, stab people the next.

Jackson: I found a machete under my side of the bed. I was like "Weird, there seems to be a lump here. I wonder if I need a new mattress." And no, I needed to remove the arsenal from under it.

Leland: It's like the princess and the pea! How cute.

Jackson: I found a spiky thingamajig in my glove box when I got pulled over for speeding the other day.

Leland: Oh noooooo. That sounds bad. Did the officer have to strip-search you?

Jackson: No! Thankfully, he knew me, and I played it off that it was a toy!

Leland: Wow, what skills you have! First you can sense peas under your mattress and then you could convince an officer that a medieval torture device was a fun toy.

Jackson: Thanks... I think.

TWENTY-TWO

JACKSON

I get out of my car just as Mason gets out of his in my driveway.

"Thanks again for letting me borrow your tent," Mason says as I wait for him to catch up with me. After work, he followed me home in his car to grab the tent I haven't used since my parents gave it to me.

"Yeah, I've had it for years and haven't used it. I'll have to get the key for the shed."

"You should go camping with us sometime," he says. "You could bring that guy of yours and the four of us could rough it. Go hardcore hiking." The cheating husband case he was working on turned out to his benefit, especially after he showed the lady pictures of her husband balls deep in another woman. They seemed to hit it off after her seperation.

"Maybe we'll need to do that. Leland would be all over it. He has the energy of three of me." I wonder if he has that energy because he's used to doing lord knows what and not being pent up in a house as he has been for the past month. In order to exercise more often, we've started going running together every morning, and he dragged me off to the shooting range over the weekend.

At first, I was against the idea, but I realized that I can't expect him to give up everything he loves. And he really does light up when he's allowed to shoot things.

"I finally get to meet him," Mason says eagerly.

Thankfully, Mason is awful at being a PI and has a shitty memory, so he probably won't even remember that Leland has already been to the office pretending to be someone else.

"I think you'll like him," I say as I pull open the front door and step into the house with Mason by my side.

When Mason lets out a strange noise, my attention snaps to the living room where Leland's lying facedown on the living room floor. The issue isn't that he's lying there, it's that he's butt-ass naked. His legs are spread, giving us a far too clear view of his balls as I realize what's going on.

He's lying in the only patch of sunlight in the living room like a fucking cat while reading a book.

"Jackson!" he shouts before rolling onto his back and cocking his head. "And... not Jackson! Hi!"

Mason starts laughing as he looks over at me. "Did I ruin a surprise for you?"

"Oh no, I was sunning my ass cheeks," Leland says, like that's an everyday experience.

"Please find your clothes," I say.

Leland grins at me. "I'm pretty sure Mason has seen a willy before, haven't you, Mason? I mean, you have one, don't you?"

"I do!" Mason says, like he's proud of the fact.

"See? Crisis averted. We all have willies."

I sigh because I know I won't win. "Let's get you that tent," I say as I grab Mason's arm and drag him after me as Leland gleefully laughs.

I quickly grab the keys and pull him back outside.

"Well, well, well... looks like you've found your match," Mason says while grinning at me.

"I've found something, alright. I'm thinking he had brain trauma."

"If I came home and my girl was like that? I would have said, fuck the tent, come back some other day."

I walk across the yard to the shed. "I am one hundred percent positive that none of that was to be sexy. That was just Leland being Leland."

"Are you talking about me?" Leland calls.

I turn to see him coming out of the house. Thankfully, he has his clothes on this time. Well... thankfully, just because Mason is here.

"I am."

"Surely about how magnificent I am, right?" Leland asks as he comes up. "It's nice to finally meet you, Mason. I've heard a lot about you."

"All good things, I assume."

"That you're fantastic at wooing women."

"Don't forget to mention his solitaire skills. Or his lack of detective skills. Basically, he couldn't find a clue if it smacked him in the balls," I joke.

Mason starts laughing as he points at me. "Yeah, that's pretty much how I would describe myself as well."

I unlock the shed and pull it open. The tent is way in the back, where I put it after my dad brought it over, so I start clambering over everything to get it.

"Need help?" Leland asks as he climbs in as well. Together, we pull the tent free.

"You two have plans tonight?" Mason asks.

"Date night," I say.

"It is?" Leland asks with wide eyes. We haven't officially gone on a date yet, so I decided it was well past time.

"Is that alright with you?" I ask.

He gives me a huge smile. "I'll go get ready," he says before rushing off.

"How'd you hook someone like that?" Mason asks.

"There are a lot of sides to that crazy man," I say as I hold the tent out.

"Well, I've already seen more parts of him than my girlfriend, so yeah... I've seen a lot of sides to him as well. Even the sides of his balls. But I like him. He suits you well."

"Does he?" I ask skeptically. "All you've seen of him is his ass."

"Yeah, but in the five minutes he was next to you, you seemed more comfortable than I've ever seen you with anyone else. Thanks for the tent, and have fun on your date night."

"Thanks. Have fun camping."

As I watch Mason walk away, I realize that he's right. I'm definitely more comfortable around Leland than anyone else. He makes me happier than anyone ever has, and we haven't even been around each other long.

I walk up to the house, surprised to find Leland waiting. "You're ready?"

"Yes! I don't want to waste a minute of this evening. What are we doing? Where are we going? Strip club? Adult store? Oh my god. Are you taking me somewhere we can film our own porno?"

"All of the above," I say dryly.

He starts laughing. "What do we want to name it? How about this: *Saggy Balls Fucks Charismatic Soul Mate*."

"I regret this date already."

He's grinning so broadly that I can't keep my own grin at bay.

"How about we go to the mall then out to eat? And if you're *still* not satisfied, we can go to a movie," I suggest.

"I can handle that. And if I'm feeling frisky, I might buy you something at the mall."

"Do you... I know we haven't been together long, so this might be inappropriate, but then again you *do* use only my money. What's your financial status?"

"Like do I have money or not?" he asks as we walk out to the car.

"Yeah."

"I have money, but why use my money when I can use yours?"

I raise an eyebrow as he looks back at me. For some reason, I still open his car door for him.

"I'm joking! I'm not going to suck you dry. Well, I'll suck your dick dry if you want. Do you want that?"

"Get in the car."

"Why do dick jokes make you flustered? Should I say peepee instead? Does that make you feel better?"

I slam the door and walk over to my side before getting in.

He turns to me with a wicked grin on his face. "Want me to suck your willy stick dry?"

"No."

"If you need money, I can get you money. Ooh, I could pay you for things. Like it'll be a rating scale telling you how good you are."

"So you're not poor."

"No, not really. I mean, I have money. I just have to get things transferred around since I'm now pretending to be a real adult."

That still doesn't answer my question, but I decide that it's good enough.

"I... I'm thinking that I'll take a test to get my GED," he says, almost like he's uncertain or embarrassed. But that's not right. Leland is never uncertain. "Then maybe I'll go to college or something."

"That's awesome."

He looks over at me and smiles. "You really think so?"

"I do. Is there something you want to study?" I ask curiously. I can't see him sitting down at a desk job, but who knows what that crazy brain of his would want to do.

"I don't know. I think maybe I'll just take the preliminary classes and hopefully decide on something along the way. I have a couple months before the summer semester would start, or I could wait until fall."

"I think that'll be an excellent idea."

"Did you go to college?" he asks curiously.

I slow at a stop light. "No, I took a year off, got a job at a factory before realizing that I couldn't continue doing that. That's when I decided to enlist."

"Did you like being in the army?"

"I did. I felt like it finally gave me a purpose to be doing something. And I felt like I was good at it."

"Then why'd you leave?"

I think about it for a moment. "I don't know... I just felt like there was something more I could be doing. I thought that I would leave while I was still young enough that if I wanted to go into law enforcement, I could. The thing is... while I was in the army, I was in a spot where I felt like I wasn't... doing anything or at the point in my life I wanted to be at. I wanted to help people. When I got out, Mason and I started talking and we came up with the detective agency idea. We honestly didn't know if we could do anything with it, but he comes from money, and he didn't mind blowing it on this, so we decided to try and see what happened. And while I definitely don't do a *lot* of crazy and mind-blowing things, I still feel like I'm helping people."

"You are definitely helping people," he says as he smiles. "In and out of work."

I look over at him, surprised by the emotion in his voice.

"Like this morning, you helped me find my underwear," he says. "How did you know where it was? Were you sniffing it?"

I sigh, although I know he did it to hide the fact that he was being too serious. He does everything he can to act like nothing ever bothers him. I know that it's a topic we'll have to focus on someday, but maybe not yet. "I... looked in the drawer that I gave you to put your under-wear in."

"Clothes don't go in drawers."

I shake my head. "Of course they don't."

"I was planning on taking all of the clothes out and putting Blow-Up Randy in there."

"I have yet to meet Blow-Up Randy."

"He's a little shy."

"A shy blow-up doll. How interesting."

I pull up to the mall and find a place to park.

"Shit," Leland says as I get out of the car.

"What's wrong?" I ask as I meet him on his side.

"We should've listened to the sex playlist I made for you as we drove here! It could have gotten you in the mood!"

"I threw it out," I lie.

He looks at me in horror. "You wouldn't dare. That was the mix I was going to walk down the aisle to."

"Aisle of what? The local jail?"

"Do you think your dad will walk me down since mine's in prison?" he asks. "I mean, I could call him up, but he probably doesn't even remember me. And your dad already loves me."

"He actually called me the other day," I say.

"To tell you he loves me?"

"No, he said I forgot my cookie dish at the house."

"And?"

"That was it."

"It was not," he says as he walks beside me. "What'd he think of me?"

"It went something like this: 'So... that guy you brought...' And then I was like, 'Which one?'"

"Not funny."

"And then he goes: 'He's... interesting.'"

"Right there!" He jabs a finger at me. "Your dad loves me."

"Yep, that's definitely what that translated to."

He starts laughing as he holds his hand out.

"You want to hold hands in public?" I ask in surprise. None of my other partners have ever asked to hold hands in public. "You know we'll get stared at."

"We already will with my overwhelming personality and our age difference. They'll just think you're my daddy."

"I'm barely twelve years older."

"Daddy, hold my hand so I don't get hit by a car," he says as he wiggles his fingers around.

People are now staring at us and we're not even holding hands yet. I pretend to grudgingly give him my hand, even though I'm more than happy to take his. He slides his fingers between mine and gives me the greatest smile.

I don't care who looks at us or judges us, it'll all be worth it to have seen that expression on his face.

"Jackson..." His smile widens. "I didn't know you were so susceptible to peer pressure. Will you finger me in JCPenney?"

"What? No! And who says *finger*. Just... no!"

"Fine! What about the bookstore?"

"I will hold your hand. Anything more gets reserved for home."

"Movie theater! The ultimate hand job location."

I stop and the connection to his hand pulls him to a stop as well. "Look at me."

"I'm looking," he says, grin just as wicked.

"Give me a normal look."

"I can't. My face is just fucked up like this."

I try not to smile as I squeeze his hand. "I'm not giving you a hand job in the movie theater. But if you're good, when I get home, I might."

"Well, we might as well both forget that, then. I don't foresee me becoming a good person anytime soon," he admits.

I squeeze his hand again and he returns the gesture. "You couldn't be good for two hours?"

"Oh no. No one can stomp out this personality."

"Good. It's my favorite part of you."

His eyes get wide. "Really? Not my hole?"

"I regret everything," I say as I start walking away. Briskly this time, so I'm dragging him after me as his laughter follows me.

Leland: Hey, Jackson, on the topic of dates, what's your ideal date?

Jackson: Oh... man, so... I like it when they're shiny, you know?

Leland: *scrutinizing* Like... down there?

Jackson: A sheen, almost. Ooh, and I like it when they purr. And when you press them *just* right, they roar.

Leland: *eyes narrowed* You're talking about a car, aren't you?

Jackson: Wait... what? Did I miss the prompt?

Leland: Your ideal date as in *what to do*, not *who* you want to do. Gosh, *sniffles* leaving me *sniffles harder* for a car...

Jackson: Ohhhhh. A date with you? Honestly? Anything with you is perfect and lovely.

Leland: Aww, you're so sweet. It would be sweeter if you didn't confess to wanting to fuck your car first.

Jackson: I don't want to fuck my car.

Leland: *mockingly* Ohhhhhh purr for me. Do you like it when I touch your rims, you dirty boy? Don't titillate me like that!

Jackson: At least my car doesn't chastise me like you do. Maybe the car will go on a date with me instead.

Leland: Don't you dare.

Jackson: I'm sorry, I can't hear you over the purr of this engine.

Leland: Jackson... my love... how could you... cough cough... how could you...

Jackson: I'm confused. Did the car attack you? Did they choke you? Is that why you're coughing?

Leland: Don't leave me... cough... like this... after... I loved you so hard.

Jackson: Do we think that maybe you're being a bit dramatic? Like what if we went on a date all together?

Leland: No! I don't want to be the third wheel! Fuck! Your car has so many more wheels than me!

Jackson: Cough, cough.

Leland: Why the hell are you coughing?

Jackson: Oh, I just... thought maybe that's how we got our way now.

Leland: Wise... Wise...

TWENTY-THREE

FOUR MONTHS LATER

LELAND

"I will fucking *murder* you if you keep doing this shit. I will cut you open and tear you apart piece by piece if you don't listen to me," I growl.

I press the "on" button on the vacuum cleaner and the red "clogged" light flashes again.

"You are NOT CLOGGED," I scream.

Household chores are clearly not my specialty. Hunting people is. But that was my *old* specialty. My new specialty is keeping the house clean, making supper, and keeping straight A's in all of my online college classes.

I don't *need* to hunt people or kill people anymore because I'm a changed man. I have changed for the better. I have changed for Jackson because I will do anything for him. Even clean the living room with the vacuum from hell.

Deep breath.

I exhale and drop to my knees before laying the vacuum on its side. Then I dutifully tear it apart like I already have once today. I clean out every tiny scrap of anything that could be making it think it's clogged.

Using my phone's flashlight, I look in every tube and every crevice until I'm positive that it's as clean as the day it was born.

Then I stand it up and turn it on.

The red light flashes and the brushes refuse to spin.

In a ridiculous fit of anger, I grab the vacuum and hoist it high into the air so its wheels nearly touch the ceiling. Then I bring it down as hard as I can, slamming the wretched piece of shit onto the floor. "Die, you stupid motherfucking piece of shit!" I yell as the base of the vacuum goes flying off, but I don't let it get too far as I begin beating it with itself in a completely uncalled-for fit of rage. "Die, you cock-sucking, pussy-licking—"

The front door opens, and I quickly look up in horror.

Then confusion when it's not Jackson letting himself in but the chief of police, Henry Johnson.

"Um…"

We both stare at the massacred vacuum that I am slightly mortified I destroyed. I didn't *mean* to destroy it. I just… it was making me unreasonably angry.

"Are you a new type of burglar who breaks things instead of taking them?" Henry asks.

I point at myself. "Me? You're the one who just let yourself in."

He points at the remnants of the vacuum. "Yeah, because I heard an awful noise and screaming. When I knocked, no one answered. The door was unlocked, so I let myself in. Is everything alright?"

"There was a spider… on the floor," I say as I toss the busted handle. "I got it!"

"I would hope you got it after all that."

"Thanks. That thing has been biting me for weeks, and I just saw it while vacuuming and knew I had to do what it takes to flatten it."

"You just got pissed at the vacuum, didn't you?" he asks.

I nod. "I did. It kept saying it was clogged and it wouldn't work and I just…" I sigh as I slump down to survey the mess. "I think I can duct tape it back together."

He starts laughing, and suddenly we're both laughing at the ridiculousness of the situation. And now that I really think about it, it wasn't worth getting that angry about.

"Please don't tell Jackson. I'll bury it in the backyard before he gets home."

"I take it he's not home?"

"No, he went into work today for something. But I can text him to see when he'll be back, if you want?"

"Sure, that would be great."

"And… you are?" I ask, since I'm not actually supposed to know who the man is. Sadly, I know him better than he could ever imagine. He's the man who wants me dead, after all.

But who can blame him?

I killed his partner.

"Oh! I'm really sorry. My name's Henry. I'm the chief of police, which is how I know Jackson. We've worked together for a few years."

"Henry! It's awesome to finally get to meet you! Jackson has said a lot about you. I think he wants to trade Mason for you so he has a partner who does more than flirt."

Henry laughs, and I can't help but wonder what he'd do if he found out. Would he arrest me right here? And if I tried to run, would he shoot me? What would Jackson do? I lied and told him that I wasn't the one who killed Henry's partner. That was just because his death was the hardest to explain. At the time, we didn't know each other very well, and I thought that if he knew the truth, he would turn me away. But even now, I don't know how to tell him.

"What was your name?"

"Leland."

He points a finger at me as his eyes get wide, and I try to think about how I must have just fucked up for him to have that expression. "You're the gunshot victim, right? I never got to meet you, but I stopped by to see what happened while you were still in surgery."

"I was."

"It's such a shame we couldn't figure out who shot you."

"Jackson said he'd been nosing too much, and I think he blamed himself. Really, I should have warned him I was stopping by. But I was embarrassed because I didn't really know him, but I just… wanted to talk. This is embarrassing. I'm sorry, you don't need to hear about all of that. I'll let Jackson know you're here."

> Me: Yo, JackJack, the chief of police is here for an orgy. He told me he wants to suck my toes and sniff my armpits. He's into some weird shit but I'm strangely into it.

I slip the phone back into my pocket. "I let him know you're here."

"Thank you."

I point to the kitchen. "Want some coffee?"

"No thanks, I don't drink coffee."

"I thought that was a requirement to join the force."

He gives me a smile. "Not for this man."

"I hope you at least like donuts, or I would think there might be something wrong with you."

He grins. "I can always handle a donut."

"We should make Jackson pick some up on the way home."

"Oh! No need, I'm fine with just some water."

"If I have to pick up the mess that's his sweeper, then he can bring us something to eat."

"Didn't you make that mess?" he asks.

I shrug, not willing to admit to any more. "It needed to die, Henry, and Jackson just wasn't going to do it himself. He loves to keep things well past their prime. I'm the only thing he owns that's still ripe."

Henry chuckles as I get him some water. That's when my phone beeps, telling me that Jackson is aware of Henry's presence. I read it as I walk back into the living room so I can clean up the mess I made while merely exercising.

> Jackson: Mother of god. No... I don't want you in the same room as him.

> Me: Why? Afraid I'll show him my dildo collection?

> Jackson: Please tell him to wait in the car.

> Me: No. I already asked him if he wanted to see the sex tape I made of us.

Jackson: I thought I told you to delete that.

Me: Why the fuck would I do that?

"Ooh, what is this?" Henry says.

Quickly, I look up and see him holding a rifle.

Me: Whoops. I might have forgotten to put a gun away.

Jackson: Please tell me it's not your rifle.

Me: Okay!

Jackson: Why was that out?!

Me: I was jerking off with it in one hand and my cock in the other.

Jackson: Tell him you're my cleaning lady.

"Man, this is a nice gun. Jackson didn't tell me he had something like this."

"Is it?" I ask as I walk over. "I don't like guns in the house. It makes me nervous, but Jackson's all military and 'look at this shiny cool gun that murders people.'" I shudder. Out of excitement. But he seems to think it's out of hatred for guns, which goes along with my story. "I really wish he'd find a safer job, you know?" What I really wish is for Henry to get his dirty fingers off my precious baby. I just cleaned her and now there are probably fingerprint smudges all over her.

"I get that. My wife has said the same thing, so I know how hard it is. Just remember that he's doing this to help people. And if you were in the victim's shoes, you'd wish for someone like Jackson to come around."

"I've already wished for someone like Jackson. Now I regret it and realize the blow-up doll was less work," I say as I open the trash bag I'd grabbed from the kitchen.

Henry laughs, although I'm positive it's out of politeness. As he starts helping me pick up the pieces of the vacuum, I realize that he might not be half bad.

By the time Jackson gets home, the remains of Mr. Vacuum are in the outside trash bin. Jackson seems slightly stressed as he comes rushing through the front door and looks between Henry and me. We're sitting on the couch sharing embarrassing stories about Jackson, and the sight of us sends Jackson to a standstill.

"Sorry… it took me so long," he says warily. I think he'd have been less surprised if he came in and we were in the middle of a duel to the death.

"No problem at all, I was just sharing everything embarrassing you've ever done," I assure Jackson.

Jackson pretends like I didn't even speak. "Can I get you anything to drink, Henry?"

"Like the time you went outside in your underwear to get the newspaper and I locked you out."

"I see you vacuumed some, thank you," Jackson says.

Maybe I need to tell Henry about the fence story. But I give in and realize that I should probably pretend to be good. "I've decided that we need a new vacuum."

"It's fine, you just have to give it a little thwack on the front and it'll start running again."

"I gave it a little thwack and it just didn't seem to help," I say earnestly.

Henry starts laughing, which makes Jackson look between us with narrowed eyes.

"What did you do?" Jackson asks.

"Nothing! I'll leave you guys to talk, I'm going to go water those stupid flowers your mom got us. She did it to torture us."

"No, she didn't."

"They're ugly too."

I head to the door as Henry and Jackson relocate into the kitchen. Instead of going outside and doing anything with the ugly plants that look like vaginas, I pretend to go outside, then sneak back in, far too curious about what Henry wants with Jackson.

JACKSON

"You didn't tell me you got together with the guy who was shot. I'm assuming you're together... he seems to live here," Henry says as he takes a seat.

"Yeah, we just... hit it off, I guess. After I got to know him at the hospital, we went on a couple of dates, and I realized that I really liked him. He moved in a couple of months ago." While it's partially true, the reason I didn't tell Henry was because he currently wants Leland in prison, for life.

I would have preferred them to have never met, especially because I can't really explain to him that Leland wasn't the one who actually killed his partner.

"He seems nice. A little, uh... easily frustrated, but nice."

"What do you mean?" I ask warily.

He shakes his head but is wearing a grin. "No reason."

"He broke the vacuum, didn't he? Dammit, you just have to give it a gentle hit."

"Oh, he hit it alright. Into about a hundred pieces."

"He's really not crazy or violent or anything. He *does* lack patience and couldn't sit still to save his life." Which is why it surprises me that he's doing so well here. He promised me that he hasn't done anything since the Gibbs incident, and I honestly believe him. Our relationship wouldn't go far without me trusting him. I know he's had to give up so much, but I can't stand the idea of having him out there where the police want him behind bars. What if he was shot again? Hurt? Killed?

"Yeah, I get it. When I was in my twenties, I didn't have much patience either. Who am I kidding? I still don't have patience. Anyway, so I wanted to talk to you about coming in as a consultant. The case you were dealing with about the missing girls, we think it's been reopened. Everything was quiet for months, but now we've stopped a shipment of illegal weapons. We believe it's tied to the same case. Since you were able to get information on Hardek and found the location of those girls, I thought you could help. We owe their lives to you."

No, you owe them to Leland.

That's when I realize what he's here for. "So, you want me to help you?"

"Yes. We need to bring this man down, whoever he is, and get him out of this city."

"Okay, yeah. I don't have much on my plate at the moment. I can push my current stuff over to Mason or work on them on downtime. Do you want me to come in tomorrow and we can go over everything?"

"Sounds perfect. Gather anything you can so you can spend some time talking to the team."

"Thank you for considering my help." I feel almost thrilled to be asked to help. I would love to get Hardek and his group off the streets and behind bars.

"Of course," he says. "Well, I better get home before the missus wonders if I've run off."

"She might get excited if she thinks you have."

He shakes his head at me and grins. "Tell Leland I said bye."

Oh, he can probably hear you. "I will."

I follow Henry toward the door before he points at the rifle Leland left out. *Why* it's out, I have no idea. "That's a *nice* gun. Where'd you get it?"

I try to guess where Leland would have gotten it. Honestly, I have no idea. "Special order."

"I can't believe you put that much money into a weapon. You're so tight with everything."

"Just a lapse of judgment." The lapse was letting Leland keep it in the house.

"Nah, not a lapse. It's *nice*."

"Thanks."

"See you tomorrow, Jackson."

"See ya."

As soon as he's gone, Leland comes around the corner. Instead of running to my arms, he runs to his gun. "Oh, precious! He put his nasty fingers all over you," he says as he grabs it and cradles it like a baby while trying to rub out imaginary fingerprints.

"Maybe that'll teach you to keep it locked up like it's supposed to be."

"How would you feel being locked in a dark room twenty-four seven? Huh? Not so good."

"I'm not a gun."

"I heard you guys talking about me," he says as he takes the gun over to its velvet-laden box and lays it gently inside. He's never treated me that gently.

"Of course you did instead of watering the flowers, you little liar."

Leland grins. "You should have confessed your undying love. 'Oh, Leland makes my heart race and blood rush to my penis. Sometimes, my butthole even puckers thinking about him.'"

"Why the butthole?"

"I don't know. It's your butthole. You tell me."

I shake my head as he walks over to me and wraps his arms around me. He squeezes me tightly, and I kiss the top of his head. "Welcome home, my sex slave," he says.

"Thanks. And what happened to the vacuum?"

He pulls back enough that he can look up at me. "Want me to reenact it?"

"Oh no."

"I'll reenact it for you," Leland says as he pulls back and grabs a pillow off the couch. "First, I was like, oh, sweet sucking creature, suck for me. And of course it wouldn't because it was clogged, *again*. Before I came along, did you use to stick your penis in it and let it suck? Is that what happened to it?" he asks. "Maybe it's clogged up with spunk."

I shake my head. "Do you think people have done that?"

"Oh, I'm positive."

"But what would you do when you got your penis stuck in there?"

"I guess you'd have to cut your penis off because there's no fucking way I'd go into the hospital dragging the vacuum after me. I suppose you could walk in and pretend like you were vacuuming the place. 'Don't mind me! Just getting a little dirt! Oh? Why's it attached to my penis instead of an outlet?'"

I start laughing at the thought. "Okay! Stop distracting me. What'd you do to it?"

"I picked it up nice and gently and then I smashed it on the ground," he says, throwing the pillow for emphasis.

"It's broken?"

"Completely shattered, but I'll buy you a new one. Or I could buy you a cleaning boy. I'll make him wear only a thong and tights."

"Why tights?"

"Sounds sexy."

"Your fetish for tights has been noted."

"Will you wear tights for me?" Leland asks eagerly.

"Nope."

"Fine," he says as he walks back to me, straight-faced and determined. "So you're going to be helping them with Hardek? Why didn't you ask me first?"

"What do you mean?" I ask.

"Well... you got to decide that I couldn't do this stuff anymore, so I think it'd be right for you to ask me if *you* should be allowed to. Hardek isn't just some horny husband who is looking for something on the side. He could kill you and not bat an eye. Any of his guys could..." Leland squeezes my arms tightly as his blue eyes hold me captive. "Jackson... I can't lose you. If Hardek got ahold of you, he could kill you. Jackson... please."

I've never seen so much desperation on his face as his words settle. He's right, though. It isn't right for me to dictate what he does and then run off and put myself in danger. I've never really worried about what happens to me, but I guess with me worrying about Leland, it's likely he'll worry as well.

"I'm sorry, you're right, that wasn't very smart of me. How about I help them with the case, but I promise to leave the dicey stuff to them?"

He thinks about it for a moment, eyes narrowed as he scrutinizes me. "*Fine.* You better be good, you hear me? If not, I'm going to spank your ass with a riding crop."

"Okay... and where are you getting this riding crop?"

"Same place I'm going to get a harness and bit for you because you'll be my little horse bitch if you fuck this up."

I snort. "Not where I thought this conversation was going, but okay."

"I'll spank you until you're whinnying just for me."

"Looks like I'm going to be good and not do anything to result in *any* of that happening."

He looks disappointed. "But… I wanted to feed you sugar cubes and wear cowboy boots."

"What else would you be wearing?" I ask, realizing that I might be able to get behind this idea depending on what he's wearing.

"Chaps."

This might be turning out for the better. "Ooh. And?"

He grins, realizing that I'm enjoying the idea. "Nothing underneath it."

I lean into him and press my lips against his. "Sounds sexy," I mumble against him.

"I'll buy a little cart for you and make you pull me around town in your harness."

I grimace at the mental image. "This is taking a turn for the worse."

"I'll rename you Bolt."

"Why I originally thought any of this was sexy is beyond me," I realize. "I think I just got so distracted by the thought of you in chaps that I lost sight of what you really wanted."

"A sex slave," he says.

"And there it is." I press a hand against the back of his head and slide my fingers into his hair as I kiss his forehead.

"So if you need to take a break from the agency… I could work on your cases for you," Leland says.

"That's okay, I know you're busy with school stuff. Mason can handle them *if* he can stop flirting with his girlfriend long enough."

He smiles at me. "Alright, need help with anything else?"

"Maybe starting the grill. Can you do that while I put on something cooler?"

"Yeah, of course."

Leland: That was the day I saved Henry's life.

Jackson: Wait… from what?

Leland: Your vacuum.

Jackson: That's why you bashed it to the ground? Busted it into a hundred pieces?

Leland: I actually wrote a death rap for it.

Jackson: Oh joy.

Leland: *My name is Leland, and this is my tale. There I was all alone, when I was forced to face the greatest enemy known. It said, hey, Leland, I'm gonna suck your fine man's ass—since it clearly had class. So I gripped that mofo, cuz no one was touching my beau. And as I brought it down to the floor, it simply became… no more…* and this is the tale of why you shouldn't stick your dick in a vacuum.

Jackson: I never stuck my dick in it!

Leland: If you hadn't, why did it want to suck your ass, Jackson? Come on! Don't lie to me like this.

Jackson: Do you ever wonder why you're never worried about people? You're never like "Oh, Jackson, who was this man letting himself into your home?" You were like "Oh, I bet the vacuum wanted your dick."

Leland: *clearly pleased by this* It's a tough life being this perfect. And what can I say? It shows how much I trust you.

TWENTY-FOUR

LELAND

I have this weird sense of guilt as I lie in bed. As if noticing, Jackson squeezes me tighter, holding me captive. It just makes me feel more guilty. More and more, I've begun to stretch the truth. Since I was forced to become someone who could talk my way into places, I became a good actor. I knew how to act to get people to see and believe what they *wanted* to see and believe.

The issue is that I've never had to do that with someone I care about. Maybe that's because I've never cared about anyone like I care about Jackson.

"Did you have a good day?" he asks as I run my fingers over his bare back. These past four months, I've gotten to know his body so intimately. I've gotten to know every part of him. He's wonderfully caring. Kind. Gentle. And the perfect participant in my jokes. He also cares too much about what I say. That's why I know that if I tell him the truth that I hate sitting in this house alone while he's at work, it would really upset him. So instead, I tell a little white lie.

"I did," I say. But it isn't a complete lie. The moment he came home, my day became so much better. Because when I see him, I can forget about doing anything. I don't *want* to do anything when he's in my arms. I only want to be with him.

I don't regret my decision to leave my past life behind, but sometimes, my active brain has trouble settling down during the long hours he's at work.

"Especially when you got home," I add.

He squeezes me tighter in response. And I know that I would give it all up again and again just for him.

"I'm happy to hear that."

"What about you?"

"Mine was boring. And Mason was annoying. But the texts you sent me kept me trudging through the day," he says as he kisses my forehead. "I can't wait for the weekend so I can spend it all with you."

"That'll be nice."

His fingers begin to move in a circle on my back, rubbing gently as we fall into silence. It isn't long before his hand stops and his breathing becomes even.

But my mind strays to Hardek. The one who got away.

I've never let a target slip through my fingers. And while I've thought about Hardek occasionally, it was never with much conviction. But now that I know Jackson is going to be dealing with him, I feel uneasy about it.

Gently, I pull away from his arms and get up. I grab one of Jackson's T-shirts and pull it on as I creep from the room. Quietly, I walk to the kitchen and open up Jackson's laptop that's sitting on the table. Then I grab my own laptop and set it up beside it.

I wish he'd let me help him with cases. That couldn't hurt, could it? But I don't want to ask because then maybe he'll start to question if I'm unhappy. Or maybe he'll start to wonder if I want to go back to my previous life. Or maybe he'll think I'm not worth the trouble.

I could never do anything that'll separate him from me.

Before going to bed, Jackson had worked on compiling some notes about Hardek, so I read through them. He's missing so much information. Things I spent weeks searching for. So, as he sleeps, I transfer every note I have on Hardek to his computer and add it to his notes.

When I'm finished, I change the background picture of his laptop before heading back into the bedroom to crawl into bed. I feel a little better now and am able to quickly drift off to sleep.

JACKSON

"This is… why have you been holding out on us?" Henry asks as he waves some papers around when I walk into the meeting room.

"I… have? I didn't think anything was that different than what we went over the last time," I say.

Henry looks at me like I'm crazy. I'd sent him the file this morning through email, but I kind of thought it was just repetition of what we'd previously gone over.

"Are you joking? You never told me the addresses of these places. Especially where you suspect the trafficking is coming from."

I stare at him a moment as everyone in the room stares at me. It's a small team, but I know a few of them just from coming in and out of here. The only ones I don't know are the FBI agents who'd started working with the police to acquire any information they could on the case. Once there was a connection between Hardek and the missing girls, they came in. But after the girls were found, they only left a few behind to work with the police until there was a need for more.

"Oh… that? Yeah, excuse me a moment. I'm going to run to the bathroom."

I slip out and pull my phone out of my pocket. I go to my sent email folder and click the document I sent Henry. I open it as I duck into the bathroom and lock the door. I scroll past my measly information before seeing that there are three more pages to the document that I don't remember putting there. And the *details*.

I quickly call Leland.

"Hey, soul mate. I just bought a new vacuum, please don't stick your penis in this one," he says. It's almost enough to distract me from the other issue.

"Did you add all this stuff about Hardek?"

"No, but I think I saw some mice gyrating on your keyboard last night. Of course I did! Who else would have?"

"Well, you should have *told me*. I shared the file with everyone in the meeting and I didn't read what you wrote."

He snickers. "Oh, yeah… that was supposed to just be for you. I didn't know you were such a sharer. You rarely share with me. I'm like 'let me see your balls' and you're like 'no, it's *my* ball sac.'"

"We were at a family cookout!"

"Eh. Fine. Anyway, I just thought that since I couldn't use the information, maybe you could."

I sigh, because even though this isn't going the way it should, the information is crucial to the case. "Thank you. This is very helpful."

"You're welcome. I get to write a paper now on any controversial subject I want. Mine's going to be on why superheroes shouldn't wear capes."

"You're joking."

"I'm not. It's a ten-page paper and this shit is gonna be good. I'm going to quote *The Incredibles* throughout it."

"Maybe… write about something else?"

"Why hitmen should be legal?"

"Capes. I like the idea of capes."

"I thought you would. Also, I want a puppy. And if you don't get me a puppy, I'm going to get five."

"What?"

And he hangs up.

Now I'm terrified I'm going to come home to five dogs. It wouldn't even surprise me. Not in the slightest.

Once I'm up on all the new information I have to pretend *I* found, I head back to the meeting. I'm sure they think I was in there taking a shit, for how long I was gone. But I dutifully sit down, open my laptop, and stare at the screen.

Henry, who'd been walking behind me, begins laughing. "Wow, I'd say you're a bit obsessed."

My background screen says "Soul mate" in gaudy, sparkling rainbow colors. And then there are about thirty pictures of Leland. None were done with attractiveness in mind, but all were taken by him because I *know* I didn't take them. There's one of him sitting on the toilet looking at the camera like he's mortified. One of him trying to pick his nose with his foot. By the time I reach the one of him curled up in an old doghouse, I have an audience.

"We don't even own a doghouse," I say. There's a sticker on it, so it looks like he crawled into it at a store and had someone take the picture for him or set up his camera.

"This is your boyfriend?" a woman, who goes by LaRosa, asks.

"Sadly."

But there's nothing sad about it.

LELAND

"Guess what?" I ask as soon as Jackson walks through the door.

He quickly looks around for some reason. "Oh no. Please don't tell me you bought ten dogs."

I grin at his slight panic. Maybe I'm a sadist. "No, I didn't. Not yet. I should've." Especially since he left me home alone while I was bored out of my mind writing about why superheroes shouldn't wear capes. I did research by binging some Marvel movies.

"So what'd you do?"

"I bought a vacuum!" This is what my life has come to. Excitement over a fucking vacuum. "It's a robot vacuum so I never have to clean again."

"You realize it just vacuums, right? It doesn't clean the counters or anything."

"Maybe. But I'll hold off on cleaning until we're positive it doesn't clean everything."

He doesn't seem very excited, which is understandable since it's *just* a vacuum. "Great. Come on. Get your shoes on."

"*For?*" I ask, dragging the word out.

"I have some errands to run. Do you want to go with me?"

"Let's see. Do I want to unbox my super-awesome robot vacuum or go on a super-awesome trip with you? I'm going with you. Fuck that vacuum."

"How much did you spend on a *robot* vacuum, anyway?"

"Bitch wasn't cheap. I could've bought a sex machine for that much. You know what... I bet I could make the robot vacuum a sex machine as well as a vacuum. What do you think of me putting a suction-cup dildo on the top? She could be like a little unicorn with a dick for a horn."

Jackson stares at me like he's forgotten how to laugh. Like my comment wasn't even remotely funny. All I know is that I can't wait for his friends to come over again so dildo Roomba can make her entrance.

"Let's go before you embarrass yourself any more."

I start laughing. "Sounds good."

I follow him out to the car and get into the passenger's seat.

"Did you like your background?" I ask with a grin.

His face doesn't even twitch. "What background?"

"Don't play cute with me. You know what background and you loved it, didn't you? Like super loved it."

"Didn't even notice it."

"Of course you did."

"I didn't."

I nudge him with my elbow. "You loved it."

"It took a lot of work."

"It did, but it was worth it, wasn't it?"

"Maybe."

"Did you leave it?'

"Of course I did."

I smile at him as I pat his leg. "Good boy."

He shakes his head, but he's grinning.

When I see the sign telling me where we're at, I grab his leg even harder. "Oh my god. You're letting me get a dog?"

"I will get you anything you ask for."

Not anything. "Fuck. I should have asked for an elephant."

"What would you do with an elephant?"

"Ride it, obviously. Snipe from its back. I'd be a badass mother-fucker with my elephant."

"Isn't the goal of a sniper to be unnoticed?"

"That's because no one's ever done it from the back of an elephant before."

His eyebrows knit. "Makes sense. How about we try out a dog first and see how that goes?"

"Fine."

He parks the car, and I jump out before rushing for the front door.

I eagerly look back at him. "Gosh, you move like an old man, hurry up."

"No, I'm just not running like you are," he says as he catches up and pulls the door open for me. He sets a hand against my back and guides me inside the dog pound.

"Good afternoon," the lady behind the desk says. "Are you guys here to look at some dogs?"

"We are," Jackson says.

She waves to a clipboard in front of her. "Go ahead and sign in, and then I'll take you back."

Once signed in, I eagerly follow after her as we walk to the back. The moment we step into the kennel area, the dogs start going nuts. Each one barks louder than the next until the noise is deafening.

The first kennel has a small dog yipping away. I slowly walk past each one—a pit bull, a mix, a hound—until I lock eyes with it.

Well, that is for the split second its body makes contact with the front fence before rebounding and lunging to the back wall. The mutt leaps off the back wall before hitting the gate again in some type of joyous, overly hyper circle. Half of the time, its feet only touch once right in the middle before hitting the next wall.

Jackson puts his hands on my shoulders before dragging me away. "Don't look at that one."

"Why?"

"*Why?* It's slightly crazed."

No. It's an energetic dog stuck in a small room and expected to behave. I know the feeling.

He takes me over to a nice-looking pit bull who crowds the fence and wags her tail. "Look at her! She's nice."

I look back at the crazy dog who has stopped bouncing off the walls and is now at the fence, front legs pawing at it.

"That thing will tear up the house the second you turn your back," Jackson warns.

I want to tell him that the dog isn't the only thing ready to do that.

"Can I at least see it out?" I ask.

He sighs. "At least it's not an elephant."

I laugh and go back to the dog so I can read the tag. "Cayenne Pepper. Look at that energy," I say as the dog paces the pen.

"Why do you say that like it's a good thing?" Jackson asks.

"Because it is," I say as I kneel down.

She rushes to the front and whines as she stares at me. She's a mutt in every sense. She's red, probably where she got her name, with one ear that stands straight up and a white one that flops down. She has short wiry hair that's mostly red, besides her black muzzle and white paws.

"Can I see her out?" I ask the woman.

"Of course," she says. She puts Cayenne on a leash and leads her back the way we came. Instead of going to the front room, she takes us to a different one with a couch and dog toys. "When you guys are done playing with her, I'll be in that room there, just knock and I can put her back or get a different dog for you."

She slips the leash off her and steps through the door.

Cayenne doesn't miss a beat; she looks between us before running over to us so fast she slams into my legs and nearly knocks me off balance, then she flops onto her back. Since we're not rubbing her stomach fast enough, she leaps back up and does a circle around us before doing it again.

I kneel down and she crawls onto my lap like she doesn't weigh forty pounds. She barely balances on my legs as her entire body shakes with excitement.

"She's ugly as shit," Jackson says as he kneels down. "Literally the ugliest dog I've ever seen."

"I know! But it's like... so ugly she's cute, right?" I ask.

"Eh."

Cayenne leaps off my lap and onto his. She wraps her paws around his midsection like she's going to keep him from moving as her tail whacks me.

My heart melts. "She already loves you. Love her back."

"She's... kind of cute," he says as he strokes her back. "See if she'll play ball."

I grab a toy out of the toy bin and toss it. She shoots off like a bullet, not caring what she tramples to get to it. She grabs it and races back.

"She's skinny," I say as she spits the ball of slobber onto my lap. It leaves a damp impression on my pants. She picks it back up before I can throw it.

"I want to make sure she lets you take it without any aggression," he says as he reaches out and holds his hand to her. She doesn't seem to care—even when he takes it from her, she willingly gives it.

I look over at him as he throws the ball again. "Did you have dogs growing up?"

"I did until I joined the military. Then I had to give her to my parents. I just… didn't get one when I came back."

He gives her a treat from the treat jar and seems pleased when she doesn't eat his hand off. He manipulates each foot, ear, and her tail, and she loves every minute of it.

"Can I have her?"

He leans over and kisses my lips. "I would give you the sun if I could reach it."

"You're so sappy and mushy," I say, like the comment didn't make me overly happy.

"Thank you. I like making you cringe."

I grin and kiss him again. "I'm so excited about my new dog."

Leland: I was so excited to get a dog. I always loved animals, but it never really worked out, you know? Like… I'd often be gone for days or even weeks, and what would I do with a pet?

Jackson: I'm glad. And I know I was a bit skeptical of her when I saw her, but she really did end up being the best dog.

Leland: She's so freaking happy all the time. Imagine being that damn happy every minute of the day. She wakes up happy, goes to sleep happy, takes a shit happy.

Jackson: Cayenne's definitely not struggling in the happy department.

Leland: She's never met a stranger. She loves everyone.

Jackson: You're a bit like that.

Leland: Oh hell no, I do not love everyone.

Jackson: No, the never meeting a stranger thing. You can make a friend out of anyone you look at. You can literally look at the most stubborn human being and decide that you want to harass them until they break down and submit to being your friend. It works every time.

Leland: Besides Ava. *shudders* Then again, Ava isn't human. She's a monster at the very least.

Jackson: I wish I had your confidence.

Leland: Eh, it's simple. Just don't give a shit what others think. And know that even if they still hate you at the end of the day, it doesn't matter because I really only need my fence climber.

TWENTY-FIVE

JACKSON

I'm waiting outside my car when Henry pulls up. Since our meeting spot was closer to my place, I told him I'd meet him somewhere nearby and then we'd drive together. He pulls up and I slip into the passenger seat.

"Thanks for coming along," he says as I shut the door.

"Of course," I reply.

Because we're both nosy, we found a possible lead and decided that instead of waiting until tomorrow, as we *should*, we'd check it out ourselves.

"How are things going with you and your partner?" Henry asks as he drives.

"Good. Leland is such a… breath of fresh air. He's so different compared to the other men I've dated. I've never gone a day where he hasn't made me laugh."

He smiles at me, giving me that "fatherly" look he occasionally uses with me. "Your entire face just lit up. I never thought I'd see the day when your face would light up talking about someone."

I shake my head. "I might be sick."

He slows the car as he laughs. "You're not sick."

"I bought him a dog yesterday just because he suggested it."

"What kind of dog?"

"The ugliest thing I've ever seen, and he already loves it to death. I told him the only rule was that she has to sleep on the floor. Before I even *got* into bed, she was already lying on my side. And even though we gave her two baths, she still has that shelter stench to her. And there she lay, inches from my face, stinking up the bed, but Leland was so damn happy, that's where I let the dog stay."

"I never knew you were a sucker."

"Oh, I am. I'm a very weak man when it comes to Leland."

Henry smiles at me. "That's good. I'm glad you found someone like that. You've focused too much on work lately, so I'm glad to see you making time for yourself."

"Thanks," I say as I get out the binoculars.

The building in question is an old factory that'd been converted into a storage facility. We talk some as he watches it, waiting for something exciting to happen. We're stuck waiting for a while before we see someone moving around.

"Now, I could be wrong," I say as I zoom in on the one guy, "but isn't the guy standing next to the semi the guy who was questioned for being a drug runner?"

"The one we couldn't find anything on?" Henry asks.

"Yeah, that guy."

"It's really far away, but I think you're right… he's driving the load," he says as the man gets into the driver's seat. "What do you think about just… snooping around a little once they're gone? We'll be quiet. The thing is, if I get a warrant and we're wrong, Hardek will know we were snooping."

"This isn't even your job," I say.

"Yeah, but I want to find this fucker, and sometimes I get tired of not taking chances."

Old me would be out the door and running to the factory with him. But I know that I have Leland to think about now. "Alright… maybe. Let me check with Leland. I told him I wouldn't do anything involving the case without checking in with him."

I get out of the car and call Leland's phone number.

"Hey, sugar nuts."

"Hey, babe. Henry and I think we might have found something worth snooping in." I don't want to say much because I don't want Henry wondering why I'm telling Leland confidential things. Not that Henry is good at keeping confidential things to himself. He blabs more than he should to me.

"I have supper in the oven. You said you'd be home in an hour." Leland sounds disappointed, and it makes me want to just tell Henry that I can't and I need to go home.

"I know, and we were going to be…"

He sighs. "Fine. Be safe. If you're not safe, I will bring my fucking machete down and hack the fingers off everyone who touched you."

That got dark *fast*. "Do you have a machete?" I ask curiously.

"I do. I also have an ancient battle-axe that I would *love* to hang over the mantel."

He sounds so excited that I hate to burst his bubble. "We don't need a battle-axe."

"*We don't need a battle-axe*," he mocks. "Keep your nuts safe, boy."

"I will."

"Please."

"I promise."

I want to tell him I'll be safe and that I love him, but I'm always afraid he's not ready for that yet. He's never said it to me, even though I *know* he loves me. But he's not always sure how to express things. I can't blame him since he didn't have an ideal upbringing.

But over the phone doesn't seem like the best spot to do it.

"I'll call you when I'm headed home."

"Sounds good," he says. "Bye."

"Bye, babe." I knock on the window and Henry gets out. "Did they leave?"

"Yeah, everyone's gone," Henry says.

We wait a little while before making our walk over to the factory. Of course the doors are locked, but we find a window that's boarded up. The nails are rusty, so it doesn't take much tugging for the two of us to get it off and slip inside.

Once on the factory floor, Henry turns to me. "You take the right side, I'll take the left?"

"Sounds good."

We start walking and searching. Most of the things in my area are storage boxes that aren't used. But when I find some that are covered, I open one. There are plastic parts inside that I shine my flashlight into. I push them to the side when Henry starts shouting about something.

I put everything back as it was before rushing over to him. He's leaning over a similar shipping container. When I peer inside, I see the hint of a weapon.

"You gonna get a warrant tomorrow?" I ask curiously.

"Oh yeah. I'm going to keep someone on watch to make sure they don't move anything until I can get it."

That's when I hear a noise that stills me. It takes me a moment to realize that it sounds like tires on gravel.

"Fuck, there's someone here," I say as I see a flash of lights.

Henry quickly covers up the guns as I grab the lid to set on top. Together, we rush toward the window we'd come in through, but I see a shadow moving toward it. They shine a flashlight through the open window, so I pull Henry back.

"Fuck. Look for another exit," I say, hoping we can find one before we get caught.

That's when I hear the door swing open.

"They're in here somewhere," a man says, and that's the moment I realize we're fucked.

"Shit... we need to get out," Henry whispers.

"Should we call it in?" I ask, but Henry looks alarmed, telling me that we *definitely* shouldn't be in here without permission.

"No! If they find out we were tampering, we could fail to use it in court."

Think, think, think.

I mean... I *could* call Leland, but... I'll be fine. I can't put him in danger.

That's when the men flood in, and I know that if I want to get out of this situation, I'll have to rely on the Sandman.

I send him a message while hoping that I can take care of all of it before he arrives, but he'll be there as backup, just in case.

To say that Leland seems ecstatic would be an understatement, but I just shake my head and quickly reply.

I hover near the door, and when the first man comes through, I grab him and tear him to the ground as a second comes in. I pull him into a chokehold, worried about doing some serious damage to him or the other guy. He struggles against me, but when I smash my gun into the side of his head, he slumps down in my arms.

I drop his slack body before turning to the first guy, who is now rising up. I'm on him in an instant and knock him out just as Henry stops a third man.

I hear someone behind me and turn, seeing yet more men holding their weapons steady. "How about you let him go and we have a talk?" a man asks.

I let the unconscious man drop to the ground as Henry puts his hands up.

LELAND

I stir my supper around as I stare at the book I'm trying to read, but it's boring as shit. They just need to fuck and move on or I'm done.

Cayenne is staring at me, wishing I'd stir my supper right into her mouth. Jackson is off snooping and being badass and saving the world, and I'm seeing how fast Cayenne can catch green beans out of the air.

This is the life.

I melt out of my chair and slide onto the floor. Cayenne thinks that means she can then stand on my body and crush my internal organs as she stares down at me with love and adoration in her eyes.

"I want to be badass too," I whine.

She wags her tail. She thinks I'm badass just the way I am.

"I want Jackson to come home so I can stop feeling like this. At least I now have you."

My phone buzzes on the table, but it's probably just Jackson rubbing it in that he's having *so* much fun breaking and entering.

My phone buzzes again.

"Fine," I groan as I push Cayenne off me and grab my phone.

> Jackson: I need your help. Immediately. They know we're here and we're currently surrounded. I'll send the address. Just distract them so we can get out.

"Oh… my… fucking BALLS!" I take off running, body overcome with glee. I'm nearly vibrating, I'm so excited.

Cayenne has no idea what she's excited about, but she's just as excited, bounding after me as I grab guns. Lots of guns.

> Jackson: Keep your face hidden and DON'T KILL ANYONE.

Wait… what? I'm supposed to go in and what? Spank their asses? Whatever.

> Me: Your motherfucking angel of death is on his way to reap the souls of the assholes who think they can even look at you with their unworthy eyes.

> Jackson: *sigh*

"I'll be back, Cayenne!" I yell as I tear off my yellow shirt mid-run and yank on a black one. I have five guns—what I'm going to do with them all, I'm not sure, but I'm going to fuck shit up. I blast through the door and run out to my car. I throw everything inside, plug in the GPS, and start driving before the GPS can even tell me where to go.

Semi-considerate of the police that might be lurking, I only slow when I need to make sure I'm not going to get caught. When I near the location, I pull off and park the car. It's in a slightly rural area, where there are no residential houses but a few other storage facilities. Since I'm not allowed to kill anyone, I grab a handgun and my rifle just because I didn't have time to find binoculars. The scope will have to do.

As I get out of my car, I hold the scope in front of me as I pull a ski mask on in an attempt to hide my features. I throw my hood up and start moving toward the cornfield that surrounds the place. The rows make it easy to move and since the corn is still fresh, the leaves don't rustle too much, but it blocks almost all of my field of vision.

I check my phone, but I haven't received another message from Jackson, which makes me feel uneasy. What if something's happened?

When I near the edge of the field, I look through the scope and scan the area. There are four vehicles parked out front. At least three men are currently visible as they walk the perimeter. They seem to be looking for something or waiting for something.

Maybe they're waiting for me.

I could snipe each of them with ease from here, but I'm *not allowed to kill anyone.*

Sheesh. Way to make this harder.

And more fun.

I slide the rifle onto my back with its strap in place and pull out my handgun. I wait until one of the three men go around the corner and the other two are separated before moving forward. Then I make my move.

The distance from the field to the building is about fifty feet of barely any cover, so I'm quick and quiet as I move. The guy pulls out his cellphone and starts staring at it, making me realize that I could have skipped over, and he wouldn't have even looked my way.

Whatever he's doing must be very interesting, because I manage to walk all the way over to him and behind him while he grins at his phone. I step up to him and peer over his shoulder to see what he's watching.

It's a video of a kitten getting scared by a boot. "My new dog is cuter," I say before wrapping one arm around his neck and my right hand over his mouth.

He thrashes, but a chokehold is a vicious thing and he goes down quickly. The only issue with choking someone is that they don't stay down for hours like they do in the movies. They generally only stay unconscious for a brief period of time. Maybe a couple of minutes at most. Which means I only have a few minutes to clear this place out and save my damsel in distress.

I wish he was wearing a dress so I could lift him up and carry him away like a lovely bride.

I let the man drop to the ground and head to the door he's guarding. I *could* hide his body, but I'd be losing precious time. I pull open the door and come face to face with a man who'd been planning on coming out the door. I pistol whip him in the face so hard he doesn't have a moment to even let out a squeak.

The issue is that he crumples to the ground like a deadweight, and I'm not supposed to kill anyone.

Fuuuuuck…

"Hey, buddy," I say as I stoop down. "You're alright, aren't you?"

He doesn't look alright.

I take his head in my hand and make him nod. "Perfect! I knew you were fine!"

And I quickly rush off before anyone can trace *that* mess back to me.

The issue is, he didn't *lightly* hit the ground. He hit it *hard*. And others heard.

"What was that?" someone asks as they come around the corner.

Thankfully, I'm trained in the art of fucking someone up because I'm on him like a goddamn spider monkey. People are always confused when someone suddenly leaps into their arms. Then, when that someone puts them in a chokehold, their brain just shorts out. I ride his body to the ground just as someone else comes to see what the first man yelled about. This guy grabs for his gun, but I'm already too close for it to be efficient. I smack it out of his hand, causing it to go flying and skitter across the ground. I yank his arm down and my knee up, successfully breaking it which makes him holler, and I lose all sense of stealth I'd previously shown.

"Shush!" I snap as I give him a smack.

He's crying now and no longer eager to play as he rushes away instead of toward me. I consider it a job well done. As I turn around the corner, I notice a few unconscious bodies just outside the door and smile at them, proud of my Jackson. I bet he looked ridiculously hot fighting them. I should make him fight people while naked for our next date night.

I reach the door the men are lying near, and when I pull it open just enough to look inside, I see about four men surrounding the man of my dreams.

He even looks handsome tied up and on his knees.

Ohhh, he's *definitely* handsome tied up and on his knees.

I have found a new fetish.

A bullet strikes the door, and I realize that I should stop getting excited and do something about the situation.

So I grab a hold of one of the unconscious men and then set him in front of the door so they can't easily push it open.

While they're busy trying to figure out why the door won't open, I notice a staircase. I head up it in hopes of finding a window that looks out on the shop floor. If not, it's going to be really embarrassing walking back down the stairs. It's dark, so I take a flashlight out and shine the light up the stairs. At the top, I am greeted with the most magnificent overview of the factory floor. There are enough lights on that I can look down and see the men eyeing the door with their two prisoners between them. There are only three men now, telling me they sent one after me. I pull my rifle off and steady it so it's aimed at the first man I want to hit.

I use my handgun to break the glass so I don't waste my rifle on it. Then I take aim and fire as the men look up in surprise. I shoot the first man in the shoulder, the second in the knee, and the third in the leg. None are vital spots, but it sends all of them down.

That's when I hear the fourth man.

I draw back just as he comes barreling up the stairs. His gun fires but misses since I'd moved. And instead of firing again, he plows into me like a damn bull. He sends me flying to the ground on my back. He grabs my arm and tries pinning me down with his leg, but I punch him in the face with my free hand. He pulls back but doesn't let go as he tries keeping me down.

I swing my leg over, hooking it around his neck and driving him to the ground. Then I press my handgun against his shoulder and pull the trigger.

It won't kill him, but it'll put him down long enough I can wander down the stairs and save my bride.

My phone vibrates, so I pull it out to check on it.

> Jackson: Are you okay? We're free and heading back to the car. Please tell me you're okay.

> Me: I wanted to carry my bride out of the building in my arms. Why did you deprive me of that?!

> Jackson: Clearly, you're fine.

I grin and rush down the stairs. I'll need to make sure the two remaining men aren't out and about and that the rest don't decide to fuck with my snugglenuts.

Leland: Tell me how hot that was.
Jackson: It was really fucking hot.
Leland: Am I a badass motherfucker?
Jackson: You're the best badass motherfucker I've ever met.
Leland: Good. That is all. We may continue.

TWENTY-SIX

JACKSON

"Mason did all that? You're always going on about how lazy he is," Henry says as we finally make it back to the car.

This lie I've made up is most likely going to come back and bite me in the ass, but what was I supposed to say or do? We didn't have much in the way of options once the men moved in on us with guns out. They didn't know who we were, they just knew that we were on their property nosing through black market items they were smuggling somewhere. So they captured us, tied us up, and were just starting the interrogation when Leland arrived and put everything on hold.

And I had to explain who the man was that came in gunslinging with a manic grin on his face. It was the only thing I could see through the ridiculous ski mask he wore. Ski mask and all, though, it was weirdly hot. Like *weirdly* hot. I never knew I had a fetish for being tied up and having Leland come save me.

"Uh… yeah? I mean, Mason was a… army—soldier! He was a soldier who was trained to fight. It's honestly not surprising, right?" Right? I'm going to give everything away with my own uncertainty.

"Yeah, that's true. You're just always going on about how he doesn't do anything, so… I'm thoroughly surprised. But thank god he could help us, or we'd be fucked. I'm going to call it in and get some people here. We might have fucked up, but I can still keep them from moving the weapons," he says as he opens the car door. "I'm probably going to stay here, but I can get someone to run you to your car."

"No, once I know you're alright here, I can just walk. My car's not that far away."

"That's up to you," he says.

As he makes his call, I pull out my phone so I can reach out to Leland. I need to make sure he made it back to his car.

> Me: You're still doing okay?

> Leland: Tell me I'm a badass motherfucker.

I sigh. Of course he's okay.

> Me: You're my sweetums.

> Leland: No! Call me badass!

> Me: I'll be home in a bit, babe.

> Leland: I'll ignore you until you call me by my proper title.

> Me: Of course you will.

I look over at Henry as he leans back in his seat. "You can head back to your car. I'm honestly good, Jackson. A bit irritated at myself for being nosy and irrational. But I'm good. Thank you for your help," he says.

"Are you positive?" I ask.

"Yes. Thank you."

"Of course."

"And tell Mason that we owe him."

Oh no. "Yeah…"

I'm going to have to give Mason a heads up. I doubt he'll care since he'd love to take credit for Leland's work. He'd love to "work" without moving from his chair.

I wait a couple more minutes until the team starts to move in before I begin walking down the road to where I parked my car at a twenty-four-hour fast food restaurant.

There's a small wooded area that hides the city from the industrial area that I have to walk alongside first, but it's a nice night. Especially with the moon lighting my path.

That's when I hear a branch crack. I freeze where I'm standing as my hand instinctively goes to my gun.

"What do you plan on doing with that?" he growls as I feel something slam into my back. The hit throws me forward. Startled, I release the hold on my gun as he wraps one hand around my neck and starts dragging me backward into the trees.

His hold isn't tight enough to choke me, but I still can't get away.

"Were you trying to run?" he growls in my ear.

"I ain't fucking running," I say as I grab his arm and yank it from my neck. I duck under it, but he moves into me so I can't push him back. It's clear he knows what he's doing as he drives me forward using my own weight to push me off balance. I quickly regain my balance and slip free.

He growls something under his breath as he grabs for me again, but I catch his arm and pull it behind his back. He's not giving it his all, because when I slam him into the tree, he doesn't fight me. I yank his mask up and bite his neck as he groans.

"You actually think you can distract me? That you can manhandle me?" Leland asks as he slams his ass into my groin.

"I *know* I can," I whisper in his ear as I tug at his pants.

Leland reaches back and sinks his fingers into my hair before roughly tugging my head to the side. "*Oh? Says the man who had to call me for help?*"

"Shut it before I make you be quiet."

"Ooh, I *do* love it when tough boys try to make me do things."

Since *I* don't have lubricant, I assume he does, because who lies in wait for someone and doesn't come prepared? He probably already raided my car or who knows what while I was dealing with Henry. I grab for his pocket when he holds up something between two gloved fingers. "Looking for this?" he asks.

I grab the lubricant but find that he doesn't have a condom.

"I want it raw and hard," he whispers, and all thoughts of safety fly out the damn window. We've both been tested, and even though cleanup is easier with a condom, the thought of doing it like this turns me on even more. As if I wasn't turned on enough by this strange and rough foreplay.

"Stop talking," I growl as I shove him harder against the tree. "If you don't stop, I'm going to make you stop." I clamp my hand over his mouth, but he responds by sticking his tongue out and running it over my fingers. "Did I tell you that you could lick me?"

I pull his head back and suck his throat as I push his pants down his legs with the hand that'd been over his mouth. My cock is hard, digging into my jeans as I settle against his ass. Even though I want nothing more than to drop my own pants, there's something sexy about pressing myself against that bare ass while *needing* to pull my cock free. I tear open the lubricant and run it over my fingers before sliding them between his cheeks. I rub my finger over his hole before grabbing onto his ass cheek with my free hand. I roughly grab one ass cheek as I push a finger inside his tight body.

As my finger works its way inside him, I reach back and smack his ass cheek. He wasn't expecting it, and I feel him clamp down onto my finger. He groans as he leans against the tree, digging his gloved fingers into it as I push another finger inside him.

"You like it rough, don't you, *Sandman*?" I smack his ass again and he responds with a pleased murmur.

"I do," he says as he pushes his ass against me, taking my fingers even deeper. He feels so tight that it's amazing he can even take my cock.

"Did I tell you that you could move?" I growl as I push his chest against the tree, pinning him there. I use my weight to hold him as I unbutton my pants and release my cock. It brushes against his lower back as I work my fingers inside him. With my free hand, I rub lubricant over my cock before pushing it against his thighs. I kick his foot, making him spread his legs so I can shove my dick between them.

"Tell me what you want," I say as he squeezes my cock tightly between his thighs.

He leans back and looks over his shoulder at me. For some reason, I find that it's the sexiest fucking thing I've seen yet. I want to pin him there and just let my eyes run over him as he looks back at me like that.

"I said, tell me what you want," I growl into his ear.

"I want… I want you to call me a badass motherfucker." And the grin on his face makes me question if *this* is now the sexiest thing I've ever seen.

Of course he can't keep it serious.

I grab his hair and yank his head back. "What's that? You dare tell *me* what to do?"

I smack his ass again, making him groan. Then I reach in front of him and grab his cock. I roughly run my hand down it as he presses into me.

"I want your cock," he says as he rests his head against my shoulder. "Deep inside me."

Without hesitation, I pull my fingers free and settle between his legs. I push the head of my cock against his hole, and he groans as my cock slides deep inside his tight body. He digs his fingers into the tree as I grab his hips and pull him toward me until I'm completely inside him. My first thrust is shallow and slow until I begin moving deeper inside him.

He reaches for his cock, but I push his hand away as I keep moving. "Did I say you could touch yourself?"

"You're being awfully cocky," he says as he pushes back into me, taking me deep. It makes him moan and sink into me.

"You're mine to do with as I please," I say as I press his hand against the tree.

"Maybe you're just moving too slow?" he taunts.

I grab his cock and wrap my fingers tightly around the base. "What's that?"

"N-Nothing," he says.

"Thought so."

I let my fingers move down his cock as I kiss his neck down to his shoulder. I want to touch and kiss every part of him, especially when it makes him lean into me. I can tell he's getting closer because he's not being as obstinate and is allowing me to do with him as I please. I quicken my strokes on his cock, knowing I can't take much more myself. He moans as cum hits the bark of the tree, running down it, and his body tightens around my cock. I thrust deep inside him until my own release hits me. I bury myself into him as I come inside his body.

He sinks into me as I release his cock and hold him against me. For a moment, I keep him there, breathing hard as I kiss his neck.

"I could never get sick of touching you," I murmur against his skin as I pull out of him.

He turns and wraps his arms around me. I think I would have held him all night if my phone didn't start ringing.

"I should probably grab that in case it's Henry."

Leland looks delighted for some reason. "Ooh, I might get to save his ass again."

I accept the call, but it isn't Henry asking for help. It's Henry wondering why I never made it to my car, and I'm left coming up with some ridiculous excuse.

LELAND

I beat Jackson home since he has to stop and talk to who knows who about who knows what. Probably about how awesome I was. I have time to get a shower and crawl into bed, but I'm nearly vibrating with excitement and know that sleep is nowhere on the horizon.

When the front door opens, Cayenne takes off barking for it, but Jackson tiptoes his way inside. He must think I'm asleep because he goes right to taking a shower before coming into the bedroom and quietly climbing into bed with me.

"How was work?" I ask as he plugs his phone in.

"Pretty uneventful."

I reach under the blankets until I find him and set my hand on his bare arm. "I heard a super-sexy man saved your ass. Tell me about him."

He chuckles as he slides in deeper until his naked body is pressed against mine. "He *was* pretty sexy, and he *did* save my ass."

I reach around his hip and take a handful of ass into my palm. "Which means this is now mine."

"It was yours before."

I give him a good squeeze to help express my excitement. "I had so much fun."

"You did?" he asks, but he doesn't sound as delighted as I am. "I'm really sorry for asking you to do that. I shouldn't have put you in danger like that."

"Danger? Literally none of them even touched me. I wasn't in *danger*. Who do you think I am?"

"I think you're Leland. My partner and the man I care more about than anyone else. That's who you are to me."

My grin falls. I realize this means he's not miraculously going to let me start beating up bad guys again, but the fact that he cares this much about me pushes it all away. He was worried I would get hurt. No one ever worries if I get hurt unless it'll somehow screw up their schedule or their life. But he cares, and I need to respect that. Cherish it.

I let go of his ass and reach up to his face before cupping it. It makes my chest feel tight as I realize how much he cares about me. "I'm okay, love. I promise." I push his hair back. How could I be so greedy? This man has given so much to me—I couldn't bear making him worry, making him feel regret. "I'm fine, babe. I promise."

He wraps his arms around me and squeezes me tightly. "All I could think about as I drove home is you nearly dying when you were shot. And then I was thinking about how *I* called you and asked you to come. And I could've been the reason you were shot again."

I mold myself against him. "Jackson, I promise I'll be careful. The only thing I can get around here is a papercut."

"Those really hurt."

"They do," I say with a grin as I kiss his lips.

Because everything I did tonight is nothing compared to a single moment with him. And that's why I will not hate my new life. I will not feel suppressed in this house ever again. It doesn't matter. All that matters is that Jackson will be by my side.

Leland: Wow, there was an incubus waiting for you in the woods.

Jackson: There sure was.

Leland: Come to penetrate your dreams.

Jackson: And it just turned weird. Didn't take long.

Leland: Oh, it was *long*.

Jackson: Oh lord.

Leland: And that was what you were a-moanin'.

Jackson: Sometimes I wonder how something so innocent can go south so quickly.

Leland: I can go north, south, east, or west, baby. Any position is the position for me when I have a fine man like you "coming" for me.

Jackson: So today at work I met this really nice guy. He was so… normal. It was weird. He asked me for my number—

Leland: Who do I need to fuck up?

Jackson: Fuck up? It looks like you're ready to murder him! Why did you just pull out two guns? Where'd you pull them *from*? And I was just joking! He wanted my number to send me some pictures.

Leland: *gasps* He was sending you *dick pics*? You know my dick pics are the only dick pics for you!

Jackson: He didn't send me any naked pictures. He's married *to a woman*. It was a joke just to get you to stop talking about… that stuff.

Leland: What was I talking about? Ohhhh, you "coming" for me.

Jackson: Fuck. Next chapter, please.

TWENTY-SEVEN

JACKSON

The turmoil at the factory makes me glad that I'm not involved with the police. While they're dealing with the weapons bust and Henry is trying to keep people from knowing just *how* far we went into the building, I'm allowed to keep sniffing out clues about Hardek.

The issue is that no one really knows exactly *who* Hardek is. We have a name because it's been given to us and referenced by multiple people quite often, but besides that, Hardek is a ghost. He has no identity. No papers. Nothing. He's just a ghost in the wind.

Mason was more than happy to take credit for my "mysterious helper." Thankfully, he's too eager about being seen as a badass hero to question who the real badass hero was.

All day today it's felt like I've had countless puzzle pieces, but none belong to the same puzzle. So when I'm finally able to escape work and go home, I'm thrilled. I used to love staying at work, spending hours looking through case after case, but now I spend the entire day dying to get home to Leland.

When I arrive home, I'm not sure who reaches me first, Cayenne or Leland. But Cayenne is more determined for my attention as she pushes Leland out of the way and dances at my feet. I ruffle her ears before stepping up to Leland.

"I missed you," I say as I wrap him up in my arms. Cayenne, not happy with the length of the petting, tries squeezing between our legs.

"I bought something today," he says as he looks up at me with the biggest smile.

The smile alone makes me worried. "Oh no."

"I know, right?"

"Sex swing? Blow-up dolls? What is it? I'm prepared."

"I want it to be a secret." That's when he whips out a blindfold. Where he was hiding it, I don't know.

"What?" I ask as he proceeds to tie it over my eyes. "Wait... *what*?"

"Road trip!"

"Oh no." This time it's a much more severe "oh no" because I'm honestly worried. Who knows what he has planned?

He starts pushing me backward and out the door. I'm terrified, but I'm also love blind and willingly let him guide me toward the car. It's all fun until something suddenly slams into me.

"What the hell?" I cry.

"Why'd you stand in the way of the door?" he asks like it's my fault.

"Because I can't *see* it."

"Huh. That's strange," he says as he gives me a not-so-gentle shove.

"Get in there," he growls as he pushes my head down. Then, instead of guiding me *into* the car, he grabs my hips and smashes his groin against my ass. "Ooh, look what I have."

"Stop violating me!" I cry as I try to feel my way into the car.

"But this ass is *fine*. We're old friends, dontcha know?"

"This really better not be the surprise," I say as I finally get away from the fondling—that I might have been secretly enjoying—and into the vehicle.

"You don't like being assaulted by my ultra-massive dick?"

I snort but don't want to break his heart.

"Fine, by my boringly average dick." He sets his knee on my thigh, digging it in as he leans into the car.

"Ow! What are you doing?"

"I'm just buckling you in, babe," he says sweetly as I feel the seat belt go across my throat like a noose. I try to believe this man I care deeply for won't choke me. Of course I shouldn't have put *any* faith into him to be sweet and loving because he presses the seat belt against my throat unlike how a seat belt should ever go.

"Don't choke me!"

"It might make you pop a boner, though," he says before I feel something on my lips.

I jerk back in terror before realizing it's his lips.

"You don't like my *kisses*?" he asks as he pokes my cheek with the seat belt clip.

"I do! I was scared!"

"And why would you be scared?" he whispers into my ear. "Scared the Sandman is here to penetrate your dreams?"

Then his tongue goes into my ear. "Dammit, Leland!"

"I'm sorry, my tongue wants to penetrate a hole and it was the only one it could find," he says before snapping my seat belt in.

"No hole penetrating."

"Maybe tomorrow, then."

"Maybe." I try not to grin since that'll just encourage him. He leaves long enough to get into the driver's side, and the car starts moving.

It feels weird having no idea which way the car is going. "I have a few pressing questions."

"I can't imagine what those would be."

"First off, where'd you get the blindfold?"

"I bought it for sex, but it ended up working out really well for this too. Like, I was contemplating putting underwear on your face, but then I remembered I bought a blindfold yesterday and if I put underwear on your face, you'd just be trying to snort them."

"So you were planning on putting *dirty* underwear on me?"

"What? *Never*. What's your next question? How am I so amazing? I really don't know. I can't say it's because of my breeding. My parents weren't much to write home about."

"No, my second question is: where are we going and what are we doing?"

"That's two questions. But I'll still answer them anyway. What do you think we're doing?" he asks, definitely *not* answering the questions.

"I have *no* idea. Like… I honestly wouldn't be surprised if you pulled the blindfold off and we were at Walmart."

He starts laughing. "I promise it's more exciting than that. Like at least a Kroger Marketplace. You know, where they sell clothes and stuff?"

I grin, and for some reason, I remain sitting in the passenger seat with my blindfold on.

"How was work?" he asks.

"It was alright. But I was excited to get home. The Hardek case isn't going anywhere until they're done dealing with the raid, so I just helped Mason on some of the stuff I dropped on him. I honestly just wanted to come home and see you, but as soon as I got home, I regretted it."

He starts laughing, but I feel his hand rest on my thigh. I set my hand on top of his and he squeezes my leg tightly.

He gives me two quick squeezes. "I'm having minor… worries. Like maybe you won't love it."

"I'm sure I'll love whatever you do."

I hear the turn signal, then the car slows down, but he drives for a short while before stopping.

"We're here, but you can't take the blindfold off yet."

He opens the car door and jumps out before coming around to my side. Then he yanks the door open and starts dragging me after him. I warily follow him as he manhandles me around until he seems satisfied.

Then he steps behind me and puts his hands on my hips. The touch makes me smile and want to lean into him. These little things he does make me feel so much for him.

"Ready?" he asks.

"I don't know," I admit.

He starts laughing as he pulls the blindfold free.

I'm not sure exactly *what* I'm expecting, but what I'm given is definitely not it. The house is *huge*, like borderline mansion. I look around, uncertain if it's some type of museum or sex house or something.

He jumps in front of me. "Ta-da!"

"Ta-da... what? Is it a brothel?"

His eyebrows scrunch up. "What?" he asks. "No, it's a house... I'm starting to question if maybe you don't like it."

"Like... what kind of house?"

"I was going to buy it for you. All I have to do is sign the papers, and it's yours."

I look away from him to stare at the four-story monstrosity. "Um... what? How would we afford that thing?" And what would we do with it?

"I'll pay for it. Do you not like it? Is it too much?"

It has *pillars* holding up the porch. There's a pond in front with a freaking waterfall. "Yeah... like three stories too much."

"Yeah, but I already have ideas. The fourth story will be a sex dungeon. I really don't care about the rest of the levels."

"Is that a *swan* in the pond? Those things alone are like three thousand!"

He sighs while looking horribly disappointed. "You don't like it."

I'm about ready to tell him I'll pay for it myself just to get the look of disappointment off his face, even though I don't have enough money for just the flock of swans swimming around. "I *do* like it, but... people will question where we got the money for this house, and we *really* don't need a house this big."

"Most of my money is legal, Jackson. The guy who took care of me... Lucas, the original Sandman, he put me in his will. He was a millionaire. I mean, anyone who looks into me would know I'm a millionaire. I just want to give you something like you've given me. But I don't have... the things you have, so I tried to think about what I *do* have. And that's money. So I'll buy you *everything*."

He looks ecstatic about the idea. But when I reach out to him, his smile falls.

"Too much?" he asks again.

The look on his face makes me want to just grab him and never let go. "Leland, I don't need big houses or fancy things. That's not why I'm with you, and it won't change how much I care about you. I could have nothing, and I know I would still be happy because you make me laugh every day. You make me fall for you a little more every day. If you want a bigger house, we can get a bigger house. When I bought that house, it definitely wasn't my forever home. It was a place for me to decompress from the army until I could move on. Unless this is what you want. I'm not going to tell you that you can't have a mansion if you want a mansion. I care about you so much that I would literally do anything you asked."

He steps into me and wraps his arms around me as he smiles. "I could live in a cardboard box as long as I'm with you. If you don't want a mansion, can I buy you a sports car?"

My interest is piqued. "I don't need a sports car."

"Your body tensed up out of excitement. Let's go buy a car!"

"But… no…"

"I'll buy you anything you want. I do want a sex dungeon, though. Let's buy a house with at least three bedrooms. One for us, one for my sex dungeon, and a third for my child."

"You have a child?"

"Not yet, but I want one I can teach to be an assassin. Do you know how cute a mini hitman will be?"

"Shush, let's just worry about simple things for now. No mini hitmen."

He starts laughing. "Deal."

Leland: This chapter makes me sad.

Jackson: Why? It was sweet.

Leland: I don't like thinking back on that.

Jackson: Leland… why? Did you want the mansion that much? I'm sorry. We could have gotten the house. We can still get it!

Leland: No… I just wanted to turn the whole fourth floor into a sex dungeon and the whole first floor into a gun shrine, but alas… I was only allowed two tiny spaces.

Jackson: **sighs** I know this might seem a bit... *foolish,* but I would think an entire *basement* and a bedroom would be adequate space, you know? Like... if you bought that mansion and turned a whole floor into a sex dungeon, think about how much space you'd have to fill.

Leland: So many Blow-Up Randys.

Jackson: I weirdly feel like one is... one too many.

Leland: Every room would be different. Swings and tables and bars and wiggly things and inflatable things and pointy things and murdery things.

Jackson: Why would there be "murdery" things in the sex dungeon?

Leland: There are murdery things in every room of our house; we can't let the dungeon feel left out.

Jackson: Makes... a ton of sense.

Leland: Imagine if your mom walked up there.

Jackson: Let's not imagine that.

Leland: Think of how many spots the garage would've had for cars for you.

Jackson: Do you... do you think that place is still available?

TWENTY-EIGHT

LELAND

When my phone beeps while Jackson is in the room with me, I stare down at it like I've never seen it before. *No* one texts me besides Jackson since I really don't need anyone else.

I pull my phone out and look down at it from where I'm snuggled up against Jackson on the couch.

> Unknown number: Please call me.

> Unknown number: It's Tucker.

I stare at my phone as Jackson looks over at me.

"Something wrong?" he asks as I tuck the phone back into my pocket.

I lean into him and kiss his cheek. "Nope."

My phone begins to ring, and I quickly silence it. Tucker *knows* not to call this number unless it's an emergency. And even if it was… he knows I'm done. He can find someone else.

"We have to leave in about fifteen minutes, are you ready?" Jackson asks as I try to squeeze myself against him like that can save me from Tucker's annoyances.

We're going out to supper with his parents, at least that's the plan, but my mind is on the phone that won't stop ringing.

"I need to change my pants," I say as I get up and head back to the bedroom. I shut the door before pulling my phone out as it begins to ring again. "What, Tucker?" I snap.

"I need your help—"

"No! I'm done, find someone else."

"I can't, Leland! I was doing some shit… nosing where I wasn't supposed to in Garrison's shit, and I just got a message from him… he's got my daughter, Leland." His voice is shaking. I've never heard him sound like this, and honestly, it surprises me, but I know I can't give in. He'll just fuck me over again and again.

"Find someone else."

"I can't screw this up. I need the best, and you're the goddamn best!" he yells, but his voice breaks in the middle.

Hearing him that way stills me, but it also makes me mad. How dare he guilt me into something when he's never done anything for me? "What have you ever done for me? You were as bad as fucking Lucas. You treated me like shit. Like I was a weapon for you to use. I was nothing to you guys. Why should I risk ruining everything for you?"

He's silent for a moment. "I… I didn't—"

"I was the same age as your daughter when you guys would send me out on hits. And you guys never cared what shape I came back in. It didn't matter how bloody or broken I was, you guys would just send me out on the next hit. As long as I could shoot, you never cared about anything else."

"You're right, Leland, we treated you like shit. I'm sorry… Just… that's how Lucas treated you, so that's how I saw you. But Garrison… he's a fucking convicted rapist. We know he's dealing with Hardek— you know what he'll do to my daughter. Please, I will give you every-thing I have."

"I don't want your money."

"What can I give you? Anything. Please." There's so much emotion in Tucker's voice. I didn't even know the old asshole could feel emotion. I thought he only understood how to be a dick. But even so, he's done more for me than Lucas ever did, and I did a whole lot more for Lucas. But now I have Jackson and… I could fuck everything up. But Jackson *is* going to his parents.

I take a deep breath. "Do you know where Garrison is?"

"I had him tracked to that old restaurant where they gamble."

"You think she's there?" I ask.

"That's where he's living, I think. I don't know where else he'd be keeping her."

"It's an illegal gambling spot?"

"No, it's just for him and his boys."

"Fine. But this is it. Don't *ever* contact me again."

"I won't."

"Send me the address and be nearby to collect her."

"I will."

I hang up on him before sinking onto the bed. I'll be quick. There'll probably be five guys there, six tops. I've handled more than that before. Jackson won't even know.

The door swings open and Jackson looks at me before frowning. "Hey, babe, what's wrong?"

I guess I don't have to fake an expression. "I just have a stomachache for some reason. It started earlier, and I thought it'd go away, but it feels worse."

"We can stay at home."

That won't work. "No! Just go ahead without me. You know how your mom will be if you don't go."

"Yeah, but if you don't feel good…"

I raise an eyebrow. "You really think your mom is going to be happy with you staying behind because I have a *stomachache*?"

He snorts. "I guess you're right… are you sure? We'll probably be late since she's wanting to go to that restaurant that's an hour away."

"I'm positive, babe. I'm a big boy. I can handle being alone."

He leans over and kisses my forehead. "Okay. Let me get you some water and something for your stomach. Then try to take a nap."

I don't know why I love him taking care of me so much. I could honestly fake being sick just to get his attention because I love it so much. It also makes me feel unbelievably guilty for lying to him. I haven't felt this much guilt since I killed Williams. But this is different. That guilt was filled with realization. Filled with regret and fear that I was a bad person. This guilt is filled with emotions. So many emotions.

But I will do one last thing just so the girl doesn't get hurt. So I can return her to Tucker and never see him again. Just one last time.

I crawl into bed feeling like I'm making the right decision. I'm not running off and doing something reckless. I'm saving the life of a girl. I know Jackson would do the same. But I still know I can't tell him. I can't do anything that could threaten this relationship because I'm not sure I could function without Jackson now that I have him by my side.

As I lie in bed, Jackson hurries around and gets stuff for me. He hands me a pill and I wash it down with the glass of water he's gotten me, even though I feel completely healthy besides the little ball of regret swirling around in my stomach. I feel so guilty for doing this to him. But I'm being a good person, right? I'm helping that girl. That's good, right? What if it's not? What if I'm being a bad person?

"Do you need anything else?" he asks.

"No. Thank you."

"I hope you feel better," he says as he smooths my hair back before kissing my forehead. "If you need me, call. I'll come running back."

"I'm fine." I'm not. I'm not fine. I want to tell him everything and stop feeling awful about all of it.

He fusses over me for another couple minutes before leaving, since he'll be late if he doesn't get going. As soon as he's gone, I'm up, knowing that I can't waste a single minute if I'm going to be back before him.

I grab my 9mm from its box, change my clothes, and rush out the door. I put the address into my GPS and begin driving. It's a thirty-minute drive, but I cut it down to twenty-five by speeding on empty roads. I drive by the address and see that it's an old bar or restaurant with blackened windows and a sun-bleached spot where the sign used to hang. It looks empty and is in a bad part of town. I could open fire down in this area and no one would bat an eye or call the police.

Hopefully, I don't have to do that. All I have to do is go inside and grab the girl. If the girl's not there, I'll beat Garrison until he tells me where she is.

Simple.

JACKSON

"Where's Leland?" Mom asks as I step into her house. It's the first question out of her mouth, and I'm honestly surprised by it.

"He's sick," I say.

She's dressed like she's going to church or some other fancy place, making me wonder if I didn't dress nice enough. "Oh... does he have the flu?" she asks.

She cares? My parents have been tolerant of Leland, but so far, they haven't gone out of their way to make him feel like part of the family. I honestly get the impression that they're hoping we break up and I go back to lone wolfing it. It kind of hurts that they would prefer that I was alone than happy with Leland.

"I don't know. His stomach started hurting him, so he decided to stay home."

"Are you sure that's why he's staying home?" she asks.

I stare at her for a moment. "What's that mean?"

"That maybe he's doing something else."

"Like what?" I ask in annoyance.

She shrugs. "He's a very... charismatic guy and young, too. And those gays are said to be promiscuous."

I stare at her in disbelief. "You think Leland decided to fake being sick to stay home so he could what, bring a guy over and fuck him? Did you seriously just say that to me? And I guess that must mean I'm promiscuous too, right?"

Ella steps into the foyer where I'm staring at my mom and debating whether I should just let it roll off or explode. I'm leaning toward exploding.

"Mom, I don't think that's very fair of you to say," Ella says.

Mom shrugs like her comment was an innocent one. "I'm just... saying."

Thankfully, Ella continues on before I explode. "Leland is super nice and funny. Yeah, he's outgoing, but it's clear he tries really hard to get you to like him. And I've known that Jackson is gay since he was fourteen. He just refused to tell you guys because he knew neither of you would support him. Can you imagine having to keep that secret from the closest people in your life until you were in your thirties? But I don't blame him."

Mom's silent as she watches us, clearly unsure of what to say.

"Maybe I'll just go home," I say. What's unsaid is, "Before I say something that I can't take back."

Ella reaches for me. "No! Please don't. It's fine. Grandma is waiting for us." She gently sets a hand on my back. "Let's go."

I hesitate, but I follow Ella out to the car even though I want nothing more than to go home and hold Leland against me until he feels better. Instead, I silently get into the back seat next to Ella as we wait for Dad.

"You know I didn't... mean anything *bad*," Mom says.

"I do?" I ask because I'm tired of just "taking" everything from her.

She's quiet, and even after Dad gets into the car, she doesn't say anything else.

I pull out my phone and click Leland's name.

> Me: I wish I'd stayed home. My mom's being a bitch and I miss you. I hope you feel better soon.

LELAND

Because of the windows, I can't tell how many people are inside. What I do figure out is that the front door is unlocked. Clearly, the men are confident that they're not in any danger, although a locked door wouldn't have stopped me.

I check to make sure my ridiculous ski mask is in order before moving forward.

The front of the building is empty except for old tables still left from the past. I hear noises toward the back telling me that someone is having a good time and someone else is pissed about something. Stealthily, I move deeper into the old building until I near the location of the noise. The door is open, so I walk down the hallway, keeping my body as close to the wall as I can while moving. What I didn't account for is the door sliding open behind me and a man stepping out into the hallway. I step back, but it's too late.

"Who the fuck—"

I grab him in a chokehold with one hand and slam the butt of my gun into his face with the other. He goes down fast, but he made enough noise that the men have quieted down.

"David, what the fuck was that?"

David doesn't say much as I step over him. The first man through the door gets greeted with a punch to the solar plexus. The knock sends him back into the wall as I slip past him and into the room with my gun drawn and aimed at the men still seated around the table. There are five of them, but all look too dumbfounded to do much.

"I just want the girl," I say calmly.

The five men leap to their feet, but I shoot the man closest to me in the hand before he can grab for a weapon.

"The girl," I repeat, in case they didn't get it the first time I asked. "You guys can either hand me the girl or I will not hesitate to kill all of you."

I find Garrison hanging toward the back, relying on everyone else to be bullet shields for him. He's a balding man in his fifties with a beer gut and little eyes. He looks like a stereotypical creeper. Or maybe just knowing what he's done makes me see him that way.

"It's five against one, what do you think you're going to do?" he asks as he gives me a grin like he thinks he has a handle on the situation.

"It's actually four, since one is flailing around about the hole through his hand."

Another moves toward me. Clearly, the man doesn't have a gun, or he'd have presumably been smart enough to use it. Instead, he flicks a knife at me and I shoot him in the shoulder. Like, really? What a fucking idiot.

"That was literally the stupidest move I've ever seen. Did you not see me holding the gun?" I ask.

"It was kind of stupid," Garrison says to the man.

The man has chosen to remain silent as he rolls around, which I feel like is the only intelligent thing he's done.

"Now it's three against one."

I rush into them as one of the men opens fire. I know they'll slow their attacks since their buddies are now in range of being shot in the crossfire. Garrison starts backing up as I grab a chair and fling it at one of the remaining men.

Garrison, realizing that he's currently on the losing end of this fight, decides to flee, but before he can get far, I shoot him in the leg, making him drop down.

"Stop your men before I kill you."

"Fine! Stop! Put your guns down," he cries.

There's minor hesitation, but the men are smart enough to drop their weapons and recognize defeat. I walk over to Garrison, who is trying to get to his feet.

"Where's Tucker's girl?"

"Are you the Sandman?" he asks.

I grin at him from behind my mask. "I am. Now give me the girl or you're all going to die."

His expression changes now that he knows who he's dealing with. "S-She's in the back room," he says.

"And before I gather my reward, tell me, what is your connection to Hardek?"

"I just transported some weapons for him. But not anymore. The police raided my warehouse. So I don't have a connection to him any longer. Please, just take the girl and leave."

"I will," I say as I grab his arm and drag him to his feet. "But you're going to take me there, and if she's not in the room, I'm going to blow a hole through your chest."

His body tenses and I can instantly tell he's been lying to me. "No... please... no!"

"I take it she's not in there. So where might I find her? Or were you planning on locking me in the room and what... shooting me? Starving me? Boring me to death? You're already on your way to boring me to death."

"I—"

I shoot his foot and he screams as I swing him around to face his remaining men. "Let's try this again. Where's the girl?"

"Upstairs!" he cries.

"And did you touch her?"

"No!"

"Hmm... are you sure?"

"Yes!"

"Oh, but how many times have you been convicted of rape?"

He shakes his head.

"You know what? I'll give you an option. Either you can shoot your dick off or I'll shoot you in the head."

"W-What?" he asks in horror.

"It's simple." I motion to the gun in his friend's hand. "Grab your buddy's gun and either shoot your dick off so you can't rape anyone ever again, or I'll kill you."

His hand is shaking as he holds it out. The man puts his gun in it and Garrison draws his hand back. He lowers his gun to his groin, body shaking.

"You better hurry up."

"You can't... I can't..."

"Then I will," I say as I press my gun against his head. "Ready?"

"I'll do it!" he cries, and that's when he decides he'll get smart with me and try to shoot me through his legs. He's not that skilled, so the bullet from his gun goes wide. A bullet from my gun quickly puts an end to that, and he crumples to the ground as I turn my attention to the remaining men.

"Anyone else interested?" I ask.

They drop their remaining weapons and hold their hands up.

"Good, go in that room there, and drag the others with you," I say as I point to the room Garrison tried getting me to go into.

They dutifully shuffle inside along with the injured men, and I slide the table in front of the doors. Then I head up the stairs and use a lock-pick to open the door. When it swings open, I step inside just as something moves toward me. I slide to the side, but when I realize that it's Tucker's daughter, I barely stop myself from breaking her nose, which leaves me open to the hit against the side of my face.

It tears my mask halfway off my face, ripping the cloth and making my eyes water.

I hold my hand up so she understands I'm not here to hurt her. "Dani, stop! Your father sent me."

The girl of about fifteen hesitates as she looks at me with huge blue eyes. "H-He did?"

"Yes. Are you okay?"

She looks shaken up but in one piece, so I grab her arm and start pulling her after me before waiting for an answer.

"Did he touch you?" I ask.

"N-No. He… he told me w-what he was going to do to me. I-I was so scared."

"You did good," I say as I point to the bar she's holding and had also hit me with. It looks like a bar from a towel rack, if I had to guess.

She notices me looking down at it and clutches onto it even tighter. "I hit you. I'm sorry."

"No, it's okay. I stepped out of the way of most of the hit, my mask is just a bit funky now," I say as I pull her down the stairs. Your father's waiting, so let's go."

I try to hurry her through the room, but when she sees Garrison, she hesitates and her eyes get wide.

"I-Is he dead?" she whispers.

"Yeah. He wouldn't listen, so he got what he deserved."

She hangs on to my arm as I push through the front door and step out of the building. "Did I cut you?" she asks as she reaches up and pushes my mask halfway up. I push her hand off before she can pull it all the way off. I quickly readjust it as I tighten my grip on her.

"I don't know where your father is, but he should…" I still, realizing that we're not alone.

"What's wrong?"

I pull her behind me as I lift my gun up and aim it at the man. He takes half a step back, and that's when I realize who it is in the light of the streetlight.

Leland: Well... it sure is a nice day out today.

Jackson: No comment?

Leland: I think it might rain... in seven days.

Jackson: We're just going to comment on every part of our story but this part, are we?

Leland: This one time, I knocked this surfer off his surfboard, and I ran out into a thunderstorm where the waves were crashing and thrashing, and I climbed up on that surfboard and I rode that fucker so hard until I could see my target on a Jet Ski, then I sniped him.

Jackson: You... sniped a man... with a sniper rifle, on a surfboard in a storm?

Leland: Sure did.

Jackson: What about Tucker?

Leland: Never heard of him... her? It? Tucker sounds like an it. Like... Stephen King's *It*, you know? Creepy, clown-like... I once killed a clown. It was right after the surfboard monsoon guy.

Jackson: Now it's a monsoon?

Leland: The thunderstorm was so excited by my sniping abilities, it escalated to monsoon levels! Obviously. So there I was, coming up on shore, dodging lightning left and right while timing my shots perfectly so the gunfire was hidden in the thunder. And there he was... Happy the Clown. He wasn't so happy when I was done with him. Some might even say he was... unhappy.

Jackson: Why was Happy the Clown just chilling on the beach in a monsoon?

Leland: I tried asking him that, but he was already dead.

Jackson: FINE, we will move on.

Leland: Oh thank god, I almost had to tell you about the time I assassinated a woman with a clown.

TWENTY-NINE

JACKSON

I stare at my phone, wishing Leland would message me back. I'm sure it means he's taking a nap, but I will honestly take anything to cheer me up from this horror of a supper.

"I don't know why you're upset with me," Mom says.

I stare at her, not trusting myself to find words that could even be useful in this conversation. Instead, I have visions of myself grabbing her shoulder and shaking her until something happens. "Why's it taking so long to get our food?"

"We've only been here fifteen minutes," Ella says.

"Oh heaven save me," I cry.

Mom sighs. "Now you're just being dramatic."

I should have stayed home and nursed Leland back to health.

> Me: Save me. My mom needs to be strangled. And no, please don't make an autoerotic asphyxiation joke.

Silence.

I hope he's feeling better.

"Don't forget about the family reunion," Mom says.

"Why? Please just let me forget about it," I say, not wanting to spend the entire day with the family while pretending like I don't want to stomp off like a teenager. "Oh, and I'm bringing my promiscuous boyfriend with me as well. I sure hope he doesn't sleep with all the men there or that'll be a real bummer."

Mom ignores me, Dad stirs his food around, and Ella pretends like something on her phone is the greatest thing ever.

Why the hell did Leland have to get sick?

LELAND

Why this man? Out of everyone, why this man?

Henry stands there, staring at me. The man who wants me dead more than anyone in this world.

With the mask on, he won't know who I am... unless he saw me when Dani pulled my mask up. My heart starts pounding as my mind races.

Fuck. Fuck. Fuck.

His expression tells me what I don't want to know. "I'm just helping this girl," I say, lowering my voice.

"Leland... Fucking Leland. It all makes sense... you're the Sandman, aren't you?" Henry asks.

My stomach seizes. "No!" I say. "No! I'm not... I don't know what you're talking about."

"Drop your gun!" he yells, and my stomach seizes.

Fuck. Fuck. What have I done? What have I done?

I've never felt like this before. Generally, I'm confident about what I'm doing, but right now, I don't know what the fuck to do.

I slowly lean over and set the gun on the ground before straightening up. "Henry, I didn't do it. I didn't do anything. I was just... helping this girl." I almost sound like I'm pleading with him. Maybe I *am* pleading with him. I would do anything to make this end.

"Put your hands up," he yells as he keeps his own gun trained on me. He's not like me, his voice is steady as he walks toward me.

I have fucked up. I have fucked everything up. He's going to arrest me; he's going to take me away from Jackson. I'll lose Jackson. "I can't live without Jackson."

"Shut up and keep your hands up!" he barks. "Lower yourself onto the ground!"

I never knew what happiness was until I met Jackson... Jackson is going to be disappointed in me. He's going to know that I lied to him. Why the fuck did I do this? I was done with this job, with this life. I promised Jackson that I was done, and I ruined all of that. I ruined everything.

Slowly, I drop to my knees until I'm on the ground.

Henry moves toward me and grabs my hand before pulling it down, gun still trained on me.

I can't lose Jackson.

"I'm sorry," I whisper as I yank his hand down and thrust my shoulder up, driving him forward. I draw his arm down hard as I loop my free arm over his neck and pull myself behind him. He thrashes and fights as he tries to get me off his neck. He even fires his gun, and I feel pain on the side of my leg. It feels like he barely nicked me, but it gives me the drive I need to squeeze tighter. His thrashing arms begin to slow, and the gun falls from his hand a moment before he sinks into my arms.

I let him drop to the ground before I kill him. I don't want it to come back that I did it.

"Wait here," I tell the girl as I grab Henry around the midsection and carry him toward the building.

"Who is he?" she asks.

"Don't worry about it," I say as she rushes forward to hold the door open. I drag Henry into the building and position him on the ground. Then I go over to Garrison and pick him up. If I shoot Henry with Garrison on the ground, they'll question it, so I hold his body up and point to Garrison's gun.

"Dani, grab that using your shirt. Don't touch it."

She dutifully grabs it and holds it out to me. I take it with my gloved hand before working it into Garrison's limp hand. Then I aim the gun at Henry's head.

This is the man who Jackson respects more than anyone. He treats him like a son and shares things with him a man of the law never should with an outsider.

And I'm going to kill him because Jackson can't know. Because if I let Henry go, I'll go to prison, and I'll never come out. And Jackson will move on and find a good man to love him.

If I kill Henry, will Jackson drag me to the funeral? Will I have to look at the dead man while facing the person I care about most and pretending it wasn't me?

"Fuck!" I cry. "Why the fuck did you have to be here? Why! Why are you so goddamn nosy?"

I drop Garrison to the ground. "Get the fucking door back open," I yell, and Dani runs for the door.

I have so many emotions racing through me that I can't separate between the anger, the hatred, and the fear.

I grab Henry and drag him back through the door. He's too heavy for me to carry, but I have enough adrenaline going that I manage to drag the man to my car.

"Dani!" Tucker yells as he runs for his daughter.

I drop Henry to the ground and grab ahold of Tucker before he can reach his daughter. "This is all your fault! Why the *fuck* did you make me do this?"

Tucker's eyes catch mine. "You saved my daughter... Thank you so much, Leland. Thank you for saving my daughter." His words just roll off me.

"Do you know who that is?" I ask desperately.

Tucker looks over at him before stilling. "The chief of police."

"Yeah, and he knows who I am because he works with my partner. Tucker... I..." I take a deep breath. "Will you kill him for me?"

His eyes grow wide. "W-What? The... the *chief* of police?"

"I saved your daughter!"

He nods even though he's hesitant. "Uh... yeah... I can do that... for you," he says. "Can I use your gun? I don't have one."

I hold it out to him, and he takes it.

"Here?" he asks.

I squat down and grab my head. "I don't know... Tucker... I don't want to go to prison. Why did you do this? I finally found a man who cares about me. I'm finally happy, and now… I've lost all of it." I want to curl up and cry. Curl up and sob. How could I have done this? How could I have ruined everything?

"I can kill him," Tucker says gently.

"No! Just… put him in the trunk of my car, I'll deal with it. Don't ever call me again."

I pop the trunk and Tucker helps me get Henry in the trunk and tied up.

As I'm turning from the trunk, Tucker sets a hand on my shoulder. "I'm sorry. I didn't mean for this to happen."

"Yeah… thanks," I say, not sure I meant any of it.

With a ball of anxiety in my stomach, I get into the car and start driving. I drive to a safe house I purchased some years back but have never used. It's in the middle of nowhere, but I pay to keep it maintained. As I'm pulling into the driveway, I hear a loud ruckus coming from the trunk. Clearly, Henry wants out.

But I can't get myself to leave the car. Instead, I hug the steering wheel and wish I could go back a couple of hours and never answer that call. I would give up everything monetary in my life to go back. Try again.

I know I have to keep moving before Jackson gets home, so I get out of the car before walking over to the trunk and popping it open.

"Let me go," Henry says. "Please, I won't tell anyone. It'll be our secret."

"A cornered man will say anything to get free," I say as I pull my mask off and toss it into the trunk. It's no use hiding my face any longer. Then I grab his arms and drag him out until his feet hit the ground. "Start walking."

He willingly does, but I can see his mind running a hundred miles an hour. He's trying to figure a way out, but he also knows who I am.

"Don't do anything stupid," I warn him.

"I won't."

"Please," I whisper.

He looks over at me but doesn't say anything as I keep walking behind him. I direct him into the house and down into the basement. I lead him over to a chair and have him sit. Then I walk over to my supplies in the corner. I grab the cable ties and duct tape. I cable tie him to the chair, then wrap duct tape over it until I'm positive he can't get free.

"I won't tell anyone if you just let me go. I'll walk away. It'll be our secret," he says, voice gentle and even, like he understands.

"I have a feeling you're going to be awful at secrets." I stare at him as I try to think about what I should do. That's when my phone buzzes.

> Jackson: Headed home from the restaurant. It'll be about an hour and ten. Are you feeling better? Do you need anything?

I have to go. I have to get home. But how will I face Jackson? I hate the person I've become to have done this to him. I turn back to Henry. "I'll be back in the morning. You can't get out of here."

I know from experience.

"Leland, please. I won't tell Jackson who you are. I promise."

He thinks Jackson doesn't know.

"I can't risk it," I say as I slip through the door and slide it shut. Then I slide the lock in place, knowing there's no way he can escape.

The drive home is as torturous as the drive to the safe house. Maybe worse, because I know that I will have to look Jackson in the eyes and pretend nothing is wrong. As soon as I'm parked, I run into the house and get rid of my clothes. There's dried blood on my leg from Henry's bullet. Thankfully, it doesn't need stitches, since that would be hard to explain. My face is red from where Dani hit me with the rod, but it hopefully won't bruise.

I get in the shower as my stomach tries to eat itself out of worry. What the fuck do I do? What the fuck…

Everything will be fine. Everything is fine.

But I know that's a lie. When did I become such a liar? No… I've always lied. It's how I've gotten close to my victims. When did lying start to hurt so much? Especially when Jackson is involved.

As soon as I'm clean, I quickly get into the bed. It's only around five minutes before Jackson comes in.

"How are you feeling, babe?" he asks as he walks over to my side of the bed.

Awful. Horrible. "Better."

He gives me a huge smile. "I'm glad." Then he leans over and kisses my forehead.

"Please lie down with me." I want him to hold me and tell me it'll be alright. That I didn't fuck up. That I'm not a bad person.

"Let me brush my teeth," he says before leaving for the bathroom.

Anxiously, I wait for him to return. He undresses and crawls into bed with me. I grab onto him and tuck myself against him. Desperately, I cling to him.

"What's wrong?" he asks.

"I just missed you."

Everything's going to be okay. Everything will be fine.

Please.

Please let everything be fine.

Leland: Looks like there's a... gust of wind coming at... nine miles per hour out of the... west...

Jackson: Why are we back to the weather?

Leland: With a sprinkling of sun and clouds. Not the pointy clouds but the big ones. The c... cumming clouds.

Jackson: Cumulus.

Leland: Close enough.

Jackson: I'm... not quite sure that was.

Leland: So yep... that is all for the weather today.

Jackson: And what about Henry? You know... Henry's disappearance?

Leland: Um... I would assume he'd have the same weather living so close to us. I mean, maybe it'd sprinkle there but not here or something. We'll have to ask him.

Jackson: Is that the only thing we need to ask him?

Leland: We could also ask him... if... he... likes chocolate. Because I like chocolate. He just... looks like he'd like chocolate.

Jackson: I was more talking about the fact that you *abducted* him and tied him up in a basement.

Leland: Oh, that? That's... something he asked for. Said his wife mentioned it and he was too embarrassed to try it out with her, so he tried it out with me. He's a fun guy like that.

Jackson: I see.

Leland: What do you see? The cloud that looks like a dick? Yep. I see it too. Cock cloud. You know, they say when you see a cock cloud, you're looking at the cock of the gods.

Jackson: I don't even know why I try.

THIRTY

JACKSON

A call wakes me up around six. I see that it's from Jeremy, the officer who has never been fond of me. It's quite strange he would bother to call me. I slip out of bed so I don't wake Leland and step into the hall before answering.

"Hello?"

"It's Jeremy. Have you seen Chief?"

Why would I be with Henry at this hour? "No... what do you mean?"

"His wife called. I guess she went to bed last night, expecting him to come in later, and when she woke up this morning, he still hadn't gotten home. I thought maybe the two of you were doing shit again."

Where the hell would he be? And why would he go out alone without telling anyone? "No. He didn't tell me he was up to anything. Well... he asked what I was doing, but I told him I was dealing with my mom. I never thought to ask why or what he was doing. Is she sure he didn't just leave early?"

"Positive."

"I'll be in. I want to help you try to find him."

"Okay. See you then."

I hang up as I hear the door behind me swing open and Leland looks out. "What's wrong?" he asks.

My grip on my phone tightens. "Henry's missing... he never came home last night. I hope he wasn't sticking his nose into Hardek's stuff."

Leland watches me for a moment. "What do you mean, he's missing? Maybe he's doing something or maybe he's... I don't know..."

I hope. I really hope he's just out, lost track of time and forgot to call his wife. Maybe he was home and she didn't realize it. "I'm going to go in right now and see if I can help."

"Okay." He comes over to me and wraps his arms around me before squeezing me against him. I grab onto him, not realizing how much I needed this hug. "Please be safe," he says, but his voice makes me question if he's worried. Or maybe he still doesn't feel good.

"Do you feel better?"

He shrugs. "I don't know... I haven't been awake long enough to really tell."

"If you need me, let me know," I say as I kiss his forehead before letting go of him. He stands in the bedroom doorway and watches me as I quickly get ready before rushing out the door, anxious that something has happened.

LELAND

I wait half an hour before getting dressed and driving to take care of Henry. I wanted to wait longer. I wanted to never go and never be forced to face what I did. Last night, I didn't sleep a moment, and I still have no idea what I'm going to do with the man.

When I walk into the room in the basement, I find him lying on his side, having tried to escape the chair at some point. He should have realized that even if he did escape the chair, there was nowhere for him to go. When Lucas locked me in here as part of my "training," I also tried to escape. There is no escape.

"Leland... hey... please," Henry says as soon as he sees me, black hair plastered to his head from where his head had been lying on the ground. "You're a good guy. I know you're a good guy or Jackson wouldn't be with you."

"I don't want to go to prison," I say as I grab his chair and pull him up. It takes a good amount of effort because he's much bigger than I am.

He looks up at me with his dark brown eyes. "Leland, listen to me. I don't want to die. If it means letting you go free so that I can live, I'm prepared to do that. You can just walk away."

I cut the tape free from his hands and direct him to his feet. "You spent *years* of your life looking for me. Wanting to see me in prison or dead. You expect me to believe that if I let you go, you'd just walk away from all of it?" He'd walk away long enough to reach the safety of the police station.

He nods earnestly. "I would to protect myself."

"You think that now because you're at my mercy. But when you're free with your mini army of lawmen behind you, what will you think then? You won't even think back on this moment. Now, this is your only chance to use the bathroom until tonight, so you'd better listen."

He continues to try to reason with me, even as he eats, and I tie him back up. But what am I going to do? Keep him as a pet? Maybe I could brainwash him as Lucas tried to do to me.

I suppose I was, for many years. But Henry's not young with a brain easily molded like mine was. Whatever I do with him has to be more permanent. I just have to figure out what that is.

JACKSON

We've found no trace of Henry in the past twelve hours. No one has an idea where he would have been headed or what he was doing. Why he chose to go out alone without notifying anyone is beyond me. I'm sure there's something on his computer or in his possession that would direct us to the right location if we could just *find it.*

"We're finding nothing," Jeremy says as he paces the room.

"Can…" I don't want to bring Leland into this. It was wrong of me to bring him in last time, but this might be the only opportunity I have of finding Henry. And this would be safe. All he has to do is look at

Henry's stuff. "I have someone who is highly intelligent and an excellent problem solver. Can I have him come in and look over Henry's things?"

Sandra, who'd been impatiently watching the analysts work on Henry's computer, looks over at me. "Have we worked with him before?"

"No, but you guys could pull him in as a consultant, like you did with me."

Jeremy shakes his head. "Henry had connections to you. We don't even know this man."

Of course he has to be stubborn about it, so I look away from him and focus on Sandra. "He can at least look at the stuff that isn't confidential."

Jeremy sighs. "Let me talk to a higher-up. See what they think." He hurries out the door and I'm left to stare at Sandra or the analysts while feeling completely useless.

I think they're desperate to find their beloved chief because it isn't long before they return to tell me that I should bring Leland in.

So I step out into the hallway and call Leland.

"Hey," he says softly.

"Hey, babe. I know you're not feeling the best, but I really need your help."

"You still can't find him?" he asks.

"No. It's already six, and we have nothing to show for it. You're the smartest person I know. Please, can you come in and see if you can figure anything out?"

He hesitates for a moment. "Yeah, of course. I'll be there in fifteen."

"Okay. Thank you."

"Of course."

I leave Henry's office and make my way to the front to wait for Leland.

When I see his car pull into the driveway, I head out to meet him. He gets out of the car wearing sweatpants and a baggy hoodie. And when he looks up at me, he's not wearing a smile. I'm not sure he's ever greeted me without a smile.

"Are you still feeling sick?" I ask in concern. I feel bad dragging him out when he clearly doesn't feel up to it, but I *have* to have his help.

"I'm okay," he says, but I know he's lying. He must be feeling very ill to not be ecstatic to help out.

I reach out and gently squeeze his hand. "I'm sorry for pulling you in... I just don't know what else to do."

His response is delayed, but he squeezes back after a moment. "That's okay. I'll see what I can do."

I lead him inside where I take him over to the next in command since Henry is gone. He goes through some stuff with him which seems unnecessary and takes too long. Are legalities really more important than finding Henry? When Leland is finally given back to me, I hurry him over to Henry's office where the analysts are still digging through his stuff.

Jeremy steps in and looks Leland over. "*This* is your consultant? Isn't this your boyfriend?"

"He is," I say. "But if anyone can find Henry, it'll be him."

Jeremy sighs, clearly not won over, but Leland is being quiet, which helps matters. "Alright, how about we give these two the room for half an hour and see if they can figure out anything we missed?" Jeremy suggests.

The analysts willingly leave, telling me they weren't close to finding anything of use. Jeremy looks over at me and nods. "Well... I wish you luck."

"Thanks," I say.

Leland sits down on the chair and looks around him.

"What do you want to start with?" I ask.

"Um... let me just take a few minutes and kind of look over things. I honestly don't know how much help I'll be. I've never just been handed the information before in the form of papers. I'm used to finding evidence in the form of actions and confessions."

I pull up a chair, and even though I've already looked over every-thing I can, I look over it again with him. He's quiet as he works, quickly reading and flipping through the documents before turning to the computer. I'm glad no one is in here to see him work, because he clearly knows his way around information that someone like him shouldn't know.

"We have to find him," I blurt out. I don't know if I'm saying it to him or to myself. I just felt like I needed to get it out there.

Leland's eyes flicker up to meet mine. "We will."

I rub at my face. "I never… told you how I had a lot of trouble when I left the army. I… was struggling with life. I was struggling to find solid ground. Mason talked me into joining him at this meeting. It was for easing soldiers back into society. I told him I didn't need it. I wasn't suffering from PTSD or anything like that. I was just… struggling. But I went and Henry was running the meeting. He helped me find a purpose. He's like a father to me. He's pulled me back into society and made me feel like I still had a reason to be here. And even when I started getting better, he didn't leave me. He's always taken such good care of me."

Leland slides a paper over to me and picks up a pencil. He circles the name of the transportation company that had been moving the weapons. Then he draws a line to another paper with the name of Garrison on it.

"He was looking for a man named Garrison," he says.

I stare at the name for a moment before I put two and two together. "That's the guy who'd been transporting the weapons, right?"

"It is. I'll get you the address of where Garrison lives."

"You have it?" I ask in surprise.

He shrugs. "I have it somewhere."

He pulls out his phone and messes with it for a moment before writing it down and sliding it over to me. "Give that to that Jeremy guy. We'll drive separately and meet them there."

Finally. Something to go on. Somewhere to go. Even if he's not there, it'll give me purpose and make me feel like I'm doing *something*.

"Thank you so much."

He nods, but he still doesn't look happy. "Of course."

I rush from the room to find Jeremy and give him the information. As soon as he takes it from me and gets a team around, I head back to the desk to find Leland staring at Henry's computer.

"Are you ready?" I ask.

He jumps and looks away from the screen. "Yes. I'll drive."

"Are you sure?"

He stands up and nods. "Yeah," he says as we head out of the room.

Jeremy is still barking orders outside Henry's office, so I stop next to him. "We'll meet you guys there. We'll stay out of the way."

"Alright. Let's hope this gets us something."

We head out to Leland's car and he gets into the driver's seat. He pulls out and starts driving.

"I really hope this is it," I say. "But... it's already been twenty-four hours. He could be... would they keep him alive?"

"Would Garrison?" he asks.

I nod. "Yeah, do you know what kind of man he is?"

Leland thinks about it for a moment. "A man who loves preying on the weak. But I don't know what he'd do with a man like Henry. I don't see him killing him unless Hardek orders it."

For a couple of minutes, we follow the police car that's in front of him before Leland turns right, pulling away from the vehicle we'd been trailing behind.

"Where are you going?" I ask curiously.

"Different way."

"Okay."

After about five minutes, I realize that we're definitely not heading toward the location he had me give Jeremy. Was that a loose end? Does he have a different idea? One where he didn't want them to see?

"Where are you going?" I ask, wishing he'd be honest with me because I'm starting to think that he's not.

"I think I know where he is," Leland says.

"Why didn't you tell them? Why give them the other address?"

"They asked where Henry might have gone, and I think that's where he might have gone, but this is where he might currently be."

I set a hand on his leg. "Okay. Thank you so much for helping me."

He glances down at my hand before setting his on top of it. He squeezes onto my hand almost painfully tight.

Jackson: S—

Leland: CHAPTER THIRTY-ONE.

Jackson: Aren't we—

Leland: That was the moment that Jackson burst into the room, clothes completely gone as he took one look at Leland his Lucious Lover and went, "Ride me, cowboy! Ride this stallion! It's the only way to save all of mankind from the invading aliens with their probing green fingers." And Leland was like "Oh, Jackson! You're such a *hunk*." And Jackson puffed out his mighty chest—

Jackson: You're just going to rewrite the entire chapter. And add aliens. Interesting twist.

Leland: You know… it's that or talk about clouds some more…

Jackson: I do see the cock cloud now that I've actually looked.

Leland: Right? I killed a guy with a cloud once.

Jackson: Alright, you win. Let's move on.

THIRTY-ONE

Jackson

When Leland pulls into the driveway of a house, I feel a sense of confusion. Why would Henry be held in a nice house like this one? Yeah, it's kind of in the middle of nowhere, but it just doesn't look like a place someone would hold a man captive.

"I think this might be the place," he says.

"Are you sure?" I ask skeptically.

He nods but doesn't explain *why* he thinks that.

"Okay. Stay in the car, I'll go look."

"Okay," he says, and I'm surprised he's willing to wait in the car.

And that's when he drops a set of keys into my hand.

"Leland… what… what is this?"

"I'll wait here," he says, blue eyes holding on to mine.

I hesitate before turning from the car and rushing up to the door. The first key I try unlocks the door and I quickly move inside. I pull my gun out, in case there's someone inside I need to be worried about, but the house seems quiet and empty.

When I see the door with the sliding lock on it, I open it and look down into the basement. The light is on, so I slowly begin to descend the stairs. When I reach the bottom, I look around, but the only thing in the basement is a door leading to a small room. I try the door handle before seeing the padlock. The second key on the key ring unlocks it. When I swing open the door, I come face to face with Henry, who is strapped to a chair.

The surprise on his face is as apparent as my own. "Jackson! Jackson, please, help me. Please!"

I rush over to him and start pulling at the tape. "What happened?"

"Your fucking boyfriend is the Sandman."

I still, tape in my hands as I look up into Henry's eyes. Everything begins to click into place as I stare at the man in front of me.

"You knew," he realizes, shock coating his expression. "You fucking knew?"

I hear a footstep on the stairs and look up as Leland slowly walks down the stairs and up to the door.

"Jackson, please, you need to get me out," Henry says. "He's a psychopath, Jackson. He's a murderer. Please."

No. No, my precious Leland is not a psychopath.

I turn my eyes to Leland. "You told me you stopped." I feel betrayed. Why wouldn't he have stopped? He *told* me he stopped.

His face is blank as he stares at us and for a moment, I'm strangely reminded that this man has killed countless people. He could swing this door shut and lock away the two people who know who he is. But he would never do that to me.

"Jackson, you need to stop him," Henry says.

Leland stumbles, then sinks to his knees as his expression cracks and crumbles. "I did! I stopped! I promise I did," he cries, and the devastation on his face is enough that I want to push away from Henry and rush to his side.

I want to forgive him even though I don't know the whole story.

"I did, Jackson. I *stopped*. I gave up everything for you. I gave it all up. And I hated giving it up, but I love you so much that I could do it. You don't even understand how much I hate being caged in that fucking house. All day I just sit there, bored out of my fucking mind, feeling like a caged animal until you come home. But I will rot away in that house as long as it means another moment with you."

Does he really hate it that much? "Why didn't you tell me you hated it? I thought you were happy." I thought I was giving him the best life he could have by keeping him safe.

He shakes his head. "I was happy! I *am* happy, whenever you're home. But when you leave… it's really hard for me. But still, I was good! I promise I was good! But my old handler reached out. His daughter had been taken by Garrison and he pleaded with me to save her. Kept talking about how Garrison was a rapist… how he would rape her and hurt her. I told him I couldn't, but… what the fuck would you have done if it were you?"

I would have saved her.

He looks away from me, eyes dropping to the floor. "I got her out, and as I was coming out, Henry saw me. He went to arrest me… I don't want to leave you, Jackson. I can't imagine living my life without you, so I honestly debated killing Henry. I was going to make it look like Garrison did it and then we could be together, but I couldn't do it… I couldn't kill an innocent man, so I brought him here. But then you wouldn't stop talking about how much he meant to you… I'm so sorry. Please, please forgive me." His voice breaks and it makes my chest hurt.

It's at this very moment that I realize I'm about to lose the man I love. And it all makes sense why Henry is here. If I let Henry go, Leland will go to prison for life, and I'll never be free with him again.

I can't lose Leland.

"Why didn't you run?" I ask. "When I went in the house, you could have left."

"I planned to. But I can't leave you."

I nod, knowing I couldn't leave him either. "Then we'll run together. I'll call someone in to free Henry later. We can run together."

Leland's eyes hold on to mine. "Jackson… I can't have you go to prison for what I've done. This is my sin to live with, not yours."

Then something hits me. "Wait… but you didn't even kill Henry's partner! You didn't even kill Williams! Tell him the truth! That the man who raised you did it."

Leland shakes his head, and I'm terrified of what he'll say. "I killed Williams."

"What? But you told me you didn't…"

"See? He's a liar!" Henry says, but I want him to be quiet. He might have lied to me, but I know that Leland would never lie without a reason for doing so. The Leland who is on his knees, absolutely devastated, is not the type of man to lie for his own benefit.

"I did lie when I didn't yet know you. Williams… Henry, before you arrest me, can I tell you my side of the story?" Leland asks as he stares at the man still tied to the chair.

Henry nods, even though he isn't given much choice. "Okay."

"I was taken in by the original Sandman. His name was Lucas Phillips. If you looked into me, you know he's the man who gave me all the money in his will. He took me in when I was young because I accidentally killed a man who tried to molest me. I'd been living on the streets at the time, and here was this man who told me he would keep me from going to prison after what I did.

"He took me home and instead of giving me a life to live for, he made me into a monster. He was just as abusive as everyone I'd run from, but it was a different kind of abuse. He knew how to talk me into things. He knew how to make me want to please him. And as the years progressed, he molded me through mental abuse until I was the perfect little hitman for him. And for some fucked-up reason, I stayed. Even after I was a better shot than him and a better fighter than him. I stayed because… I thought I meant something to him. But I didn't. He'd send me out to do things without caring whether I'd come back alive. I was a toy and if the toy broke, he'd just find another one. I was still carrying on this… sense of being a good person, though. I wanted to be like the superheroes in the books. Save people who needed to be saved. Kill one to save a hundred. And that's what I thought I was doing.

"That was until Williams. Lucas told me Williams was a corrupt cop. He spun these tales of the women and children he hurt. Of the people he illegally imprisoned and killed. And I believed him. Then he sent me off to kill him. He already had the note written up that I would leave with his body, and I realized later that it wasn't for Williams or the cops that would find him, it was to fool me. To make me think he really was a bad guy. So I shot Williams because of those lies, but something he said as he was lying there bleeding to death got to me. It was simple: 'He's lying to you.' At first, I thought it was just... a dying man's last attempt at life, but it hit me so fucking hard. It was like a blow I needed to wake me up. And for the first time in a long time, I felt so much guilt. I remember falling to my knees as those words left his mouth. And I tried to save him, but I was always too good of a shot. As I leaned over the man, compressing his wound while covered in his blood, something... changed inside me. It was like... I realized at that moment that I hadn't left an abusive life for a better one. I'd left one abusive life to join another.

"Williams died within a couple of seconds, but I held his wound for at least an hour. And then I got up, cleaned myself up, and went home. Lucas was proud of me. So proud of me. He praised me and treated me like I was worth something. But when I started digging into Williams, I learned that the cop wasn't corrupt. No... Williams was close to uncovering exactly who the Sandman was, and Lucas was terrified that Williams was going to put him in prison.

"The issue is, Lucas created a monster. A monster who was stronger than him. A monster who he abused and never cared for. It didn't take me long before I planned exactly what I was going to do to him. And I killed him. I promise that I have never killed another innocent man since the day I killed Williams. But I still understand that I killed him. I don't feel guilty for any of the other men I've killed. The only one I still wear guilt for is Williams. While I can't bring life back, I'm excellent at taking it away. And I don't feel guilty for that.

"Last night, I killed a man who would have raped a girl of fifteen because he believes it's his right to ruin that girl's life. I gave him a choice, but men like that only care about themselves. I told him he could shoot his dick off so he couldn't rape again, or I would kill him. And I was shown again that people like him *don't* deserve to live. If the police caught him, they would take him to the prison and give him a warm bed and food, and then what? Why should he get that while his victims are left living with what he's done to them?

"I know and I acknowledge that what I did to Williams was wrong, but you cannot *ever* force me to believe any of the others that I killed were wrong. They deserved to die. And I knew how to do it."

There's so much honesty in his voice that I can't even find it in myself to blame him for any of it. But while I love Leland and know that he's a good person, that doesn't mean Henry will. Yes, I feel upset that he lied to me, but I know that he believed it was in his best interest. If I'd known that he had killed Williams, would I have been as willing to let him into my life?

I might not have. And I never would have seen how amazing of a person he is.

We'll definitely have to have a *talk* about all of this, but if I have to decide between being mad and losing him for the rest of my life or being upset that he lied, but understanding why, then I know what I'll choose.

Leland

I look between the two men, honestly unsure of what else to say. "I know it doesn't help, but I truly am sorry for all the pain I caused. I've lived with the guilt for many years. But I was a seventeen-year-old who thought every word Lucas spoke was to be obeyed."

I find that I honestly only care what Jackson thinks of me. Yes, I feel guilty for what I've done to Henry, but if Jackson left me or if I had to leave him…

Jackson takes a deep breath before turning to Henry. "I'm going to go with Leland… I'll call someone in a couple of hours to let you go."

My stomach clenches as I stare at him in disbelief. "You'd still go with me?"

Jackson's eyes catch mine. "I would."

It makes me overwhelmingly happy, and I feel like we've suddenly thrown all our emotions out before us. Like something had been holding us back before, keeping us just out of reach of each other, but now… now we truly understand each other. "Thank you, but I can't let you do that. I would run… I thought about running, but if I ran, I'd never see you again. At least… if I go to prison, you'll visit me, right?"

He shakes his head. "I won't let you go to prison. I'll do everything I can to make sure that you never do. Henry, please… you run a group dedicated to helping others. You've helped me so much. Please… extend that kindness to Leland. I beg you."

"He's not a soldier, he's a killer," Henry says.

"But he can do so much good. You know it. You've been in this life long enough to know that the bad guy doesn't always get what he deserves. You've come to me when men walk away with a smile on their face even though you *know* they deserve to rot in prison," Jackson says.

That's when I get an idea. I stand up and walk over to Henry before kneeling in front of him. "Let me stop Hardek. It won't make up for what I've done to you, but let me do this. And then, if you still think I deserve to rot in prison, I will walk with you right to the front door."

Henry watches me closely. "You'll run."

"I could run at this moment, yet I haven't. Let me do this. Let me keep more girls from being abducted. Let me save the people that would die by his weapons. Let me at least try to do that," I say.

Henry is silent as he watches me, but I can tell he's thinking. Honestly, I'm surprised he didn't immediately agree, then as soon as we let him go, call the police on me. Maybe this means he really might let me walk.

"Henry, please. I know Leland is a good person. I know you've already done so much for me, but please do this for me," Jackson says.

Henry's quiet as he thinks about what to say.

"Henry, I've never needed anything as much as I need Leland. I don't... I know it's hard for you to trust him or believe him after what happened. But you've known me for quite a few years, and I know you've helped me time and time again, but I need you just one more time. I need you now more than I ever have."

"Jackson, he's a *killer*."

"But that's not all he is! He's a wonderful person who makes me laugh every day. Who treats me better than I thought anyone would ever treat me. Henry... I'm willing to give up everything for this man; that should tell you how far I'd go to protect him."

"What if he's lying again? He lied to you here."

"I know he did, and that hurts, but I know that he did it because he thought he was doing the right thing. Please... just... give us a chance. You know who he is now. If he messes up, you could have the entire police force searching for him."

Henry turns to me. "Since you've lived with Jackson, how many people have you killed?"

"Just Garrison… and I might have accidentally killed one when helping you guys." Henry gives a start as he realizes that it was me at the warehouse and not Mason. "I hit him too hard because he surprised me. But if I did, that's on you guys. Honestly, you didn't see the cameras as you went waltzing in? It was even apparent that they're motion activated. How you two accomplish anything is beyond me. You were like two horny bulls busting through looking for the ladies."

Jackson grimaces. "We might have missed some… minor details. But in *my* defense, those cameras were triggered by Henry. Even though he's chief and supposed to bark orders and not break into places."

"I hate sitting behind a desk," Henry says. "I miss being out in the field."

Oh, do I know that feeling. "So do I! We can be field buddies if you like. I'll even hold your hand if you need guidance. Which you clearly do so that you don't run in front of motion-activated cameras."

Henry sighs. "Alright. Do *not* make me regret this. If you fuck up even the tiniest bit, the police will find you."

"Stripper police or real police?"

Jackson gives me *the eye* like I should be serious. But I can't. I'm overfilled with happiness that he cares enough about me that he would give up everything for me.

"They'll throw you in prison for life," Henry warns.

"M'kay." I crawl the two feet over to Jackson and wrap my arms around him. "I think you might love me."

"I do love you," Jackson says.

I'm startled still. I'd been joking around, but… does he really love me? "You do?"

Jackson, who'd apparently been thinking about freeing Henry, who looks like he'd really enjoy being free, turns to me. "Of course I do."

"I love you too. Henry, do you want to be my best man at our wedding? Or you can walk me down the aisle since my father's in prison and if I ever saw him, I might punch his face in and break our promise to never hurt someone."

Jackson sighs. "We're not getting married—"

"Yet," I remind Jackson. "I'm going to name our daughter—"

"Is he always like this?" Henry asks.

"Unless he has a gun in his hand, his brain doesn't work right."

I grab Jackson's face in my hands and kiss his unresponsive lips. They're probably unresponsive because I'm squishing his face while drawing it close to me. "My brain always works unless you're in the room. Then the love I feel for you turns my brain to mush. Romantic love mush."

"This is who you were prepared to throw your life away for?" Henry asks skeptically.

"I promise he's not actually insane… he just acts that way."

"I love that within the same two minutes of telling me that you love me, you tell me that I act insane," I say.

He pulls my hands off my face and gives me a smile. "That's how you know this is true love. I'm to the stage in our relationship that I'm brutally honest."

"What else do you want to be honest about?"

"Those purple pants you own are hideous."

My grin widens. "I'll wear them to our wedding where Henry will walk me down the aisle."

"Are you… are you sure he's the Sandman? Like… I think he might be pulling your leg," Henry says.

"I know, right? But he has these notebooks filled with all this genius-level stuff."

"Why are y'all acting like this is surprising?" I ask sourly as I take the knife from Jackson since it's clear he likes his supposed buddy all tied up. Maybe it's a kink for him. A kink I can definitely get behind. Or in front of.

I cut Henry free and he quickly stands up while rubbing his wrists. "So you will forget that I'm the Sandman, and I'll try to forget I saw your penis." I hold my hand out, confident that this was a good enough exchange for a handshake.

"What?" Jackson asks. "How'd you see his penis?"

"I had to take him to the bathroom where I had to keep a close eye on him to make sure he wasn't up to anything."

Jackson glares at me. "You didn't have to look at his groin while doing that."

"There was nowhere else to look, Jackson! It took up so much space. I was like 'look away!' but even the shadow of it was shocking. I started calling it Godzilla, and then—"

Jackson sighs. "Please tell me none of this actually happened."

"I now understand why you told me to put Godzilla back in my pants," Henry says.

"I'm really sorry," Jackson says, for some reason.

"That he has a huge dick? Nah, baby, people *like* big dicks," I say as I pat Jackson's arm.

"I was apologizing that he had to deal with you."

I smile at the naive man. "Everyone loves me. You just said it yourself. I'm glad we're all friends now. We might have started off the day with a minor misunderstanding, but we'll end the day as best friends, Henry."

"Leland... while I think you were originally on the right track to keeping yourself out of prison, you've begun to redig your grave," Jackson warns.

"He... He did just compliment my dick," Henry says.

Jackson stares at Henry like he's never seen the man before. Like he's an alien.

"Stockholm syndrome," I explain to Jackson.

Jackson nods like he understands. "It really can be the only reasonable explanation."

"I'm sure my wife is worried sick about me, so is it okay if we get going?"

I nod, but Jackson seems uncertain. Before Henry can slip past, Jackson puts a hand against his chest and stills him.

"Henry, please... I've never cared about anyone as much as I care about Leland. I've lived my entire life feeling like I never fit in. I was never the person my parents wanted, and I had to be a different person than the army wanted. Even when I came back, I felt like if I just buried myself in work, I could stop worrying about what kind of person I should be. But since Leland came into my life, he's made me feel like I don't need to worry about that. I just need to be myself. Nothing else matters."

Henry reaches out and sets a hand on Jackson's shoulder. "The main reason I'm letting that man walk is you. I'm not even sure you've realized how much happier you've been since he moved into your life. And that tells me that even if it goes against everything... every *single* part of me, that he must be a good person to make you so happy. Let me pray that neither of us is wrong." Henry looks at me. "Do you understand?"

"I don't know, I just got so unbelievably happy after you said that *I* made Jackson happy that you could tell me to do anything at this moment and I would do it," I admit.

"Are you sure that's the badass Sandman who can snipe someone farther than I thought was humanly possible?" Henry asks.

No wonder he's concerned, because I'm currently smiling like we're all involved in the weirdest Hallmark movie ever created. "It's all so sappy and I love it so much."

"He has a few quirks, but he really does make me happy, and I know that he's a good person... well, at least a decent person."

"Okay."

"Okay," Jackson repeats, and he steps out of his path. "Let's go."

I don't think I walk a step back to the car. Instead, I float on pure happiness. Who knew how well this disaster would turn out? Maybe I should start abducting and tying up people more often. Jackson's mom would be the next on my list. She needs a severe attitude adjustment.

Jackson takes us back to the station where we part ways so he can deal with Henry and I can take the car home. The farther I get from Jackson, the more I wonder if this is all a ploy so that Jackson isn't there when they arrest me. Now that he's not by my side, small insecurities and anxiety creep back in as I pull a chair up to the window and wait for his return. Thankfully, Cayenne crawls onto my lap and gives me some comfort, even if she's not meant to be a lapdog.

JACKSON

I'm dying to leave, but I know that I have to stay to keep things some-what smoothed over. Especially since we sent the team off to find Garrison, who they found dead, and I brought back Henry from some other place.

After about an hour, I'm allowed to leave. The entire drive home, my mind is filled with information Leland gave us. But it's also filled with fear. Someone else knows who Leland is, someone who has spent years wishing to find and capture him. Henry could ruin everything in merely a moment.

When I pull into the driveway, I park beside Leland's car before rushing for the front door.

I pull it open and find Leland waiting there. Before I can do anything, he dives into my arms, grabbing onto me painfully tight. He squeezes me to him as he buries his face against my shoulder.

"I'm so sorry. Please, please forgive me. I didn't know what to do, and I made a mistake and it was such a stupid mistake. I told Tucker to never call me again no matter what happens. I thought you were going to hate me."

I wrap him in my arms, startled by the quake in his voice. He's always so strong and sure about everything, but maybe he's just as weak about me as I am about him. It makes sense. While my family hasn't always supported me, they've always been there for me. He's never had that. "I could never hate you, Leland." I let my fingers slide down his back. "I don't blame you for saving the girl. If you'd have talked to me about it, I would have helped you."

"No, you would have insisted on doing it alone. I was so scared you'd hate me about Henry. I was terrified I would have to leave you." He looks up at me and I realize that his eyes look watery.

When a tear falls down his cheek, I reach up and wipe it away with my finger.

"What are you doing?" he says as he tucks his head against my shoulder. "I'm not crying. I'm too manly to cry."

"You're very manly by showing emotions. Anyone who says that showing emotions is not masculine is an idiot."

"They're idiots. And I only care about what you think, now. And if you think it's manly for me to cry then I might be sobbing because I was so fucking scared, Jackson. And I feel so stupid for having lied to you."

"I'm upset you lied to me, of course I am, but I also know that you thought you were making the right choice by lying. What did you think would happen if you told me the truth that you weren't happy in the house doing nothing?"

"I don't know. Now it feels so stupid, but I thought you would be upset... that you'd think I would leave you and go back to being a hitman. That you'd realize I wasn't worth all of this. I've never had anyone like you, and I'm so terrified of fucking it up and losing you that I fucked it up anyway."

"You haven't fucked anything up, but you have to promise me that you'll never lie to me again. There can only be truths between us from now on. Understood?"

He nods. "I do. And I promise I won't."

"I'm sorry for keeping you locked up in this house. I... I didn't know you hated it so much. And hated not being able to do the things you used to... you always act so happy that I thought you really were happy."

He tightens his grip on me. "I am happy here! I'm happier than I've ever been... but I also feel caged in. Like I can't... move or go anywhere. I want to be out there. I want to help. I want to do something."

"I'm sorry. I was more worried about keeping you safe than thinking about any of that. If I really thought about it, it was clear you wanted to help me with cases or clients. You're phenomenal at it... it was just... every time, I'd think about you in that hospital bed and the possibility of losing you and I would get this sense of panic. But I also want you happy. So what if you start working at the agency with me?"

He pulls back and looks up at me as he wipes at his eyes. "Yes! I will condemn all the rotten men and send them to the depths of hell!"

"Or... you could just, you know... tell their wives that they're cheating."

"Sounds boring. I'll leave that stuff to you guys. I want danger, adventure, theft, murder—"

I smile at him. "You're going to be *very* disappointed."

"If you're by my side, nothing can disappoint me."

"That's a lot to live up to."

"Not even when you're old and can't get it up anymore."

"I'm not old."

"You'll be in your forties dating someone in their twenties. What a creep."

"I'm starting to regret saving you."

His eyes go wide like I was actually serious. "No! Don't regret my love!"

I kiss his forehead. "Fine. I'll put up with your crazy antics if I *have* to."

He squeezes me tightly. "It's a requirement."

Requirement or not, I know that I'll always go along with anything he does.

Leland: And they all became the best of friends.

Jackson: Did they?

Leland: Like best friends in the whole world. You know… Henry did cave much quicker than I expected. I bet it's my charismatic attitude.

Jackson: Could be. Or could be the fact that he was frustrated by so many people getting away with things and he finally found a way to make them pay.

Leland: No, no. Totally my charisma. I'm like level OP in charisma. If I was a D&D character, I'd be chaotic neutral, with high stats in Badass Motherfucker and Charisma. And atrocious in things like Patience or Reading the Room.

Jackson: I don't think those are levels in D&D.

Leland: They are in my D&D: Dungeons and Dicks.

Jackson: Oh wow, that's definitely different than the game I remember playing as a kid.

Leland: Oh yeah, only an exclusive group can play Dungeons and Dicks. I'll let you play if you want.

Jackson: I'd love some clarification. Are we... fighting dicks? Like is that the main enemy?

Leland: No, that's what we're fighting with.

Jackson: Like... with our own dicks?

Leland: No, the dicks of our enemies.

Jackson: Are we... hacking them off?

Leland: No, you heathen. They're still attached.

Jackson: You will go to *any* extreme to avoid talking about this Henry thing, won't you?

Leland: The weather looks pretty nice... there's a chance of sun in an hour... that'll be fun.

Jackson: Just go back to talking about your Dungeons and Dicks. That was at least fun.

THIRTY-TWO

JACKSON

As I walk into the meeting room with a nearly bouncing Leland by my side, I begin to wonder if I've made a mistake.

"Don't forget our talk," I whisper.

"What talk and why are we whispering?" he asks as we step into the room.

I sigh because I *know* he knows what talk. "The talk where you decided to be good and quiet and just listen, almost like you aren't here at all."

"Hmm… Definitely don't remember any of that talk. Was that when I distracted you with my penis?"

He has found my weakness. "Yes."

"Ah. Well… don't remember any of that. Just remember you saying something like, 'Wow! What a mighty tool you're wielding!'"

"None of that happened."

Before Leland can say more, Henry comes in and sees him. He looks as apprehensive as I feel. "What's he doing here?"

"I missed you," Leland says with a huge smile as if he actually missed the man. "So much."

"I thought you wanted Leland's help," I say.

"I'm already regretting it," Henry says.

Leland gives him a not-so-innocent smile. "I'm going to be perfect." Then he heads over to find a seat. Before I can direct him anywhere, he picks a seat next to Jeremy.

I rush over before he can ruin anything.

"Hi, I'm Leland," he says.

Jeremy looks at him. "We've met."

"Huh… I vaguely remember that. Were you in that porno they wanted me to do a couple of years ag—"

I slide Leland's chair over with Leland in it. Then I push a chair between Jeremy and Leland so I can create a nice blockade since Jeremy already dislikes me. We *really* don't need Leland adding fuel to the fire.

"Shhhh…" I coax Leland.

Leland is grinning. "I'm so excited to be here."

"Don't be *too* excited."

He turns to his neighbor on the right. "Hi! I'm Leland."

She smiles, not caring that he was talking about pornos just because he has a charming smile. "Hi, I'm Jennifer."

"You're going to *love* working with me because unlike Jackson, I make things fun *and* get work done."

"How about you stop introducing yourself?" I suggest.

"Shhh," he says, clearly mocking me. "Jennifer and I have a thing going, don't we Jenny?"

She gives him a smile. The kind of smile someone gives when they realize that they don't care what the other person is saying, because they would like to fuck them.

Thankfully, Henry saves the day by walking up to the front of the room, which grabs Leland's attention.

"Alright, we have a new consultant working with us who can hopefully give us some more insight. This is Leland," Henry says as he halfheartedly motions to him.

Leland is ecstatic.

"Isn't that the guy from your computer's background?" Ronnie asks.

"Sadly."

After we're finished with the meeting, we head to the agency to do some research. When we reach the agency, Mason is there "working" on something. I'm not sure if there is a difference between working or texting his girlfriend. All I know is that I've really never seen him grin this much about anything that has to do with work.

"Mason!" Leland calls like they're long-lost buddies.

"Hey, handsome!" Mason says as Leland rushes over to greet him. Mason even puts down his phone long enough to converse with him.

"Guess what! I'm moving in!" Leland says.

Mason leans back in his chair. "Jackson told me that! You can have his desk. He rarely uses it anyway."

Hold on... "Wait a minute, I'm the only one here that actually works!"

Leland walks over to my desk, clearly not hearing me at all. "Mason, we could be desk mates. Sorry I can't be your soul mate, I already have one, but desk mates is open."

Mason laughs. "I like that."

I sigh as I realize that I've given Mason another excuse to not do anything. "I'll go downstairs and see if I can borrow a spare chair," I say as Leland peers down at the files I have spread across my messy desk. I don't really want to use the client's chair in case we need it.

Leland nods. "Okay! Mind if I move some of this?" He waves at the mess on my desk.

"Yeah, you can move it all."

I head downstairs and find Rose sleeping behind her desk. She's forgotten to switch the sign from Closed to Open. Not wanting to wake her, I head over to a stray chair and grab it. I carry it up the stairs only to find Leland nestled right in my spot.

"I brought you a chair," I say as I scoot it up against my desk that already looks remarkably clean. He's basically taken all of my papers and piled them up into a wavering tower of paperwork.

Leland looks down at the chair apprehensively. "Oh… honey… that looks really hard."

"Yeah, it's wooden."

He grimaces. "Hmm… yeah… My butt might get sore and then we could never have sex again," he says, like that's a thing. Like it isn't the stupidest excuse I've ever heard.

Mason snorts as I stare at Leland.

"I don't think the chair is planning on fucking you," I say sarcastically.

Leland leans forward with wide eyes. "If it *was*, I would be on top of it so fast, but alas. It's just a hard wooden chair."

I sigh as I look down at the chair. "Do you want me to sit in the *hard* wooden chair?"

He innocently nods.

"Of course you do."

I sigh again. As long as we get some work done, I suppose it doesn't matter. As soon as I sit down, I open up Amazon and start searching for comfortable chairs because there is *no way* I'm using this chair.

Leland: I was immediately accepted, Jackson.

Jackson: It's because they didn't know the real you.

Leland: Excuse me?

Jackson: The you who wants a sex dungeon, raves about a fence, and has a robot vacuum with a dildo running around the house.

Leland: When you sum me up like that… I do sound fucking amazing.

Jackson: You are. There's only one thing that would make you even more amazing.

Leland: Yeah?

Jackson: If you had a flamethrower.

Leland: You're not burning down The Fence. Honestly, Jackson, your obsession with The Fence is kind of concerning. Like... don't you ever think about anything else?

Jackson: You... I... ha... Leland... *youuuu...*

Leland: Honey? Studmuffin? My hunk? Sugar teats? Did I break you?

Jackson: You... you think *I* think about the fence too much?

Leland: Maybe... but the look on your face is making me question if maybe you love the fence *more* than me.

Jackson: Yep. That is the issue here.

Leland: Thought so, my wild stallion.

THIRTY-THREE

LELAND

I'm trying to see how many pans I can fit into the oven when Jackson's phone beeps. It's sitting on the counter and he's in the shower, so I walk over to check out what it is.

> Mason: Need u now. Meet at work in 10 min?

I scroll up to previous texts sent by Mason. While I don't know the man overly well, I've exchanged a couple of texts with him, mostly when I want some cute pictures of Jackson hard at work so I have something to jerk off to.

I hit the oven off and run to find Jackson. "Jackson!" I yell as I rush into the bathroom and yank the shower curtain open.

He screams like his nuts never dropped and slips before nearly wiping out. The only thing that saves him is the handle on the wall.

I cover my mouth in the worst attempt to stifle laughter.

"Holy shit, you terrified me!" he says.

That's when I remember what I came running in here for. "Mason's been abducted," I say as I shove Jackson's phone in his face.

He stares at it in confusion. "What part of this says, 'I'm abducted'?"

"He used the letter 'U' instead of Y-O-U."

He cocks his head like Cayenne does when she hears a strange noise. "Wait... what?"

It wasn't a "wait, what? You're right!" but more of "wait... you've lost your mind," so I decide that I need to explain. "Has Mason ever sent you a text and abbreviated *anything*?"

I can almost see Jackson's mind racing as he thinks about it. "You really think something's happened?"

"I don't know. We'll tell him we can be there in twenty. We'll arrive early and see what's happening," I say.

"Okay," he says as he quickly turns the shower off.

I'm glad he believes me. While I could be one hundred percent wrong and Mason has acquired some hip new lingo, it feels like something's off.

Even though I would love to see Jackson get dressed, I head off to grab my gun—or *guns*, if I have to be specific.

By the time I have my stuff gathered, Jackson's dressed and ready, so we rush for the car together.

"Did you text him back?" Jackson asks.

"Yeah, I told him twenty minutes. He never replied. Why was he even there?"

"He had an extra case he was dealing with. He told me he'd probably be working until late," Jackson says as he gets into the driver's seat.

It's getting dark out since it's already seven o'clock, but there's still enough light to see by. When Jackson pulls up near the agency, he parks at the bar down the road in case there's anyone watching out for us.

"Now when I peeped on you previously, you know, that time I bought you the flowers? I was able to do so from the top of that building there," I say as I point. "I could see right into the agency from up there. We could go there and check it out."

"The issue is, do we have time?"

He's right. Playing it safe might not be what we need to do to get

Mason out alive. "I don't know. What if you go up there, and I'll check out the building?"

He looks at me like it's a stupid idea. "Fuck no," he says.

Why's he always so stubborn? "Jackson, Mason's life could be in danger and between the two of us, I'm better with a gun."

"I'm not putting you in danger," he says. "We're going in together or you're waiting in the car."

He's crazy if he thinks I'll wait in the *car*. Maybe he'll even crack a window for me to sniff out of like a dog. "What? Now, I like it when you order me around in the bedroom, but this is my stomping ground."

His eyes stare right into mine. "I will tie you up and shove you in the trunk."

I sigh, even though a bit of bondage sounds enticing. "Fine. We'll go together. But when we get home, will you tie me up and make me beg?"

"Sure."

I lean forward and give him a kiss. Then I turn to look at the building I need to infiltrate. "I'm going in the back door," I say.

"That's what he said."

And I fall even deeper in love with him. "From the moment I saw your butthole, I knew we were meant to be, and this just confirmed it."

"You *didn't* see my butthole that day, but yes. We're meant to be."

"Come on," I say before leading him down an alleyway so if they're looking out for us, they won't see me.

It's not often that I have anyone go out with me on a mission, so it's quite different having him trail behind me as I make my way up to the door. When I reach out and try the handle, it easily turns in my hand. "Shouldn't this have been locked?"

"Yes, Rose always locks it even if we're still here," he says. "She's scared someone will steal her books."

I snort. Since no one seems to want to *pay* for her books, I can't imagine anyone stealing them. "I don't think there's anyone still here, though."

"Why else would they call us?" he asks.

"Unless… they did something to Mason," I say as I push the door open so I can look inside in case I'm wrong about no one being there.

"I'm going to call the police and have an ambulance headed here just in case."

"Sounds good," I say as I slip into the bookstore. Books are scattered all over the floor and shelves have been knocked over, making it hard to move toward the stairs quietly.

"I don't hear anything," Jackson whispers.

"No… and that's what I'm worried about." Mason should be making some noise at the very least.

I step onto the top of a bookshelf that's lying on its side and quietly move toward the stairs. I make my way up them before pushing the door open without moving inside. I want to make sure there's no one waiting for us, ready to ambush us if we make a mistake. Jackson stands by my side, one step down from where I'm at. When I don't hear anything, I peek inside and see Mason lying on the ground.

Jackson must see him too because he yells, "Mason!" and rushes past me before I can stop him.

I check the corners, but we're completely alone besides Mason, who is lying on his back, blood pooling out around him. What I do notice is that Mason is lying right in front of the window. The same window I had looked through way back when I had been peeping in on Jackson when I'd bought him the vase of flowers.

"Mason, please," Jackson says so desperately it hurts me.

Blood trails lead from Mason's desk to his current spot, telling me that someone dragged him there. Almost like he was positioned.

"Jackson, stop!" I yell as I run for him. I grab his arm and tear him back just as the glass shatters. I push him to the ground, throwing my body over him, ready to do anything to protect him. I will protect this man with every ounce of my life if I have to. "These fucking assholes think they can catch me off guard? Jackson, stay down and don't move."

I jump up and rush for the door as another bullet comes in, but I'm too far from it.

"Leland, don't!" Jackson yells, but it's too late. I only have my handgun, and I don't know if I would be able to hit them from this distance, so I *have* to leave the protection of the agency. Anyone who would threaten to shoot Jackson *will* regret it.

"Leland, please, you don't know how many are out there," Jackson begs, but my attention is fixated. I will not let this asshole get away with trying to kill the man I love, even if I have to hunt him down.

I rush down the stairs and out the back door where the sniper doesn't have a clear line of sight. I rush forward into the darkness, hell-bent on making this man pay.

JACKSON

I want to follow Leland, but if I get up and move toward the door, I'm in the direct line of fire, and there's still a possibility of helping Mason if I stay. Keeping my head down, I stretch out until I hook Mason's leg and drag him toward me.

A groan escapes him, making relief flood through me. Once I've pulled him a safe distance from the window, I try to believe that Leland will be okay and that I need to focus my attention on keeping Mason alive.

"Mason, can you hear me?" I ask as I pull him to the side and flip him onto his back. His face is bloody and his nose looks broken, but that can't be where the blood is coming from.

Mason groans and tries to lift his hand. He's apparently weak, which results in him barely moving it away, but he reveals the gunshot wound in his stomach. I push his shirt up when I hear another bullet hit the glass still hanging in the pane.

My mind is telling me to race after Leland, but I know that if I leave Mason here, he'll probably die. So I put pressure on the wound and pray the police and ambulance hurry up.

Jackson: You were so sexy, Leland.

Leland: Ooh. No, *you* were sexy.

Jackson: I was sexy running right into the sniper's line of sight?

Leland: Well… I mean, I didn't say you were being *aware*, I said you were being sexy.

Jackson: … Thanks.

Leland: You are most welcome. It would have been better if you were shirtless.

Jackson: The next time Mason is lying there bleeding, I'll be like "Hold on, hold on" and whip my shirt off.

Leland: Yesssssssssssssss.

Jackson: You're such a goof.

Leland: Shhhhh honey, don't talk, I'm envisioning you naked. Perky nipples glistening as you run.

Jackson: Why are they glistening?

Leland: They're moist.

Jackson: *Why*?

Leland: I don't know, Jackson! They're your nipples!

Jackson: I can show you my nipples. They don't glisten.

Leland: *gasp* No! They sparkle! They're blinding me, Jackson! It hurts so good!

Jackson: For fuck's sake. Let's finish this.

THIRTY-FOUR

LELAND

Thankfully, I'd been on the building back during my Jackson harassment days, so I know exactly where the man is at. I also know that when someone is using a rifle with a scope, they have tunnel vision. The only catch is if he has a spotter with him, but I'll deal with that hurdle if I come to it. The telling factor will be if I get shot when I cross the street. Will he see me?

Because I can't see him.

I watch for a moment before rushing across. No bullets rain down on me, telling me that he probably doesn't have anyone with him. Or that person is an idiot.

That's likely as well.

The building has an old fire escape leading up it, and he even sweetly pushed a trash can over to aid my ascent. The main issue I now have is that the old metal fire escape is anything but quiet. I have to move slowly, judging each step as I go while also keeping my attention above me in case he hears me and is interested in putting a bullet between my eyes. If only Jackson would have allowed me to bring my rifle, this would already be done with.

Either I'm like a fucking ninja or Hardek is hiring deaf men, because when I reach the top, he's still lying down, fixated on his scope. But he's also on the phone, so I guess my ninja and deaf theory are out.

"They're taking cover... none of them have moved since I missed the first shot. He fucking ducked! I didn't *plan* on missing it... I apologize... I'm sorry for being rude..." the man mumbles.

I slowly walk up to the man who is prone on the ground.

Instead of alerting him to my presence, I step on each side of his body before sitting down on his back. He hollers out in alarm as I kick the rifle out of his right hand, press my gun to his head, and snatch up his phone.

"Hello?" I purr as the man struggles beneath me. He seems to be having a hard time with my weight between his shoulder blades. Every time he gets an arm under him, I kick it out.

"Who the fuck is this?" the man on the other end says urgently.

"It's the Sandman, who has come to visit your dreams. And who might this be?" I ask slowly, toying with the man on the other end of the phone.

"Who hired you?" he growls.

The man I'm sitting on stops struggling when I announce who I am, telling me that I might be a bit famous. It's almost enough to make me blush.

"Who hired me... Originally? Wilson. But I killed him, as I'm sure you're aware."

He's silent for a moment. "Wilson wanted me dead? How interesting..." He snorts. "Of course he would want to stab me in the back to take it for himself."

I try to pull anything out of his voice that I can. Anything that might give him away. An accent, dialect, any familiarity. I've dealt with a lot of people, but there's nothing about him making me think he's familiar in any way.

"Wilson is a bit of a bummer like that. So you must be Hardek. A pleasure to finally speak with you," I say.

"If you have no client, then what are you doing snooping in my business?" He sounds a bit irritated, yet I have no idea why. The man under me has decided to try his hand at becoming one with the ground because he's stopped moving.

"Hmm… who said I didn't have a client or a stake in the matter?" I ask.

"And what's that client want you to do?"

"It's really none of your business… you'll be too dead to care when I'm finished."

He scoffs. "You're a man who works for money, are you not?"

"I *have* been looking at getting a new pair of shoes. They're pink with rhinestones. Do you think that'll look gaudy? Should I go for the blue?" While I'm sure he thinks I'm just being annoying, I want to see if he's easy to push into anger. Is he a sensible man? Or will I easily irritate him? Men who are easily irritated make mistakes.

"How much are they paying you?" he asks casually.

My rambling clearly didn't affect him. "Why?"

"Well, maybe I have something you'd be more interested in."

"Would I? What would that be?"

"Just come work for me."

"And when I walk in and you shoot me between the eyes, what then?" I ask.

He chuckles. "Then, I suppose, you'd be dead."

"I like my head. And I currently have the perfect amount of holes in it."

"Mr… Sandman, I think it would be in your best interest to just walk away. Maybe we can come to an agreement another time, perhaps." He's very calm, a man who has been in this business a while. Confident, even.

I consider agreeing to meet him, but I'm about ninety percent positive the meeting will be a setup. Men don't like things stronger than them, and Hardek will have to know that I've come too close to hunting him down to just walk away. If he knows my name, he'll also know that I don't kill innocent men, no matter how much he's willing to pay.

"What do you want to do now?" I ask. "You could tell me where you're at?"

He snorts. "I could tell you that I'm sending men your way to kill you."

"I'm not worried. I mean, your *sniper* is currently on his hands and knees while I ride on his back. He's like a little pony. Do I *really* need to worry about the others?"

"Hmm..." He seems to be thinking about something. "How much money do you want just to tell me who's paying you?"

"Oh, don't worry, I'm not that money hungry."

"Are you sure? Every man can be bought."

The man I'm sitting on is trying to reach for his gun, so I tap the side of his head with mine. "I'm not like other men. How about a trade? You turn yourself in to the police, and I won't kill you."

"Oh? You're awfully confident, aren't you?"

I grin as I grind my heel into the sniper's hand. "I might be. Or I might know exactly what I'm talking about."

I can hear the sound of sirens in the distance. Hopefully, they're here in time to save Mason, because it looked like he was still alive when we arrived.

"I'll be around if you change your mind," Hardek says.

"How will I find you?"

"Don't fret. I'll find you."

"Is that a threat?"

"That *is* a threat, Mr. Sandman." And then he hangs up. I slide the phone into my pocket and look down at the man who's lying beneath me. It's clear he's scared of me since he hasn't fought *too* hard. He'll likely break easily.

I grab his arm and roll him onto his back as he looks up at me with wide eyes.

"Let's play a game. For every question you refuse to answer, I will hurt you."

He shakes his head, eyes nearly popping from their sockets. "I don't know anything! They hired me from an outside source!"

"Hardek isn't that trusting. Why would he hire someone he *doesn't* trust?"

"I don't know!"

"Let's start with the agency you were shooting at. What's your interest with them?" I nod at the window he'd been shooting through.

He shakes his head, diligent about playing the innocent card. "I don't know anything!"

No one's innocent in this line of work.

I punch him in the face, sending the man's head slamming into the roof. "What's that?"

He looks up at me with wide eyes. "I-I don't know!"

I punch him again.

"I-I think because the PI was getting nosy or something! I think someone hired the detectives to look into Hardek!"

I hesitate as I think about it. "So they must be getting close if Hardek is getting nervous about a simple little PI, huh?"

He shakes his head as blood bubbles from his nose. "I don't know!"

"Who is your boss?"

"Please! I don't know anything! Please!"

I pull a knife out and make a show of opening it before grabbing his hand.

I didn't think his eyes could get any wider, yet he proves me wrong. "W-What are you doing? What are you doing with that? Please! Please don't!"

I grin at him, since a person who is grinning *always* comes across more confident. "Who do you report to?"

He shakes his head, weighing his options. What's scarier? Giving away information on Hardek? Or me?

I set my foot against his throat, pinning him there as I stretch his arm toward me while standing up. Then I push the knife under his fingernail. For some reason, fingernails and eyeballs are generally the tipping point for people. There's something about cutting a fingernail off that makes them second-guess everything and makes me *much* scarier.

He thrashes beneath me until the foot on his throat makes him hesitate. "Stop! I'll tell you!"

"Oh?" I ask as I glance down at him.

He's quiet, so I step down on his throat, making him gurgle something out before I let up.

"I'm listening," I remind him.

"T-The person I report to is called Buddy."

"Buddy? Is he a dog?" I ask.

"No! I don't know their real name, really, that's all I have!"

"And where did you meet 'Buddy'? The dog pound?"

"It's how I get jobs."

"I see," I say as I pull his phone back out. I grab his hand and put it against the fingerprint sensor before checking out his texts. He definitely does have a contact named Buddy, but he's wiped all his messages clean. It's probably something he does before every job in case he gets caught. I click on Buddy's name and text: Done.

While Buddy will probably know that this guy is in my caring custody, he might not be up on it *just* yet.

"Alright, let's…"

I hear a noise behind me. Someone is on the fire escape, making their way up. I don't want to be caught as the "Sandman" and have my real identity be known, so I wait for them to make their appearance as I hide beneath my hood, unsure if I should run. When I see just a sliver of a head, I realize that there is only one man with that amazing hair.

Jackson looks at me, but I hold a finger up to my lips. The man I have pinned to the ground doesn't need to know that I'm familiar with Jackson.

I drop my hold on the man. "Oh, Detective, come to arrest me? Maybe I'd love for you to put me in handcuffs."

"Stay where you're at," Jackson says, but I drop my hold on the man and rush away from him. Jackson goes for the sniper and pins him to the ground as I make my great escape. Once I'm down the fire escape, I pull my hood down and take my hoodie off. Then I step to the side and watch the men work. The ambulance is already gone, but I see Jeremy, so I head toward him.

"Jackson is dealing with the sniper up on the roof," I say.

He glances at me. "You didn't help?"

"Me? Um… do what? Help by staring in terror?" I ask.

He sighs like it's such a nuisance having to do his job, but he gathers a couple of people to assist Jackson. I stand back as they bring the handcuffed man down the fire escape and over to a police car. When Jackson is away from him, I make my way over to his side.

I slip my hand in his and squeeze his fingers. When he instantly responds in kind, it makes me strangely happy. "Is Mason okay?"

He looks pained but optimistic. "God, I hope. He lost a lot of blood and was in severe shock as they were loading him in the ambulance." He lifts my hand up to his face and kisses the back of my hand. "Thank you, Leland. Or I'm positive I would have been lying next to Mason. When I saw Mason hurt, my mind just went blank and I stepped right in front of that window. I *knew* better, and that's what's killing me."

"When someone you care about is hurt, you never make the best judgment call. It's human weakness," I say.

He pulls me up to him and wraps his arms around me, squeezing me tightly. "I'm glad you're okay. I was scared something happened when you still hadn't returned by the time the ambulance showed."

"Sorry, I was… having a talk with Hardek and then the shooter."

Jackson looks at me in surprise. "Hardek?"

"Yeah. This guy tries telling me he's basically never even *heard* of Hardek, yet he was on the phone with him. But I did get a name of who he works directly under. A man by the name of Buddy. Man or dog, I'm not sure." I hold the phone out to him, and Jackson takes it.

"Buddy, huh?" he asks with a grin.

A man I don't know mutters something under his breath as he moves by. Surely something about the way Jackson is holding me. I start to pull back, ready to destroy this man's ass, when Jackson locks me in tight. "Nope."

"He sassed us," I say.

"Yep, he did, but I need you to just let it slide on by."

I stare at the back of the man. "*Or* I could whap him across the back of the head. Knock his knees out from under him, give him the ultimate wedgie."

"While I would love to see you do all of those things, I think we need to just allow his arrogant ass to walk away."

"You're such a better man than me."

"Not better. Let's say… I can keep my head about me better. Let's get you on the phone with Henry and you can tell him everything you can while I drive to the hospital."

"Sounds good."

JACKSON

I'm exhausted, but hearing that Mason is stable is the boost I needed. We've sat in the waiting room with Mason's girlfriend for the last two hours, just anxiously waiting. Leland has already chatted her ear off by the time the nurse comes, but I think she needed that since it was something to distract her.

Since only two are allowed back at a time, Leland stays behind while Mason's girlfriend, Mattie, and I go back to see him.

He's in the ICU, but when we reach his bed, we find that he's awake.

"Hey," he mutters groggily.

I can't help but smile as I see him. "You gave me quite the scare."

He stares at me for a moment, like he's trying to process my words. "I don't even… I don't even remember you being there. How'd you get there?"

"Long story," I say before sighing. "The man who shot you sent us a text as if it were from you. Thankfully, Leland realized it wasn't you."

He's pale and his eyes are heavy, but I can tell that he's trying to think this through as the monitor beeps behind him. "Through a text?"

I nod, still not sure myself. "Because the man had used the letter U instead of spelling out the word."

Mason lets out a laugh that quickly dies down. "Ow… no… I think I love your boyfriend."

I smile. "Don't be moving in on my man," I joke.

He closes his eyes and falls quiet. I think he's fallen asleep until he mutters, "Tell him I said 'thanks.'"

"I will."

After Mason falls asleep, I head back to the waiting room to find Leland asleep in his chair. *How* he fell asleep, I'm not sure, especially in those crappy wooden chairs. There's no one else in the waiting room, so I find myself watching him for a moment. His brown hair stands up on the side from where it's pressed into his hand that's supporting his head. I want to rush over to him and never leave his side.

Whenever he leaves me like he did tonight, I feel an overwhelming amount of anxiety that something is going to happen to him.

If anyone saw this man curled up in the chair, head tucked against his arm that's leaning on the armrest, they would never imagine what goes on in his brain. Or what this man could do.

But all I see is someone I want to protect, someone I want to love, and someone I want to be loved by.

"How long are you going to stare at me for? Long enough to jerk off?" Leland mumbles.

A smile touches my lips as I shake my head. "You just ruined the moment."

He slowly opens his eyes and grins at me. "I did? By what? You were the one creeping and leering."

"You say that like you don't want me creeping on you."

"I love it," he says with a grin. "How's Mason?"

"Good. He said to thank you for saving him."

"Oh, well, you're the one who saved his life. I didn't keep him from bleeding out. I ran off and left his life in your hands."

"How about we decide it was a joint effort?" I suggest, even though I'm positive he deserves all the praise.

He holds his hand out to me so I can pull him from the chair. Once on his feet, he gives me a hug I feel like I really needed.

"I can handle that," he says.

Jackson: You were so badass, Leland.

Leland: Thank you. The real reason I was so badass was because I was thinking about your moist nipples.

Jackson: I thought you'd forget about that by now.

Leland: They sparkled their way into my heart and left an impression that I can't forget.

Jackson: And chapter thirty-five!

Leland: Wait! No! I wasn't done talking.

Jackson: Chapter *thirty-five*.

Leland: No! Embrace the nips!

THIRTY-FIVE

LELAND

I know Jackson isn't convinced about going to his family reunion while Hardek is still on the loose, but I'm positive his mom would lose her mind if we didn't show up. And we're only two hours away if we have to rush back for any reason. Like… in case we *have* to make sure we turned the stove off.

I turn to Jackson as he slows the car down to turn into his parents' driveway. "So… if you're mad at your mother, *why* are we all packing into the same car together for a two-hour drive?" I ask curiously as Jackson parks behind his mom's car.

"Leland, sometimes you just have to… bite the bullet and do what the monster wants to keep the monster happy."

I grin at him. "Can I call her monster too?"

Even though I know he's upset about the whole thing, I see his lips quirk up. "Not to her face."

"Well then that's no fun," I say with a grin.

He sighs as he grips the steering wheel so tight his knuckles turn white. "Why aren't you more angry at her? She literally thought you were off jumping from cock to cock."

I nonchalantly shrug. "Maybe I feel flattered that she thinks I have that much stamina."

Jackson shakes his head. "You shouldn't feel flattered about any of it."

We get out of the car as Jackson's parents and sister come through the front door of the house.

"I already miss Cayenne," I say as I head to the back to grab our overnight bag. I'm positive that Jackson thinks the night will be full-on torture.

"She'll be fine. Henry seemed more eager to deal with her than you."

"Can you imagine how much he must love her, then, if he loves her more than me?" I ask with wide eyes.

Jackson starts laughing. "He's warming up to you. He was proud of the information you got out of that guy since he's gotten nothing from him."

"You just gotta stuff the knife under the nails. Tell Henry that's my pro tip."

Jackson stares at me with wide eyes. "Seriously?"

"Yeah. You just take the knife and put it right under the nail so they can *just* feel the tip of the knife. And then you tell them you're gonna pry their nail up and that's when they spill. Works every time."

He shudders. "Oh god. That makes me cringe just thinking about it."

"You're so cute," I say before looking at the family that's getting close enough to hear us. I'm not sure his mother would be any happier knowing about torture techniques. "Hey, guys!"

"Hey!" Ella says as she rushes over and hugs Jackson as I hold my arms open.

"Hey," Jackson says as he gives her a quick hug.

"How could you go to him first?" I ask with wide eyes, like I'm hurt that she hugged him.

"Aw! I'm sorry!" she says as she rushes over and gives me a bear hug. It's rib-crushingly tight.

"You'd be good at torture," I tell her as she releases me.

"Huh?"

"Ignore him," Jackson says.

I reach out and grab her bicep to get a good feel. "You could just hug them into submission."

"I've been exercising a lot. Like I get up once every hour to eat a snack," she says. "And my snacks are up really high, so I have to stretch far."

Jackson laughs as he takes the bag from me and carries it over to the trunk of his father's car.

"How's Mason doing?" Ava asks as she looks through me to her son.

Jackson nods as he pulls open the back door. "He's headed home today."

"That's good," she says.

"And you're being careful?" Lewis asks.

"As careful as we can be. Thankfully, Leland was there to help us or I'm afraid Mason... and I wouldn't have made it."

Jackson looks over at me and the emotion there startles me. It makes me feel strange knowing he's that grateful to me.

"Nah, you'd have been fine," I say as I try to dismiss it since I don't know what to do with the heaviness of the situation. "Do you want me in the middle?"

"Isn't that the position you take when you're out on the town without me?" he asks as he glances at his mom.

I grin at him. "You know me so well."

"Can we not talk about being spit roasted?" Ella asks.

"Depends. Are you going to be in the front or the back?" I ask.

She starts laughing. "Neither!"

"Fine, fine," I say as I slide in, but Jackson pushes me over.

When I look at him in surprise he says, "I'd like to try the middle position for once."

"Ooh, kinky. I'm sure you'll like it."

"I'd prefer it wasn't with my sister, though. But you know how us gays are," Jackson says.

He's just *trying* to get his mom to say something, and I don't know whether I should encourage it or tell him that we should tiptoe. I've *never* been good at tiptoeing around awkward subjects, though.

Once we're all packed in, the car starts moving and we begin our road trip of silence. His parents stare straight ahead, Ella stares at her phone, and Jackson's eyes burn holes in the back of his mom's head. While it *would* be pretty neat if he acquired laser vision, I'm not sure this is the way to go about it.

Just think of the mess inside his father's car.

The issue is that I'm not very good at the whole silent act. I'm having enough trouble sitting in this small of a space without fidgeting and flopping around. Thankfully, Jackson knows that I can't sit still to save my life and doesn't even notice anymore. I'm determined that he loves me shifting around, even if I step on his foot and elbow him a time or two.

"How far do we have to go?" I ask curiously.

"We still have two hours," Jackson says.

I look at him in horror. It's enough to still me. "Seriously? We've been driving for what seems like hours."

"Patience."

"What's that word mean?"

He looks over at me and grins. "It's that thing I'm always telling you that you don't have."

"Hmm…" I make a show of thinking about it for a moment. "So… they're like boobs?"

His eyebrows knit. "What?"

"You said it was something I didn't have."

Ella starts snickering but his parents are dead quiet. Clearly, they love me.

"That's alright, Leland, I don't have those either," Ella says as she pitifully looks down at her chest.

"Aw, yours are perfect," I say.

"Please stop talking about my sister's chest," Jackson says.

"Shush. It's not like I'm asking to touch them, unless she offers, then all bets are off."

He glares at me, so I innocently grin at him.

We continue the drive of awkward silence in the smothering quiet of the car.

"Is this what it's like to have a family?" I whisper in Jackson's ear.

He gives me a pained look even though I was trying to be funny. "I'm really sorry."

Now *I* feel bad even though I was just hoping to make him laugh. I forget that he thinks I suffer from missing my family. I don't. He's more than enough for me. "No! Don't apologize. Apologies make me feel gross. I was trying to be funny."

He sets a hand on my knee and squeezes it. "I know, but it's true and it sucks."

"That's alright," I say as I pull out my laptop. "Let's find Buddy."

"Who's Buddy?" Ella asks.

"Probably a gangster who wants to murder us." I like the way the comment makes Ella's eyes go wide.

Jackson sighs. "A man involved in the current case we're working on."

"That's all you have to go by? The name Buddy?" Ella asks curiously.

"I personally think it's a dog," I whisper. "Dogs can be tricky little things."

Jackson stares at my computer screen where I have a Word document up that I've been doing my ramblings on since I've been required to share it with others, and everyone complains that they can't read the "craziness" of my journaling. "Did your, um... consultant get back with you?" Jackson asks.

Since Tucker owes me, I have him looking into "Buddy" as well.

"Not yet," I say.

When we reach the family reunion, it's already started by about fifteen minutes. I'm sure Ava thinks it's our fault we're fifteen minutes late even though the invitation says to come at any point of the day.

We leave our bags in the trunk even though we'll be spending the night, which sounds borderline insufferable. But I will live through torture and hell for the man I love.

As a family—the word almost makes me giddy—we walk to the backyard where two huge tents are set up and people are wandering around socializing. I excel at both of those things, so I'm positive I'll fit right in.

When a lady who looks like Ava walks up with a smile, Ava is the first to greet her.

"Hey, Darla. Sorry we're late," she says as she hugs the woman.

Darla shakes her head. "Oh, hush, you're not late at all. And you brought someone new!"

Ava sets her hands on my shoulders, which I find to be an oddly intimate gesture for her. "Yes, this is Ella's boyfriend," Ava says.

"What?" Jackson says, but before anything more can be said, Darla smiles at Ella, who is staring at me like she's never seen me before.

"Oh! You didn't tell me, dear!" She elbows Ella and whispers overly loud, "Looks like you hooked a good one."

"Um… I did?" Ella asks, clearly still trying to figure out if I'm alien or man.

When I look at Jackson, he's looking away like he hasn't even heard his mother, but I can tell by his posture he's not happy about any of this.

I decide that it's up to me to make the situation the best it can be. "Ella, my sweetpea," I coo as I grab her hand. "Sugar dollop, do you need anything?" I pull her in my arms and hug her in tight as she stands there like she has no idea what a hug is.

"Um… no… thank you?" Ella says, clearly muted by my overwhelming love.

"I need a drink," Jackson says as he wanders off.

I pull Ella in even closer and kiss her cheek loudly. "Don't fret, my lovely bride, but I'm going to see what ails your brother."

"I know what ails him," she mutters. "And I'll go with you."

Hand in hand, Ella and I find Jackson at the drink table where he is scavenging for something to erase his memories of his mother.

"Babe, it's going to take more than a beer to forget her," I say.

He whirls around and for a moment, I wonder if I said something wrong. "She just fucking pisses me off. We should've stayed home. If I'd have driven, we would be halfway back by now."

"We can set her straight," Ella suggests.

Jackson gives a defeated sigh and I don't like the way it makes his shoulders hunch. My usually confident man seems to have been utterly defeated by this, and it royally pisses me off. I wouldn't mind trying some torture techniques out on his mother to see if I can straighten her ass up. I clearly don't understand the significance of having a caring mother, but Jackson seems very bothered by it.

I put a hand on his arm, hoping it gives him some reassurance. "Jackson, I can—"

He shakes his head. "I don't want to deal with it. Congrats, Ella, you got yourself a boyfriend."

I squeeze his arm before turning to Ella. "I'm kind of high maintenance," I warn her. "But I'm amazing in bed. I stay on the right side of the bed, I don't steal the covers—"

The strained look on Jackson's face softens a bit. "No, you just give them all to the dog."

I grin. "But she's cold. I *do* have one question. Do I need to be well-behaved?"

He thinks about it for a moment before shaking his head. "No. Not in the slightest. I'd actually prefer if you weren't," Jackson says. "Want a beer?"

"A pop is fine, but thank you. I don't want your mother to think I'm a lush as well. I'm already promiscuous enough without it."

Jackson smiles, but I can tell there's weight behind it. He's upset that no matter what he does, his mother doesn't seem to accept who he really is. I reach out and squeeze his hand gently. "You've gotta give her time. You can't expect someone to change overnight."

"We've been together for almost six months. I would think that would be plenty of time."

"Yeah, but when you're as old as she is, six months isn't much time."

He shakes his head but at least I see a hint of a grin. "You mean when you're a witch like her, right?"

"Maybe."

"Now do me a favor and be as disgustingly flirty with my sister as you can be," he says. "I want my mom to regret it."

"Got it," I say with a devious grin.

"I don't 'got it,'" Ella says, looking worried.

"Don't worry about it, Ella. Leland will handle it."

She raises an eyebrow. "That's what I'm worried about," she says, but as we head over to the table where Ava and her husband Lewis are sitting, she lets me take her hand and squeeze it.

"Your hands are so tiny that it's weird," I inform her.

She squeezes my hand. "Oh?"

"Jackson, her hands aren't all sweaty like yours."

"My hands aren't sweaty!"

"Clammy."

He sighs.

"Sticky."

"Not sticky."

There are only two open seats at the table, but Ava reaches for an extra chair.

"No need!" I assure her. "Ella, sit."

Ella warily sits, and then I sit on her lap which makes everyone at the table stare at us. Jackson looks away to hide his laughter as Ava stares at us.

"Leland, why don't you pull up a seat?" Ava suggests.

"That's okay! My sugar plum and I are practicing this relationship style called Close Love. It's where we try to constantly be touching each other. That way, her spirit will flow up through the part of my body where we're touching. Right now, her spirit is flowing out of her legs and into my butthole."

Ella presses her face against my back as she tries to hide her laughter. She could never be an actress. Jackson is covering his face and Ava is staring at me like she'd enjoy murdering me. The feeling is currently mutual. Too bad for her, I would win.

Ava abruptly stands up and grabs a chair before slamming it into my leg like a savage.

"Oh my god, my leg!" I cry.

"Please have a seat, *Leland*."

"If you insist."

I sit down on my chair before leaning into Ella so I can whisper sweet nothings into her ear. "Wanna hear a secret?" I whisper.

"My mom's going to murder you," she whispers back.

"I wore rainbow socks today."

"Oh?"

"Did that turn you on?"

"Me?" she asks in alarm.

"Don't matching socks turn women on?"

"I'm… not sure they do."

"They have naked leprechauns on them."

"What?"

"Wee little penises."

"Is this how you hooked my brother?"

"No, I actually shot at him with a rifle."

She laughs, thinking I'm joking.

Thankfully, before long we're able to get our plates of food. We stand in line with Darla and her daughter in front of us.

"What do you do for a job, Leland?" Darla asks, out of curiosity.

"I've been working with Jackson at his agency."

"Like a receptionist?" she asks.

"No, he's my lead detective," Jackson says from where he's at, three people back.

"Oh? You don't look like a detective!" Darla says.

"What do I look like? Maybe a scientist?"

"Oh, wouldn't he be adorable with some glasses?" Darla asks. "You should wear glasses."

"I'll wear anything my baby doll wants me to wear. Or nothing," I say as I wink at Ella.

Darla and her daughter just laugh while Ava contemplates how hard it'll be to get rid of me. Joke's on her, I've already figured out how we could dispose of her body.

We get our food and sit down, but before Ella can start eating, I grab her fork and stab a piece of watermelon before directing it toward her mouth.

"Open wide, sugar plum."

Ava drops her plate. "Jackson, a word."

Maybe, just maybe, I went too far.

Then Ava hurries off. Jackson sighs, but gets up and follows her. Instead of waiting behind, I get up and follow after them at a safe distance. She's close enough that I could grab the spoon off the table next to me and throw it at the back of her head. I should get an award for resisting. She takes Jackson into the house and I follow after them. I stop in the foyer as I hear her start talking.

"Your *friend* is making a fool of this family. How could you let him act like that? If you were with a nice, polite woman, none of this would happen. You need to open your eyes and see that this is *wrong*."

I start to walk into the room, knowing that there is *absolutely* no way I'm going to let this woman talk about Jackson like that. Ava looks at me as I step in, but Jackson moves in front of her, breaking our eye contact.

"That's enough!" Jackson snaps. "Leland's not my *friend*. He's my boyfriend. We've been together for nearly half a year now. I don't know if you think by saying shit about him or doing shit like this that you think you'll make me move on or find a woman or die alone, but all you're doing is making me hate being around you. I'm so happy when I'm with Leland, and you're too far up your own ass to even notice it! Being with Leland makes me unbelievably happy. It's dealing with this shit, it's having to put up with you hating who I am that makes me unhappy.

"Mom, I love you, but sometimes, I question how real that love is. Because I feel like someone who loves me would never treat me like this. Leland has never made me feel like this, so why you think you can get away with him being the 'bad guy' I don't know, and I'm sick of it."

She shakes her head, like she's still not bothering to listen to what Jackson has to say, and I want to shake some sense into her.

I don't know if it's in my rights to say anything now that Jackson has said what he wanted and needed to, but I feel like I need her to understand my side of it as well. "You try to make Jackson feel like he's a bad person for being who he is. All Jackson does is love me. So how can that make him a bad person? I've had a shitty life. I never had a family as amazing as yours. But how you could ever think badly of

Jackson, I don't know. I know who goes to hell, I've dealt with them time and time again. So if you think any part of Jackson isn't perfect enough, it's because you haven't seen enough bad shit in your life. And maybe you need to wake up and see that your son is pretty damn perfect."

She won't look at me, but I know that she's heard me. Jackson reaches back and holds his hand out to me, which I take.

He squeezes it tightly as he stares at his mom.

She's silent as she watches Jackson. I have my doubts she's used to people talking back to her. "I... I don't want to see your life harder than it has to be. When you came back from the army, life was already hard enough for you. You struggled to fit back in. To have a place to stand. And this... this could ruin all of it. I just want you to be normal and happy."

"Why do you think I'm not? I *just* told you how happy Leland makes me."

She bites her red-lined lips. "I don't know, but I never meant to make you feel unhappy with yourself. I wanted everything to be better for you."

"There isn't anything better for me than Leland," Jackson says, and my chest tightens. "Please, please just trust me on this."

She takes a deep breath. "I'll... try to be understanding. I may not... agree with it, but I will try to be understanding. Okay? Can we start there and see where it takes us?"

"Okay," Jackson says with a nod. "I can work with that."

She gives him a soft smile. "Thank you... for making me see reason."

"Thank you for listening."

She hesitates before Jackson pulls me after him and we walk into the foyer.

"Thank you," he says as he grabs me and pulls me into his arms.

"You're the one that did it all."

"Yeah, but I've never cared about anyone enough to stand up to her before now. So thank you. And don't think I didn't notice you running to my rescue."

I grin. "No idea what you're talking about."

"Of course not."

I sink into his arms as I squeeze him tightly. "Now my food's getting cold."

He kisses my cheek before releasing me, but instead of pulling away, I hold on tighter. "You can go eat," he says.

I honestly don't want to let go. "I was, and then you made me feel all weird inside and it creeped me out." I urgently look up at him. "Are you sure this feeling doesn't mean I'm dying?"

He chuckles. "I'm positive you aren't dying."

I dramatically grab my chest. "It hurts."

He shakes his head as he grins. "It doesn't hurt."

"I'm dying, Jackson!"

"You're not the Grinch. Your heart isn't growing, and you're not dying. Let's go eat," he says as he lets go of me.

I grudgingly let go before heading back out to the yard to find my plate of food. As I near the table, I notice Darla's back is to me while whispering hushed words to Ella.

"I think your boyfriend is cheating on you with your brother," she says. "I saw them *hugging*."

"That's because he's not Ella's boyfriend, he's Jackson's," Lewis casually says.

Everyone at the table is silent, especially when we walk up and quietly take our seats.

Without a word, I start eating even though I'm *dying* to say something. As soon as Darla scurries away, I look over at Lewis, who seems proud of himself as he eats.

"Lewis?" I ask with a raised eyebrow.

"These things are always ridiculously boring. Let's stir some things up."

I point my fork at him. "I like the way you think."

Leland: You know, Jackson, I'm so thankful that I was able to give Ella a brief glimpse into what it'd be like to have a badass motherfucker boyfriend like me.

Jackson: I'm... I'm sure it's a memory she'll never forget. My mom won't ever forget it either.

Leland: Shhhh, don't speak those words in this house.

Jackson: What words? "My mom?"

Leland: Jackson, stop! You don't want to summon evil into our life. It's like... a curse.

Jackson: Saying... "My mom" is a curse?

Leland: I'll go get the guns.

Jackson: You already have like four guns, why do you need more?

Leland: I have to exorcise the evil that you've invited into our home.

Jackson: Are you going to hunt down my mother? I'm so confused.

Leland: Shhh, that's the demon trying to pry into your brain.

Jackson: I... don't think it is.

Leland: Gonna fuck that demon *up*.

Jackson: What if we just cuddle instead? I can protect you from her.

Leland: I do like to cuddle. I bet if we were both naked the next time she came over, she'd never come over again.

Jackson: Shhh, just cuddle.

Leland: I'll be sitting on Blow-Up Randy's lap when she comes in. Our Dickavacuum chugging along.

Jackson: You going to be practicing "close love" with Randy now?

Leland: Well, you'll be under Randy. It'll be you, Blow-Up Randy, and then me. We'll just be like a tower for when your mom walks in.

Jackson: I... I think we need to finish this as soon as possible. You're clearly tired and delirious.

Leland: That's fair. Very fair.

THIRTY-SIX

JACKSON

I'm not sure if I've ever been so happy to be home. Leland yanks open the front door and immediately falls to his knees.

At first, I think something's wrong and reach for him before realizing that he's just being dramatic. I press my foot against his ass and push him farther inside before shutting the door.

"Home! Home, sweet home!" he cries before hugging the rug to his chest.

I stop beside him and drop to my knees, realizing that this situation does deserve drama. "I've never been so happy to be home."

He starts laughing as I lie down right there in the foyer next to him.

"The only thing that would make it better is if Cayenne was here. I told you that Henry was going to steal her. He's never going to bring her back."

"He's not stealing her. He said he'd bring her over later."

Leland grabs my head in his arms, hugging it to him.

"I didn't think we'd make it," he says as he turns the head hug into leaning on me since he can't sit still for even a minute. I've become a type of backrest for him, but I'm so happy to be home that I'm satisfied with whatever he wants.

I glance back at him as he kicks his shoes off like he's preparing to get comfortable. "Hey."

He glances at me, blue eyes holding on to mine. "Hey?"

"I... just... it really meant a lot to me that you helped me with my mom." It really did. It meant the world to me that he cared enough to stand up for me and give me the strength to say something to her. "I... I'm trying not to be optimistic, but I hope she'll learn from it."

He reaches out and grabs my hair between his fingers. "Just give her time and I really think she'll come around." He rolls over before crawling forward until he's lying on top of me, smashing me into the hard ground. The balled-up rug is now digging into my thigh, but I don't say a word because I will let him do anything he pleases to me, even if that means treating me like a cushion.

"I hope."

"I think she just needs to loosen up," he says as he grabs my shoulders and squeezes them.

It feels good, so I submit to it. I should have remembered that Leland was allergic to niceness because just as I'm relaxing into his touch, he sticks his finger in my ear.

I bat at him but miss. "No! Be *good*."

"I can't, Jackson. It *hurts*," he cries.

"Being good hurts?"

"So much! Almost as much as it hurts when you're sweet to me. I don't know what to do with it. It feels sticky and strange."

I sigh. "Just rub my shoulders some more as I lie in the doorway."

There's a knock on the door, so I look over at it. "Get up so I can get that."

He grabs onto me. "Nope."

"It's probably Henry and Cayenne," I say as I push myself onto my hands and knees. I *assumed* both my movement and the mention of the dog would be enough to get him to his feet, but he just readjusts so he's now riding on my back like I'm a horse. "I'm *not* answering the door like this."

"Walk on, my wild stallion!" he shouts as he smacks my ass. "You know Henry will find it hilarious."

The moment I realize that I'm ill—that Leland has made me ill—is the moment that I crawl over to the door with him on my back, eager to see the look on Henry's face. Leland pulls it open and smiles, but what I realize is that it's *not* Henry but our mailman, who stares at us with wide eyes. I'm positive my eyes are just as wide as his. What has love done to me? What has happened to my brain? Maybe my mother is right, and I need to find myself a sweet woman who wouldn't ask to ride on my back.

"Good morning!" Leland says as I try to stand up, but Leland puts both of his feet on my hands so I can't push myself up.

"Um... can you... sign for this?" the man asks in horror.

And if the mailman wasn't enough, that's when Henry pulls in.

"Leland, get off!" I hiss.

"Shh... I can't spell my name with you trying to buck me off," he says as he pets my head like I'm a real horse. "I'll give you an apple when we're done."

I try to push myself up but Leland clings on tight, bare feet pinning my hands down. I decide that I would rather die lying facedown than deal with any more embarrassment. So when Henry walks up with Cayenne, I've given up on everything and am becoming one with the floor.

"Do I even ask what's happening here?" Henry says.

Leland nudges me with his heels. Of course he's still on my back. "I... I thought I bought a wild stallion but when I got it home, I realized it was an old nag," Leland says as he gets up.

"Jackson... you've changed," Henry says.

"Shush," I whisper. "I'm letting God take me to heaven or hell or wherever, so I don't have to be here at this moment."

Leland laughs as he squishes my ass with his foot. I grudgingly get up and face Henry, although I can't look him in the eyes. I'll have to put in a request for a new mailperson as well.

Cayenne wiggles at Henry's feet and I realize that I can't even look *her* in the eyes.

Leland kneels in front of Cayenne and ruffles her ears. "Hey, baby.

Did you miss me?" Then he looks up at Henry. "You too. I missed you too, Henry."

He then wraps his arms around Henry, who doesn't seem to know what to do with it. "Um... Can't say the same."

That makes Leland laugh, but he doesn't cease his hugging. "Jackson dragged me off to his evil family who was pure evil."

Henry looks over Leland's shoulder at me in concern. "What happened?"

I shrug. "Normal shit. My mom just being my mom."

"Are you alright?" he asks, while pretending like Leland isn't still hugging him.

I shrug before nodding. "Yeah, I guess. Leland... stood up for me and had a few words with my mom when she wasn't listening to what I was saying."

Henry seems surprised. "Good." He looks down at Leland who is finally pulling away, then he gives Leland a single gentle pat. "Thank you for doing that."

Leland looks clearly pleased as he gives him a soft smile. "Well, she shouldn't say anything bad about Jackson. I mean, there is nothing wrong with him! He's almost perfect."

"You just called him an old nag," Henry reminds him, but since he's joking with him, I know that Leland just gained a bit of respect from Henry. For some reason, it makes me unbelievably happy. Maybe I care more about what Henry thinks than I originally told myself.

"I did, but *I'm* allowed to say mean things about him—no one else is."

"That's understandable," Henry says. "Is everything alright with your mom now?"

I shrug. "Yeah, she's better. To start with, she told everyone Leland was Ella's boyfriend, but by the end, she acknowledged that Leland was with me."

"I'm not sure why she felt the need to do that, but I'm glad things are a little better. Have you heard from Mason today?"

"Yeah, he's doing good. He said he's already bored, which is surprising because he doesn't do anything at work so I can't imagine him *ever* getting bored," I say.

"I'm just glad you guys made it there in time. And I'm glad Leland kept you from getting shot." Henry sets a hand on my shoulder and squeezes it tightly. "I couldn't lose you."

"I'm fine. I promise," I say.

"Good."

"Was Cayenne good?" I ask as I glance at Leland, who is petting the dog while grinning like a fiend. Probably from all the indirect praise.

"Excellent. She has a *lot* of energy though, doesn't she?"

"Leland was only happy with the craziest one. I was like, look at this little sweet dog, and he's like 'No! I only want the most neurotic one.'"

Leland cups Cayenne's ears. "Shush, she'll hear you." He stands up. "So... anything on Buddy?"

Henry shakes his head. "Nothing. I was hoping you had something."

"Not yet. I do have some people on it, though, that might have something worthwhile."

"Let me know if you do. Well, I'm going to head out. I'll let you know the next time we're calling a meeting," Henry says. "See you guys later."

After he's gone, I turn to Leland. "I think Henry likes you."

Leland smiles at me, but he looks sad. "I hope... I know he can never forgive me for what I did, but I truly hope that someday he'll at least understand that I would never have hurt that man if I hadn't been pushed into it."

I wrap him up in my arms. "I'm sure he will."

"Now let me ride on your back again," he says, unable to stay near an uncomfortable topic for more than ten seconds.

LELAND

I'm pressed against Jackson, tracing a circle around his nipple and considering pinching it or something equally mean, when my phone rings.

I roll onto my side and pick it up. "It's Tucker. Maybe he has something good for us, but don't hold your breath. Tucker is like stupid smart. But mostly stupid." I accept the call and put it on speaker so Jackson can hear. "Hello?"

"Hey, I have a name for you," he says.

Maybe he's not so bad after all. "Ooh. Spill."

"Barter."

I still, smile falling from my face. "Oh?"

"Are you home?"

I think about what exactly I should say. "Not at my apartment." I give Jackson a shove and jab at the dresser. "So, do you know where I could find him?" I quietly get up and make my way over to the dresser where I grab the first thing I can and quickly pull it on. As Jackson also gets dressed, I reach under the bed and pull out my rifle. Jackson looks at me in surprise, but I just shrug like I have no idea how it got under there.

"Why don't we meet and we can talk about it? Where are you?"

"I can't at the moment."

"You must be with the *detective*."

He knows about Jackson. Not good. I decide to play dumb. "Who?"

"The detective."

"I... don't know a detective, do I?"

"Wait for me, I think I might have an address for you."

"Got it."

He hangs up as I drop my phone back into my pocket. "They're holding Tucker for information. They wanted to see if I was with you, and though I didn't answer, they probably assume I am and are likely to raid the house at any moment."

Jackson cocks his head. "Wait... *what*? You got all of that from... the same conversation I just listened to?"

"I did. The name Tucker gave me is a name we agreed on before. It means, get the fuck out, shit is going down. Get anything you can't live without."

"Live without?"

I hear a window break somewhere deeper into the house and Cayenne starts barking as she rushes for the door. I grab for her, but she slips past before I can and rushes toward the noise.

Jackson quickly looks into the hallway. "What's that sound?"

"Are they in the house?" I ask as I go to the closet to get my handgun since the rifle won't work well in the tight hallway. There are too many things the barrel could get hung up on.

"Not that I see... and Cayenne is quickly fleeing from the guest room."

"What—" I start to ask just as the window behind me breaks. I slip into the closet and Jackson steps into the hallway to get out of line of the window just as I see what has happened. Someone has broken the window and tossed a goddamn Molotov cocktail through it. When it hits the blinds, it falls to the ground, spilling liquid from the bottle everywhere the moment it hits the carpet, allowing the fire to race across it.

"Leland, get out of there," Jackson snaps.

If I move, I'll be in line of the window, but the blinds are still blocking it, so I quickly slip into the hallway to meet up with Jackson as I hear another window break.

"Are they planning on burning us alive?" Jackson asks as he grabs the rifle from me since I'm not using it.

"It's highly likely that they want to flush us out. Is there anything in the house you can't live without? Because it looks like it's about ready to go up in flames," I say as I carefully make my way to the living room that's already on fire. The curtains are like matchsticks and currently burning hard as I snatch up my laptop and stuff it into its bag. Jackson returns with a similar bag and looks at me.

"If we leave, they're going to kill us. We should have moved into one of my safe houses where I have multiple exits," I say thoughtfully.

"Go to the garage," Jackson says as he heads toward the connecting garage.

"Cayenne, hurry up," I say as I pat my leg. She finally follows after me as Jackson goes over to his car.

Jackson grabs a rope off the workbench and tosses it to me. "Get her in the back seat and tie her head to the ground so she's not standing on the seat."

"Good idea," I say as I yank open the rear car door. I push Cayenne inside, tie the rope to her collar, then tie her so she can't jump onto the seat. She seems confused and a bit panicked but stays where I put her.

By the time I finish, Jackson is already in the driver's seat, so I get into the passenger seat. It's a good thing we backed into the garage to unload the groceries, or that would have added to the difficulty.

"I want you on the ground," he says as he tries shoving me down.

"How can I shoot people if I'm on the ground?" I ask as I fight against his hold.

"You don't. You just get on the ground."

"They'll be waiting outside that garage door. The moment you open it—"

"I'm not opening it, I'm going through it," he says.

I manage to sit up long enough to stare at him in disbelief. "My car is in front of it! You won't be able to see, and if you hit my car, we're fucked."

"I'm hoping luck is on our side. Are you ready?"

A tricky question, but I have no option but to be. "Sure," I say as I take the rifle from him so I have both guns in case shit starts happening.

He backs the car up until it begins to crush the junk behind it. I hear something pop beneath the tire. Then he puts it in drive. I wait for the acceleration, but instead of doing anything, he turns to me. "I just want to remind you that I love you."

I stare at him in horror. "Oh my god! Don't pretend like we're about to die! Just go!"

He gives me a half smile. "Alright."

"I do love you, though," I mumble.

His halfhearted smile turns into a full one. "I know you do. Ready?"

"Sure," I say.

He slams down on the gas and his tires squeal before gaining purchase. The car crashes into the garage door and he yanks the wheel hard, narrowly missing the front end of my car as pieces of garage door disrupt our view. For a moment, there's silence before the sound of bullets pinging off metal and glass.

They'd parked their vehicles in a way to keep us from going far, but Jackson turns the car sharply to the right so we go between two trees before taking our fence out. And then we're off.

"Are you alright?" I ask since his window is quite damaged.

"Yeah... I'm sorry I got you into this mess," he says.

I look over at him in confused surprise. "Wait... you're blaming yourself? Literally, my guy probably told them where we're at. Tucker's a good guy, but if anyone threatens his daughter, he'll throw them info they don't even want."

The car leaps off the curb and onto the road. "I'd do the same for you."

"You'd better not."

"Hmm... I still would, and I'm blaming myself because you were clearly good at staying undercover, and I made you leave that life."

"Made me? You didn't make me do anything. I saw your butthole hanging over that fence and knew we were destined to be soul mates." I glance in the mirror just in time to see a car behind us fly right through a stop sign. "Now, not to concern you, but we do have someone following." That's when I realize what this is. "Oh my god. Are we going to be in a car chase? I've never been in a car chase before! I'm so excited!" I clap my hands out of glee before looking over at Jackson, who looks less than enthused. I wonder if I should dial it down a bit. Then I remember that he loves me and with love comes acceptance for all of one's faults. My fault is that I mentally never know what's good for me.

"Please don't be excited about this."

Poor Jackson, back to thinking I'm a better person than I am. "But it's so hot. You're like... bad boy Jackson, and I'm very turned on right now."

He sighs, but I see a teeny hint of a smile, which tells me that maybe he's kind of pleased. That's until a bullet hits the car's mirror. I start to roll down the window before Jackson elbows me and rolls it back up. "What the hell are you doing?" he asks as he takes a corner going at least twenty miles per hour faster than he should have.

"I was going to shoot them."

"You're working with the police now, and I'm in a vehicle registered under my name. You can't just... shoot people!"

I glance at the red car gaining on us. I'm kind of disappointed it isn't black like most of the bad guy vehicles in the movies.

I jab at the window button, but it won't work since Jackson has his finger on his side to keep it up. "Jackson, I have a license to carry. Nowhere in that stupid little seminar did it say that I could not shoot out of a moving vehicle at people trying to murder us," I say.

"Are you sure?" he asks as he makes a sudden turn. What really gets me is when he puts his arm across my chest like he's going to protect me from flying around the corner. It's oddly sweet and makes me want to kiss him and shoot the assholes following us even more. What it also does is get his hand off the button so I can roll the window down. Which I do before swinging my rifle out of it.

I barely have the tire in my sights before I pull down on the trigger. Their car jerks to the right, catching the rear bumper of a car that'd been parked on the side of the road. It throws their car off course, causing them to come to a metal-crunching halt. I'm no worse for wear as I sit back down in my seat, stroking my rifle for a job well done.

"No wonder Hardek wanted me to join him," I say as their car slows down. "They shot our car up, what? Fifteen times. One bullet from me and they were out of commission... I should have waited, shouldn't I? Gosh... I ruined the fun."

Jackson glances at me with a look of disbelief on his face. "You didn't ruin the fun, you *saved our lives.*"

I chuckle. "I know. I'm joking with you. Kind of. Not really. I wanted explosions and the car was supposed to flip! And then the cop cars would come in but they wouldn't realize there'd be more than one cop car on the scene, so they'd slam into each other but be perfectly fine. And then we and the bad guys would still be at it. And then some *motorcycles* would—"

Jackson pats my leg. "I get it, you think our life should be like an action movie."

"I think I overhyped the situation, you know? And now I'm honestly a bit disappointed."

"Would it make you feel better if I took this turn faster than I need to?" he asks.

I look up at the intersection. "It would!" I say excitedly.

He slams on the brakes and skids around the corner, and I joyously hang on before remembering that we had poor Cayenne in the back, who isn't enjoying a lick of this.

That's when I hear the sirens and see the flashing lights.

"Oh, fuck me..." Jackson says, nearly deflating in his seat. "Why'd I do that? Why do I let you talk me into the stupidest things?"

"It was your idea," I remind him as I try my hardest to wipe the huge grin off my face as the cop car comes barreling down on us, but I absolutely can't.

"But *why?*" he cries as he slows the car.

I pat his leg. "It's like you're a teenager trying to show off to your first love."

"But... I'm *not* a teenager!" He stops the car and looks at me desperately as his words sink in.

"AM I YOUR FIRST LOVE?" I ask, rather loudly for some reason. "You said you weren't a teenager, but you didn't say I wasn't your first love!"

He seems to stop fretting about the flashing lights as his rich brown eyes watch me. "Of course you are. I pretended I was straight until I was thirty, and then I've never been in a committed relationship."

My heart is clearly melting. "I'm getting that weird feeling again, Jackson! I think I'm having a heart attack!"

He sighs as the officer gets out and walks up to the car. He looks in at us with arched eyebrows. I recognize him from the police station, but I can't remember his name. "Jackson, what the hell happened to your car?" he asks in concern.

"Are you talking about the bullet holes?" I ask.

Jackson looks over at me. "Of course he's talking about the bullet holes. What do you think he'd be talking about? The amazing wax job?"

"Maybe he's a wax man! We can't assume anything about him, *Jackson*. That's... hmm... it wouldn't be racist... hobbyist. No..."

I trail off, not because I'm done with trying to figure this out, but because there's another vehicle careening around the corner.

Jackson pulls out the mature voice card. "Hi, Miller, we just... you know..."

I smack Jackson's arm to get his attention. "Not to rush you, babe, but it looks like we have company."

"Fuck," Jackson yells as he throws the car into drive. "They're trying to shoot us!"

And then we take off.

"Now *this* is more like it," I say, very excited. "We have the police *and* more bad guys. Something just needs to blow up and something else needs to flip!"

"Stop being so damn excited!" Jackson snaps.

"Don't tell me what I can and can't do! How dare you try to suppress my emotions like this!" I cry as I roll the window down.

Before I can even shove my gun out the window, their car slams into ours, shoving it into a car that'd been parked along the side of the road, sandwiching us between them. Jackson throws the car into reverse but the engine only revs and the tires spin.

"I got this," I say, but before I "got" anything, the police car comes flying up, boxing us all in as the officer gets out.

"Put your hands up!" the officer yells at the two men in the car. They're hesitating. They're not the ones who originally shot at us, and while I'm sure they have weapons in the car, they would get less time by just saying that they accidentally ran into us.

They raise their hands and I stare at them in disappointment. "How shameful. They have shamed their families."

"They've decided to not murder us or the police officer. Yes, how shameful," Jackson says sarcastically.

I lean over and kiss his cheek. "I love you."

"I have *no* idea how you were able to sit in the house for this long without anything life-threatening happening to you. And the only thing you killed was the vacuum."

"I don't know either. But that should prove to you how much I care about you." I lean into the back seat to check on Cayenne, who looks like she's eager for a new home. "Hi, baby, it's alright." I stroke her head in hopes of comforting her.

"I'm going to call Henry and see if he can get us out of this."

As he deals with that, I stare at the cop and his victims. When the driver gets out, I notice the passenger door open, even though I'm pretty sure the officer didn't tell the passenger to get out. Eagerly, I grab for my door.

"Hey, Leland?" Jackson asks.

I keep my eyes trained on the man who is trying to sneak away. "Yeah?"

"Can I do something badass for once, or does it always have to be you?" he asks.

I grin as I look away from the man to Jackson, who looks amused. "I *suppose*."

He tosses the phone to me and pushes his car door open before taking off after the man who is now leaping the neighbor's fence. "Miller, I got this one!" Jackson shouts.

I put the phone to my ear. "Hey, Henry," I say.

"Oh... no."

"One of the guys got away and Jackson is chasing after him, but he has to face his archnemesis first."

"What's that?"

"The fence. Did I tell you how we met?"

"I'm pretty sure you've told everyone that story by now," he says. "Can you unload your weapons and set them aside while you wait for me to get there?"

I sigh. "I suppose. Jackson looks so hot running. I wish he didn't have his shirt on."

"Hmm..."

"Oh man, those muscles."

"I'm going to hang up now."

"You're missing out."

"I don't think I am."

"He's so hot."

And he's hung up.

Leland: Neigh for me, boy!

Jackson: Let's skip this talk.

Leland: *talking with a horrible Southern accent* You're one fine stud.

Jackson: Please make this end.

Leland: I could have ridden you into the sunset and back. Let me get my boots and spurs. I'm gonna lasso myself a pretty wild thing.

Jackson: Please don't.

Leland: Shhhh, horses don't talk.

Jackson: This one does. This one wants to complain.

Leland: Got my boots, stud. I'm gonna tame you good.

Jackson: This is miserable. What about my moist nipples? I actually preferred talking about that. Funny, huh? How perspectives change?

Leland: You a wild one, ain'tcha? I think I'm gonna need to tame you real good. You wanna sugar cube? You can lick that sugar off every inch of my body.

Jackson: I'm… confused… worried… and what is with this horrible accent? It's like you've never heard anyone from the South *in your life*.

Leland: Shhhh, stud. You don't have to worry about the simple things in life. Just enjoy my carrot and let me hear you neigh.

Jackson: I'm just moving on.

THIRTY-SEVEN

JACKSON

I hope Leland is looking as I clear the fence in one easy leap. Thankfully, no private body parts are put on display as I jump over and chase after the man. When I hit the ground, I find that the man isn't too far ahead of me. As he's climbing the far side of the fence, I grab him and tear him down. I pin him to the ground until he's well aware that I'm not fucking around. Once we have some rules established, he lets me walk him back to the car.

Thankfully, this mess doesn't take long to clear up and all too soon, we're asked to give our statements. Henry picks us up in his car with the news that the house fire *was* put out, but the house might be too damaged to save. After we give our statements for both the house fire and the car chase, we're allowed to leave.

Thankfully, Henry had sent someone else out to get a car for us, which we find waiting in the parking lot when we leave the station.

"We can head to one of my houses," Leland says as he walks Cayenne over to the back door of the rental car.

"The one you kept Henry at?" I ask curiously.

"No, we'll go to a different one. That one might not be safe at the moment."

There is so much about Leland that I still don't know, but I guess when you build your life around never being known, it makes sense. "Mind me asking how many places you own? Just… out of curiosity."

"You can ask me anything. Want to know my shoe size so you can buy me a new pair of boots? My stalking shoes got all full of dumpster trash."

"I'll buy you whatever you want."

He smiles. "Lucas was a strange man. When he passed, he had a total of eleven places spread out in multiple states. I sold all but three. The one you saw, another out in New York, and the last one is the place we'll go to when we're positive no one is out to murder us. They might have followed us out here, but I think once we start driving around, we'll be able to tell if they're still around."

"My concern is, how did they know we were together? Do you think Tucker told Hardek?" I ask.

Leland seems hesitant. "Honestly, I don't know. Hardek might have already known, or maybe Tucker sold us out to keep his daughter safe. I honestly didn't think he knew I was with you, I mean, yes, he knows I'm with someone, and it's the reason I quit… but he didn't know who. Now, I probably have to save Tucker too, but who knows where he's at. I mean, how do you find a man who's with another man who no one can find?"

"I don't know," I admit. "But we'll find them. For now, Henry wants us to lay low." He'd asked if we wanted someone to keep an eye on our location, but Leland was adamant about it being safe and he didn't want anyone to know about it.

He gives me directions as I drive, taking me toward the far end of town as my mind races. Why can't I figure anything more out? How can this man remain so hidden?

"I'm sorry about your house," Leland says as he sets a hand on my lap. I place my hand on top of his and squeeze it tightly.

"I don't know why you're apologizing. It's not your fault."

He leans against the window, pulling his legs up like a child. "I know, but it has to be hard losing everything." Honestly, with all of the shit going on, I hadn't thought about the house much. I had definitely *thought* of it, but being shot at by two crazy people seemed to stand out a bit more. Henry didn't want us going to the house in case someone was watching it and said that he would make sure to get out anything valuable that hadn't been ruined.

"Yes and no. Things can be replaced. I grabbed my laptop, which has most of my pictures on it. My important documents were in a fire-proof safe, which Henry said he'd retrieve for us. As long as I got you and Cayenne out safe, I'm happy."

He smiles at me as his grip tightens on my leg. "I'll buy you a house and everything that goes in it. Sex dungeon. Blow-up dolls, sex swing. Armoire for your dildos. Can you think of anything else you'd like?"

"Maybe a fridge would be nice."

He slowly nods. "Yeah, a fridge sounds nice. You could press me against it and fuck me. That would be tolerated. Anything else?"

"Maybe a bed?"

"We could sleep in the sex swing, but if you want a bed, baby, I'll get you a bed," he says with a grin.

"You're so generous."

"I know, babe. I'm just amazing like that," he says before laughing.

It feels good to hear it after the stressful day.

"If you can think of anything else you just absolutely need to have, I'd be more than happy to give it to you," Leland says.

"Clothes?"

"That's where I draw the line. No clothes for you. I want you naked all the time," he decides.

"Even in public?"

He nods earnestly. "Even in public. Everyone can look at your sexy body and be jealous of what they can't have. You should get a tattoo that says, 'Belongs to Leland.'"

"I don't really want a tattoo."

"I thought you loved me."

"I do."

"Then get a tattoo. I want it across your ass cheeks. That'll be fun."

"Sometimes I feel like we have wildly different ideas of fun," I say.

He adamantly shakes his head. "See, we actually don't. You're just too unsure yet to let others know what you see as fun."

"Is that what it is?" I ask skeptically.

"Guaranteed," he says with a grin. I shake my head because there's no "guarantee" that I want Leland's name tattooed all over my body.

"Turn here," he says as he motions to the next road, so I make my turn and he points to a small house off a country road. I pull in and drive up to the garage. "Let me open the garage door," he says before jumping out.

Once I have the car put away, I head inside. While Leland situates some things, I nosily look around. The house is stocked with necessities of every kind. The food is all packaged or canned, but not even close to expiring.

"There's a safe room in the basement, so if anything happens, that's where I want you to go. No bomb, nothing is going to get through those walls. There are also weapons if you need them... like awesome weapons. Anyway, I've convinced the guys who take care of the place that it's my apocalypse house. They laugh, think I'm weird, but keep everything in tip-top shape."

"You have all of this figured out, don't you?"

He shrugs. "I don't know. Lucas just taught me how to be a nobody. How to disappear. But I don't want to be a nobody anymore. I want to be your bride."

I roll my eyes and head toward the kitchen for some water as he cackles behind me.

"I'm exhausted. Like... why has life been so exhausting?" I ask.

"That's what it's like living with me. Let's take a shower to wash away the smell of burnt house and snuggle like a married couple who still loves each other," Leland decides.

"I'm all for that," I say.

I follow him to the bathroom where he hunts for shampoo and bodywash while I get the shower going. Then I turn to Leland, who leans against me.

"Are you tired?" I ask. It's already three in the morning, so it's no wonder that he's tired. I also want to crawl straight into bed, but I can smell the smoke clinging to his clothes and hair. "That can't be right. You don't *get* tired, do you?"

"Rarely," he admits. "I think I'm... mentally tired. Like I just want to stop having to think about this mess, since I'm getting nowhere."

I slide my hand down his back to the base of his shirt and push it up. His arms willingly go up as I pull it over his head. The moment he's free of the shirt, he collapses into me as I push his sweatpants down.

Leland shakes his head. "I just feel useless. Like I've never been so bad about figuring something out. I mean... I know I took a four-month break from Hardek, but before I met you, I'd been spending weeks trying to find him. I feel like I'm no closer, but he's closer to us. He *knows* us. And whoever has more knowledge generally comes out on top."

"Yes, but they don't have you on their side."

"That's true. I am pretty scary," he says as he grabs my ass and squeezes it.

"Are we going to stand like this all night, or do you want to let me get undressed?"

"I suppose you can undress, but only because I like to see your naked booty. But then again... it looks like too much work," he says as he steps back toward the bathtub.

While I enjoy the view of his ass, he climbs in and I'm left to undress and follow after. When I step in behind him, he looks at me incredulously.

"What took you so long?" he asks as he pours shampoo into his hand and attacks my hair before it even gets wet.

"My hair is still dry!"

"I was wondering why it wasn't sudsing very well," he says before pulling me under the water. When he promptly gives up washing my hair and wraps me in a bear hug, it becomes apparent that my only purpose is to hold him up. Which is fine because that means I get him to myself. I pour soap in my hand and run it down his back since that's pretty much all I can reach.

"I just don't get it," he cries.

"Get what?" I love the way it feels to run my fingers over his bare shoulders down to the small of his back.

"Fucking Hardek! We *have* to be missing something. This is going to drive me nuts."

He's such a better detective than I am. I'm over here so preoccupied with touching him and feeling every part of him that I've pushed Hardek to the wayside.

"I think you should rub my head, maybe that'll help my brain work," he says.

Okay, maybe he isn't immune to my touches either.

Even though I'm pretty sure he already shampooed his hair, I pour more into my hand and begin to work it in.

"It's not working, but it feels amazing," he says.

"Maybe sleep will help."

"Maybe. Or I'll wake up feeling angry that I still can't figure anything out. And then you know what must happen then, right?" he asks.

"I'm not sure I want to know."

"I get to spank your ass."

"Lovely."

He reaches around and smacks my ass cheek for good measure. Not expecting it, I jump and manage to drop a glob of shampoo right into Leland's eyes.

"Oh my god! My eyes!" he cries as he pushes me out of the way. "Why? Why are you trying to kill me when all I've done is love you?" He dramatically grabs the showerhead and sprays it into his eyes.

"Sorry, but you startled me."

Clearly, it wasn't as life threatening as he first thought because within a couple of seconds, he uses his not-so-damaged eyes to glare at me. "Someone lovingly caresses your ass and you shove shampoo into their eyes?"

"Lovingly?" I ask skeptically, which results in him spraying me in the face with the showerhead.

I battle it out of my face before glaring back at him, but he looks so smug that I can't do anything but smile.

"There was so much love in that love tap," Leland tries to assure me.

"Ah, it's now not a caress but a love tap. I see."

"Right? You now understand how dramatic that was to try to blind me, right?"

"Oh yes, very much so. Come here, baby. Let me make it up to you," I say as I pull him into my arms and hug him close. He's still holding the showerhead, so it's sandwiched between us. I gently stroke his cheek. "You poor, poor baby. I'm so sorry."

He tilts the showerhead and sprays me in the face again.

"Dammit! I was being nice!" I say as I grab it from him. Or at least try to, but before I can, he's slid behind me, showerhead hose wrapped around my throat, gently of course. What gets me is not the hose, but how easily Leland slipped past me and basically put me in a chokehold.

"Choose your next words carefully," he whispers in my ear. For some reason, it kind of turns me on. It makes me realize that I'm either a kinky bastard or have a few screws loose to find it hot that my partner can manhandle me.

"You are a cute asshole," I tell him.

He hesitates. "I don't know if I should choke you or not! I've never come to this kind of dilemma before. To choke or not to choke?"

"I called you cute," I remind him. He's behind me and I want to turn around and face him, but he holds me there.

"But you also called me an asshole."

Suddenly, the water turns ice cold as he aims it right at my ass. Startled, I jerk forward, but that just causes the hose to tighten around my neck, choking me.

Leland releases the hose as he shuts the water off, but it just amplifies his laughter. "What'd you choke yourself for? Is that a new fetish I'm not aware of?"

I turn around and glare at him. "You're just so damn proud of yourself too."

"I am," he says gleefully as he turns the water back on long enough to rinse any remaining soap off before getting out. I shut the water off and follow him out. He's patting himself dry with a towel while digging in the cupboard with his free hand.

"Toothbrushes!" he exclaims as he holds them up. "Sorry, they don't vibrate, so you can't get your rocks off."

"So... you think I like to masturbate with, what... a vacuum in one hand and a vibrating toothbrush in the other?"

The grin on Leland's face instantly makes me smile. "Sounds like a Friday night to me," he says as he hands me a pink toothbrush.

I brush my teeth with him next to me, and even though we've lived together for six months, I'm not sure when the novelty of it will wear off. Doing anything domestic together really drives home that he's with me for a long time to come.

"You know what I just realized?" I ask as soon as I spit the toothpaste out.

"Huh?"

"We already brushed our teeth."

"Huh... We did, didn't we? Oh well. Definitely not the worst thing that I forgot I did and did again."

Instead of getting dressed, Leland heads out the door and into the bedroom. I soon follow him and find him staring down at the bed before looking at me.

"What's wrong?"

He looks over at me. "I wish I saved my pillow."

"I'm... not sure the pillow was that important."

"But... my pillow... I love it so much. Call Henry and ask if my pillow is safe."

I sigh and yank the covers back. "Get in the bed."

"I can't. I'm overcome with sadness. It wasn't even my house, and now I'm sad," he says as he looks over at me. "All of our first memories were in that house together. The first time I came over."

"You drove into my tree while bleeding to death."

He smiles fondly at the memory. "The first time I stayed over."

"You lay on my couch half-dead."

He sighs as he crawls onto the bed, which makes Cayenne leap onto it and curl up at his feet. "The first time you set up a camera to watch me masturbate."

"Yeah, that's definitely not why that camera was set up," I say as I climb into the other side and turn to face him. He's watching me closely with his vibrant eyes.

"The suppers, the time on the couch, the bedroom... All of it..."

I reach out and push his hair back. "Why do you think it's all gone? Yeah, the house might be gone, but all of those memories don't just evaporate because it's not there."

"Yes, they do."

"Don't be stubborn," I say as I push myself close enough that I can kiss his forehead. "It's all still there."

"I suppose."

"You wanted a bigger house anyway, remember? With a sex dungeon?"

His worried expression fades away into a grin. "Ooh, sex dungeon. I can have my sex dungeon?"

"I'm not sure we need one, but I've already come to the conclusion that I'll give you anything you ask for."

"Those are some brave words."

"I know. I've lost vital parts of my brain since meeting you. For some reason, I give in whenever you're involved."

He doesn't seem disheartened about that at all as he presses against me until nothing could slip between us.

Jackson: You know, Leland, I think that fence climbing should rewrite all fence climbing I've ever done in my life.

Leland: I don't know what you're talking about. All I remember is your tush on The Fence.

Jackson: No, I climbed that fence as I was chasing that guy. I scaled it with ease.

Leland: I don't remember any of that.

Jackson: Well, I did.

Leland: Hmm... try to refresh my memory. How did you do it?

Jackson: I just ran up and climbed over it.

Leland: That's... that's not jogging my memory. Maybe more detail?

Jackson: I... *clears throat* There I was... heart pounding in my chest as I laid my eyes upon my nemesis.

Leland: Oooooooh. And then what happened?

Jackson: I turned to that motherfucker, and I ripped my shirt wide open.

Leland: OH MY GOD. And then?

Jackson: And with my glittering nipples on display, I faced that fucking fence, and I went "I will mount you this very day!"

Leland: And did you mount it?

Jackson: I mounted it so fucking hard. It tried to knock me down, it tried to snag my pants, but joke's on it... I didn't have pants on.

Leland: OH YESSSSSSSSSSS.

Jackson: I clambered to the top, defeating that motherfucker so hard.

Leland: SO HARD.

Jackson: And that's the end.

Leland: I remember it now. I do! I remember all of that.

Jackson: Of course you do.

THIRTY-EIGHT

LELAND

Jackson sits up so quickly that I know something's wrong. I grab my gun and aim it at the doorway before remembering that we're in a different house and I'm pointing the gun at the dresser.

"What the fuck?" Jackson yelps.

"Huh?" I grumble.

"Where are you pointing that gun?"

"I was gonna fuck the dresser up," I tell him as I switch the safety back on and melt into the bed.

"Why? Can I ask that? I need to know."

"You jumped up like there was someone rushing in to murder us, and I was going to murder them first. My tired brain forgot we weren't home."

Jackson grabs my arm just as I'm fading back off to sleep. "We need to get up and face the day."

I shake my head. "The day doesn't want to be faced." The warm bed while being pressed up against his nakedness is the only thing I want to face.

"It does. Henry just sent me a message that we need to meet up.

But first I need to swing by the agency and grab some stuff. So… let's face the day."

"Fuck the day," I grumble as I pin my pillow to my face in an attempt to never face the day again. It makes me miss the perfect pillow that I lost.

Jackson pulls it off like the savage he is and gets up. I grudgingly get out of the bed and get dressed in clothes that were stored in the house. Because I had only planned on needing badass clothes, I'm decked out in black. Jackson is decked out in black as well, but the pants are high-waters and the shirt is so tight his nipples are trying to tear their way through.

"My god, you're beautiful," I say.

Jackson glares at me before looking down at his clothes. "And you're a liar."

I grin at him. "I would never lie to you."

"And you confirm you're a liar in a statement about never lying while *smirking*. Cute."

"Thank you. I *know* I look cute in black," I say as I turn so he can see more angles of me. "Wanna smack my booty?"

Jackson grunts. Clearly, he's impressed. "I can barely walk."

"You don't need to walk. You need to strut."

"I can't do either. Every step I take, I feel like I'm crushing my balls."

I raise a judging eyebrow. "I got shot and nearly bled to death, and I didn't complain this much."

He shakes his head as he follows after me out to the car. We drive through McDonald's for breakfast before going to the agency. He parks out front since we'll only be a few minutes. When we walk in, he smiles at Rose, who is looking busy by dusting the counter. Thankfully, it seems like everything came together alright after we helped her put her bookshop back together.

"Hey, Rose," Jackson says.

"Oh, you boys better not be up to any trouble again!" she says as Jackson turns to the stairs.

"We're not."

"Could one of you lift this box for me?" she asks.

I hesitate with a foot on the first step leading up. "I got it," I say. "Jackson, go get your stuff."

He nods and heads up the stairs, so I follow Rose over to a box of books.

"I didn't think you guys would be in today," she says as I pick up the box. "It's a blessing you two weren't shot up as well!"

"Yeah… you're talking about when Mason was shot?" I ask.

She quickly nods. "I've been scared of coming here every day and have been leaving early."

"How'd you know I was here?" I ask curiously.

"What?" she asks.

"It wasn't released to the press who was here with Mason."

Her eyes flick up to meet mine. "I just assumed since you're *always* with Jackson."

No… she can't be… *can* she? I mean, she's like seventy. But I suppose a person doesn't have an age quota where they just *stop* being evil.

Yeah, but…

Wait a minute…

Wait a minute…

Rose*bud*.

Buddy?

No…

I'm a genius. That's all there is to it. But I have to be sure first.

I guess there's one way to find out.

The *smart* thing would be to go upstairs and quietly tell Jackson that his landlady is a possible psychopath, sociopath, or maybe just a drug dealer. Who knows? But then he'll be all, "Let's practice safety!"

Or I could blurt it out in her face.

Or… I suppose I could just stand here with a dumb look on my face until she whips a massive revolver out from behind the counter that looks as old as she is.

"What the *fuck*?" I yelp.

I quickly step backward, knowing there's a box of books behind me so that I can dramatically fall over them and pray the noise is loud enough Jackson comes to save me. I hit the ground in a shockingly amazing fashion. I pull my phone out of my pocket as I flip onto my stomach and slide it under my shirt, tucking it into my right armpit so she isn't as inclined to take it if she can't see it.

"Get up!" she snaps.

Clearly, my amazingly perfect and handsome man needs his ears checked because he's not rushing to my rescue.

"I'm getting!" I cry as I keep my arm tucked tightly to my side so the phone doesn't fall out as I push myself to my feet.

Honestly, I could take her. She's a bit shaky and looks like she'd break a hip if I hit her just right, *but* she could take me straight to Hardek.

"You don't want to kill me; Hardek would want me alive."

"I *know*. Because you're the Sandman."

"Oh my god. I gave you the book, didn't I? The graphic novel that I had you give Jackson... this is kind of embarrassing. How long have you known?"

"I figured it out... a few days ago."

"Phew. Gosh, that would have been really embarrassing if you knew this whole time."

"Shush your mouth and put your hands up!" she barks.

"Careful yelling so much or your dentures might fall out—"

She whaps me across the side with a book, so I put my arms up while keeping my elbows to my side to stop the phone from tumbling out.

Then she quickly pats me down, removing my gun and knife before moving to my legs. She goes up them before getting a huge ball grab in there that shocks me.

"Are you patting me down or violating me?" I ask.

"You could only wish," she grumbles, even though she *very* clearly went for a testicle tickle.

"To be fondled by a grandma? Maybe."

"I ain't no one's grandma," she growls.

"But you *could* be."

"Now shut up and head for the back parking lot."

"Don't you want your cane?" I ask.

She glares at me. "If I had a cane, I'd shove it up your ass."

"Ooh. I would enjoy that very much."

The look of shock on her face tells me that she clearly doesn't understand a good joke if it hit her in the face. "Hurry yourself out to that car, right this instant!"

And so, with my hands still up, phone still tucked under my right armpit, I shuffle out to the car while the man of my dreams is obliviously doing something *very* important just upstairs.

She puts me in the car then assesses me, since abducting people must not have been on her schedule for the day. That's when she yanks the string out of my hoodie like a heathen.

"Do you know how hard those are to put back in?" I ask.

She ignores me.

"Granny, I asked if you knew how hard it is. Then again, you probably haven't seen anything hard in *ages*, have you?"

"I used to like you," she says.

"Thanks."

"Not anymore."

"Well, that's brutally honest. You may be suffering from early signs of dementia if you've forgotten how amazing I am."

"Fuck off," she says as she ties both hands together and then to the door handle. She's moving at the speed of a sloth, and I literally could have taken her gun from her at any point, but because I'm a good boy, I just let her tie my hands as loosely as she can. She's clearly not the brawn of the group.

But she's kind of cute, so I let her get away with it. All the while the man of my dreams *still* hasn't noticed that I've been kidnapped. As she starts driving, I let my phone drop out of my shirt and onto the seat. The string around my wrist is so loose, I easily slip one hand free before reaching down to my phone, and that's when she takes off.

When my head slams into the window, I realize that she's clearly not a sloth while driving.

JACKSON

"Mom, I'm really busy, can't this call wait?" I ask as I try to figure out where I put my files. Better yet, where did *Leland* put them when he "cleaned" my desk? He cleans off desks as well as he vacuums.

"I just... I've been thinking, and I don't like this... gap that's grown between us since Leland came in," she says.

"If you are calling to tell me I need to get rid of Leland—" I'm going to be so pissed.

"No! No, that's not it. I was calling because I don't like this gap. I feel like I don't even know what's going on in your life anymore. Do you think we can start getting together for suppers? The four of us?"

"Uh..." I'm honestly shocked by her suggestion. "Yeah... sure." Unless "the four of us" means her, Dad, and some random chick off the street. "We could do that. I'm kind of busy at the moment with stuff from this case, but as soon as it's over with, why don't we start that? I would have you at our place, but with the house burning down—"

"WHAT?"

Whoops. "Oh yeah, our house was lit on fire last night, but we're fine."

"WHAT? And you didn't tell me? Who burned it down? Where are you staying?" she asks in apparent shock.

"I'm sorry. It was late, and there was just a bunch of stuff going on. It's been a bit of a mess, but we're alright. Henry has someone staking out the house."

"I wish you would have told me. I mean... we've been talking for five minutes and you never thought to mention that your house *burned down*."

"I told you that life has been ridiculously busy, and things between us have been strained."

She sighs. "That's my fault, isn't it? That you don't talk to me anymore."

I sigh. "I really don't know. Just..." I rub my head. "I'm in the middle of something. Can we just... sit down and talk about this later? We'll do that supper some day this week."

"Do you have a place to stay?"

"Yeah, I'm staying at one of Leland's places."

"One?" she asks.

"Did I not mention that Leland is a millionaire?" I ask. I don't even know why I tell her beyond the fact that it feels a little bit like I'm getting to brag about him.

"Uh… nope, you didn't… mention that."

"Yeah, so we're fine. Leland can take care of me if I need anything."

"Okay… we're here if you need a place to stay… or need anything."

I know she's trying. But for some reason, I feel like I have to keep pushing up my defenses. I'm too concerned there's a catch to it. Like she's trying to butter me up so she can try to slyly get me away from Leland. It's stupid. I know she's not doing anything of the sort, but I can't stop feeling that way.

"Thank you. I'd like this tension between us to leave as well… I just want to be treated like I used to be," I say.

"I understand. I'll let you go. I love you."

"I love you too."

I hang up and look over at the door, surprised Leland isn't up here yet. Rose must have gotten ahold of him.

I dig through the piles of paper stacked on my desk when my phone beeps. I pull it out and look at it.

Leland: I've been abducted. Lol

Leland: By…

Leland: Wait for it…

Leland: Wait!

Leland: Want to guess?

Me: What are you talking about?

Leland: I've been abducted by Buddy. Lol

Me: Why is this funny? Is this a joke? Are you joking? If you're joking, I'm going to shake you so hard.

> Leland: No joke. I've been kidnapped. At what point does it change from being kidnapped to abducted? How old do I have to be? Am I kidnapped? Or abducted?

> Me: WHO THE FUCK HAS YOU?

> Leland: Are you ready for this?

I may strangle him if someone else doesn't get to him first. He's clearly waiting for a response.

> Me: SPIT IT OUT.

> Leland: Rose.

> Leland: Rose is Buddy. Hilarious, right?

Is that hilarious? Clearly, he's pulling my leg.

> Me: Funny. Now tell me what's really going on.

> Leland: I.

> Leland: Have.

> Leland: Been.

> Leland: Abducted.

> Leland: She smells like licorice. Why's she smell like licorice?

I rush down the stairs, *positive* Leland is pulling my leg. There is *no* way Rose just… what? Abducted a trained hitman—unless he *wanted* to be abducted. Dammit! He wanted to be abducted!

"Leland? Rose?" I call as I look around the clearly empty bookshop.

> Me: If you are hiding somewhere, I'm taking Cayenne and leaving.

Leland: What part of "I have been abducted" don't you understand?

Me: But she's letting you just chat on your phone?

Leland: She's old, she doesn't know that I'm on it.

Me: She's not that old!

Leland: I'm a sly motherfucker.

Me: Where are you at?

Leland: I don't know, she put a shirt on my head since she thinks I can't see through it.

Me: Then how are you TEXTING?

Leland: She didn't tie it, so I can look down and see my lap.

Me: If this is a joke, I'm going to be so pissed.

Leland: Not a joke even though it's HILARIOUS.

Is he really not joking?

Me: Did you LET her abduct you?

Leland: Oh I definitely did. My hands are currently free because she tied me so loose. She has NO idea. I mean, she does have a gun, but I could have taken it fifteen times.

Me: WHY?

Leland: She's taking me to meet Hardek! Come save me!

Oh my god.

Only Leland would think this is a good idea.

> **Me:** Why the hell did you do that? Get out now!

> **Leland:** This is our chance. They're not going to kill me, babe. I have skills that they want.

> **Me:** Please, Leland. Please get away.

> **Leland:** I'm okay. You just have to find me.

> **Me:** Go into your maps and send me your location every minute.

> **Leland:** You're so smart!

After a moment, my phone gets a message telling me Leland's location. I rush out to the car as I put the address into my GPS and turn the car on. Once I'm sure I know where I'm going, I call Henry.

Jackson: I really wish you wouldn't put yourself in dangerous situations, Leland.

Leland: Then I wouldn't even be able to get out of bed, Jackson! The whole world is dangerous!

Jackson: You know what I mean.

Leland: I nearly got murdered by your car the other day. Your car looked at me and was like "Jackson's mine, motherfucker" and it tried crushing me with the car door! I was screaming and like "He's mine, not yours! Ooh. Why's it feel sooooo good?! Did Jackson teach you this? Ohhhhh, I'm so sensitive right there!"

Jackson: None of that happened.

Leland: It did! If I was safe "all the time" I would just… live such a boring life.

Jackson: There's a difference between living life and *letting yourself get abducted by the bad guy.*

Leland: Oh, Rose? Nah, that shit was easy to deal with. That was like a child's game.

Jackson: There were guns.

Leland: My life was more in danger when I got into your car.

Jackson: Sometimes... I just wonder if anything I say sinks into your brain.

Leland: I love you.

Jackson: And then you distract me just like that. I love you too.

Leland: You da best.

Jackson: Just try to be safe... but yes, yes, you're also the best.

THIRTY-NINE

LELAND

The car stops, and I patiently wait while Rose comes around the side and opens the door. She forgets that my arms are tied to the door and nearly yanks them out of their sockets since I'd slipped them back into the loose tie.

"Ow!"

"In all my years, I've never heard anyone complain as much as you." She unties me and leads me after her while moving at hyper speed.

"At this speed, we'll get there sometime tomorrow," I mutter.

She yanks the shirt off my face so she can glare at me. "Your generation is just so rude."

"Oh? I'm not currently the one tying people up and abducting them."

She continues to stiffly walk toward the house. Why she didn't choose to park closer, I'm not sure. It's a nice house, but one I don't recognize. The last map location I sent Jackson was as we were pulling into the driveway, so he should be able to figure out my exact location.

The house almost looks too nice to be a bad guy's place. There are pretty flowers and neatly trimmed hedges around a porch clearly created for hosting.

She takes me into the grand house, looking pretty pleased with herself.

A man comes around the corner and stares at us in apparent shock. He has a couple of lackeys behind him, telling me that he's most likely Hardek. "Um... hello?"

"Hi!" I say as I pull my hand free of the hoodie string and hold it out to him. "I'm the Sandman, and you must be Hardek." The man is sadly boring. He looks like any old businessman off the streets. He has graying hair with brown eyes hidden behind glasses, and is wearing dress pants and a button-up that's borderline too tight for him.

Oh, and he's currently gaping at me. "Rose, what the fuck is this? What the fuck? You thought it was a good idea to bring a goddamn hitman into my house?"

"I had him tied up! He's a squirrely one. I bet it's because he's gay. Those gay ones like the kinky shit. He's probably used to being tied up," she decides.

"You don't think it might be because he's a HITMAN?" Hardek seems a bit dramatic to me. But who am I to judge? I love creating drama.

"How *dare* you speak to your mother with that tone!" Rose growls.

"Rose is your mother? How cute!" I say. "Rose, I think you should ground him."

Hardek doesn't find me funny, for some reason. "Put your hands up. Men, tie him up. Norm, call in backup, get them here immediately. Kenny, pat him down and make sure he doesn't have anything on him."

"Ooh, I get frisked again. Please pick the cute one." I survey the bodyguards until I set my eyes on a *very* buff man. His shirt looks painted on, so I point at him. "Can he frisk me, please?"

Instead, the ugly one steps forward and grabs me. "No! I want the other one!"

I reach forward and run my fingers across the fine man's tight chest before grumpy pants can tie my hands in front of me. A *huge* mistake. They should always go behind. "Hardek, you're *really* missing out if you don't think I'll be of good use. You should *see* what I can do in and out of the bedroom. I might be too much for you to handle."

I wink at him, which makes Hardek look confused. He must not understand "flirting."

While Hardek has a mini freak out, the man whose face looks like it's been beaten in with a boulder takes the hoodie string from me and starts wrapping it expertly.

"Oh! You know your way around a rope, dontcha?" I ask.

He makes sure it's ultra-tight, probably to show off his bondage smarts.

I grin at him. "What else do you know how to tie up?"

"Titties," he says, and I start laughing.

"Kenny, don't talk to him," Hardek snaps, mid-panic. He'd seemed very confident when I was on the phone with him, but I guess having a hitman on the other end of a phone is much different than having one in the house.

Kenny shrugs and starts patting me down. He's a lot more vigorous than Rose, so it's a good thing I left my phone in the car. He even checks under my armpits before moving his hands down my legs. That's when my balls get slightly brutalized, like he thinks I'm hiding a shotgun up there or something.

"Ow! Those are my *balls*," I cry. "I don't like it rough like your girls."

"Man up," he says as he yanks my shoe off and searches in it.

"You have a foot fetish too?" I ask curiously as I wiggle my toes.

"Rose, who the fuck is this kid?" Hardek asks.

"He's the Sandman!" she exclaims.

Hardek stares at me *very* skeptically, and that's when Kenny feels my foot over.

"Oh!" I moan. "Send that piggy to the *market*."

He promptly drops my foot.

"Kenny, that's enough!" Hardek says before Kenny can get to my left leg.

The thing I've found with men is that by making them uncomfortable, they're easily flustered and commonly stop a pat down. He doesn't even bother checking my left ankle.

I shove my foot back into my shoe and turn to Hardek, who is suspiciously staring at me, like he's trying to figure out if I'm even human.

"Have we talked?" he asks.

"You already forgot our call? Or are you just really trying to see if I'm the Sandman?" I ask.

"Who hired you?"

"I told you, originally it was Wilson."

"But you killed him."

"I did."

He shakes his head. "I shouldn't have trusted him. But he never was happy looking up to me. He thought if he killed me, he could take over. But I have plans. Big plans."

"Wanna tell me about those plans?" I ask.

"Oh yes, let me tell you all about my plans," he says sarcastically. "So why are you hunting me down now?"

"Because you've been harassing my partner. You tried to kill him. And I don't take it lightly when someone tries to kill the man I love."

"He was getting nosy."

"Well, that's what he was hired to do. *But* I do have some pull with him. The man loves me, so I can get him to stop... for a price."

"You want me to hire you?" he asks.

I give him my most confident smile. "I can outshoot every person in this room."

"I'm sure you can. The thing is, it's not always smart to have someone so powerful who can't be controlled. If you aren't loyal to me, who's to say you won't stab me in the back?"

"Money. I'm a man of money."

"Last time we talked you didn't want money."

Whoops. "Well... then I didn't. Now I do. Can't a man change his mind? The thing is, a person like me does what the person who hires them wants. If you keep me paid, I'll kill anyone you want me to kill."

"Then what happens when someone else hires you to kill me?"

"Then I'll kill you. Do you not understand what a hitman is? I kill who I'm paid to kill. If you don't want me to kill you, you can either pay me off or keep me employed."

"See? You have no loyalty."

"You're right, I don't, because no one has ever given me a reason to be loyal to them. You just need to give me that reason."

"You sound like a lot of work."

"If you expect everything to be easy, you're not going to make it far in this corrupt world you're paving a way through."

"Hey, boss," a man says as he comes in with something in his hand.

Hardek's attention is drawn to it. "What do you have?"

"There was a phone hidden between the seat and the door. I can't open the phone, but from the lock screen, it looks like he's been sending someone his location."

"Fuck."

JACKSON

I've gotten within half a mile of the place when I pull off. I'm not sure if they have cameras or what to expect, but I don't want to get too close and jeopardize the entire situation. I called Henry, but he's a good fifteen or so minutes behind me. And who knows how soon he can get his team together.

Leland might believe that Hardek will keep him alive for his skills, but men like Hardek don't always like someone stronger than them. They see it as a risk. And Leland isn't only skilled, he's smart. Hardek wants people who follow, not someone who can outsmart him.

I rush around to the trunk, wondering what other weapons Leland has in the rental car. When I pop the trunk, I realize that I'm very wrong. Leland is *not* a smart man. At what point did he pack all of these into here?

I sigh and grab a rifle as I tuck the handgun into its holster on my side. Henry told me to wait for him no matter what, but I *cannot* sit in my car and pray they won't kill Leland. I have to do something.

I sling the strap of the rifle over my back and start moving into the wooded area that must surround the property. It reminds me of my army days and my training. But this time, it isn't a drill. Even when I was deployed, I didn't get into much action, but right now, I have only one thing on my mind, and I know that I'll tear this city apart to keep Leland safe.

I keep moving along the trees, keeping my body down to the ground and pulling up my hood to make my body as dark as I can to not stand out amongst the trees.

When I see the outline of the house, I slow down and move along the ground until I have a good focal point. That's when my phone begins to vibrate.

Expecting Henry to call and tell me to not be stupid and rush in alone, I'm surprised to find that it's Leland. Has he already taken down the entire syndicate and stopped for ice cream?

"Hello?"

"Ah, you must be Jackson," the man says, sounding far too confident.

Worry swirls in my stomach. He must have found Leland's phone and knows I'm headed there. He might even know that I'm outside, staring through the rifle's scope.

"I just want him back, and I'll turn around. If you don't, I'll call the police and tell them your location."

"And you want me to believe you haven't already called them?" Hardek asks.

"Whatever I've done, I can deter them long enough for you to get away if you give him back to me," I say as I see a car pull in and people get out. Clearly, he's called reinforcements.

"Or I could just kill him."

"I will kill every one of you if he has been harmed in any way," I growl.

"Who did you tell?"

"No one yet because I didn't know what I was getting into."

"Don't lie to me," he growls. "Tell me what you know!"

"Jackson! My love!" Leland calls in the background.

"Shut up!" Hardek yells.

"I'm gonna take these guys down!" Leland says.

"Shut that fucking guy up!" Hardek yells. "Shoot him in the foot."

And that's when I hear screaming and the first gunshot. Then the call goes dead.

Panic hits me as I see the guards turn to run for the building, and I know that I need to figure out what I'm doing immediately. I aim with the rifle and shoot the man closest to me in the leg. He drops down as I swing my gun up and shoot the next man. All thoughts of legality and Henry's warnings fly out the window. All I know is that I need to get to Leland as quickly as I can. I will not stop until he's back in my arms.

LELAND

I draw my leg up and pull the knife out of the shoe Kenny never checked. Hardek's attention is stupidly on the phone, so I step up to him and try to slam the knife into the side of his neck. He pulls back at the last moment so I drive it into the base, closer to his shoulder and missing anything vital. He yells out and shoots at me, but I'm close enough that I slip to the side as he fires. I wrap my bound hands over Hardek's neck as I pull him back.

Hardek slams his elbow into my side, shoving me back. I still have the knife, but I've never been a master knife wielder, seeing as guns are my forte.

Sexy buff dude grabs me and tears me backward, but since I'm attached to Hardek's neck, I yank him back with me. He falls into me, crying something about his bleeding neck. With the way he's struggling, he's going to make blood pump out so much quicker, but he doesn't seem to notice.

Kenny and the sexy guard grab me as I tighten the binds on my hands over Hardek's neck.

Hardek lets out a gargled sound as I tear him back, but Kenny manages to get my hands off Hardek before throwing me to the ground. I still have the knife, so I reach out, pulling Kenny closer to me as I ram the knife into his leg. He howls out as he falls back, but Hardek stands over me, a gun aimed at my head, his other hand holding his bleeding throat.

"You... *fucker*," he growls.

"You don't threaten to shoot me unless you want me to bite back. But do you *really* want to kill me?"

"No, you have some information I wouldn't mind having. Imagine *all* the knowledge you have going on in that brain of yours. But you don't need hands or legs to give me that information, now do you? What do you want to lose first?'

"Oh? I get to pick? I'll let you trim my hair if you want."

He aims the gun for my hand as I realize that I might have fucked myself. But I wasn't going to just lie there and let him shoot me in the foot. And stabbing him really made me feel a bit better.

"Or maybe you're not even worth it," he says as he moves the gun up toward my head.

That's when the gun fires and I flinch back, but the pain never hits me. Instead, Hardek drops to his knees, hand going slack enough that his gun falls from it. He groans and grabs his side as he rolls onto his back, wallowing around in pain. Directly behind him stands Jackson. I watch with wide eyes as he stands there looking like God dropped him directly from heaven.

"If any of you move, I *will* kill you," he growls, and I realize that I've never been so turned on.

One of the men moves, but I grab Hardek's gun and shoot him before he even gets the gun raised. Then I'm up and running for Jackson, who grabs me with one arm and pulls me behind him like he's going to protect me with his body.

"You saved me," I say, mystified and turned on and far too excited.

His eyes leave mine to watch the men in case they get any ideas. "If any of you move, I'll kill you all," Jackson growls. "Leland, get out."

"I'm not leaving you," I say as I grab onto the edge of his shirt with my left hand just because I want to feel a part of him. Even if that part is only what he's wearing. "I will only leave if you're leaving with me."

"Alright, watch my back. Henry's crew should be here momentarily," he says.

"I could watch your back all day," I say.

"Don't make me want to hug you when I'm holding these guys at gunpoint," Jackson says.

"Fine, but Kenny knows how to tie a mean knot. He says he can tie up titties, maybe he can teach you a thing or two."

"I don't have any titties to tie up."

"I suppose."

The sirens start and people begin flooding the building. Jackson directs them to Hardek, who is trying to crawl away while simultaneously trying not to bleed to death.

"Don't say *anything* until we talk to Henry," Jackson says as he reaches down to my hands and quickly unties them. "I don't know what he wants to do about the legalities of things. He'll keep us out of jail."

Henry walks up as other people come in and handcuff Kenny and the buff man.

"Let's let them work. Are you two okay?" Henry asks.

"Oh my *god*, Henry," I say as I grab his arm. "It was so fucking hot. There I was lying on the ground, Hardek had a gun aimed at me, was about to shoot me and here comes Jackson. I'm on the floor, quivering in fear. Who is going to save me? Jackson will! He busts in on top of a white stallion and screams, 'Don't touch my lover!' And POW pops him. Hardek falls to his knees and Jackson rips his shirt off so I can see his muscles. There was a slight shimmering of sweat, which is not as sexy, but I'm still rolling with it."

"None of this happened, did it?" Henry asks.

"Very little," Jackson admits, but he wraps a secure arm around my waist and pulls me back to him.

"Shut up, Jackson. It was sexy! Let me bask in the sexiness of it. Do you think you can reenact it?" I ask eagerly as I press my body into him. I love the protective grip he has on me.

"I think we should be quiet so we can remain as innocent as possible," Jackson says. "We have no idea who shot them. They took Leland hostage. I came in to save him. By the time I came in, everyone was already half-dead."

I look up and find him closely watching me. "That story sucked. It didn't have anything about your heroic efforts or the chubby I got watching you."

"We don't need any of that information," Henry says. "Are you positive both of you are unharmed?"

"I am. Leland?" Jackson asks as he pulls me in front of him so he can look me over.

"I already told you I was fine," I assure him. "More than fine! *You* were more than fine. You were *sexy*."

Henry pats my back. "You did good."

I look over at him. "I did? Do you… tolerate me now?"

"I guess… because Williams would have wanted it. He was the kind of guy who forgave everyone. Now we need to keep anyone here from blurting about who you are," he says.

"Men like that don't talk, especially to the police," I say. "And without Hardek to protect them, they're probably a bit scared to talk. If no one asks the question, I doubt it'll come up. But if you want me to go in there and threaten them, I can. I like threatening people. Wait! Let Jackson threaten them. That sounds sexy."

"No threatening. You guys have done plenty. Just go wait by my car; I'll come talk to you after I have a better handle on things."

"Alright," Jackson says as he directs me over to the far side of Henry's car before pulling me around to face him. Then he grabs me and draws me close to him as he squeezes me tightly. "I was so scared, Leland. Dammit, don't make me worry like that ever again!" He pushes my hair back and grabs my face in his hands.

That's when I realize that this isn't Jackson being dramatic. He's *really* upset. "Hey, I'm okay. Jackson, I promise I'm okay."

His hands are quivering as he brushes his thumb over my cheek. "He could have shot you… I could've lost you," he says as he tucks his head against my neck. "Why did you go with them? Why did you do that?"

I pull his head back so I can look him in the eyes. "Jackson… I'm sorry I put myself in that situation, but I need you to stop and think about how many people we've saved. Hardek moved both weapons *and* people through the black market. How many girls did we save? How many people did we save that could have been shot by those guns? Jackson, I know you love me and that means so much to me. But we can save people. We can save lives. You and me? We have skills and abilities that many don't have. And sitting in a safe, padded room won't save anyone but ourselves."

He lets out a deep breath before setting his forehead against mine and closing his eyes. "I know. You're right. It was just… I was scared."

"I know, and that probably will never get any easier no matter how long we do this. I would have felt the same thing if that was you lying there. Because you mean so much to me. More than you'll ever know. Before you, I felt like I wasn't even living. I *thought* I was happy. I thought I was living life to the fullest. But... it was because I was resigned to thinking that I would never have this. Never have these moments with you. Never have someone who cares and loves me the way you do. But you've proven to me that there's so much more to life," I say earnestly. I'm not sure words could ever portray how I feel, but I think he still understands.

"I know," he says before tipping my chin up and kissing me.

I lean into his lips, wanting to feel more of him. "It's hard, but I know that together we could accomplish many things. But I promise I'll be less reckless next time. I *maybe* jumped into things there and could've done it differently."

He raises an eyebrow. "Maybe?"

"Tiny bit," I say with a grin. "Teeny, tiny bit. Like nipple-sized bit."

He shakes his head like he doesn't believe me. Like I could be *exaggerating*. "That must have been one big-ass nipple."

I grin. "Nope."

"Let's do things together from now on. Like... talk things through."

"I bought you a sports car, but since I didn't talk to you about it first, I'll take it back," I say.

He sets a hand on my arm. "Starting *now* we'll talk things through."

Leland: And that is the moment... the mistress came between us.

Jackson: Stop calling my car "the mistress." She prefers madam.

Leland: Dammit. I never knew what a grave mistake I was making buying you that car. I never knew how much you'd love it. How it'd come between us!

Jackson: Well, you have the fence and I have my car.

Leland: Yeah, but The Fence also wants your ass. Everyone wants you. You're just so delectable but you're mine. You tell those thirsty bitches you're mine.

Jackson: I'm all yours... Don't worry about the car. Don't worry about what the car said about you. Only ever worry about me.

Leland: What did the car say? I bought it! I used *my* money, and it betrays me like this.

Jackson: Shhh, I thought you were sexy being all badass.

Leland: I was?

Jackson: So sexy.

Leland: You... maybe will be forgiven.

Jackson: Then again, you did run off without me and get abducted. My car has never left me.

FORTY

JACKSON

I pull into the driveway of our new house. We'd gone middle of the road once we decided we *really* didn't need a mansion. At two stories, it's still bigger than my two-bedroom house that is currently being rebuilt for sale.

The issue with Leland paying for the house is that I felt like I had to give him more leeway when he designated the rooms for specific things. When he wanted a "gun shrine," I couldn't say no. So one of the four bedrooms was immediately turned into an "If the police came in, we'd immediately go to prison for the number of illegal weapons we're currently setting out on display" room. At least I talked him into making it the most secure room in the house—nobody's going to be casually strolling into there.

My phone starts ringing as I put the car in park, so I accept the call.

"Hey, Henry."

"Just thought I'd give you an update," he says. "Now that he's stable, they've moved him to prison to await his trial date. I'm not even sure why he needs a trial. The amount of evidence we have on the man is a mile high. He orchestrated so much of it. The smuggling, the illegal trading, the abductions—he was behind all of it. He didn't physically do much of it, but he was very organized and kept things progressing."

"I know it all seems to be moving at a sloth's pace for you guys, but I'm glad that it's clear things *are* moving. It's only a matter of time before everything falls into place."

"Yes. There's always the concern that we didn't get all of them, that someone will take over what he started, but I'm glad we cleaned up a good amount of it."

"I agree."

"I'll keep you updated as the case progresses, and if we ever need your help again... well, you *and* Leland, I'll let you know."

"You know where to find us. And Leland is chomping at the bit to help with something, so never hesitate to ask. No matter how ridiculous, I'm sure his answer will always be yes."

"Thanks. I really am very glad to see you so happy."

"Thank you, Henry. You've been like a father to me."

"Don't get all sappy on me. I don't know how to handle it," he jokes.

I chuckle. "Alright, I'll let you go. Leland said he has a surprise for me. I have no idea if the surprise is a bubble bath, a rocket launcher, or it might even be a terrorist he has tied up."

"Your life's never boring, huh?"

"Not with Leland in it."

"Good. I don't think you handle boring very well."

I smile, glad that Henry really is starting to like Leland. "That's true."

"Have a good night. I hope it's not the terrorist."

"Agreed."

"But if it is, call me. I'm always up for some action."

I laugh. "You're almost as bad as Leland!"

He chuckles. "Not yet."

We say our goodbyes before hanging up, and I head into the house. Cayenne is the first to greet me, tail wagging as she dances at my feet. As soon as Leland comes around the corner, she shoots off to visit him like she also hasn't seen him *all* day.

"Welcome home," Leland says with a cocky grin.

"What are you up to?" I ask.

"Fun things."

"Rocket launcher?" I guess.

He starts laughing. "Not that fun."

"Hmm... I'm worried."

"Don't be," he says as I grab him and pull him close. He wraps his arms around me, and I realize that if I keep him like this, I might not have to deal with whatever he has planned.

Then again, I'm too curious. "What horrible thing have you dragged us into?"

He starts laughing before smacking my ass. "Nothing! Come along. I have *things* to show you."

"Oh no," I say, but I eagerly follow him through the house and over to the door leading into the basement.

He dramatically yanks the door open and throws the lights on. Then he steps behind me and clasps his hands over my eyes.

"I have to go down the stairs like this?"

"Correct," he says as he knees me gently in the ass. "I'll catch you if you fall or I'll laugh. Just expect one or the other."

"I honestly don't expect one *or* the other. I expect laughter," I say as I take my first timid step forward.

"Why are you moving so slowly? I'll be an old man by the time we reach the bottom. Is this how you're going to move in the next couple of years?"

"Yes, because I'm on the brink of being elderly," I say sarcastically.

He chuckles as he follows me down the stairs. "Last step!"

"Oh, thank god."

"I know, right? I didn't get to laugh at you tumbling down the stairs, either. So disappointing." He pushes me forward by slamming his groin against my ass. "Want me to hump you into position?"

"Or you could just direct me."

"Boo. Boring. But fine." He pushes me into position. "Are you ready?"

"I don't even know how to answer that," I say.

"Of course you are!"

He sounds so excited that I *know* I should be worried. He yanks his hands away before slipping beside me so he can do a dramatic motion toward what I'm supposed to be staring at.

"Ta-da!"

"It's…" I stare at the huge tripod in the middle of the finished basement, straps hanging here and there from it. And right in the middle is a male blow-up doll.

"Sex swing! And that's Blow-Up Dandy."

I'm trying not to grin at the ridiculousness of the situation. "I thought it was Randy?"

"Fuck if I know," he says. "I bought him on Amazon." He rushes over to the sex swing and kneels next to it. "Look at his blow-up penis! I nearly died blowing him up. When his penis popped out, I was laughing so hard on top of already being air deprived from blowing him up that I nearly passed out."

He yanks him free from the swing and holds him in front of himself. There's a twelve-inch blow-up schlong aimed at me.

"I want to penetrate," Leland says in a robot voice for some reason.

I can't help myself at this point and start laughing. "My god, what's wrong with you?"

"I really don't know," he admits. "A lot? A little? Who knows?"

LELAND

I toss Blow-Up Dandy Randy and step in front of Jackson. "Are you ready?"

"To try out the sex swing?" he asks with a grin. Clearly, he's ready.

"Oh yeah. I assembled it, so if it falls apart mid-coitus, it's not my fault. I called Henry and asked if he would help me put a sex swing up and he hung up on me, so I think he's busy."

"Please tell me that's a joke," Jackson says.

I smile, since I don't want to lie to him ever again. Lying is not a good thing, especially in a relationship as perfect as ours. "Now let's get you undressed so we can try this out!"

He grins as he grabs my arm and pulls me to him. "We can have a *lot* of fun with this tonight."

"I'm glad you like it. It's only the first thing in my sex dungeon. More to come!"

He gently kisses my lips, but when he pulls away, he's grinning. "I look forward to it." Then he draws me in for a deeper kiss. One that makes me push into him and leaves me breathless. One that makes me almost forget about everything but him.

Oh, and the sex swing.

Can't forget the sex swing.

As his tongue brushes against mine, he pulls my shirt up. Sliding his fingers over my bare sides and up to my shoulders, he takes the shirt with him. Then he pulls it free and drops it to the ground as I unbutton his pants.

I'm not sure we've ever undressed each other so quickly. There's barely any foreplay, just frantic undressing while we still try to manage to get a few kisses in between fabric flying. I think I kiss his shirt at one point.

Naked, we stand side by side and stare at the sex swing.

"I don't have any experience with sex swings," Jackson says.

"I do! I watched some people use it in porn! I would consider myself an expert."

"Those two straps for the thighs and back?" he asks as he assesses the swing.

The swing didn't come with one large seat like the ones I've seen in the pornos. This one comes with multiple smaller straps. It appears like one body strap should go under the thighs and the second body strap should go behind the back. "I think. That's how I shoved Randy in there."

"Alright," he says as he grabs me by the waist and picks me up.

There's nothing sexier than seeing the muscles in his arms bulge from my weight as he lifts me into the air. I wrap my legs around his waist, his cock brushing against my ass as he smiles at me. He carries me while pressing gentle kisses against my lips.

He lowers me onto the swing as he gives me another kiss, then lets me go. That's when I realize the straps must not have been in the right place because I drop down between them. The only thing keeping me from hitting the ground is grabbing onto the back strap with my arm and hooking my ankle so I'm dangling an inch above the ground.

"Shit! Are you okay?" Jackson asks as he grabs for me.

"Maybe this is how it's supposed to work," I say as I use my arms to swing myself some.

Jackson starts laughing. "That's definitely not how it's supposed to work."

"But you have full access to my ass, right?"

He starts laughing harder as he stares at me. "Why is it every time we do something sexy, it turns out like this?"

"Hurry, Jackson! Penetrate me before my arms get tired of holding myself up!" My hand starts to slip. "Oh no... Jackson! I don't know if I'm going to be able to do it! I don't know if I'll be able to make it!" I let my arms drop and my back touch the ground, but my ankles are still in the air which means my ass is too. "Look! New position!"

"You're going to hang upside down while I do you?" he asks.

I flip over and push the strap down to my lower stomach. "Here we go! I could swing into your dick! Just stand behind me!" I start swinging back and forth as Jackson just laughs. "Stop laughing, Jackson! Get into position."

I reach back with my toes and slide my foot through the stirrup and then the other before grabbing onto the handles and lifting myself up. "They call this one the Flying Squirrel."

"They do *not*!"

"Hurry! Get on my back! We'll fly toward ecstasy!"

He reaches over and grabs Blow-Up Dandy Randy before shoving him on my back. "There you go."

I start laughing as I kick my ankles free. "Why do I feel like you're not into this?" I ask as I drop back down to my feet and stand up.

"I was until I savagely dropped you on the ground."

I grin at him as I move toward him. "I have a new idea. I want you on the swing."

"I'm honestly scared," he says, but he's grinning as he looks at it.

"Good, I like men when they're frightened," I say as I push him toward the swing. He sits down on it and we make sure he's properly positioned and isn't going to fall through. I grab the lubricant and toss it at him. He catches it before going back to admiring my craftsmanship or maybe the fact that I know how to read directions. Who am I kidding? I tossed the directions in the trash, which is probably why I fell right through the swing.

I climb onto his lap as he looks at me in worry.

"We're going to break this thing."

"What are you talking about? I assembled it. This fucker will stand for eternity," I say as I grab the chains and pull myself forward to get it swinging, but it won't move because he has his feet on the ground. "Get those feet up."

"I'm worried," he says, but he gives us a push then lifts his feet.

"There we go," I say as I grin down at him. "This is already so much more fun than I could ever imagine."

"All we've done is swing. You could have done this at the park."

I raise an eyebrow. "I think that's how you get arrested."

He starts laughing. "Not... this, but... you know what I mean."

I grin as I lean down and kiss his lips. "I do."

He pops open the lubricant before squirting some on his fingers. Then he pushes us off again, probably because it makes my grin widen.

"Put your knees on the strap my back is leaning against and grab onto the handles."

"I have no idea what we're doing, but I'm into it," I say as I try climbing up his body. It puts my cock right in line with his mouth and I realize that I'm *really* into it. Especially when he pulls my ass toward him and runs his tongue up my cock.

I clutch tightly onto the handles above my head as he grabs my ass cheeks in each hand and squeezes them. But when I look down to see him staring up at me, my excitement overtakes me. His fingers slide between my ass cheeks until they find my hole. Then he begins rubbing a circle around it while his tongue runs around the head of my cock. My body doesn't know if it wants to push forward, deeper into his mouth, or back onto his fingers as the swing rocks beneath us.

His finger slides into me, stroking just inside as his hot mouth and tongue slide over my cock. A second finger joins the first, opening me up and making pleasure fill me as I see the lubricant tube sliding down his chest. I decide that I could probably reach back and rub it along his thick cock.

He pulls his mouth from my cock and kisses my thigh. "You like that?" he asks.

"I do," I say as I let go of the handles just as he gives a huge kick off with his feet. I'm not sure where he was planning on sending us sailing, but the swing careens through the air.

Neither of us expected what the other is doing. I lose my balance and fall forward as I head dive off the front. I easily catch myself, but when I look back, I realize that I've smashed my balls into his face as I straddle his head. I clearly help the situation by collapsing onto him while laughing. Slowly, I slither off him as I curl up on the ground, laughing so hard I can't even stand.

"I didn't know you wanted to look at my balls so closely," I say.

He looks back at me in shock. "I think I got your nut hair in my teeth!"

"Shut up! No, you didn't!" I say as I crawl back to him. "I'm sorry! I got eager!"

"You're the one who's fallen for the second time, so I'm not sure why you're apologizing. Are you alright?"

"Yes! Stay there!" I say as I grab the lubricant off the ground before going between his legs. With lubricant in my hand, I rub it down his shaft while trying to keep the laughter on the down low. "You're going to have a nut-sized bruise on your face tomorrow."

He starts laughing. "Shush. Go back to the sexy."

"I'm trying," I say as I climb back onto his lap. This time, I don't go too far; instead, I grab onto the handle with one hand and his cock with the other before lowering myself until I can feel the head against me.

"This is why I love you," he says.

"What? My clear inability to succeed at the sex swing?"

"Because you never fail to shock me, make me laugh, and be sexy all at the same time."

I grin down at him as I let my fingers run up his cock. "I'm good like that." Then I lower myself onto him, his cock opening me up as I sink down. I grab the second handle with my free hand. Every time we swing forward, I slide down onto his cock, using my momentum to push us back. Jackson sets his hands on my thighs, moving them up until he has my cock in one hand and my hip in the other. He moans as I sink onto him, rocking my hips as his fingers tease the head of my cock.

"I want to try another position," I decide. "I want to try them all!"

"I... don't think I can hang on for *all* positions. But we'll have plenty of time," he says as he stops the swinging with his feet. He sits up and wraps one arm around me, cock still deep inside of me as he uses the chain of the swing to pull himself to his feet. He turns around and lowers me onto the swing, never losing contact in case he decides to throw me on the ground again. As he stands up, he pushes my foot into the stirrup before the other one. Then he grabs onto the straps as he swings me back, drawing his cock out of me before pulling the swing back to him until he's buried deep inside of me.

My head drops back as I moan and realize that he's *very* right. There is *no* way I'm going to hold on much longer, let alone for more positions. And the way he's pulling me into him with the swing and driving himself into me with his hips has me writhing in pure pleasure. I reach down and grab my cock, stroking it while the only part of his body touching me is his cock as he pushes deep inside me. I rub my cock with one hand as I hold tightly onto the strap with the other.

"Harder," I moan. He's right there, so close, and it's driving me crazy.

He begins thrusting forward, meeting with the swing as he pulls me into him, and I realize that maybe I shouldn't have asked for it even harder because it's making me feel so much pleasure. *Too* much pleasure. It's driving me crazy.

He buries himself inside of me as I realize that I'm already at my limit. There's not much more I can take as my balls tighten and cum shoots from my cock. He groans as he buries himself inside me, moving quicker as I throw my head back as my orgasm rushes through me. I can hear him moan as his cock pulsates inside me. It feels like he pushes unbelievably deep inside me as I let go of my cock and grab onto him.

He's panting as he leans over me and kisses me gently.

"Did you like the swing?" I ask with a grin.

He smiles at me before kissing me again. "I love the swing. But we'll have to put a lock on the door if you're really making this a sex dungeon."

"Imagine if your mom came down here."

"Don't talk about my mom when we're like this," he says.

"So picky," I say, but I don't want him to run from me, so I decide to be good.

Jackson: Flying Squirrel, eh?

Leland: I mean... have you *ever* heard of a sex position that's better than that?

Jackson: There are a lot of sex positions that are far superior, like... Sex in a Bed, or Normal Sex, or Oh, Look, Here's a Bed, Let's Get Naked.

Leland: Jackson, how could you make sex sound so boring? I fell asleep while you were talking. Now say "Flying Squirrel" to me.

Jackson: *sighs* Flying Squirrel.

Leland: Fuck, yeah, baby. The desire is surging through me. The lust is tingling through my body.

Jackson: You literally get the same way when you look at weapons, so I'm not quite sure what to think about this.

Leland: You... you want to do the Flying Squirrel... while playing with paintball guns? Oh, Jackson. You know the way to my heart.

Jackson: I think this book is nearly over and we need to skim the rest of it. We have three seconds; think we can finish it in time?

Leland: I can make *you* finish in three seconds.

Jackson: Please... no...

Leland: You ready? I'm going to read the epilogue with an accent just for you. That'll make those nipples moist again.

Jackson: And they lived happily ever after. The end.

Leland: If you sass me too much, I'll start back at the beginning. DARK NIGHT, lone PI, panties ready to snag, heart ready to capture, lust raging—Jackson! Jackson, don't fall asleep! No! Fine, I'll move on!

EPILOGUE

JACKSON

I'm like a child on Christmas morning as I lead Leland up to the agency. Since Rose isn't going to be back to selling books anytime soon, Leland bought the building. I'm not sure what we'll do with the lower level now that I've persuaded him that we can't have *two* sex dungeons.

"But… think of how cool it'll be—our clients walking in and being like 'What's this?'" Leland says as he walks up the stairs behind me to the second floor.

I reach back and grab his hand to tug him after me. "No, they'll just leave."

He sighs. "Whatever. So picky."

"Yes, very picky," I say sarcastically.

I push the door open and pull him onto the second floor. He stops as he sees what Mason and I moved in last night.

"Is this… my own desk?" he asks with wide eyes.

I smile at him as he wanders over to it. "It is."

"I have two desks now! I'll let Cayenne sit at the other desk."

My brows furrow. "Um… no, the other desk goes back to me."

He presses his finger against my lips. "Shush, my sweet, sweet man. Now, how many desks do I get?"

He's giving me that loving smile, the one that generally makes me weak and give him anything he wants. "You get one."

He walks over to my desk, grabs it, and drags it over to his. "One *huge* desk. Thank you, honey! I love it!"

I shake my head. "May I sit at your second desk?"

"Eh." He looks over at it and seems to be thinking quite a bit before shrugging. "I *suppose*."

I walk over to him and push him against the desk until he sits on the edge of it. "You're so sweet."

"Thank you."

"Don't make me regret working with you."

"I've been thinking of starting my own agency and competing against you."

"I wouldn't even be surprised."

Leland had wanted to quit all of his college classes, but I suggested that he take some forensics classes or other classes that could help him in this field because I think he needs more to keep his attention than just cheating husbands or wives. While he claims that he doesn't want to stay long enough to get a degree, I'm sure he could do anything he sets his mind to. He's obviously spent a lot of time in the field, but he doesn't know as much about the forensics side of things that seems to interest him.

Leland reaches up to my face and cups my cheek. I *believe* he's going in for a kiss, but instead, he smiles at me and I know I should be worried. "So... I was talking to Tucker—"

"Why the hell were you talking to him?"

"Just checking to see if he got away or not."

"And?"

"He was talking about this guy—"

I sigh. "No."

"Who has been assaulting—"

"We're PIs now. Not hitmen."

"Women—"

"Fine, we'll check it out. JUST check it out."

His smile widens as he wraps his arms around me. "Why are you so easy to persuade?"

"Only when you're involved," I admit.

Definitely only when he's involved. I'm weak to anything he does or says, and he knows it. But it doesn't matter because I know that I'll go anywhere with him. I lean in and gently kiss his lips as I wrap my arms around him.

"I like that," he murmurs against my lips. "I like you weak to me."

I grin. "I wouldn't say *weak*."

"Weak and horny."

I shake my head. "Yes. Weak and horny whenever you're around."

He chuckles as he digs his fingers into my back and holds me tightly. "I love you so much."

His words fill me with so many emotions. "I love you too."

"Since Mason comes back to work tomorrow, let's bring Blow-Up Randy and put him in his chair."

I grin at the idea. "Yes."

I feel like I could stay like this all day, wrapped up in his arms even as his fingers creep down the back of my pants. I never thought I'd be lucky enough to be in a relationship. And never with someone as amazing as him.

I have no idea what my future holds, but I know that as long as I have him by my side, I'll face it head-on with a smile on my face.

Leland: Boo.

Jackson: What? You literally didn't like our life, Leland? How we met?

Leland: Boo, it's over. It does make me in the mood for another Flying Squirrel, though.

Jackson: One Flying Squirrel is all I can handle.

Leland: Nah, think about how far you've come, Jackson! You went from a man who can't even climb a fence, to a wonderful but sketchy partner who refused guns and sex dungeons, to the man you are today. We have a sex dungeon packed full, you recently even took a class on how to climb fences, and you've hooked a badass motherfucker.

Jackson: I *have* come a long way. Although… I kind of came across as pretty normal before I met you.

Leland: Yeah… but were you happy?

Jackson: Not as happy as I am now. Weird how that works.

Leland: It's magic.

Jackson: I think it's called love, not magic.

Leland: Ew, no, gross. It's magic. I wanna magic all over your face.

Jackson: I'm just… confused now.

Leland: It's my favorite state for you.

Jackson: Okay. That's good, then. Well… even if the road to each other was… a unique one, I'm glad that you saw me that fateful night.

Leland: Are you… admitting that you're thankful… to The Fence?

Jackson: I guess… if it led me to you… I'll tolerate The Fence.

Leland: I love you.

Jackson: I love you too.

Leland: Now let's read the next one!

Jackson: Oh hell no. I'm not reliving Sasquatch Jackson. Once was enough for me.

The following snippet is best enjoyed if you've read through at least three books in the Hitman's Guide series seeing as it includes some characters who don't make an appearance in this book.

Cassel: Ew.

Jeremy: We could burn the book.

Cassel: Why the hell did they give me a book about how they met? And why did they think we'd want to read about them doing it. Ew. Gross. *WHY*? Jeremy, my EYES.

Jeremy: I told you not to read it. I told you to burn it the moment he handed it to us.

Cassel: I know but Leland was so excited, and I was tricked! He told me it was sweet and cute and fun, and it was just fucking *torture*. I thought dealing with Leland was bad enough but reading his thoughts? Seeing him harass Jackson? AND THE SEX. MY EYES.

Jeremy: Honey, stop focusing on the sex.

Cassel: I'm never going to be able to get it up again. And the FLYING SQUIRREL. God and then I was thinking about you eating a squirrel and then I was confused.

Jeremy: Why'd you keep reading? Did you read the whole thing?

Cassel: I skipped the sex, but the book was like a train wreck. I couldn't look away.

Jeremy: You should have looked away.

Cassel: Jeremy… do you think you could hold me?

Jeremy: Come here.

Cassel: Henry, what'd you do with your copy?

Henry: I threw it at some guy trying to stab me. The man ended up stabbing the book, making it impossible to read. Leland was extremely thrilled that I took down the bad guy with it. It stopped him from ever asking if I read it.

Cassel: *holding the book like a boomerang* I'm gonna fuck up some assholes. You're right, Henry, if it's coated in blood, the pages will be unreadable.

Henry: Is… that what I suggested? I… don't think it was. Oh fuck, here they come. Act natural.

Leland: Sooooo, how did you like the book?

Cassel: MY EYES. *chucks the book*

Leland: Why the fuck did you just throw it at me?

Jackson: Leland, don't tell me you gave them the book.

Leland: I did! I also went through and highlighted every time your ass was mentioned. Cool, huh?

Cassel: J-Jeremy, I don't think I'm long for this world. P-Please… take me away.

Leland: I'm so pleased everyone loved it!

Henry: Did they?

Jeremy: Did they?

Jackson: But *did they*?

Cassel: They didn't.

GET THE AUDIO SNIPPETS

Go to: https://dl.bookfunnel.com/uvhv4vg0uc to access the audio version of the snippets. In order to access the file, you MUST be a newsletter subscriber. If you are not, you can become one by going to www.alicewintersauthor.com and joining the newsletter at the bottom. (Or by following the steps on the Bookfunnel page.)

A MESSAGE FROM ALICE

This link takes you to a special audio for the owners of The Hitman's Guide to Making Friends and Finding Love special edition. Please do not share this with others. It took a lot of time and energy from my illustrator, narrator, editor, and myself to make this possible. I chose to not charge for the audio version as a special treat to my wonderful readers and listeners who purchased the special edition. But if I see the audio being shared, I will add a fee to it as well as any future audios similar to this!

A MESSAGE FROM LELAND:

Leland: Yeah, don't steal shit or I will find you—

Jackson: Please don't threaten them.

Leland: No, they love it! They love knowing how serious I am. I am a badass motherfucker and you do *NOT* want me coming after you.

Jackson: Please, no... stop the threats. Is this even legal? I don't think it's legal. Just enjoy the audio.

Leland: And if you pass the code off... I hope you can't sleep.

Jackson: That was so much tamer than I thought it was going to be.

Leland: You forced me!

ACKNOWLEDGMENTS

Jackson: And now it's time to thank all of the people who made this possible.

Leland: I would like to thank Jackson's booty—

Jackson: NO! Thank REAL people! People who made this nonsense you call your life story possible!

Leland: You're so picky! FINE. Ummmmmmm… I… guess… I'll thank Court-nay.

Jackson: It's Courtney.

Leland: Yeah, but that's boring. No one even reads the acknowledgements, so if we start making up shit, they might! So Court-Neigh, thank you for like flicking your fingers at the book with your editing wand.

Jackson: She's not a mage.

Leland: Well… to make some of your lines readable she has to be. HA HA.

Jackson: FINE, we can pretend she's made of magic. Thank you, *Courtney,* for your wonderful editing.

Leland: Let's see… who is next… Alice's mom. Thanks, bro.

Jackson: Don't call someone's mom "bro."

Leland: Why??? It's sure nicer than what she calls Alice! You should hear the shit she calls her!

Jackson: That's… true. Okay… A huge thank you to Savannah.

Leland: Ooh, I remember Savannah. She likes it when I'm ruthless.

Jackson: That makes her sound like she likes violence.

Leland: She does! And let's thank Kat. All I have to do for that is say "Badass Motherfucker," and she's pleased. And Sam... hmmm... Oh! Sam has a horse! Sam, did you see how well I rode *my* pony? Made you whinny, didn't it?

Jackson: You're not even *thanking* them.

Leland: Who else is on the list? Claudia, Jenn, Leslie, and Mildred. I bet they also liked my horse-riding skills. Look at the stallion go!

Jackson: For fuck's sake. Why does Alice even let us do this?

Leland: And then we have Lori who did the proofreading. Lori, I will name a gun after you. That is the best of compliments.

Jackson: No! Only you would think that!

Leland: Oh! Lucia, thank you for the artwork. Daaaaaaamn they made my man look *FIIIIINE*. I am a bit like... did he really have to have clothes on in every illustration? I asked for you to be naked in them all but was told "that was wildly inappropriate."

Jackson: Thankfully, that didn't happen!

Leland: I bet more people would have liked it.

Jackson: Oh yes, just me naked at the dog shelter. Balls out in the street while you're shooting. Oh, and you might ask why I am naked at the fence! That was just me comparing wood.

Leland: Hee hee. Sounds delightful.

Jackson: Move on.

Leland: And then we have Michael.

Jackson: Thank you, Michael, for allowing Alice to torture you with all of these songs.

Leland: *gasps* My songs are not TORTURE. They are pure MAGIC. Jackson, you are my MUSE and with my muse naked before my very eyes, I will compose the greatest of songs.

Jackson: Michael... I'm so sorry.

AUTHOR'S NOTE

Check out some free short stories by joining my reader group or my newsletter:

    Reader group: facebook.com/groups/alicewinters

    Newsletter: alicewintersauthor.com

Thank you for reading! I hope you enjoyed!

ALSO BY ALICE WINTERS

Shadow's Lure

Cast in Shadows

Casting Light

Vexing Villains

A Villain for Christmas

A Hero in Hiding

Mischief and Mayhem

Monstrous Intent

Hunter's Descent

Medium Trouble

Ghost of Lies

Ghost of Truth

Ghost of Deceit

Phoenix's Quest

Nixing the End of the World

Winsford Shifters

Of Secrets and Wolves

Of Betrayal and Monsters

Of Redemption and Vengeance

The Hitman's Guide

The Hitman's Guide to Making Friends and Finding Love

The Hitman's Guide to Staying Alive Despite Past Mistakes

The Hitman's Guide to Tying the Knot Without Getting Shot

The Hitman's Guide to Righting Wrongs While Causing Mayhem

The Hitman's Guide to Codenames and Ill-Gotten Gains

The Former Assassin's Guide

The Former Assassin's Guide to Snagging a Reluctant Boyfriend

VRC: Vampire Related Crimes

How to Vex a Vampire

How to Elude a Vampire

How to Lure a Hunter

How to Save a Human

How to Defy a Vampire

In Darkness

Hidden in Darkness

A Light in the Darkness

Deception in Darkness

Dancing in Darkness (short story)

In the Mind

Within the Mind

Lost in the Mind

Demon Magic

Happy Endings

Familiar Beginnings

Malicious Midpoint

Seeking Asylum

The Sinner and the Liar

The Traitor and the Fighter

Standalone Titles

Unraveling the Threads of Fate

The Last Text

Dear Cassius

Just My Luck

Never Have I Ever Ridden a Bike

Other Titles

Rushing In (Ace's Wild Book 3)